OPERATION ORPHEUS

BY PAT MONTEATH

A Quill Publishing Book

Published by Quill Publishing in 2005

ISBN 0-9545914-3-7

2nd edition 2006

First published in 2005 in the United Kingdom by
Quill Publishing
The Haven Eskdaleside,
Grosmont,
Whitby, North Yorkshire YO22 5PS.

Although based on real events, characters, names, dates, times, companies, organisations, and agencies in this novel have been changed and are either the product of the author's imagination or, if real, used fictitiously without any intent to describe their actual conduct.

'Remember today is the start — of the rest of your life!'
Enjoy the read.

Pat Monteath

"Observe your friends carefully for they may well be your enemy!"

Pat Monteath
2005

Prologue – the story so far

It is on Richard and Paul's return to Ireland that Richard becomes embroiled in a situation that spurs him into renewing his contact with Sean O'Donald. Through this renewed friendship Richard meets Major O'Rourke and Colonel Ash both men will have an impact on Richard's life forever.

'Operation Orpheus' is the second one in the trilogy involving Richard James and his friend Paul Jones and although it would prove beneficial to have read the book *'Who pays the Ferryman?'* prior to reading *'Operation Orpheus'* it is not necessary as both books are self contained stories in their own right. *'Operation Orpheus'* opens where the book *'Who pays the Ferryman?'* left off and it takes the reader into the world of the 'Circus' where it's every man for himself, where dog eats dog.

In 1970's and 80's World Politics took a turn for the worse. In Ireland there had been a proliferation of paramilitary organisations and the 'Provisional' wing of the IRA had stepped up its campaign and the 'Troubles' escalated. In its efforts to combat these events the British Government recruited numerous Agents, 'Agent Provocateurs' and Informers all of whom worked for different handlers and agencies, so it was no wonder that from time to time lines of communication became confused and things went wrong. At home the bigger picture was one of the 'Cold War', where relations between the UK and the Soviet block had deteriorated to a point where even the Territorial Army was busy training units in guerrilla warfare in readiness should there be a Russian invasion.

Richard James returns to Ireland where he meets a man called Jimmy and very quickly they become good friends, or so it seems! Whilst in the Republic he again meets up with the lovely Fionnuala who certainly hasn't lost any of her Irish charm and he is surprised to learn that she has a brother called Danny who works for C3. There is a surprise encounter with the troubled Noel and a brief meeting with his old adversary Breandán O'Shea, but times have changed and things have moved on since his earlier visits to the Republic, but not for the better.

Chapter 1

You could have been forgiven for thinking that the farm was derelict. The outbuildings alone gave the impression of having been abandoned long ago. The roof of one of the outbuildings had collapsed completely reinforcing the image of dereliction. Add to this the lack of livestock and the illusion was complete. Closer inspection would have revealed otherwise.

Inside the large barn, careful construction work had been carried out. The exterior had been completely untouched, unless of course you saw the aerial array carefully camouflaged within a small copse nearby. In fact the aerial array was a clue to the real identity of the barn and what it housed. It wasn't a barn at all, but it was one of the most advanced electronic centres outside of GCHQ!

The front door of the farmhouse opened spilling light onto the shingle drive. One by one five men emerged and stood chatting in the pool of yellow light. It was evident by the white powdery deposit on the leaves of the bushes that the night had seen a heavy frost. Dawn was fast approaching and fingers of light, from the east, clawed their way across the dark sky. Birds in the trees started to chirp and in the distance the unmistakable throb of a helicopter's engine could be heard. One of the men looked towards the north, nodded.
'Sounds like your transport's approaching Sir.'
'Yes. I think you maybe right J'. He also glanced northwards, before turning to address the other three men. 'Well gentlemen have a safe journey all of you, and Richard, welcome to the Circus. Whatever you do, don't forget what I said about keeping in touch with Control. At least once a week without fail. More if possible.'
'Colonel.' A Sergeant emerged from inside the house. 'The chopper is en route for you.'
'Thank you Sergeant I'll be...' the rest of his sentence was drowned out by the sudden deafening noise of a Lynx helicopter as it circled overhead then quickly dropped in below the roof line. The Colonel turned, raised his hand. 'Gentleman, 'till the next time.' He walked back into the house followed by Major O'Rourke.
'Richard good luck.' Sean O'Donald, a man over six feet tall, extended a large hand towards his friend. 'Don't forget now, like the old man said, keep in touch. Should you ever need anything, well you know what's what. Just keep in touch that's all.' He turned his attention to the other guy, a slightly built individual, a quietly spoken Irishman. 'Eamonn keep him out of trouble and I'll see you around.'

3

'See you S...' the roar of the helicopter engine drowned Eamonn's words as it suddenly appeared above the rooftop. It banked to the right and climbed rapidly away heading Northeast. The three men watched in silence until it became a mere spec in the cold light of dawn.

Sean had already started the engine of his car as Eamonn and I made our way over to the blue Volvo parked nearby. Within minutes we had gone our separate ways and the illusion of what appeared to be a deserted and run-down farm was once again complete. Yes you could be forgiven for thinking it was just another derelict farm!

Chapter 2

It seemed only yesterday since that night in the Safe House in Ulster, but in fact it was several months ago. Since then I had spent many weeks in training. I attended centres in Gosport, Hereford, Ashford, Borough High Street and even one in Suffolk. The first hurdle was over. I along with about thirty to forty others had passed the selection process. Having got to this point we were all invited to change our Christian names to one of our choice, but because commissioned ranks were the exception, I was fortunately able to retain 'Richard'. Our training was now to start in earnest.

'This weekend is yours to enjoy, but remember that on Monday you will be met at the station at 20:00 hours. You will be transported by coach to what will become your new home for the next few weeks and whilst at your new home you will be taught many new skills. Some of you will pass but others will fall by the wayside. As you pass each stage you will move on to the next location. As we operate on a "need-to-know" policy you will never ever be told the exact location. As of now you will not communicate with any member of your family, friends, wives or lovers anything that you hear, see or learn. Good luck to you all and enjoy.'

I left the selection on a high with those immortal words 'Good luck' ringing in my ears. My mood was buoyant as I made my way home to Kent.

The first training stint was at Fort Monkton near Gosport. We were met at the mainline railway station by coach and travelled through the dark to a camp situated in the middle of nowhere. Once we had all dumped our gear in the accommodation block we were given a brief guided tour around our new home. Armed MoD police patrolled the area backed-up with passive infrared and closed circuit television cameras. Everywhere was geared to security and at no point was the camp visible from the road.

Tuesday morning saw our group lined up in front of a number of different cars whilst a small group of instructors stood nearby. Each instructor called out three individuals by name and with their trainees walked over to one of the vehicles. Eventually it was me and two other guys named Jason and Ed. We were joined by our instructor with a Saab 'Right lads my name's Mick and my job is to teach you how to drive our way. I am your instructor in advanced driving. From time to time you will be taught by other instructors, that way we will all have a chance to view your driving technique. Whilst here you will be taught the skill of driving at high speed but safely. You will all be tested and should you fail the test or I deem you unsafe to take it then I'm afraid you are of little use to us. Technique is important at all times, concentrate on that for now. Although we call the course "advanced driving" it isn't quite the same as Joe public learns for his or her advanced driving test. Any questions?' Mick looked around at the three of us and we all shook our heads. 'Good, then lets get started.'

He started the engine and we moved off down the camp road heading towards the main gate. At the gate Mick checked for traffic in both directions and pulled out onto the road. He gently accelerated away until we settled down to a gentle cruising speed of about fifty.

'Now remember, the best position for your hands should be the ten to two position. As you turn the wheel always feed it through from one hand to the next by pushing with one and pulling with the other.' As we cruised along at a steady fifty I thought to myself this is basic stuff. We slowed to forty as we came up behind a heavy truck, which had entered into a double bend with us behind it. As we entered the bend I watched Mick to see if he followed his own doctrine and kept his hands at ten to two and fed the wheel through. We went into the left hander and the Saab started to drift off to the right. We were now heading round the bend on the wrong side of the road!

'Of course you can always come out and take a good look ahead – but make sure you've left yourself enough room to dive back in should something be coming.' Sure enough, right at that moment a red sports car was heading towards us a great speed, Mick moved the wheel quickly and dabbed the brake tucking us back in again behind the truck. We all grabbed hold of something and waited for the collision that never was. As the sports car drew alongside us, Mick was already checking his rear-view mirror and before it had fully passed us he swung the Saab out into the right hand lane, changed down into second and with the engine revs increasing we could see the road straightening out. Coming towards us at a reasonable closing speed was a stream of traffic. The obvious option was to brake and tuck back in behind the truck but that was not Mick's choice. Instead he floored the accelerator and with full power of the engine the Saab surged forward taking the needle of the rev counter into the red section.

Mick shouted over the roar of the engine. 'Always take it to maximum revs when overtaking otherwise you're not fast enough, also make certain by taking a really good look before you commit to a move, if you're uncertain, don't!' I was convinced we were going to hit head-on the lead vehicle of the fast approaching stream of traffic, but as we continued to accelerate towards them. Mick changed up into third. The car surged forward again, at the very last second we slipped in front of the truck and effortlessly drew away as our speed neared ninety-five. I expelled the breath I had sub-consciously been holding onto through my pursed lips. "Phew! That was too close for comfort."

Mick carried on talking to us as if a near miss such as that was common to everyday life. 'Notice how I only briefly touch the gear stick. That enables me to keep both hands on the wheel for the maximum time. Never take your hand from the wheel until the very second you are going to change gear. Read the road ahead, as far ahead as you can see. Use markers to guide you, the hedgerows, telegraph poles and the trees to give you a clue as to which direction the road is going in next. Don't brake too soon or you waste power. Power is speed – wasted speed is time. Use your brakes to reduce speed not your gears – once your speed is right for the bend, change down, then on the apex, power out.'

We continued with the lesson travelling at high speed through the countryside, all the time Mick talking us through the manoeuvres. Each manoeuvre was as second nature to him. We entered the town and slowed our pace, but Mick still kept up his commentary. He showed us how to chop in and out of traffic overtaking sometimes on the inside, but always aware of where the dangers were and of the pedestrians. After travelling through the town we were again out on the open road with our speed now up above a hundred. Not once did Mick let up on his monologue as we hurtled into chicanes, right then left-hand bends, up hills and passed cars, trucks and coaches.

After a few minutes of driving at breakneck speed, Mick swung off the road and into the training area of our camp. We continued along a tarmac road then off onto a dirt track through the woods, 'Of course there is always the situation where the car goes into a skid. This can happen for a variety of reasons, whether by accident or by design. Sometimes you may wish to use a skid to your advantage, for instance the handbrake turn. Brace yourselves and I'll demonstrate.' Without further warning Mick slammed the palm of his hand flat on the centre of the bottom of the wheel and spun it hard on full lock. The front dipped down dramatically, the tyres screeched, and the tail end swung violently out. My natural instinct was to brace myself, Jason was slung against my side and Ed held on for dear life, as Mick pulled on the handbrake. We were now travelling backwards with tyres screaming, Mick commentating as we continued 'We have now turned completely in the opposite direction. The back has travelled through 180 degrees. I'm going into first gear, foot hard down on the throttle…handbrake released now…clutch released now…As the wheelspin stops and the wheels bite, you can feel the car accelerating. Don't worry about all the blue smoke. The front wheel drive is doing its job and is now pulling forward in a straight line.'

'That was a handbrake turn where you use the skid to your advantage. It has enabled me to travel at fifty miles an hour in one direction and in less than ten seconds I have changed direction completely and we are now travelling at fifty miles an hour in the opposite direction. Very useful manoeuvre, especially if you're being chased! Now lads it's your turn!'

We continued being evaluated, instructed, pushed and coerced for two weeks. Each day we learnt something new until at the end of the two weeks, hard and fast driving was second nature to us. At the end of two weeks, secure in the knowledge that we were now competent drivers, we were able to execute all the manoeuvres both safely and at speed.

The following morning we were directed to a small group of buildings on the other side of the camp. Two guys met us outside the entrance to one of the buildings, a tall wiry looking individual called James and a short stocky person who introduced himself as Will. Both men were from the Royal Observer Corps. Will, the Sergeant, unlocked the main door and ushered the group in. Inside the building was a photographer's dream come true. There were video cameras of all shapes and sizes, tiny specialist cameras, the old style 'two and a quarter by two and a quarter' and the modern 35mm Single Lens Reflex cameras (SLR). Within the darkrooms there was everything needed to process any type of films plus some equipment that I didn't recognise!

'Ok everyone, let me have your attention.' Gradually the talking subsided and the group fell silent. 'Thank you. Now, your next couple of weeks will be spent on learning all about photography, like everything else you have and will learn in the future, this will become second nature to you. In your operations it will, at times, be necessary to take photographs. Each time will be different. There will be a different set of circumstances and different environments that you will work in. However, regardless of where you are, or the circumstances, one thing will never alter and that is time. You can always guarantee that the time available is limited. To carry out a detailed observation on somebody, or place takes time. That is why we use photography. A good photographer can capture the merest detail in a split second. Photographs can be 'shot' in rapid succession, they can be shot from a distance using telephoto lenses without the target's knowledge, they can be 'shot' from a moving vehicle with high-speed film. The advantage of all of this is that once the photographs, or video, of the target have been processed then the result can be examined at your leisure and details that you would otherwise have missed, are in fact caught in the frame. You will learn about shutter speeds, apertures, f-stops film speeds, and focal lengths. If you are in an observation post you will need to know how to get the best shots of your target; know about depth of field, when to use broad depth of field and when not to. We will teach you about IR film and IR flash. You may remember what you were taught in science whilst at school. Infra-red is the wavelength beyond visible red so is invisible to us, but black and white IR film used with IR flash will pick up an image at night just as an ordinary black and white film with flash will see an image. The major difference between the two is that with ordinary flash at night the target would be aware of it, whereas with IR flash the subject is unaware of the photograph being shot. Imagine how useful this is in your line of work. Let me show you an example of what I mean'

He then picked up an ordinary flash unit and placed a dark gel over its lens. Then he dimmed the lights until everywhere blacked out. 'Now watch carefully.' He fired the flash several times without a glimmer being seen. 'You see, or rather you don't see, any sign of light, but you can be certain that each time the flash was operated the room was flooded by infrared. The reason is that the gel blocks out any white light and only allows infrared to pass through. Now come with me.' We all crowded into the biggest of the darkrooms. 'Now as you will notice we have two light sources in here. One is the normal white light – this we only use when all processing has been completed. Once the prints have been passed through developer, hypo and water, it is safe to turn on the white light. Because photographic paper is light sensitive to white light, the same as films, we have to be careful when we switch the light on. Our second light source is a low wattage red light. Now ordinary photographic paper is not affected by the red wavelength within the spectrum so we illuminate the area with red light, that way we can see what we are doing without fear of 'fogging' our photographs. But beware, IR film is affected by ordinary red light so you are going to have to get used to loading and unloading your cameras in total darkness.' For two weeks we studied all aspects of photography to such an extent that using a camera, like using a firearm, became second nature to us all, and like the Browning 9.00mm, the camera became a tool of our trade.

Our final week was spent learning techniques used in sabotage such as, the vulnerable points in a sub-station where a small amount of explosive would cause maximum disruption. The use of timers for small explosive charges to cause fires. Remote control devices and when and where to use them. How to maximise the explosive power available to blow open doors etc, where and when to use stun grenades, in fact we were taught how to use anything that would cause havoc to the enemy!

After five weeks in camp it was time for our group to go our separate ways. We said our farewells and moved on to the next stage in our training. Mine was to be Borough High Street in London, a centre operated by MI5.

'Good morning lads and lasses, whilst here with us you will learn about surveillance,' said Andrew in a soft Edinburgh accent. He moved over to a flip chart and continued. 'Today we'll start with the basic follow technique where we usually refer to the main target as Bravo 1.' Andrew wrote the letter B in red on the flip chart. 'We refer to the main target as Bravo 1 because B stands for body. Now our target lives here.' He wrote a capital A on the chart in brown. 'His abode is known as Alpha 1. We know he drives a car and we use the first letter C to identify this.' He wrote a blue letter C on the flip chart. 'This vehicle is now known as Charlie 1, where the C denotes car. We want to find out what Bravo 1 is up to, so we stake out his home, or his place of work, or club. In fact anywhere we know where he is, or will be at any given time. We then wait until he moves from there and follow him. In order to do this task successfully you will require tools for the job and in this case your tools are two radios, one for in your vehicle and the other on your body. Now you need to use the tools correctly; by as such I mean the language used in communicating your information to your buddy or back-up team located in a vehicle or a control room. The language used must be in code and spoken rapidly to minimise the risk of a third party being able to make sense of what you are saying. Ok everyone?' At this point Andrew passed out maps of town centres for us to look at.

'You'll notice that each street has been coloured according to a key. Now should our target live on the street marked in Orange and he walks along the street towards the High Street, we could in this case colour it in Red then our commentary would run along the lines of, Bravo 1 is foxtrot on Orange towards Red. Get the idea? There was a general murmur from the group that Andrew took as a 'yes'.

'Good in which case I would like you all to look at these packs,' he passed out a number of plastic wallets each containing a full set of Ordinance Survey Maps and Town Centre plans all with the same colour coding. 'By the way you will need to learn all the numbers, colours and locations before the end of the course.'

A noticeable groan went up from the group and someone actually voiced what we were all thinking, 'What! There must be at least fifty or more?'

Andrew grinned, 'That's right, but you've got a couple of weeks, there's no rush! So folks I'll see you tomorrow.'

On the day of our first mobile surveillance I was paired up with Jan, a slim dark haired girl in her twenties with a slight trace of an accent, which sounded as if she may have come from up country. We were given a grid reference of the target building and were told where our target lived. We were also told that he used the 'Rising Sun' and given a further grid reference. We were allocated a vehicle fitted with a covert radio. We were shown how to use the radio before leaving the garage at Borough High Street on our first assignment. Another two teams along with Jan and I had been set the task of staking out the 'Rising Sun' car park which we found to be off the Old Kent Road. We did not have to wait long before the target appeared, got into his car and moved off. The task of following the target in traffic and continually passing an accurate commentary on his precise location proved much harder than I thought. Add to this that, in order to avoid detection, we had to constantly change pursuit vehicles with those who were not involved in the actual tail. It was whilst doing this I suddenly realised that all the driving skills I had recently acquired were needed. We constantly had to drive like the devil and in such a way as not to draw attention to ourselves. We were always trying parallel routes to stop our quarry from escaping. Also we had to drive at high speed, constantly watching for pedestrians and passing traffic either by overtaking on the right or if needs be on the inside, but at all times safely. This was the only way we could stay close enough to take over the tail at any time. By the time I had left Borough High Street and Andrew our instructor I knew how to dress so I blended in with my surroundings, how to use effective disguise and how to carry out a successful mobile surveillance.

It was raining when I arrived at Bradbury Lines at Hereford. It was here that I spent my time learning about weaponry and how to use my developed skill accurately. Here we were schooled in all aspects of target practice. How to break down your weapon in double quick time and how to clear a jam, but more importantly to be able to recognise who was 'friend' or 'foe' this was vital in a hot theatre. It was whilst at Hereford that I was introduced to the 'Killing House' a three-story construction where as a group we were instructed in hostage rescue and rapid entry techniques. We were also taught about Close Quarter Battle otherwise known as CQB for short, using the 'Killing House' for our role play. What this meant was that every single one of us was taught how to enter defended buildings from the ground level and from the roof. Inside the building there was always a room set aside, as it would be in the real world, in which hostages might be held. Inside this room, live 'hostages' – SAS men in reality – would be indiscriminately dispersed among 'terrorist' dummies. Invariably the set would be in darkness and the rescue team was expected to burst into the room, in less than a blink of an eye and be able to distinguish friend from foe and shoot the enemy. Even whilst training we used 'live' ammunition so that the stress factor would be similar to a real life scenario. Add to this that no role play scenario was ever the same twice, and it is no wonder that we soon developed very fast and accurate reactions – we had to otherwise we could end up killing our colleagues who were acting as hostages! What this course did for us was that it made us very proficient in marksmanship, speed and accuracy. Upon completion of our time in the 'Killing House' and our basic course in marksmanship each and every one of the team could unleash a full clip of thirteen bullets from a Browning 9mm automatic pistol in under three seconds. That is approximately four times the rate of fire claimed by the manufacturer. These sorts of figures alone are quite an achievement, but add to them the fact that every shot fired had to be precisely placed, then you have some idea of the high level of competency the team achieved. This sort of level was necessary because once operational in the Republic of Ireland capture was always close to hand and for that reason our instructors showed us valuable pointers on escape and evasion techniques. Also, I could be part of a rescue bid to free one of our people being held hostage at any time. It was easy to see how all the basics could also be applied to an operation where the team was going to act as a 'snatch' unit. For example if it was necessary to snatch a target from the safety of their surroundings, whether their home or some other building they felt secure in. In the latter situation surveillance and detailed planning at all times was the key. During our second week at Bradbury Lines, we were introduced to unarmed combat. It was felt that in our theatre an in depth knowledge of unarmed combat was as much a tool of our trade as carrying a Browning 9mm. The seriousness of our situation was underscored when Alan - a lanky fair-haired instructor – lined us all up one evening at the start of one of our PT sessions.

'This evening, we're going to look at some basic unarmed combat', he said as he walked up and down in front of us. 'Imagine that you are on your own and the other lot has sussed you. You've been pinged by the opposition as to what you are, so one of them strolls over to you and suddenly you are staring at a pistol and he tells you to put your hands up. What are you going to do? Here Jack.' Alan called over to one of the lads to join him. Alan then produced a Browning pistol, slid back the top cover to indicate it was unloaded and then passed it to Jack. 'Stand close in Jack and cover me with your weapon.'

Jack held the gun pointing it directly at Alan.

'If he squeezes the trigger he will hit me at this range – that's obvious. But notice where he is pointing it, he is pointing it at my side, so it's not rocket science for you to realise that he does not intend to kill you where you stand. Therefore you have breathing space. In fact it's long enough for you to do something …'

In a flash, Alan grabbed the body of the pistol and twisted it outwards away from his body. He brought his other hand up and raked it down Jack's face momentarily blocking his view and distracting him. In that split second he had taken Jack completely off guard.

'See how I gripped tightly the body of the weapon. Because the Browning is a semi-automatic you will cause it to jam after the first shot simply by applying a hard downward pressure on the working parts. Had it been a revolver then I would have gripped it around the chamber and in that case he could not even fire one shot. Another method would have been for me to have grabbed further along the body and stick my thumb in front of the hammer, which would have prevented it from hitting the first round that was in the chamber to begin with. Also notice that as I reached forward I turned sideways to the threat so reducing the possible target area offered. Then as I dragged my hand and fingers down his face I would have used my nails to scratch his eyes and face. This action would certainly have blinded him momentarily. Another method would have been to push my fingers and thumb as hard as I could into the eye sockets. Both methods would work equally as well. Now in pairs I want you to practice the first move over and over again until you are proficient at it and can do it at speed without even thinking. Now move!'

Ashford was an interesting course for it was here that everything I had learned was effectively put together. It was at Ashford that the group was taught about psychological and physical torture and how to block out pain. One very effective way of breaking a prisoner's resistance to interrogation was by using self-inflicted pain. This was achieved by making the individual stand, legs apart, away from the wall so that the only way they could touch it was by leaning forward until they were supported by their fingertips for long periods of time. If this method was used in conjunction with hoodings, temperature variations from hot to cold, sleep deprivation and continuous white noise the process of breakdown could be greatly accelerated. Also we were instructed in the use of LSD known as 'sensory deprivation' as practised by the CIA. In fact I was no stranger to the latter having already spent a short time in Suffolk on a joint training program run by the CIA. Also whilst at Ashford I was taught fast response techniques and how to manufacture explosives. Using everyday products, readily obtained from the local shops, it is possible to manufacture home-made bombs. If you were involved in agriculture, as I was, HME explosive could easily be made from diesel and nitrogen fertiliser. By producing home-made explosives in the field the risk of detection by the opposition was greatly reduced. At the end of all this raining I became a fully paid up member of the Circus. I was now one of the Operators and it wasn't long before I was called upon to carry out my first duty.

Chapter 3

It was a cold and damp typical November day when a handful of people gathered in the main arrivals lounge in Terminal 2 Heathrow. All eyes watched for the first of the passengers from Dublin to appear through the doors from the Customs Hall. The automatic doors swung open and a fair-haired slightly built man was framed in the doorway. He momentarily paused. His blue eyes hastily scanned the few faces before him as if he half expected someone to be there, then with a purposeful stride he headed off towards the public telephone booth nearby. As he made his way towards the phone booth, a small man detached himself from the handful of people and likewise headed towards the same booth, both persons arrived simultaneously. A short interchange followed. The small man stood aside allowing 'blue eyes' the use of the phone, whilst he, the small guy stood at a discreet distance away, but just close enough to be able to overhear the conversation without being obvious.

'Hi Keith, yeah it's me…Yeah just arrived…What d'you say? No don't worry I'll get a cab… Yeah should be there about four. Ok see you then.' He picked up his bag and moved off in the direction of the Taxi rank.

'Tango 3 to Ferryman over.' The short guy spoke quietly into a throat microphone carefully concealed beneath his clothing.

'Go ahead Tango 3. Over.' I replied.

'Bravo 1 slight build. Five seven, five eight. Fair hair. Blue eyes. Dark jacket foxtrot Taxi. Yours. Over.'

'Roger Tango 3. Ferryman to foxtrot. Out.' Without realising he'd picked up a tail 'blue eyes' passed through the exit doors and headed towards the Taxi Rank. I followed at a discreet distance, pausing now and again to allow others to get between us so reducing the chance of him realising he was being shadowed. As I watched from a discreet distance I saw 'blue eyes' board a black cab. Before the cab's door was closed, I ran to the firm's car nearby. My driver saw me and threw open the front passenger door as I reached the car. 'Go, go, go.' I shouted as I scrambled in. 'That black cabs our target so for Christ's sake don't lose him Pete.'

'Ok. I see him, no problem.' Pete replied in an even voice as I slammed the door behind me. The black cab indicated and pulled out onto the feeder road closely followed by a second. We then accelerated off in pursuit, keeping the second black cab between the target vehicle and us.

'Ferryman to Control over.'

'Come in Ferryman. Control over.'

'We are mobile. I repeat we are mobile. Target in black cab heading towards M4 motorway. Ferryman over.'

'Roger Ferryman. Tango 2 receiving. Control over.'

'Come in Control. Tango 2 over.'
'Position Tango 2. Control over.'
'Parked on bridge at roundabout junction three on M4. Tango 2 over.'
'Roger Tango 2. Standby. Ferryman receiving? Control over.'
'Go ahead Control. Ferryman over.'
'Did you hear Tango 2's report Control over?'
'Roger Control. Heard Tango 2 strength five. Whereabouts is Tango 1? Ferryman over'
'Tango 1 receiving. Control over.'
'Go ahead Control, Tango 1 over.'
'Advise current position. Control over'
'Roger Control. Junction four Bravo M4 Tango 1 over.'
'Ferryman receiving. Control over?'
'Go ahead. Ferryman over.'
'Did you get Tango 1's position? Control over'
'Affirmative. Target now approaching M4...He's right, right, right. Target heading East towards City. We are still in contact. Speed sixty. Ferryman over.'
'Roger Ferryman. Standby. Tango 2 receiving? Control over'
'Go ahead Control. Tango 2 over.'
'Target and Ferryman heading East, should be approaching your position ETA five minutes. Control over.'
'Roger Control. Tango 2 over'

The closer we got to the city the heavier the traffic became. I glanced at my watch decided that by the time we reached Hammersmith the 'rush hour' would be well and truly underway. I wasn't wrong. Traffic was nose to tail as cars spewed from feeder roads onto the wide Hammersmith Broadway. The cab was now indicating to turn off and started to manoeuvre across the flow of traffic. It slowly approached Fulham Palace Road and we did likewise. Peter, a highly skilled pursuit driver, had no problem in keeping close tabs on our target even in this heavy traffic. Once into Fulham Palace Road traffic eased a little. We hadn't gone far before the target turned left into Fulham Road. After a short distance he was again indicating, this time right into Pursers Cross Road. 'Tango 2 receiving? Ferryman over.'
'Go ahead Ferryman. Tango 2 over.'
'Target is right, right, right into Pursers Cross Road. We are following. Proceed to Parsons Green station and wait. Ferryman over.'
'Roger Ferryman. Tango 2 out.'
We had just turned into Pursers Cross Road when we were confronted by the stationary black cab about fifty yards down on the left. Pete braked harshly slowing our pursuit vehicle to walking pace. As we crawled passed

the cab I managed to get half a dozen rapid photographs of our target, one with the house number in the background. I made a mental note that I needed to check out the property 56 Pursers Cross Road.

That evening, a small group of highly influential people including the Minister for Defence and Lord Sackville, attended a dinner party at Lady Caroline's house in fashionable Kensington. Also on the guest list was a somewhat unlikely candidate, a young man of slight build with light brown hair and blue eyes. Yes the very same 'blue eyes' who had arrived at Heathrow earlier.

'Ferryman to Control over.'
'Go ahead Ferryman. Control over.'
'Bravo 1 arrived Lady Caroline's residence. Await your instructions. Ferryman over.'
'Standby Ferryman. Control out.'
'What do you reckon Pete? What's our beloved leader's interest in this bloke?'
'Dunno. Ours is not to reason why…'
'Ferryman from Control over.'
'Go ahead Control.'
'Bravo 1 has previous. Name Kenneth Austen. Known to Met Sierra Bravo and to the RUC. Wanted for questioning in armed robbery. All charges dropped. Also known to Mother. Alpha 1 County Louth Bravo 2 connections OIRA. O'Shea may know Bravo 1. Keep obs. Acknowledge. Control over.'
'Roger Control. So Bravo 1 'blue eyes' known. O'Shea never mentioned Bravo 1 Austen, but that's not to say he doesn't know him. Keeping OBS. Ferryman over.'

A young man of slight build, light brown hair and blue eyes took the glass of wine being offered and made his way over to Lady Caroline. His hair, though not long, could certainly have done with a trim, but he wasn't there to win the best-dressed male award. He was there to negotiate with Her Majesty's Government. He was there to trade with Lord Sackville and the Minister for Defence. He had information that he was sure would be of interest. Information that would hold him in good stead. 'Blue eyes' or Kenneth Austen as he was known back home had quite a reputation. People back in Kerry saw Austen as a 'big spender' a bit of a 'jet setter' so to speak. He worked for a clothing company in Dublin, but the company – in which he had an interest – had run into financial difficulties and because of this he had to sell his luxury house in Kerry and buy something a little less

17

ostentatious. He had recently purchased a modest house in County Louth thus curtailing the opulent lifestyle he had been used to. However, whilst living in 'bandit country' he managed to ingratiate himself into the local community and develop strong links with the Republican Movement. It was through these links he quickly learnt about the weapons used by the Official IRA. He had even managed to find their source of supply. Yes, he was sure that this information would be of interest to Her Majesty's Government. What is more he felt certain it was worth money – a lot of money and money was what he was "desperately in need of"!

It was later that night, whilst at the dinner party, that Kenneth Austen managed to convince his hostess to introduce him to the then Minister for Defence. He lost no time in launching into, what he felt would be of great interest to Her Majesty's Government, the subject of the "IRA". During his meeting with the Minister, Austen told him that the Official IRA had managed to obtain AK49 assault rifles and that he would identify the Official's source of supply provided he, the Minister for Defence would arrange a meeting with the right person. The Minister now convinced decided to arrange a meeting with his Army Minister. It was during this meeting that Kenneth Austen not only advised the Army Minister that the Officials had now obtained AK49 assault rifles, but he also suggested that there would be an assassination attempt on Ulster's Minister for Home Affairs. Having been told of this development the Army Minister was convinced that Kenneth Austen had something worth listening to.
'Having listened to what you have told me I am impressed by your knowledge, and may I suggest, Kenneth isn't it?'
'Yes that's correct Kenneth Austen.'
'Well Kenneth may I suggest that I fix up a meeting between you and a gentleman by the name of Jackson-Smye a very senior officer in Special Branch.'
However with Austen's past dealings with Special branch he was far from keen to renew that 'former' relationship and was quick to turn the offer down. 'I'm sorry sir, but that arrangement…Err shall I say is not really what I had in mind, especially with my experience of Special Branch. Perhaps another department?'
'Well I'm not sure…' Austen cut him off in mid-sentence. 'Well in that case, I'd best get off.' Austen stood up as if to leave. At this point the Army Minister caught hold of his arm. 'Now, let's not be too hasty Kenneth. Here, please sit down again.,' the Army Minister indicated to the chair, 'Can I offer you a drink of something?' Austen paused, not sure what to do. 'Come on Kenneth let's talk about it. If you're adamant about not speaking with Special Branch then there are others you know.'

That was enough to convince Austen to stay. 'Well, if that's the case then who do you propose minister?'

The Army Minister pushed his hands deep into his jacket pockets, looked up at the ceiling and thought about it for a moment or two, before replying. 'How about,' he paused thinking that he needed to pick his words carefully, 'Yes, how about if I arrange for you to meet someone from 'the appropriate authorities' then?'

Austen seemed to warm to that idea. 'Who have you got in mind?'

'You'll have to leave that to me, but I give you my word it will not be Special Branch.'

'In that case I'll agree to that, so when?' He asked with a sense of urgency, 'and if I meet this person and give them details then will I be…err…paid for my information? The Army Minister smiled benignly at him and said, 'That Mr Austen depends…yes Kenneth that will depend on a number of factors…'

'Such as?' he interjected.

'Such as how useful my contact views the information and how accurate it is. In fact if it is deemed as good as you suggest it be, then there may well be something in it for you! I'll be in touch Kenneth. Leave it with me.' The Army Minister stood up and smiled at Austen as he extended his hand. That was Austen's signal to go. He stood up and shook the outstretched hand, 'thank you sir for your time, and I'll trust you on this one.'

'That Kenneth, I think you will have to do, and now I must get on. Will you be at home tonight?'

'At my brother's sir.'

'Good. I believe that my secretary has your brother's telephone number can we contact you there?'

'Yes sir.'

'Good then we'll be in touch.' The Army Minister opened the office door to let Austen out and returned to sit at his desk, whereupon he buzzed through to his secretary on his loudspeaker phone. 'Yes minister?'

'Janet would you get me Colonel Ash on the secure line. That's Colonel Richard Ash at Ashford Military Intelligence HQ.'

That night Kenneth Austen or 'blue eyes' received a telephone call. 'Is that Mr Austen?' a voice with a slight but distinctive Irish accent asked, 'Mr Kenneth Austen?' Kenneth Austen hesitated momentarily, wondering who the voice belonged to, 'Oh, I'm sorry Mr Austen, it is Kenneth isn't it?'

'Yes it is Kenneth who's this?'

'You don't know me Kenneth, but I was asked to give you a ring by my boss. My name is O'Rourke, Major O'Rourke.' O'Rourke hurried on quickly to avoid any interruption from Austen. 'I believe you had a meeting with the minister today and I have been asked to set up a further meeting with one of my men. Please remember these instructions Mr Austen. Tomorrow buy the Guardian newspaper and in the afternoon take the tube to Cannon Street station, make sure you arrive by 12:30 at the latest. Make your way to the mainline station Taxi rank and look for a newspaper vendor. Give him your Guardian newspaper and he will give you the Evening News. Inside you will find a sealed envelope with an address in it. Take a cab to the address, do not discuss this with anyone otherwise you will be getting a visit from some very unwelcome people. Do I make myself clear?'

'Yes but…' the phone clicked and for a moment there was silence. Austen rattled the receiver rest…'Hello, hello…O'Rourke…O'Rourke.' The silence was replaced by the dialling tone.

The following morning Kenneth Austen left 56 Pursers Cross Road to take a walk in order to clear his mind and to mull over yesterday's telephone call. Whilst on his walk he called into the newsagents and purchased The Guardian. He then decided that he was onto something big, but exactly how big, he wasn't sure.

Chapter 4

Gradually the constant throb of the ferry's engines deep in the bowels of the ship changed and a new note emerged. A slower gentler pace ensued and the crash of the waves beneath her bow subsided to more of a slapping noise as we slowed in our pace. Up ahead was the entrance to Dublin's Ferry terminal. Because the crossing had been good, and the Irish Sea had behaved itself for once, you could be forgiven for forgetting that it was still winter, even if it was at the tail end. As we neared the Port of Dublin the surface of the sea was uncannily calm, like a millpond. There was a slight bump as we came alongside and men scurried along the deck busying themselves with the docking process. The ship gave a shudder as the propellers again started to turn and a dull throb came up through her plates as she slowly reversed. The bow rope went taut and twanged, flicking a fine spray of water everywhere as the tension increased. The low throbbing stopped as the stern rope started to be winched in by the stern capstan winch on the after deck. Slowly, under protest, the stern pulled in towards the dockside. Another short burst from the engine room sent a judder up through the ship's plates. The water at the stern boiled and frothed as we pulled in tight to the side. The ropes, that were as thick as a man's arms, now creaked and groaned as the tension increased stretching them beyond belief.

On the car deck the noise reached a fever pitch as doors were slammed and vehicle engines kicked into life. Members of the crew were shouting directions to each other. Chains rattled through their channels as bulkhead doors were raised. The smell of hot oil and diesel fumes greeted the air as I passed by the open doors that gave access to the ships engine room. Slowly the bow door of the ship was raised and the ramp was lowered. A crew member then started to wave the first few vehicles forward. Gradually row by row vehicles disgorged from the belly of the ship, up the concrete ramp and onto the dock. Soon I was moving, and joined the rest of the throng as we headed nose to tail along the road out of the dock gates toward the city.

It was still fairly early as I headed along the road towards Julianstown and on to Swords. My brief was to proceed to the Tara hotel and wait there further instructions. This trip I was on my own, no Paul, no Mick or Terry, just me. It was a little different this time as I was prepared for any eventuality. This time I knew what to expect and had a network to help me should I have need of it. For instance I had a small army issue communications set called the PRC 319, which used a high speed digital signal via a communications satellite making it useable virtually anywhere.

I also had Eamonn, who was not too far away, as a contact point, and as additional back up there was Sean up in the Province. Finally if all else failed there was always 'our man' at the Ambassador's office in Dublin. So this time I was both prepared and well equipped.

I swung into the tree-lined lane that led to the Tara feeling as if I was coming home. As I reflected on the familiar surroundings, I wondered to myself if the beautiful Fionnuala was still working for O'Shea as the receptionist. Ah, she was really pretty! I parked the car close to the entrance grabbed my case off the back seat and bounced up the steps to the entrance. As I walked up to reception I couldn't believe my luck. There she was, the beautiful Fionnuala, still as pretty as ever with her long fair hair and oval face with the biggest brown eyes I had ever seen.
'Any chance of a room?' I enquired.
'I won't be a minute sir.' She said as she finished off what she was doing. 'Now sir, would it be a single room...' She casually looked up in my direction, gave a little squeal of delight. 'Richard. What on earth are you doing here?'
'Nothing much, just came back to see you.' I said jokingly.
'To be sure you did. Now tell the truth, what are you doing back?'
'Ok, if you insist. I'm here to see Breandán O'Shea.'
'Where's Paul?' She asked with idle curiosity.
'Ahh... back home, why are you disappointed?'
'No. Just curious that's all.'
'I'm here all on my own this time, so how are you keeping?' I asked changing the subject.
'Oh I'm fine. You know nothing's changed since last time you were over.' She smiled, 'How long are you staying for this time?'
'I'm not too sure I've got some local business to attend, which shouldn't take too long and then I'm off back.'
'To be sure you're lucky.'
'Why?'
'Well I'd love to travel around the place. To stay in hotels, be waited on and be pampered.'
'Oh sure I'm pampered. I'm away from home. Living out of a suitcase...'
'To be sure 'tis a hard life Richard, dining in the Restaurant, spending the night in the bar. In the nightclub flirting, and dancing the night away. I wish I could have some of that.' She said jokingly, as she looked through the reservations. 'Ah, here you are, in the same room as before' She reached up to get the key from off one of the hooks behind her and passed it to me. I took hold of the key and held her hand in mine for a moment or two. I looked into those big brown eyes of hers and said, 'You could always join

me when you've finished.' I don't know whether I imagined it or not, but I am sure she was up for it. 'Richard James I'm a respectable young lady.' She said with mock indignation.

'So do I take that as a no then?' She shook her head and laughed. If only you knew how wrong you are Richard James.

Upstairs in my room I unlocked my case and started to put my clothes away. I had brought a lot more clothes than I really needed which meant I had somewhere to secrete my weapon and transceiver for the time being. My next job was to figure out where in the room I could use long term, without either item being discovered. I quickly realised there was nowhere really suitable. 'Sod it.' I mumbled to myself. I walked over to the bathroom thinking there must be somewhere, when there was a creak from one of the floorboards. I pressed the same spot again. Again it creaked. I tried it again and this time I could have sworn I felt it move slightly. Fortunately the room did not have a fitted carpet, but a very large rug. I locked my bedroom door and carefully lifted the rug back to reveal a small section of floorboard that had been purposefully cut for some reason. This was loose and if I could get something under the edge I was convinced I could prise it up. 'Damn' I had left the ideal thing in the car, an old pruning knife. I wondered if there was anything in the bathroom I could use, but I drew a blank. I searched through the drawers of the dressing table, again nothing. I was just about to check out the chest of drawers when there was a gentle tap at my door.

'Who's there?' I called out.

'It's me Richard.' The soft dulcet tones of Fionnuala's voice drifted to me through the door. I hastily pushed the rug back into place.

'Hang on.' I called as I tugged off my clothes and shot into the bathroom. I turned on the taps to run a bath. Grabbed one of the bath towels and wrapped it around my waist.

'What are you doing in there?' Fionnuala called.

'Just coming, just coming.' I unlocked the door and opened it just far enough so she could see the towel.

'Oh, sorry Richard I didn't realise…shall I come back later?'

'It's ok, I was just running a bath.'

'Err I'll come back later then…'

'No it's all right come in.'

'Are you sure?'

I opened the door wide, stuck my head outside and checked the corridor. ' Come in.' I grabbed her arm and quickly pulled her into my room shutting the door as soon as she was inside. She half stumbled and fell into me. Instinctively I grabbed hold of her to stop her falling, and the next I knew

23

she was in my arms. Her face turned up towards mine, her mouth looked inviting as her body pressed close to my nakedness.

She thought I was asleep as she slipped from between the sheets. Through half open eyes I caught the reflection of her beautiful body as she darted in front of the mirror on the way to the bathroom. I heard the click of the bathroom door as she closed then the sound of the shower running. The smell of her perfume still lingered on the pillows next to me. Her clothes strewn across the floor where they had fallen in the frenzy that followed her entering my room. All this had happened unexpectedly and for the moment I savoured that time. Now I had no regrets, but would it always be? How could I know, after all tomorrow is another day. Strange, I still didn't know why she had come to my room. She had said no more about it and I hadn't pressed her on the subject. I must have drifted off because the next thing I remember was hearing the door to my room quietly close and she was gone. The only evidence of her ever having been here was the delicate smell of her perfume that still lingered in the air and a wet bath towel on the towel rail in the bathroom. I stretched and got up to run the bath – which was a genuine bath this time.

Half an hour later, having had a good soak, I emerged from the bathroom got dressed and opening the door to my room I checked the corridor in both directions for anyone heading my way, but there was no one in sight. Having made certain that the coast was clear I closed and locked the door, it was now time to put in my first call to base. I removed the PRC 319 from my case, it was a marvellous piece of electronic wizardry measuring no more than six inches by twelve which enabled me to communicate with my base from anywhere in the world almost instantaneously. On the front of it was a Liquid Crystal Display beneath which was a small keyboard. I switched the set on and typed in my codename: -

FERRYMAN ARRIVED TARA. PLEASE ADVISE
INSTRUCTIONS? OUT.

I read what I had in put and pressed the 'send' button. Straightaway the writing disappeared and within a few seconds all that was visible was a slight 'glow' from the blank screen. This was soon replaced with a new signal: -

YOUR MSG RECEIVED STANDBY ......NOTHING
FURTHER. CALL IN FOR NEW UPDATE 2 HOURS.
CONTROL OUT.

Without either news or instructions life could become a little difficult and I could not afford to stay around too long just in case O'Shea turned up, but I couldn't go too far a field either. I switched on the television in my room whilst I resumed my search for something to prise up the loose section of floorboard. Ah, just the thing. I had found an old wire coat hanger laying in the bottom drawer of the chest of drawers. I quickly rolled back the rug to uncover the loose section of floorboard. Inserting the old coat hanger under the edge of the floorboard, it only took a moment to prise it up to reveal the ideal place to hide my equipment. I placed the PRC 319 in its new hiding place, replaced the floorboard and the rug making sure nothing had been left out of place and then sat down just in time to hear the evening news.

'We are just receiving reports of an attempted escape by prisoners from Mountjoy Prison. It is believed that the two Englishmen Kenneth and Keith Austen have attempted to escape from Mountjoy Prison where they had been serving a prison sentence for the Allied Irish bank robbery. More on this story later.'

Maybe this news story had something to do with my presence at the Tara. I couldn't swear to it, but I was sure that I had heard something about Kenneth Austen and his brother being in the pay of Her Majesty's Government. There was also a whisper in the Circus about two brothers acting as *agent provocateurs* by carrying out a number of robberies around Ulster and the Republic. In fact rumour has it that they were well known to the Gardai, who not only left them alone but watched on with bemusement as they skipped around the countryside carrying out different raids. Word on the block was that as a spy Kenneth was pretty useless, his information was, in the main, totally inaccurate but, I suppose until the Dublin job they must have had something going for them or else Her Majesty's Government would have arranged their departure. In fact I count myself as being very lucky that their demise did not impact on me, especially as I had met Mr Austen's controller, and to a certain extent had 'business' links with the man.

It all seemed to happen about the same time as Paul and I were working for O'Shea. Austen was fighting his extradition in London and his controller suddenly found himself in trouble in Dublin; when he, along with one of his contacts, a Sergeant in the Gardai's Special Branch was arrested and charged under the Irish Official Secrets Act of 1963. In fact I would go so far as to say that his arrest coincided with the arrest of Paul and my involvement with the Gardai in Dublin.

One of the claims made at the time was that there was a second British intelligence officer also involved and sought by the Gardai but was never found. For a short time Paul came under suspicion, however they'll never realise how close they were, but that's another story for another day. It never rains but it pours and there seemed to have been a lot of problems for MI6 all about the same time.

I switched off the television and decided that as it was now quite dark and a trip through the crudely alarmed woodland to the rear of the Tara to check out O'Shea's place would be in order. I checked the corridor in both directions and took the rear stairs down to the kitchen area. With dinner over some time ago, all was quiet and I was able to slide out the back way unnoticed. I checked carefully to make sure no-one was around before I headed towards the woods at the back of the hotel. To minimise possible detection I kept in the shadows as far as I could then at the last minute ran across the open space between the woods and the grounds of the hotel. Once inside the tree line I had to move forward carefully, trying to picture in my mind's eye the layout of where the alarms were. I paused straining my ears for the slightest noise, but it was as quiet as a graveyard. Nothing stirred save a slight breeze in the trees. Convinced that it was now safe to do so, I took the small torch out of my pocket and switched it on. It didn't take long for me to navigate a path through the trees and the undergrowth to Breandán O'Shea's farm. By now the moon was bright and high overhead throwing the outbuildings into stark relief. Everywhere was quiet, too quiet for my liking. I edged forward towards the first of the buildings. Still no sound. It was unnerving. The building cast a long shadow in the moonlight. I stopped and listened – nothing. I started to walk over towards the house. Everywhere was in darkness. The silence was uncanny. No dog barking – nothing.

I was walking through the shadows thrown up by the last shed towards the house when I suddenly felt the cold steel of a gun's barrel jammed against my neck.

'And who have we here then? a harsh threatening whisper came from the shadows. Shit I thought.

'Now just yer keep walking slowly forward like t' good fella yer are. No looking back mind or it be too bad f'yer.' Just at that precise moment we came out of the shadows into bright moonlight, 'b'Jesus Richard it's yer!' the person behind said in a surprised voice that I immediately recognised. It was the voice of Noel the union man who I had come to know on my last trip. Boy was I relieved because he already owed me a favour from when I had kept safe his 'Seven wonders of Four'.

'Christ Noel you scared the shit out of me. What the hell are you doing creeping about in the shadows,' I looked at the small handgun he was holding, 'and with a gun as well?'

He quickly pushed the gun back into the waistband of his trousers so it was out of sight.

'Jesus Richard I'm sorry, I didn't know it was you. What are you doing over here?'

I had to think quickly. 'I'm…I'm just on my way to say hello to Breandán. Is he in Noel?'

'To be sure he's in. I'd just popped out for a breath of fresh air. Did he know yer were coming?'

'Hmm, can't…I mean I don't think so. It was err…sort of spur of the moment. Haven't been here long. In fact just arrived a little earlier.' Shit I hope he doesn't ask Fionnuala when I arrived. 'Like I said not been here long. Just stopped off on the way up north. Got some work to check up on.'

'I'll bet the big man will be pleased to see yer.'

As we neared the house I could hear other voices so I used this as an excuse for going no further.

'Look Noel, it sounds as if he's got company. Perhaps I'll leave it for tonight and try and get to see him tomorrow.'

'I t'ink Richard yer might be right to do that. Shall I be telling him I saw yer?'

'No don't tell him. Don't say a word then it'll be a surprise for him.' Noel thought about it for a moment or two, then smiled at the idea of having one over on O'Shea.

'Ok 'till tomorrow night then, see yer Richard.'

'See you then.'

I started to walk off when Noel called after me.

'By the way Richard, just what were you doing over by the sheds?' His voice now had a slight edge to it. I stopped and turned to face him and started to retrace my steps just in case our talking would be heard inside the house. Again he asked the question.

'Well Richard, why were you over there when anyone else would have come up the lane?'

'As I said Noel,' I answered in a low voice, 'I have only just arrived and I came across from the back of the hotel, it's quicker than coming around by the lane when you're walking.' I mentally held my breath hoping that he wouldn't see through my bluff.

He mulled over my answer for a little while before replying.

'Yeah, t'inking about it logically I suppose t'at would be right.' His tone lightened, 'to be sure it's quicker I've done it myself many times. Good night now.'

'Yeah I'll see you Noel.' Phew! That was close I thought to myself, as I set off once again towards the lane. A couple moments later I heard a door close in the darkness, I looked back but there was no sign of Noel so I gave

27

it a good few minutes and then returned to the house. Stealthily I crept through the shadows until I was next to the window where a chink of light showed through partially opened curtains. Listening carefully I could just make out the low murmur of voices and crouching down below the level of the window I edged my way forward until I reached a second window. Here the voices were quite clear and judging by what I could hear there was at least three if not four people present. Breandán was now talking.

'So we've got a load coming in from Libya?'

'Yes we've got an arms deal, but not from Libya direct. Northern Command set it up, they've managed a really good deal with a Libyan in Malta. I've been told that this contact is supplying us with rocket launchers and automatic weapons.'

'When?' Breandán asked.

'It's on the way now.'

'Are you sure?' Breandán asked.

'Certain. It's already been confirmed. It's on a ship called *Sea Gem* that sailed from Malta and destined for Killala Bay over on the west coast end of the month.'

'How do we land the consignment Noel?'

I wasn't sure whose voice that was.

'The arrangement is t'at the arms cases will be dumped over the side of the ship and we'll have a fleet of fishing boats out t'ere fishing, so all they have to do is to dragnet the cases and land them with their catch, it's as simple as t'at'

'Good.' Breandán spoke again, 'so that should help us with the stocking of newer weapons then, and will these then be held locally Noel?'

Already I had heard enough to convince me to get a message off to control, so keeping to the shadows I made my way as quickly as possible to the lane and back to the relative safety of the hotel.

I reached the Tara without any further mishap, but decided against using the main entrance and returned to my room through the back door and via the kitchens. Once back inside my room I checked the time and as I had only been out for just over the hour it meant I had a further two hours to wait for my scheduled call into Mother. I decided that what I had overheard was important enough to warrant my calling in much earlier than planned so without giving it a second thought I rolled back the carpeting, lifted the floorboard and retrieved my communications set the PRC 319 and keyed in the following message: -

MSG CODED SECRET
FROM FERRYMAN

ARMS SHIPMENT FROM TRIPOLI SHIP'S NAME *SEA GEM*.
SAILING MALTA.
ETA KILLALA BAY END MARCH
M.O. PLAN TO USE FISHING NETS AND LAND BY FISHING
FLEET. CONSIGNMENT CONSISTS OF ROCKET
LAUNCHERS AND SEVERAL TONS OF SMALL ARMS.
FERRYMAN

I pressed the send button and the screen went blank. The message had been despatched. All I had to do was to await the acknowledgement. It must have taken all of one minute before I received the acknowledgement, which read: -

MSG CODED SECRET
FROM SPECIAL OPS LISBURN
MSG RECEIVED. NOTED *SEA GEM* DUE FROM MALTA OFF
WEST COAST KILLALA BAY.ARMS SHIPMENT FOR IRA.
QUESTION WHERE IS ARMS ULTIMATE DESTINATION?
CONTROL

I read the message then inputted the reply: -

MSG CODED SECRET
FROM FERRYMAN
ARMS DESTINED FOR NORTHERN COMMAND.
POSSIBLE FARM KNOWN AS *HOLIDAY CAMP*.
WILL ENDEAVOUR TO ASCERTAIN AND ADVISE.
FERRYMAN

A few seconds elapsed before I received an acknowledgement which asked me to standby. It was closely followed by a new message indicating that Kenneth Austin, the man who the Prime Minister denied had anything to do with the UK's Security Forces, had escaped from Dublin's Mountjoy prison. The message read: -

MSG CODED TOP SECRET.
FROM CONTROL LISBURN
MSG RECEIVED FROM MOTHER JITC ASHFORD
CODE NAME *IGNIS*
MSG BEGINS.
RECEIVED INFO.

REQUIRE SPECIAL DELIVERY PACKAGE TO NORTHERN
ADDRESS.
POSTMAN WILL DELIVER TO ROSIE'S IN SWORDS DAY
AFTER TOMORROW ADDRESSED AUSTEN FOR
COLLECTION. PLEASE ARRANGE ONWARD SPECIAL
DELIVERY. ADVISE WHEN WE CAN EXPECT DELIVERY
AT HOUSE.
MOTHER

My guess, that my trip here was connected to what had been reported on the
television had been right, I was to rescue Austen. So then let play
commence!

Chapter 5

The time was 22:30 and it had been over twenty-four hours since I had received the message about Kenneth Austen from control. I had arrived here in Swords only a few minutes ago and parked my car not too far from the house known in the Circus as Rosie's. A detached single story building with a small yet tidy front garden comprising of neatly maintained lawn with flower borders and a concrete drive leading to an adjoining garage. There was nothing untoward about the property and from the outside it looked like any other detached bungalow in the area, an area well known for its poor radio and television reception. Because of poor reception it was not unusual to see unusually large aerials, installed on various properties to aid signal strength and Rosie's was just such a property. This in itself was of no consequence, except Rosie's place didn't suffer from a poor radio signal, in fact her reception was exceedingly good compared to others in the neighbourhood, however the aerial here was used for another purpose. Nobody knew much about the youngish couple who lived there apart from the fact that Rosie, a slim brunette, did not appear to work. Her husband Howard seemed to spend a lot of time away and it was rumoured they weren't really married, but other than that they kept themselves pretty much to themselves.

I checked my Browning pistol making sure the safety catch was on and that I had spare magazine clips in my weatherproof wax jacket. I switched on my small torch and made my way up the front drive, rang the bell with three short rings followed by three longer rings then three more short rings. This Morse code SOS signal was the prearranged signal that I was to use in order to announce my arrival to Rosie. I turned off my torch and withdrew into the shadows where I waited patiently. The plan was for me to take Austen by road to the Tara, where I would park at the far end of the car park well away from the main entrance. Once there we would wait in the car for an opportunity to get into O'Shea's alarmed woods where we would set off away from his house towards the orchards at the northern part of his land. From there on it should be relatively straightforward.

At two in the morning I parked at the far end of the hotel's car park and leaving Austen sat in the car I set off to check that the coast was clear. From the car there was a short distance of exposed terrain that we would have to traverse before we got into the shadows thrown up by the car park's wall. Keeping to the shadows I followed the line of the wall to the arched entrance that led to lawns situated at the rear of the building. Using the shadows cast by the main building I silently ran along the lawn to another archway that led through into a backyard. Here I paused for a moment or

31

two just to make sure all was clear then I crossed over the yard and passed the staff-quarters then on into kitchen garden. From the kitchen garden I could just make out the outline of the woods. I paused and listened – everywhere was quiet. Everything was still, not even a breeze stirred through the treetops. I retraced my footsteps back to the car.

'Psst, Austen.' I called in a load whisper. Carefully he opened the car door and got out. 'Right, wait for me over there in the shadows.' He bent double and ran quietly across the exposed area into the shadows and pressing himself up against the wall he waited. I locked the car up and then did likewise joining Austen in the shadows. 'Now follow me and stick close.' I whispered, 'do everything I do and no talking. Understood?' Austen nodded. 'Right let's go and remember follow me exactly, because if you don't do what I do when we enter the alarmed woods…'

'What will happen?' He whispered to me.

'You'll find out….' I left my answer hanging like the sword of Damocles. We travelled swiftly and silently. In next to no time we were across the lawn and into the yard where the staff quarters were.

'Right we cut across here to the kitchen gardens, but go as quietly and quickly as you can because this is where the staff quarters are and there could be people still about. Ok?' Austen nodded. Again I stuck to the shadows as much as possible. We had nearly reached the kitchen garden when we heard voices approaching. I grabbed Austen and pulled him into the one of the doorways where hopefully we would not be noticed. I held my breath as the voices got closer. My heart pounded deep in my chest so much so I was sure it could be heard. There were three of them, two blokes and a woman. They were approaching where we were concealed. Just when I thought they were coming to our doorway they stopped short. I heard one of the lads rattle some keys. 'Ah well it's been a long day. See you two tomorrow.'

'Yeah goodnight Colm.'

'Goodnight Damian, goodnight Donna.'

'See you.' The girl answered. A door opened and suddenly everything was bathed in yellow light. Then as the door closed, once more blackness enveloped everything. I could hear Austen let out the breath he'd been holding.

'Ohh, Damian…'

All we could hear was the noise of this couple kissing. In fact they were so close I was convinced I could have touched them. 'Ooh Damian. Hmmm.' Damn you take her inside and get on with it in there I thought to myself, but they were far too engrossed in the moment to stop. In the end I risked taking a peep. He was too busy fondling her to notice me. This was our chance. I tapped Austen on the arm and indicated for him to follow me. I gave a quick glance to my left just for reassurance, but the moans from the pair of them were sufficient to tell me that they were oblivious to anything or anyone else around them. We moved swiftly and silently towards the kitchen garden and on to the woods. At the edge of the woods I paused.

'Look Austen I need to go back and move my car so you stay out of sight. I'll be back here in fifteen minutes or thereabouts.'

He nodded to indicate he'd understood and withdrew into the shadows of the trees.

Fifteen minutes later I returned complete with map, compass and small Maglite torch. I entered the line of trees and in the shadowy darkness I gave a soft whistle. Over to my left I heard a similar soft whistle so headed towards it.

'Everything all right?' I asked in a low voice.

'Yeah.' Was all he said.

'Now listen to me carefully, this wood is alarmed so don't wander off my track. Follow me carefully and stick close to me.'

'Does the wood belong to the hotel?'

'No. A bloke called O'Shea owns it.'

'Who's he?'

'He is a very wealthy landowner. He also owns the hotel.'

'So why is it alarmed?'

'Well let's say he doesn't like nosey sods creeping about in his woods.'

'Ha, ha. Very funny. So what's the real reason, does he have pheasants or something?'

'You really don't know do you?' When they said this bloke was useless as a spy I could see why now. 'I thought you lived in Louth?'

'I do, but what's that got to do with this bloke O'Shea?'

'Nothing really apart from the fact that he's one of the top people in the IRA.'

'You're joking....' He waited for me to say yes, but I didn't. 'You are joking aren't you?'

'No. I'm deadly serious. He is the top official in the IRA. In fact he is the IRA, he's the main man. Now can we get on with things?'

'Shit. You do mean it. You must be mad. Why have you brought me here?'

'Number one because the Gardai won't even consider looking here. Number two, it's well off the beaten track and number three we have good cover and it's the quickest route to the disused railway line. So if you're ready we'll get going.'

At this I set off in front walking deeper into the woods towards O'Shea's farm. Austen fell in behind and we walked on in silence. About a couple of hundred yards in I turned left and struck out along a parallel route to the edge of the woods in a northerly direction. Occasionally we would pause so

33

I could take a quick compass bearing to make sure we were still maintaining our heading.

Gradually the trees started to thin and eventually a lighter band of darkness ahead confirmed that we were fast approaching the edge of the woods. At the boundary wall we paused just to take stock. I checked my watch. It was now three in the morning and we hadn't got very far!

'Right, we need to speed things up a little as we are behind schedule thanks to the amorous cavorting of the couple back there.' I nodded in the general direction of the Tara. 'Once over this wall we'll be in O'Shea's orchard and we'll be able to talk safely. So, we head straight across this and the next orchard before we turn to our right. I'll warn you now, these orchards eventually give way to some rough old brush land further on, it's a bit messy but passable. We've got a small stream to cross, then over a stone wall then we're at the old railway line. Once we are on the railway line we turn left and follow our noses. From here it's about ten or eleven miles at the most, so if we get a move on I reckon we should be across the border by daybreak at the latest. Any questions?'

'Can't think of any?'

'Good, then I'll just send off an update and an ETA to control, take about five minutes, then we'll make a move.'

We had now left the woods far behind and had made up on the time we had lost. Our progress was good, having crossed the orchards we were now well into the rough terrain I'd spoken of and slipped and slithered our way down bumpy and rocky banks. We scrabbled up clay and brush covered hills, forced our way through brambles and undergrowth until we eventually emerged onto a flat lush area of grassland. Here the going got stodgy as we trudged through a boggy region to firmer ground. One last bank and we were at the stream. I shone the torch on the face of my watch the time was now approaching ten minutes to four. Thankfully we were over the worst part of the journey but we still had about six miles to go.

'Hmm. Just over two hours before we're due. We might just about do it. How you doing Austen?'

'I think I've got some blisters on my feet, but otherwise fine.'

I didn't like the sound of blisters that could ultimately slow us right down.

'Well I'm sorry but we've still got to press on, blisters or no blisters.'

'I know' was all he said.

Within twenty minutes we had reached the railway line and headed due north. We'd been walking along the track for a good forty minutes or so when Austen called to me.

'I'm sorry it's no good, I'll just have to rest up for a minute, My feet are killing me.'

I had been expecting this since the minute he said about getting blisters, in fact I was surprised he'd lasted as long as this.

'Ok. Take ten minutes but no longer otherwise we will be behind schedule.'

The sky was a lot lighter now as the cloud base had started to break up allowing the moon to shine through from time to time. Austen sat down on the rusty track and unlaced his right shoe. At that moment there was a break in the cloud and I could see clearly what a mess his foot was in. The blisters had burst and his foot was a mass of bloody cuts and weeping wounds. I then noticed his footwear.

'Jesus no wonder you've got lacerated feet, what do you call these?' I said holding up a flimsy looking canvas shoe with half the sole cut to shreds from the rough terrain. The canvas upper was soaking wet and in one place had a large split.

'Do you know, I knew there was something I'd forgotten,' he said sarcastically, 'I was in such a hurry I forgot to pack my best walking boots. Now isn't that a fucking shame!'

'Whoa, hold on a minute. Now I didn't ask for this job but having been given the task it is my intention to deliver the goods, so sunshine cut the crap and the sarcasm. Ok?'

'Ok but there again these were the only ones we had issued in prison.'

'I'm sorry Austen but I didn't realise you were still wearing prison issue flimsy footwear, if only I known before hand I could have brought something a little more suitable with me.'

'That's ok.' He said meaning it. 'You weren't to know.'

'What about your other foot?' I asked feeling more than a little guilty.

He unlaced the other canvas shoe and removed it for a closer inspection.

'Hmm, not as bad as the right foot,' he muttered to himself, but I wasn't convinced.

'Here let me take a look.' Austen twisted round so I could examine his left foot, he was right, it wasn't as bad as his other foot, but nevertheless bad enough. 'Do you think you can make it?' I asked.

'Yeah, it'll be all right.' He answered but he didn't sound too convincing.

I looked at my watch and we'd been stopped for more than ten minutes. 'Sorry to have to say this, but we need…'

'I know, we need to get going,' he said cutting me short, 'just give me a chance to get my wonderful walking boots back on and I'll be with you.'

He gave a half-hearted attempt at a laugh, but I could see him wince in his face as he forced his canvas shoes back on to his lacerated feet.

It was just after six when we crossed over the border from the Republic into the Province and night was fast disappearing as the steely grey of approaching dawn spread across the sky. Austen was now really struggling, so much so I had to help him over the last couple of miles. One canvas shoe was caked in blood and the other was not much better. Both his feet were severely lacerated and swollen. At last we could get off the railway track for a short distance through the town of Dundalk, which I hoped would help to ease the pain that he was experiencing. As we walked, stumbled and staggered our way towards the centre I noticed, down a side road off to our right, a small shoe shop. Suddenly I had a brainwave. 'What size shoes do you take?' I asked.

'Why?'

'Never mind why, just tell me the size.'

'Eight.'

The place was deserted. It was like a ghost town. Nothing stirred. 'Stay here.' I said propping him against a wall.

'Where are you going?' He asked.

'Never you mind. Just stay there.' I disappeared back the way we had come then turned into the side road where I had seen the shoe shop. In a matter of minutes I arrived outside the shop and quickly checked it out, I was in luck, no alarm. I reached inside my jacket and withdrew my Browning and after a quick look around to make sure that nobody was in the vicinity, I smashed the butt of it against the window of the door and with a crash it exploded, splinters of glass flying in all directions. I reached through the gaping hole where the window had been and unlocked the door. It took me less than thirty seconds to break in and with my Maglite torch switched on I hastily scanned around for something in his shoe size, but the only thing I could see in the short time available was a pair of Wellington boots. They would have to do. In less than a minute I had been in, found the Wellington boots, out, re-locked the door and back up the road to where I had left Austen.

'Here,' I threw him the Wellington boots, 'Sorry, but it's the best I can do.'

He started to laugh. He laughed and laughed to such an extent that I started to laugh as well. Between bouts of laughter he managed to get the boots on.

'Well?' I asked, 'Do they fit?'

He immediately put on a show of walking or should I say attempting to walk back wards and forwards.

'You could have brought me a mirror so I could see what they looked like,' He quipped.

'Whoah, don't push it…'

'Thank you. They're fine. Much more comfortable.'

'In that case let's go.'

'How much further do you reckon?'

'I'm not too sure, but all things being equal we should be there in about thirty to forty minutes. Can you hang on that long?'

'Yeah I'm fine.'

It was about quarter to seven when two dishevelled looking individuals landed at the rendezvous. We were about ten minutes from the house, but Austen was about all in. His feet were far too bad even for me to contemplate pushing him any further. I sat him down out of sight in a small copse not too far from the road.

'Wait here I won't be too long. Should be back within the hour.'

Ten minutes later I had arrived at the farm's front door, our ultimate destination. I pressed on the bell push and waited. I could just about detect a slight whirring as the carefully concealed miniature CCTV camera panned around to examine who it was ringing the bell. A few moments later a metallic voice sternly greeted me.

'You're late Ferryman.'

Even the metallic overtones didn't conceal the welcome sound of Sean O'Donald's voice.

'Ok smart arse, let me in.'

The door was opened by the big man.

'Christ Richard, you look as if you've been through the mill.'

I entered the hall and felt the welcoming warmth emanating from the radiator. It was only then that I realised how chilly it was outside.

'How you doing Sean?'

'Fine and you my friend, how are you?'

'I'm ok, but I need a vehicle for a special delivery.'

'Austen?'

'Austen.'

'Is there a problem then?'

'Only a minor one, but it's really immobilised him.'

'Ok, I'll get it organised. Rick,' He called through to the kitchen area. 'Rick are you through there?'

A blonde-headed guy stuck his head out of the kitchen door.

'Just taking five Sean, can I help?'

'Ok Dan, can you organise a car, a driver and go with Richard we have a collection to make.'

'Sure Sean. I'll be there in two.'

A little later a blue rover 3500 SE pulled up near a small copse. It wasn't long before Dan and I managed to half carry and half bundle a scruffy looking slightly built man into the back of the car. Kenneth Austen was really out of it when we got to the farm and it took about an hour to an hour and a half before he was really aware of what was going on around him.

'Hello. Pleased to meet you Mr Austen.'

'Err where am I?'

'You're in Ulster. A safe house over the border. We're just going to get the Doc to take a look at your feet ok?'

'Yeah, err, I mean sure thanks.'

Half an hour later with something in his belly, penicillin gauze on his lacerated feet and a new pair of soft-shoes Austen was a different man.

'Feeling a bit brighter now Mr Austen?'

'Yeah, a lot better thanks.'

'Good, because we are ready to take you on the final stage of your journey.'

'Where's that to?'

'We need to get you to Lisburn for debrief, then we'll ship you off abroad somewhere for a short spell. So if you're ready Mr Austen we'll go.'

'Ok, I'm ready.' He turned to me and offered me his hand. 'Cheers mate, do you know I don't even know your name. But thanks whoever you are. I've left the Wellingtons in case you need them for someone else.'

He struggled to his feet and in a chirpy mood shuffled his way out to the waiting blue Rover.

'How you getting back?'

'Walking?'

'Come on Richard, I'll give you a lift back to…where is your car?

'The Tara.'

'Back to the Tara then.'

Chapter 6

Having got Austen over the border into the Province my job was done, or so I thought. On the drive back Sean took a slight detour along a narrow country lane that wound its way up to the top of a hill. Once at the top he pulled into a gateway and parked. As he got out of the car Sean grabbed a high-powered pair of binoculars and walked over to a nearby field gate.

'Here Richard I want to show you something' he called back to me as he fixed the glasses on something in the distance. I joined him at the gate and the view was quite breathtaking. To our left the valley gently rose upwards through a layer of mist into the foothills of the Mourn Mountains. To our right it dropped dramatically down towards Dundalk Bay. In the distance you could see the glint of the early morning sun on the calm sea. It was so serene out here, nothing moved, nothing stirred, and yet a stones throw away, the violence continued. In the peace and quiet of this beautiful countryside 'Orpheus the king of the underworld' was at work.

'What a view Sean.'

'I know, but that is not why I stopped. Here.' He handed me the binoculars. 'Can you see that small area of woods on the other side of the valley.'

'Yes,' I said as I focused on the woods with the binoculars.

'Now move up the hill above the woods there's a farm. See where I mean?' He pointed towards a small number of buildings in the distance.

'I see.' I answered. 'What about them?'

'Focus the binoculars on them and take a really good look.' I did what Sean asked but I still wasn't sure what I was looking for.

'Ok, so what's so special?'

'A guy called Riley, a John Francis Riley also known as 'Slab' Riley, owns that farm. Does the name ring any bells with you?'

'I can't say it does why should it?' I asked.

'Riley is an IRA commander. That farmhouse is in County Louth so like O'Shea and many others he lives in the Republic. That is when he is actually there.'

'But that's Dundalk, isn't it?' I asked as I lowered the binoculars and pointed to a conglomerate of houses further down the valley.

'Yeah, that is Dundalk but the border isn't a straight line. Although his farmhouse is to our left and quite a distance from the town it's still inside the Republic. In fact the road you can see is the South Armagh Road, which if you follow it crosses into the Republic as it passes through those woods. Those woods actually straddle the border and his farmland is half in Ulster and half in the Republic, which of course is very convenient for the IRA.'

'So even though his farm is above the woods it is still south of the border?'

'Yeah, you've got it. Now trace back along the road from the woods.'

'Ok.'

'Now those fields you can see either side of the road belong to Riley.'

'I see, but so what? After all there are many farms like that.'

'Ah yes but not quite the same as this. If you now follow the line of the road passed the woods and pick it up again on the south side, you'll see a field with a track passing through it. Have you got it?'

I traced the road down like he said and looked for the field with the track.

'Have you found it?'

'I panned slightly to my right and there it was, the field came into view and the track jumped into focus.

'Right. I've found it,' I said.

'Now follow the line of the track and you should see a barn. That barn is definitely in the Republic and is big enough to hold a large herd of cattle. Now sweep from the barn northwards.'

'Ok.' I said as I scanned with the binoculars towards the north.

'Now you should see the track continuing. That track continues through one field into the next one, which is once again north of the border...'

'Ahh I get it, so he can claim hefty European subsidies for moving his cattle across the border.'

'Right. But he's no fool. To avoid any arguments he doesn't leave them in the second field. If you swing up to the road you can see there is a gateway into that field, also right opposite on the other side of the road is another gate into the other field. I know for a fact that he moves his animals from the second field over the road into the field opposite so he is well inside Ulster. Also if you notice there is another track in that field leading to another barn.'

I panned to my right sweeping the across the field and quickly picked out the second barn and the track. I panned back to my left following the line of the track every inch of the way and it was just as Sean said.

'So how does he work it?'

'Easy. The herd's driven into the barn. His foreman calls in cattle trucks from Murphy Haulage. Paperwork is issued to say so many head of steers transported from A to B. Murphy takes them from one barn to the other and drops them off. The paperwork is the evidence and Riley claims the subsidy. We're not talking small scale here; we're actually talking large sums of money which he then places into IRA funds. Once the cattle have been delivered he then uses his own transport to move them from the holding barn back across his own land to where they started from then, a few months later, he repeats the sequence. So you see he runs a nice little scam.'

'In that case, why doesn't he get a visit?'

'That's the problem. Why should he, what's he done wrong?'

'Claimed subsidies on the same beasts!'

'Prove it? No Richard, you can't. In fact no-one can prove anything other than he has claimed what he is rightfully due. His paperwork is all in order and he's used an outside contractor what more can be asked? No Richard, to all intents and proposes what he has done is strictly legitimate and legal! Nothing can be done to stop him.'

'Nice one.' I commented, 'on that basis he must make a fortune.'

'Oh he does. In fact we know that most of that money goes towards their arms deals.'

'Why hasn't he been taken out?'

'Problem number two. Riley doesn't actually live on the farm because his main income is from a civil construction company in the Republic.'

'Is that where he got his nickname 'Slab' from?'

'No, it's because Riley is such a common surname in this area they tended to give families nicknames to differentiate between the different groups. The nicknames were usually based on some family trait or trade. In our man's case His father, Seamus Riley, was a huge bloke, a regular slab of a man hence the family being known as 'Slab' Riley. John Francis Riley shares the family trait on physique so the name has stuck.'

'I see, but I would have thought being in the building game would have been the reason, not because of his stature.'

'Ah well there you are. Anyway, we know he has a base in Dundalk, but we're almost certain that's not his main office. We suspect he lives in, or close to Drogheda, but as yet we're not sure. So the only way we can grab him is whenever he comes north of the border, which is seldom.'

'What about when he visits his farm, couldn't someone snatch him then?'

'Fine in theory, but in practice very difficult. It's fraught with a number of problems.'

'Such as?'

'Ah Richard such a simple question, but difficult to answer. First of all he has quite a few men working there under the guise of farmhands, some are but in the main we are talking security personnel.'

'How do you mean 'security'?' I asked.

'Well we have noticed that at night the farm is brightly lit with security lights and there is always people about. He also has two or three dogs with handlers patrolling the out buildings. Now tell me how many farms do that. Also take a good look at the buildings again. Do you see anything strange?'

'No can't say that I do.'

'Look above the roof of his house and what do you see?'

'Ahh. I see what you mean. A bloody great aerial array. So what's going on there then?'

41

'At the moment we are not too sure, but we assume it is some sort of control centre or communications centre for their northern command.'

'Hmm a bit of a problem then.'

'As you say Richard, a bit of a problem, anyway let's go.'

I handed Sean the binoculars and we returned to the car. A few minutes later we were heading towards Dundalk.

That evening I decided I would have a meal then head off up the lane to O'Shea's place I felt it was important to say 'hello' so that I could avoid any awkward questions as no doubt Noel, the union man, would have told him that I was here. However before then I had something more important to attend to and that was to make my peace with Fionnuala. The last thing I wanted was for her to think that I had used her that night in my room, when in fact there was nothing further from the truth. Oh sure I had enjoyed the time we had together, but I felt she deserved something a little more than a one night stand. I valued her for more than just an easy 'lay' so to speak, and I sure as hell didn't want her thinking along those lines. Besides, the practical side was that she could be of use to me in the future. Yes, it was very important that I made my peace with her and encouraged the relationship I had started, and it was with this in mind that I went back to my room and phoned down to reception.

'Hello, is Fionnuala around?' I asked.

'Sorry Mr James, she's not available at the moment. Can I be of assistance?' The voice on the end of the telephone asked.

'Err, not really. Can you tell me when she'll be around?'

'I'm not too sure Mr James. Are you sure there's nothing I can do?'

'Yes. I'll give a call a bit later.'

'I'll let her know you called.' The phone clicked as the receptionist replaced her handset. It did occur to me that perhaps Fionnuala was embarrassed about the other night and was now avoiding me. Now I wasn't too sure what to do, whether to write it off or to try and speak to her again. I was in a quandary. In the end I decided to leave things as they were for the time being and to head off up to O'Shea's.

This time I decided to take the lane. I secreted my Browning along with my communications set under the floorboards and set off on my walk. On the way I thought back to the last time I had walked up here and how I'd spent an enjoyable couple of hours with the young nurse who had taken Noel up to the clinic in Ulster, listening to the Beatles album and drinking her coffee. I fondly remembered her infectious laughter and how we had made love in her front room. I wondered to myself if she still came down from the north on her days off. Ahh, good memories. Good memories. My thoughts

42

then turned to the farm and its outbuildings for it was there, in the flattened grass, where I found the empty 9.00mm magazine case which, linked to the arc lights, aroused my curiosity and prompted me to take a look inside the sheds.

I had been so immersed in my thoughts that I had not realised how far I had walked. Suddenly I found I was alongside the gate to the very same cottage where the nurse had been staying. I wondered if she was in and for a moment I was tempted to knock on the door to find out, but the feeling soon passed. Another ten minutes found me through the gate at O'Shea's and walking towards his house. Suddenly I stopped dead in my tracks because parked alongside his old Fiat and Mercedes was a third vehicle, a Volvo, could it be the very same Volvo that belonged to his brother Dr James O'Shea, who ran a clinic in Ulster. If that were the case, then why would it be here unless his brother was also here as well? Having told Breandán on my last trip how well I knew his brother, when I didn't at all, I now needed to check this out. The last thing I wanted was to come face to face with the person I had fabricated a story about. This could spell trouble with a capital 'T'. I cautiously moved over towards the cars and when I thought it safe to do so I pulled out my small Maglite and shone the beam quickly over the Volvo. It was blue all right. The colour was the same so what about the number? I shone the torch on the number plate. 'Shit' it had a Belfast number. My worst fears had just been confirmed. I wondered if Breandán had remembered our conversation when I told him that I knew his brother Dr. O'Shea and if so had he told him? I could just imagine Breandán's reaction when he realises that what I had said was pure fabrication. If he has found out about my bluff, then I knew I was in a dangerous situation and then what? I pondered over my options. I could go back to the hotel and leave straight away, but that was out because Noel would have already told O'Shea I had said that I was going to come over. I could hope that Breandán had forgotten all about our conversation involving his brother, but that was a major risk that I wasn't prepared to take. I could presume that Breandán still remembered the conversation, but had not bothered to mention me to his brother. No matter what I thought, all options were fraught with problems and the situation was not good. I then wondered why Dr James O'Shea was here, what was he up to? There was no getting away from it, the O'Shea's must be up to something and I needed to find out what it was. Quickly I weighed up all the risks involved and decided that this was too good an opportunity to pass up so I just had to stay regardless. I tucked myself in as close as possible to the wall of the house and I stealthily moved off through the shadows, stopping below the widow of the lounge. There was a thin strip of yellow light, which spilled out from a chink in the curtains. I could clearly hear voices emanating from the same room. I cautiously raised my head to look through the chink in the curtains. I could clearly see three men, Breandán, Noel and one other whom I took to be Dr. James O'Shea. They were deep in conversation about something.

'No I don't think that's a good idea.' the one who I assumed was James O'Shea said a little brusquely. The good doctor seemed a little annoyed about something.

'Why not James?' Breandán asked in an even voice, 'After all what better place could there be to hold him? You've got the medical knowledge and the facilities to keep him out of the way and what's more, you have access to drugs that will keep him sedated. So why not?'

'Because I think it's too dangerous to keep someone with as high a profile as Thomas Niedermayer in our clinic.'

Who was Thomas Niedermayer I wondered?

'But Dr O'Shea, surely the clinic is the last place they'd think of. We can keep him there sedated forever and a day and no one would know. After all, we run a private clinic and who's to know who the patients are?' A woman's voice, a voice I was sure I'd heard before, asked. Was it Jenny O'Shea the wife of Gerry, Breandán's other brother, or was it somebody else? I wasn't sure. Maybe it was Noel's wife, but I wasn't convinced. I knew the voice but I just couldn't think who it could be. I craned my neck, but the left-hand curtain cut off my field of vision just short of her. I could just about see the side of the armchair but that was all. Then my prayers were answered as the owner of the voice suddenly came into view. It was none other than the nurse whom I had spent a very enjoyable time with on my last trip. She hadn't changed a bit and was still as pretty as ever. Seeing her had answered two questions that had been at the back of my mind since our last encounter. Firstly did she still rent the cottage, obviously she did and secondly, how involved was she in O'Shea's set-up? If appearance was anything to go by, she was very much involved with the Republican Movement!

I decided I had seen and heard enough so I quietly withdrew back into the shadows. Now I had to decide my plan of action, but the situation I was in gave me cause for concern. The same old questions were still there, how much had Breandán said to his brother? I couldn't risk meeting James O'Shea just in case he had been told about me, nor could I not see Breandán, because that would only impact on my current situation. Whichever way I turned it was a problem. I was on the horns of a dilemma. In the end I decided that the best way would be for me was to try and bluff my way through, after all I had done it before. I was about to knock on the door when the die was cast. The decision was taken out of my hands as I heard footsteps of people approaching the door. I instantly dived back out of sight melting away into the shadows. I retraced my footsteps back around the corner of the house and waited with bated breath. The front door opened and Dr James O'Shea shook hands with his brother.

'Ok, I accept the majority decision, but I still don't like it and I still think we are taking a big risk in keeping Niedermayer locked away in the clinic, just hoping our demands will be met.'

'Don't worry James. As I said before the risk is minimal. Anyway enough of that, have a safe journey back and I'll see you in the next few weeks when I'm next up at the farm.'

'Ok see you Breandán and look after yourself.'

'Bye Breandán.' I heard the nurse call. There was a double clunk as both car doors were pulled shut. I heard the engine start, saw the light from the headlights and heard the slight chatter of gravel being thrown up as the car accelerated away from the house and out on to the lane. I gave them chance to get well away and a few minutes later I again approached the front door and gave a sharp knock. There was a ferocious barking and snarling as Breandán's dog rushed to the door.

'Quiet. I said QUIET.' The barking ceased as suddenly as it had started and was replaced by a snuffling sound as the dog sniffed at the bottom of the door. 'Bed, BED.' With one last snuffle the dog retreated back from whence it came and the door opened.

'B'jesus it's you Richard. What are you doing here?'

'I thought I'd pop up to see you as I was over.'

'To be sure, it's good t' see you. What brings you here then?'

'I had to come over to check out what was still left to do up at your neighbours place.'

'Who do you mean?'

'Mike McCluskey's farm and Ross O'Toole's place.'

'Well you best come in.' Breandán held open the door. 'You've just missed my brother James, I could have introduced you if you'd been a couple of minutes earlier. There again, I wouldn't have needed to, would I, as you already know him.'

We made our way into his lounge.

'Look who's here Noel.'

'Evening Noel, how are you keeping?'

'I'm fine Richard and you?'

'Fine.' There was a decided awkwardness on my part, had Noel told Breandán about my recent visit, or had he kept it quiet?

A couple of hours later I was back in the Tara trying to work out whether Breandán was humouring me, or whether he actually believed me about my being over here on my way to Mike McCluskey and Ross O'Toole's. I decided that either way I would have to brazen it out. Just then I caught sight of Fionnuala now was my chance to find out whether or not she was avoiding me. As I approached the reception she looked up and smiled.

'Hello Richard, what can I do for you?'

Had I imagined it or was her mood a little on the cool side toward me, I wasn't too sure.

'Fionnuala, did you get my message?' I asked.

'What message would that be?' Her response was certainly not very warm.

'I telephoned earlier and your colleague said you were unavailable, didn't she tell you?'

'No. Anyway what was it you wanted?' she asked.

'I just wondered if you would like to go to the club after you finished, that was all.' I said more as a statement rather than a question.

'I'm not sure.'

'Fionnuala, what's wrong?' I asked.

'Nothing.' Was all she said.

'There is. I know there is so come on out with it. What's wrong?'

'All right, I'll tell you what's wrong. I got the impression that after the other evening you had what you wanted and since then you've been avoiding me. In fact I didn't even see you at all yesterday or last night.'

So I was right, she did think I had used her. How little did she know?

'Oh Fionnuala, how wrong you are. If only you knew the half of it, no way have I been avoiding you. Let's start again. Come on, come with me to the club tonight after you've finished. What d'you say?'

'Hmm. I don't know. I'll think about it.'

I felt there was nothing to be gained by badgering her, so I decided to go to the bar and have a drink.

At just after eleven I decided that Fionnuala wasn't going to show so I finished my drink and got up to leave, when to my surprise she turned up.

'Where are you going Richard James, I thought you were taking me to the club?'

I think my smile said everything.

'Well come on then what are you waiting for?' She asked as she grabbed my hand and led me away down the corridor and through the back labyrinth of corridors to the staff door that led into the club. Here she stopped pulled me to her, her mouth wet and inviting, her eyes full of longing as our lips met. I could feel the gentle rise of her breasts against me as we kissed.

'Oh Richard, I am sorry for doubting you.' She said between kisses. 'Let's leave the club for tonight and let me make it up to you for my stupidity. Come on, come with me.' She took me by the hand and led me off back along the corridors, through the kitchen and out across the lawn to her room in the staff quarters.

It was a good job that Fionnuala had the day off, because it was nearly ten when I woke up. She looked peaceful lying there asleep her head nestled on my chest. I gently kissed her eyelids. She snuggled closer pushing her naked breasts up against me. Her perfume was delicate to my senses. I kissed her again and this time she stretched and opened her eyes.

'Hello.' She said sleepily, 'What's the time?'

'Ten o'clock.' I replied.

'Hmm. I love you Richard James.' Was all she said. I gently kissed her and slid out of bed. As I went to the bathroom I knew that she meant more to me than just a passing fancy. I was becoming involved and just couldn't help it. Once I was dressed I leaned over and gently kissed her.

'I've got to go.'

'Why?' was all she said.

'I have to meet with some people.'

'What people?'

'Oh some people before I go home.'

'Be careful Richard.'

'Why do you say be careful?' I asked.

'Because. Just because. That's all.'

'How do you mean, just because. Is there something I need to know?'

'Richard.' She was now wide awake. 'Please be very careful of Breandán O'Shea, you don't know who you're dealing with. He is a very powerful man and you don't know the half of it.'

'Why are you so concerned about me? Anyone would think….' She cut across my conversation. 'I know Richard. I know.'

'What do you know Fionnuala?'

She then shocked me. 'I know who you really are. I know you are working for the British Government. So please be careful.' I tried to make light of what she had just said, but she was not being put off. 'Richard, I've known for a long time about you and who you are. You see my brother is in the Gardai Special Branch...'

'What?' I exclaimed unable to hide my surprise. 'I didn't know you had a brother.'

'Yes I have a brother and for some time now he has worked with one of your people in Dublin. Like I was saying, he's in the Special Branch in the department that deals with terrorism and subversion. I think it is called C3, anyway he passes official information about different people and O'Shea is one of the people known to him, but he is too powerful, he knows too many people in high places. Also my brother knows of you and what you're doing here. I try to help where I can by telling him who comes and goes through the hotel, who sees O'Shea and so on and so forth.'

I couldn't help thinking back to my first trip to the Tara when my room had been searched and how photographs and a letter had been removed to eventually turn up in the Circus with 'Mother'.

'So was it you who went to my room and removed my letters and things?'

'Not really. I told my brother about you and Paul. He did the rest.'

I was totally confused. How deep she was in God knows.

'I don't know about you telling me to be careful, I think it's you who needs to be careful.'

What she had told me put a whole new complexion on things.

It was well after eleven thirty when we said our goodbyes. Fionnuala had made me some sandwiches. I went up to my room, retrieved my equipment from under the floorboards and once again packed them carefully in among my clothes. With my case packed, I checked my room to make sure I hadn't left anything then made my way to reception to pay my bill. Ten minutes later I was on my way again, I swung the car down the tree lined lane towards the main Dublin to Dundalk road. At the end I turned right and headed off in a northerly direction. My journey to Dundalk passed with out incident and I was soon heading out of the town on the road to Belfast and Mike McCluskey's farm.

It was around this time that things really started to jump in Ulster. 14th Intelligence Company. The 14th had always used the bases of regular Army regiments as cover, and they now became the forefront of covert operations. Using the name 4 Field Survey Troop of the Royal Engineers, or the Northern Ireland Training and Tactics Team and equipped with unmarked civilian cars and non-standard weapons our operations became far more intrusive. A Captain, whose name escapes me, but he later moved on to command another Special Force in the Middle East, headed up the main thrust of this team. Towards the end of the year the IRA declared a cease-fire which held good over Christmas, but this was not catered for in the overall scheme of things, nor did our beloved leaders accept it. They felt the only way to defeat Breandán O'Shea and his followers was through an all out military operation rather than political negotiation. So it was decided that the Circus would step up its operations by taking matters into their own hands as *agent provocateurs.* So it was that early in January a three man cell of British Operators crossed over the border into the Republic and visited a deserted farmhouse which just happened to belong to a known IRA commander. The three man cell kicked in the door of the farmhouse and emptied their weapons into the victim's body and left him in a pool of blood. This action seemed to have the desired effect insofar as the cease-fire was called off within a matter of days.

It was during this heightened activity I returned home I had been home about a month when I received a telephone call from a very distressed young lady called Jean. Sean O'Donald's wife had telephoned me out of the blue.

'I…I'm sorry to call you Richard, it's Jean…Jean O'Donald…Sean's wife.' Her voice was strained, 'But I needed to speak to you.'

She gave a sharp intake of Breath.

'What's wrong?' I asked.

'It's Sean….'

'What about Sean?

'He's …he's…Oh Richard …he's dead.' She then started to sob uncontrollably.

I really didn't know what to say. I waited until she gained some of her composure.

'I'm…' I paused picking my words carefully. 'I'm so sorry Jean. How…?' The question was heavy in the air. I suppose deep down I knew what she would say.

'Killed…he was killed Richard by those murdering bastards…' Again she gave a sharp intake of breath whilst she fought to gain her composure. She spoke quietly yet a little more composed. 'He was killed Richard…'

I cut across her. 'How?' I asked.

'By a bomb.' There was a heavy silence as if both of us were trying to avoid the obvious.

'Shit Jean. I am so sorry.' I hurried on before she could say anything. 'If there's anything I can do you must tell me.'

'Thank you Richard.' Her voice was steady now. 'I will. Of course I want, no, Sean would want you to come to his wake. I trust…'

'Oh … that goes without saying. Of course I'll come.' Again a heavy silence. 'Jean how…I mean where was he killed?'

'Outside the house. A car bomb.'

'I don't understand. Sean was so meticulous about checking everything. What happened? What went wrong?'

'I don't really know, unless he was tired. He'd only been home a couple of hours when he got a shout. I guess he was careless, no tired. Oh damn you Sean damn you. Sorry Richard. I'm sorry, but he was never careless you know that.'

'What about the business?' I asked trying to change the subject. 'How will you manage, will you sell it?'

'Like hell.' She said vehemently. 'That will be the last thing I'll do, even if it kills me, I'll run the business. You know, Sean built that company from nothing and there's no way will I let it go. It was his life, our life and IRA or no IRA it will continue.' She had suddenly become very determined and it sounded in her voice.

'Good I'm glad about that Jean. Look don't forget, should you need me all you have to do is give me a call.'

'Thank you Richard. Sean would want that. Now I must let you get on with whatever you were doing. Speak to you soon. Bye'

'Bye Jean. Look after yourself and Jean...'

'Yes Richard.'

'Be careful.'

'I will. Goodbye.'

'Goodbye Jean.' I replaced the handset and thought about the conversation I had just had. I felt numb. The big man was dead. I hadn't known him that long, but I certainly knew him as a friend. 'You stupid bastard Sean. Why?' I muttered to myself, still feeling dazed from the news I had just received. Because of this latest twist I felt that my role in the Republic was even more important. Now it was imperative that I get even closer to O'Shea and his Republican cronies.

Chapter 7

Hardly a day would pass without some reference in the media to Ireland, whether it was about the Republic and the Taoiseach response to terrorism, or the troubles in Ulster, it was now a major issue. In fact it was so much so that I was summoned to Ashford in Kent for a high level meeting of the Circus.

It was fine but blustery on the morning I set off to meet with Major O'Rourke, Colonel Ash and with Sean's replacement whose death had left a hole in the network. With little traffic on the road I made it to Ashford in good time and was early for the meeting. The Corporal on duty at the main entrance checked the registration of my car against his list, then proceeded to book me in.

'Thank you sir. Park your vehicle over there,' he pointed to an area away from any buildings, 'then sign-in with the duty Sergeant on the desk in the Guardroom.' He then indicated to the armed soldier to raise the barrier so allowing me to enter.

The phone on the desk in front of Colonel Ash rang several times before he picked it up.

'Ash.'

'Guardroom here Sir.' The duty Sergeant's voice barked down the phone. 'Mr James, Richard James here for you Sir.'

'Thank you Sergeant ask Mr James to wait there and I'll get someone over to pick him up.'

'Yes Sir.' The voice rattled back the answer. Ash replaced his handset, buzzed through to the outer office.

'Sir?' The voice of his adjutant answered.

'Bill, Richard James has arrived somewhat earlier than expected, so pop over to the Guardroom and take him over to the Mess there's a good chap.'

'Certainly Sir.'

'Damn nuisance him arriving so early.'

'Yes Sir.'

'Still it's better than being late, and tell him I'll join him there shortly.'

'Yes Sir. Will that be all?'

'Yes thank you Bill.' Ash replaced the handset for the second time and returned to the buff file stamped TOP SECRET lying on his desk. He opened the front cover and started to read the first page headed OPERATION ORPHEUS. Beneath the title was a description of a farm situated in County Louth, not far from Dundalk in the Republic of Ireland with land stretching across the border into County Armagh. He looked thoughtful as he flicked through the file to the last page which he proceeded to read in detail:

(Bravo 1) is John Francis Riley.

Farm believed to be IRA stronghold.

Bravo 1 known to be a staunch IRA supporter and a senior member of the Northern Command.

Also known as O'Hare, O'Hanlon and O'Dowd. Wanted in connection with terrorist activities. Nickname(s) 'The Boss' or 'Slab'. Trademark(s) are 'explosive devices' & kneecapping with paving slabs!

Personal Details:

Riley's Dob believed to be 1949 (although has used 1944 and various other dates). Unmarried lives with his mother. Religion RC. Height 5 ft 10 in. Big strong build and balding.

Other factors:

Extremely wealthy. Main source of income from smuggling although farming & construction work are also known to contribute.

Currently employs in excess of 100 persons, all believed to have IRA connections. Cross-border pig movements, cattle, grain and oil. All used to obtain European subsidies. Most of this money used for IRA funding for weapons.

Key negotiator with arms dealers abroad.

Background Information: Profile

Known to RUC and Garda Siochána (Irish police) Special Branch as a "Smuggler with IRA connections." VAT and Tax evasion on both sides of the border always pays bills in cash.

Wanted in Ulster: -

1. *For terrorism.*
2. *On suspicion of extortion and racketeering also suspected of kidnap and organised crime.*
3. *In connection with South Armagh train hijack.*
4. *Believed to be connected with the O'Connor brothers known IRA bombers and nephews of Breandán O'Shea – Head of operations 'Official IRA'.*
5. *Links with Libyan arms deals.*
6. *Wanted in connection with Ulster sectarian killings.*
7. *Wanted for questioning about disappearance of German Industrialist Niedermayer (Note no known whereabouts since disappearance).*
8. *Wanted in connection with car bomb death of business man and UDR member Sean O'Donald*

Brief/Action Required:
1. Farm under close surveillance. Covert operation requires full information on movement of personnel. Photographs of persons and details of surroundings. Long term surveillance
2. Input from SIS agents in the Republic required. Advise on contacts in Eire and any connections with O'Shea (Bravo 2)
3. Agent 296 to advise on connection with O'Connor's (Bravo 3 & 4 nephews to Bravo 1 refer Ferryman Op).
4. Investigate possible Security Forces hit squads. (4 Field Survey Troop)
5. Train 'snatch squad' for 'collecting' Target Bravo 1 (known by Riley, O'Hare, O'Hanlon & O'Dowd) and bring north of the border. (14th to handle in conjunction with 6)

Comments from Field.
1. Initial covert obs carried out suggests Bravo 1 uses farm as ops HQ and apparently as some sort of training camp.
2. Believed to be extremely wealthy **but** unable to trace any bank details as believe accounts held in various bank and offshore accounts by relatives and in aliases.

The Colonel read and re-read this last page until he knew it perfectly. One thing was for sure, he was going to get this bastard one way or another. He glanced at his watch, closed the file and placed it back in the lockable filing cabinet. The last thing he wanted was for any cock-ups to happen.

'Richard dear boy, good to see you. How are you keeping?'

'Good morning Colonel, I'm fine. How are you?'

'Fine. I'm fine. No doubt you've heard about O'Donald.'

'Yes, Jean called me.' Ash raised an eyebrow.

'Jean?'

'His wife.'

'Bad do Richard. A really bad do. Still we must learn from it. Now to more pleasant things, what can I get for you?'

'It's a bit early for me.'

'Nonsense. How about a Bushmills?'

'No thanks I'll just have a coffee if you don't mind.'

'Well at least make it an Irish Coffee.' He smiled at what he'd just said. 'Oh dear, no pun intended.'

I just nodded recognising a pun when I saw one regardless of what he said.

'Ok, I'll have an Irish Coffee, and that was a terrible pun. By the way, who else is coming Colonel?'

'There's O'Rourke who you know. Two or three from the Irish desk, but I can't think of their names at the moment, and Eamonn.' He looked at his watch 'Goodness is that the time? I really must get on. Lot to do Richard so please excuse me won't you?'

'Of course.'

'Make yourself at home and if you want anything tell Blake and he'll sort it out. Blake.' The Colonel summoned the duty steward.

'Yes Sir.' The steward looked up from what he was doing and walked smartly over to the Colonel and stood smartly to attention.

'Blake. Make sure you look after my guest and anything he wants book to my Mess bill.'

Blake gave a slight nod of his head, 'yes Sir.'

'Thank you Blake that will be all.' The Colonel then turned back to me, 'I'll get my adjutant to come and find you nearer the time.'

I was ushered into a room within the Tactical Operations section where the meeting was to be conducted. In the centre of the room was a highly polished oak table with seating for a dozen or more people. At one end of the room a white screen had been pulled down in front of the wall and at the far end of the table, already set up for the meeting, was a slide projector. Across the windows hung heavy brown velvet drapes that matched the leather covered seats around the table. Entry into the room was through a single doorway that was made to house two doors that opened independently of each other. This configuration formed an inexpensive yet efficient method of soundproofing further enhanced by having the door that opened into the meeting room lined on the inside with thick padded brown leather. The walls and ceiling were lined with acoustic tiles in order to deaden any sound to avoid eavesdropping. This was the room always used for meetings of a 'sensitive' nature and today was just such a meeting. Around the table sat eight individuals whose collective decisions could influence and shape the future of Ireland.

'Gentlemen,' Ash addressed those present, 'some of you already know each other, but a couple of you are newcomers so perhaps we could take it in turn to introduce ourselves to the meeting, just name and a brief background should do the trick. I'll start the ball rolling. My name is Ash, Colonel Ash Military Intelligence.'

'Good afternoon everyone I am Major O'Rourke. London Desk Military Intelligence.'

I stood up and introduced myself to the meeting. 'Hello gentlemen, my name's Richard, Richard James codename Ferryman.'

Next to me a slightly built Irishman stood up and with a softly spoken voice introduced himself. 'Gentleman, my name is Eamonn and I'm from the Republic of Ireland. Known as Agent 256 or codename Ferry Pilot.'

Next to Eamonn sat someone I hadn't seen before but I knew of him. He was possibly slightly older than me with ash blond hair and of medium build. He seemed ill at ease sitting here with us. 'Gentleman.' He paused and looked about him. 'I also come from the Republic of Ireland, and my name is Danny. I'm from C3.'

'Gentleman,' Ash interrupted, 'for those who are not familiar with C3. That is Special Branch in our parlance, but not from here or in Ulster. Danny is our man in the Gardai – of course he is…hmm…shall we say here incognito. As you probably all know the Gardai does not officially assist us in any shape or form so Danny has risked himself by coming here. He is based in the anti-terrorist and subversive unit of C3 and passes us information via his controller. Suffice it to say that Danny is taking a grave risk in attending this meeting and he is doing it in order that we may have his input direct from the 'horse's mouth' so to speak. So please consider his situation and where he stands should Dublin find out he has leaked information to us.'

Now I knew why he looked so ill at ease with us. Suddenly it dawned on me who Danny was. I realised, from what Fionnuala had said, that he must be her brother. Alongside Danny and sprawled back in his chair with his eyes half closed, was another man I hadn't seen before. One could be forgiven for assuming he was a mere youngster for he had thick black wavy hair and a clean-shaven boyish face which belied his years. His slim youthful build further compounded the deception. He had a certain attitude that some would see as arrogance. It was now his turn to introduce himself to the group, he thrust his hands into his pockets, his brown eyes flicked around the room and eventually alighted on me.

'Hi,' he said nonchalantly, 'my name's Racain, Bob Racain, Northern Ireland Training and Tactics Team.'

Immediately I recognised the name. It was his cell that had taken out a number of known targets south of the border. In fact just recently, along with two of his companions, he had paid a late night visit to a farm in the Republic, where between them they pumped their victim's body full of bullets. They had emptied two 9.00 mm Browning magazines into a known IRA target and left him in a pool of blood. Racain had taken two or three pictures of the scene to pass back to his commander, just for the records! Yes I knew the name all right.

Next to Racain was yet another face I had never seen before. A face full of character heavily lined and finished off by the square jaw giving him that stamp of determination. His piercing pale blue eyes cold and calculating gave the impression of him being able to see your very soul. They were the eyes of a killer! Unlike Racain, you had no doubt that this man had your number. His eyes paid careful scrutiny to those around him. You instinctively knew that nothing escaped his gaze! He was alert and upright in his chair and when he spoke it was with a quiet confidence.

'Good afternoon Colonel and others.' He spoke with a Glaswegian accent. 'Jock Williams from 4 Field Survey Troop of the Royal Engineers.'

'Gentlemen, some of you already know me.' The owner of the voice looked around at the people gathered. He looked toward Danny and gave an imperceptible nod of his head. 'Danny.' He looked toward Ash and O'Rourke, 'Colonel, good afternoon. Major, good afternoon and of course Mr Racain, and how are you?'

'Get on wi' it mon.' Jock muttered in his Glaswegian accent. 'Some o' us wanna be away hame t'day.'

There was a slight pause as the person introducing himself gave a little half cough as if to clear his throat. 'Yes well, where was I. Some of you already know me but for the benefit of our Scottish gentleman and our other gentleman,' he looked straight at me, 'my name is Wyman. Field operative London and Irish desks; I am Agent 222 and link man for Austen.'

Now I knew him. Of course Austen's control, the man from Cavil Street in East London. He was the one who, along with the Army Minister and the rest of the Circus, had brought in that small time crook Austin as an *Agent Provocateur*. What was his other name? I racked my brains, Smith, Wyndham or Smit. Then it came to me Smythe, Hamilton-Smythe. Claimed to live in Chelsea, but never did.

Ash was on his feet again and I was brought back to concentrate on the meeting.

'Right then Gentleman with the introductions out of the way let's press on.' He walked towards the other end of the table where the projector was. 'Major would you kill the lights.' O'Rourke got up and switched off the lights. 'Thank you. Now if you would all like to look this way.' He switched on the projector and a blurred coloured image was thrown up onto the white screen, which he quickly brought back into focus. The image was of a fairly tall, broad shouldered white Caucasian with curly brown hair. In the photograph he sported an open neck shirt with short sleeves and around his neck he wore a spotted cravat or necktie. 'This gentleman is Bravo 1. He uses different names or aliases. His name is John Francis Riley, also known as 'The Boss' or 'Slab' Riley. Other names used are O'Hare; O'Hanlon and O'Dowd. His Alpha 1 is a farm near Dundalk. At this stage I'll hand you over to Danny who can give you more details. Danny.'

'Gentleman, this man is dangerous. He is already known by C3. Believed to be wealthy, main income gained from civil construction and building plus 'other' dubious activities. Our sources tell us he is wanted by RUC for questioning on conspiracy, murder, protection and extortion. Also he has not been above running other rackets. He is known to the Gardai for previous. When younger he ran a few girls in the Docks in Dublin, but since those early times he has moved on to bigger and more profitable scams. Was at one time very much involved with O'Shea, but today he has marginalised himself from the Officials. His leanings are more towards the new up and coming Provisionals.'

'Thank you Danny for your input. What about you Eamonn, have you anything to add?'

'Only to confirm what Danny said that he is more aligned to the Provisionals than to O'Shea. In fact there is no love lost between O'Shea and Riley. There are major differences between the two factions and O'Shea blames Riley for the major split. As you know O'Shea has never condoned drug dealing and we know that Riley is not beyond dealing in drugs to raise further funds for the Provisionals. It might just be worth mentioning that part of the problem was that the Belfast Boys wanted to arm themselves and Dublin was refusing their requests. The reason being that O'Shea and the Officials needed to retain tight control on finances and they felt by allowing arms to Belfast not only would it eat into the Officials depleted stock, but it would also run away with the finances. In addition to this, the Officials felt that a Political solution was their way, not rule by the gun!'

'Just for the record,' Ash interjected, 'We believe Riley was involved in the murder of Sean O'Donald and I think at this point, it maybe an idea to get Major O'Rourke to tell you the background to why it is we believe that Riley is implicated,' he turned to O'Rourke, 'so if you wouldn't mind Major.'

'Thank you Colonel.' O'Rourke stood up to address those present. 'Well gentlemen in order to understand the rationale behind Riley and our belief that he was instrumental in O'Donald's death we need to go back a couple of years. As some of you may know O'Donald had a thriving haulage company in the Province and employed a number of drivers all of whom were very loyal drivers to him and the company, many of them had been with him for many years and as such it was an open secret among his drivers that he was a member of the UDR. Unfortunately one of his most loyal drivers Reg Snow, also a UDR man and a great friend of Sean's, was targeted by the IRA and it was Riley and his lot who broke into his house one night and took Reg and his family outside. Once they were outside a couple of his mates held Reg down and Riley took a paving slab from the back of their vehicle and proceeded to smash Reg's kneecaps, then he got his mates to hold Reg's arms out so he could use the same technique on his hands. This was carried out in full view of his family. Reg's wife distinctly heard one of the men call Riley by name before she was shot. Fortunately the gunshot was not fatal and after a few weeks convalescence Mrs Snow was well enough to be interviewed. Of course that was officially done by the RUC. However because of Reg's connection to the security forces we undertook our own investigation. Obviously as Reg worked for O'Donald, it wasn't too long before Sean knew what had happened. Because of that incident O'Donald made it his crusade to hunt down the men who had done this act and it wasn't long before he had targeted certain individuals, friends and supporters of Riley, and had them either arrested and banged up in the Maze, or permanently removed. O'Donald became a major problem for Riley, but until recent times Riley did not know who his arch enemy was and all credit for that must go to O'Donald. Of course all this happened some time ago whilst Riley was still in the OIRA, before the Belfast Boys split away. However it was only a matter of time before Riley and the Belfast Boys split from the OIRA and became the Provisional IRA as we now know it today. Once this happened Riley became much more powerful and through the PIRA intelligence he set about trying to find out who it was who had cost him dearly. We suspect that someone close to O'Donald may have been the leak, it was either that or Riley just got lucky, but either way we are certain that he found out about O'Donald and was instrumental in his murder.'

All this time I had been sitting just staring at the coloured image thrown up on the screen. The image was of a well built man with a shock of curly brown hair and a round face of ruddy complexion. Around his neck he wore a spotted necktie or cravat tied in a knot to one side. He was dressed in an open neck shirt with sleeves rolled up emphasizing his biceps. This was a man of brute strength and his arms showed that. In this photograph he was laughing and it was hard to imagine that such an innocent looking face belied such a dark persona. So this was what Riley looked like.

'Thank you Major. By the way Riley got the name 'Slab' from his build and not as you would expect from the episode of the paving slab, I am led to believe that his father's father and his father were all big men and the young John Riley grew up no different.'

'A real 'slab' of a man you could say!' Racain interjected in a disinterested way as he leaned back on his chair his eyes half closed.

'Exactly. In fact he has two brothers, one known to be five or six years older and one about seven years younger and both of them are of a similar stature although John is the one that the name 'Slab' is primarily associated with. Unfortunately this photograph is a little out of date now, but from my understanding he hasn't changed too much. Please do not underestimate this man, not only is he dangerous and cunning, he also employs a considerable number of men, the majority of them being nothing more than paid thugs, criminals and PIRA operatives. However in addition to these 'employees' he also runs a legitimate building and construction company in the republic, so he does employ legitimate workers as well. The business in the south is a fairly large operation so Riley is not short of a few bob, but most of his wealth has come from his, err shall we say, farming activities and the European subsidies raised by cross border dealings. We know that he has loaded up lorry loads of pigs in the Republic, filed claims for the European subsidy of £8 per pig at the UK Customs Post in Newry and then driven them back ready for the next round trip. In fact his pigs have spent so much time on the road being moved backwards and forwards across the border that it's a wonder they didn't collapse from fatigue!' Ash paused allowing the hint of a smile as a ripple of laughter went around the room. 'But gentleman, his activities have moved on since the days of pig and grain subsidies, he is now heavily in the oil industry and it's the smuggling of oil that has netted him untold wealth. In fact so much so that he has built an ingenious gravity fed system on his farm with tanks both sides of an interconnecting underground pipe. This enables him to move the oil undetected to the side that is most beneficial to him and sell it at a vast profit without paying any VAT etcetera. I won't bore you all with the details at this stage, but suffice it to say that without this income Riley would not be such a problem. Riley is no longer just a foot soldier, a known IRA sympathiser or small time thug, he is now emerging as a top PIRA player and as such a major force to contend with. In fact we have built up quite a dossier on our Mr Riley, haven't we Major?' Ash looked toward the Major as if for reassurance O'Rourke smiled briefly and nodded. 'I believe Mr Wyman personally knows quite a bit about Mr Riley and I think at this point I'll ask him to give you his slant on things, so if you wouldn't mind Mr Wyman...'

Wyman stood up and looked around, taking a moment or two to gather his thoughts before speaking.

'Yes Colonel, you're absolutely right to say he is very much an emerging force for us to contend with. In fact we now know that the narrow split between the Officials and the Provisionals has now widened to a major gulf, and that with the help of Riley and his money, the PIRA have more small arms than the Officials, although admittedly the Officials still have the quality of arms, and it's for this very reason that Riley has in fact help polarize the split. As far as his personal involvement in the actual operation we have limited knowledge, but as has already been said we do know that he employs a large number of men on his farm. In fact far more farm labourers than you would expect to find on a farm of that size. Another thing, the farm itself is a veritable stronghold so a lot of our information is based on conjecture and assumptions. Some information is readily available from our observations but other is based on patterns of events. For instance we must assume that the farm is a training operation for the PIRA, so the majority of the men on the farm are Provos or some form of security. From covert surveillance over the months we have seen that the farm has round the clock security in the shape of floodlights at night and twenty four hour dog patrols. Also, from the surveillance, we can ascertain that there has been a high level of non farming activity taking place, with considerable movement of personnel both on and off the farm. We have noted that the farm seems to have a major aerial array which indicates some form of communication centre in operation there. So what is so special about this farm to warrant having it lit up like Blackpool illuminations at night? Why does Riley need twenty-four hour dog patrols, what is he hiding and what is such a large aerial array required for if it is not a communication centre? I think you will all agree that there are a lot of unanswered questions.'

Racain spoke quietly. 'Perhaps we ought to pay Riley a visit and find out some answers, what do you think Jock?'

'Aye maybe yer right Rabby.'

'Thank you for that Mr Racain, Jock.' Once again the Colonel addressed the full meeting. 'Well gentlemen that conveniently brings me to the real reason for our meeting which is to inform you we are to hit Riley hard. And gentlemen I mean hard. We hit his farm; we go in and take him out permanently...'

'With respect how exactly do you propose we do this?' Racain asked.

'It won't be easy but in this job nothing is easy. Because the farm house is situated in the Republic we cannot send in a large force so we can only send in a small unit and because of that surprise has to be the key, would you not agree?'

'Och aye, but what about his lines of communication, what about power to the farm and what are his movements can ye tell us any o' these things?

'All I can say Jock is that Sean O'Donald put together a lot of data before he was killed so we can answer some of your concerns. For example we know the route of the telephone cables connecting the house to the exchange; also we have managed to discover the route taken by the power lines supplying electricity to the farm. Unfortunately, the power is a three phase supply, but we have found a sub-station about a mile away that supplies a couple of small farms in the area as well as Riley's place. So gentlemen, this is my proposal. We mount a three man cell attack on the farm with a view to taking out our Mr Riley. The hit squad will be Racain, Jock and Richard. As I've already said it will not be easy, but it can be done and to enable it to be a successful operation they will need backup teams, you will need a full dossier on Riley of which Major O'Rourke will advise you further on the details.' He looked towards O'Rourke who nodded in agreement. 'The team will need to know detailed layout of the farm, where the telephone line runs, power lines etc., etc. That will be your input Mr Wyman.' Ash looked at Wyman who nodded his agreement. 'We will require a back-up team south of the border to carry out detailed surveillance of the surrounding area and to arrange for the necessary delivery of equipment and recovery of the same. Eamonn that will be for you to organise ok' He looked over to Eamonn whom also nodded his agreement. 'Danny and Mr Wyman between you, will be responsible for data on Riley. We will need to know Riley's movements, contacts, dates, names, places and even when he farts; is that clearly understood?' He glanced over to Danny and Wyman both men nodded. 'We shall also need some form of back-up team just in case the whole shebang goes tits up. Any questions?'

'What about having some form of fast car nearby plus driver?'

'It's a thought Richard, but we also need something more than that. Anyone else any ideas?'

'Och, sod the Republic, put a small unit south o' the border.' Jock said with a broad grin on his face, 'lets blast the bastard's t' kingdom come.'

'Hmm, nice idea Jock. Unfortunately I think we would get some political repercussions if we did that. So anybody...' Ash looked around the meeting but no-one had any ideas. 'Well the only thing is we have a standby unit in the north just in case.'

'But that will take too long.' Eamonn interjected.

'I can't see any way round it Eamonn, can you?'

'No, I suppose you're right Colonel.'

'So that's it then. Everyone clear on what they are doing?' Ash looked around the group. 'Good then the operation will be known as 'Damocles' and will be co-ordinated from the Irish desk in Lisburn with overall responsibility to London and Major O'Rourke. Shall we say ten days to execution, which will allow for nine days preparation time, everyone in favour?' There was a murmur of approval. 'Right gentlemen, in that case we are at Damocles minus ten. Thank you all for attending and good luck to everyone.'

I had eventually got into where the small oil filled transformer was within the fenced off area of the sub station. The time was twelve-thirty at night and everywhere was pitch black not a star in sight, an ideal night really. My transceiver crackled into life, 'Romeo Juliet from Alpha Whisky 22 over.'

'Romeo Juliet receiving.'

'In position over.'

'Roger Alpha Whisky. In target area now lights out in ten. Over.'

'Roger Romeo Juliet. Ten and counting. Out.'

I searched around to find the best place to lay the charge where it would do the maximum damage so definitely taking the power out. We had no second chances on this one. I had two jobs to do, one was to kill the power by blowing up the transformer and the other was to cut-off his telephone, neither presented much of a problem. I found the ideal place and laid two charges of Semtex just to make sure. We were using Semtex to make it look like the Officials had done the job so, if, and when they found Riley's body the Gardai would assume it was a case of retribution by the Officials on a renegade Provo unit and that O'Shea's boys were responsible for his murder.

I pushed the transmit button on my transceiver.

'Alpha Whisky 22. Romeo Juliet over.' My transceiver crackled. I called again.

This time the reply came loud and clear.

'Go ahead Romeo Juliet over.'

'Charge laid. We are now at ten and counting. Out.'

'Roger Romeo Juliet. Standby...Standby. In position above farm over.'

'Roger Alpha Whisky. Proceeding to telephone now. Stand by ... Standby.'

I hauled myself up a nearby telephone pole and swung precariously from the harness.

'Alpha Whisky 22. Romeo Juliet over.'

'Go ahead Romeo Juliet over.'

'Now in position on telephone pole. Standby...Standby.' Forcing the cutters hard up against the insulator, I squeezed and with a twang the wire parted company. Now for the other one. Again I forced the cutters as close as possible to the insulator and again I squeezed, there was another resounding twang as the second wire parted company. With a sense of satisfaction I pressed the transmit button on my transceiver. 'Alpha Whisky 22 over.'

'Alpha Whiskey receiving.'

'We have positive over.'

'Roger. Comms are dead confirm. Over.'

'Affirmative. We are now twenty seconds and counting.'

'Roger.'

'Five...four...three...two...' my voice was drowned out by the explosion. 'Go...go...go. Romeo Juliet out.' I didn't wait for their reply before starting my rapid decent. As I hit the ground and discarded my harness I could hear the sound of rapid fire. I ran down the short hill to the farm and was over the wall in next to no time. More automatic fire. Suddenly everywhere was bathed in brilliant light. Screams from someone shot. What was happening? The lights. Why?

'Richard go...go...go...' It was Jock shouting as he ran toward me. 'Get out mon. Go...go...go!'

'What the hell...'

'Rabby's dead so fu…' He was cut off by a rapid burst of machine gun fire. Jock teetered. Stumbled then as if in slow motion fell towards me. Instinctively I grabbed him. I pulled, half carrying and half dragging him towards the lowest part of the wall.

'It's n' good Richard y' best get out while y' can.' His sentence ended in a fit of coughing, but I wasn't about to give up on him just like that and with a superhuman effort I dragged him up on his feet. I half pushed him and he half scrabbled up the wall. Whilst he rolled over the top I turned and opened up with a three second burst of automatic fire in the direction of the lights. I heard a scream of pain as my fire power hit someone. There was a thud and a scream from the top of the wall. Another bullet had hit home in Jock. I scrambled up the wall and effectively kicked Jock over. He grunted as he rolled off the top of the wall. There was a dull thud as he hit the ground followed by his crying out in pain. I jumped down and landed close by.

'Ok Jock my old mate not far now.'

I Grabbed him under his armpits I wrestled him back away from the wall into a small copse. He was ominously quiet now. His moans of pain had stopped.

'Jock.' I called his name with a sense of urgency, but nothing. I tried again, 'Jock.' Still nothing. A desperate situation called for desperate measures. I grabbed hold of him shaking him and calling to him as loud as I dared to under the circumstances. 'Come on Jock,' I called, eventually he groaned. 'Jock, come on. Come on.' I shook him again. 'Come on now. Come on, wake up, wake up. Don't you dare pass out on me. Come on Jock speak.' I grabbed my transceiver and pressed the send button. 'Control, control. Romeo Juliet. Over.'

All I got was atmospherics.

'Control, control come in. Over.' Still nothing. Suddenly there was a new sound, the sound of baying dogs. 'Shit' I half shouted the expletive. I tried again, pressing my transceiver's send button. 'Control, control come in. Over.' Holding my breath I waited. At last my transceiver crackled into life.

'Romeo Juliet. Go ahead. Control over.'

'We have casualty. Need back-up urgently. Romeo Juliet over.'

'Roger. What is current status? Over.'

'Outcome of Damocles unknown. Racain dead. One injured. One fit. Over.' The dogs were sounding closer now.

'Roger Romeo Juliet, we have backup team on way. ETA fifteen minutes. Over.'

'Control we have further problem. Dogs loose need ETA sooner. Over.'

'Roger Romeo Juliet. Helicopter scrambled please give co-ordinates. Over.'

At this I lost my temper.

'You are joking Control. Now you're taking the piss. I am sat outside Alpha 1. We have taken heavy firepower. We have one dead and one badly wounded and you have the cheek to ask for co-ordinates. Ask someone man, ask someone there. I am sat on the north side of the farm close to the South Armagh road but stuff you're co-ordinates. Just get us out.' Suddenly there was a torch off to my left. I waited for the rapid fire, but nothing came save for a low whistle.

'Richard. It's me Wyman.' Was I relieved to hear his friendly voice. 'Come on Richard, this way quickly.'

'What about Jock, he's taken a packet?'

'How bad is he?'

'Pretty bad, but can't really tell. Have you a Medic Pack with you?' I asked in a low voice. Just then Wyman appeared.

'In the car. Between us we should be able to pull him out.'

I knelt down beside Jock and put my mouth close to his ear.

'Jock old mate, Wyman has a Medic Pack in the car, but we need to get you there, so we're going to move you as best we can. Ok?' Jock squeezed my arm.

'Ok Rich….Arghhh.' He screamed in pain as I manoeuvred him to a sitting position. Wyman crouched down at the other side, pulled jock's arm over his shoulder, slipped his arm around Jock's waist, and I did likewise.

'Ready Richard?'

'Yeah. Hold on Jock this may hurt.' I said in a low voice to my wounded buddy.

'Right Richard we lift on the count of three. One, two three.' We both stood up, Jock screamed in pain and we both took his weight between us.

The dogs' barks and growls were getting closer. I could hear the dog handlers off to my right. There was the noise of dogs crashing through the undergrowth which spurred us on. I forced Jock's cries of pain from my mind as we half pulled, half dragged him through the undergrowth. All the time the dogs got closer. Suddenly we were out in the open. Mercifully Jock must have passed out with the pain or loss of blood because his screams had stopped and he was a dead weight.

'Not far now Richard…' Wyman's breathing was getting laboured.

'What do you call not far?' I asked.

'About twenty yards.' He gasped, 'see that wall ahead?'

'Yeah.'

'Well, we've just got to get to the other side.' He gasped a lung full of air. 'Car's over there on the South Armagh Road. Carl, my driver is there.'

As we reached the wall I stole a quick glance over my shoulder. I could just make out the bobbing lights of torches as our pursuers emerged from the wood.

'Quick Wyman they're out of the wood.'
With a superhuman effort we half pushed and half pulled Jock's limp body over the wall.
'Right I've got him.' A voice beneath me softly called. 'Let him go.'
Carl caught hold of him as we lowered his unconscious body gently down to him. He lay him gently down on the ground and waited until Wyman and I had scrambled down beside him, then between the three of us it took next to no time to get Jock to the car and made as comfortable as possible on the back seat. Carl had the engine started. Wyman gave our poor unfortunate buddy an injection of morphine for the pain.
'Right Carl go…go…go.' With a roar from the powerful engine we started to move. The tyres squealed in protest and there was a smell of burning rubber as we accelerated off up the South Armagh Road. The engine screamed as Carl redlined it on the rev counter and in no time at all we were doing over eighty. We heard the noise of rapid fire as the first of our pursuers cleared the wall onto the road, but within seconds we rounded a bend in the road so cutting off their line of fire. Carl kept up his speed just in case our pursuers intended to give chase but after a short time it was obvious that they had given us up as a lost cause. As we slowed to a more leisurely pace I suddenly remembered that control had scrambled a helicopter and it was probably looking for us now.
'Wyman I better cancel that chopper they were sending out…'
'No re-direct it.' He interrupted me before I could finish. 'Tell them we're on the South Armagh Road heading north should cross border in ten minutes. Ask them to watch for out for us, we should be easy to spot as so far we are the only vehicle on the road. Say we'll rendezvous with them.'
I switched on the car's RT set. 'Control, are you receiving? Romeo Juliet over.'
'Go ahead Romeo Juliet. Control over.'
'Control, with agent 222. Now heading north on South Armagh Road. Have badly wounded on board need rendezvous with chopper for urgent transfer to hospital. Romeo Juliet over.'
'Roger Romeo Juliet…Standby…standby.' There was a short silence then the metallic voice from control started to speak again. 'Romeo Juliet, chopper crew alerted will watch for your Charlie 1. Control out.'
'Roger control Romeo Juliet out.'
Fifteen minutes later, an army helicopter, with Jock safely stowed aboard, lifted off from a field north of the border as in the east the cold light of morning started to spread across the sky, announcing the start of yet another day.

Carl turned into a street on the outskirts of town and pulled up outside a fairly nondescript house.

'I'll just drop you two and get some petrol before I come in.'

'Ok. We'll see you in a few minutes then. Come on Richard this is the place,' he said and with that he got out closely followed by me. I turned and raised my hand to Carl as he drove off down the street to get some petrol.

'Where are we?' I asked Wyman.

'This is Jon's place he's one of 'our' friends and his place has been used as a safe house by us for some time now. We're safe enough here for the next few hours and should be able get cleaned up, have something to eat and get some sleep.'

We'd managed to get a couple of hours sleep, a bath apiece and a good breakfast at Jon's place. The time had now come for us to make a move, it was just after eight-thirty in the morning as we casually walked through the front door towards the parked car. All three of us were in a light-hearted mood, knowing that this was the last stage of our journey to Lisburn Barracks. The job had been a catastrophe, but at least we had managed to get Jock out and escape ourselves so there was no point on dwelling on the past. Carl unlocked the car doors whilst Wyman and I wished our host goodbye. The engine kicked into life. We turned to walk to the car. Suddenly an almighty bang and a ball of fire ripped the car apart. The blast threw both Wyman and I off our feet. Windows in the house shattered and I could taste the cordite in the air. Then silence. I struggled to my feet realised I was dazed but otherwise unhurt. Wyman, who had been slightly closer, lay still. Jon, our host, held his hand to his head as blood oozed through his fingers and dripped onto what had previously been a clean step. He looked dazed and confused. Where the car had been parked was now just a pile of twisted metal. Pieces of car were strewn everywhere across the street. There was even a door about thirty or forty yards away, still spinning around where it lay. Flames licked at the remains of the wreck. There was a strong pungent smell of burnt flesh heavy on the air. In the distance the wail of a two-tone horn drifted on the slight breeze. Having now gathered my wits, I checked myself again. My shirt was torn, and my trousers were ripped but otherwise I was fine.

'How are you Jon?' I called to my host.

'I think I'm ok.' He moved his hand, which was red with blood, reached into his pocket and pulled out a handkerchief, which he used to staunch the blood flowing from the gash he had received to his head.

'A bit shaken, but really I'm fine.' I walked over to Wyman, who was now just beginning to stir. He gave a low groan and suddenly he was conscious. He tried to get up, but promptly slumped back down again.

66

'Easy, easy.' I said, 'just sit up a minute and get your breath.'

'What happened?'

'The car was booby trapped.'

'Car…what car…booby trap…what are you talking about?'

'Shut up a minute Wyman. More importantly how d'you feel, does it hurt anywhere?' I asked, as I quickly tried to check him over for cuts and lacerations. Like me he had no physical damage save for a slight cut to his hand. We had all been extremely lucky except for poor Carl, Wyman's driver. Obviously he hadn't been so lucky. He was dead. Wyman shook his head to try and clear his thoughts.

'What happened?' he asked.

'Like I said the car was booby-trapped. Do you remember where we are?' I asked.

Wyman looked about him. He struggled to his feet, saw Jon. Then his memory started to return.

'Yeah I remember. Come on Richard let's get back inside before this place starts hopping.'

It wasn't long before people started to emerge from their houses to see what damage had been sustained. Curtains started to twitch as people looked out of their windows. At this point we went back inside Jon's house to get cleaned up for the second time. Wyman immediately started to quiz Jon.

'How about strangers Jon, have you noticed anyone taking a great interest in this place anymore than normal?'

'Can't say that I've noticed.'

'Any strange cars that you've noticed around here lately?'

Jon shook his head.

'Are you certain? Think man think because as sure as eggs are eggs, that bomb was not an indiscriminate device. Someone knew exactly what they were watching for. So think carefully. I'll ask you again, have you noticed any strangers in the area or any strange vehicles?' They were both silent for a while.

'Jon,' he looked towards me, 'it's important that you remember. Now does anyone you know, know what you do?' I asked.

He shook his head, started to say something then stopped.

'No' was his reply.

'Jon what were you about to say?' I asked.

'It's just that the other night…'

'Yes Jon.' Wyman interrupted, 'What about the other night?'

'I remember now, someone in a car stopped and asked me where the nearest filling station was that's all.'

'Hmm. Didn't you find that a little strange Jon?'

'Not really. Why?'

'Well why would someone turn off the main road come down here just on the off chance for directions t a filling station?'

'Come on Wyman now you're being paranoid.' I said 'he could have been visiting or something.'

'If you'd been visiting wouldn't you ask your host or whoever you were visiting where the nearest petrol station was?'

'Yeah but...'

'There's no 'but' about it you would.'

'I think your grabbing at straws.'

'Maybe, but I still think that may have been the car.'

'Ok. Let's assume it was where do we go from here?' I asked, not sure where Wyman's questions were leading us.

'Jon I think you have been rumbled.' Then as if to confirm Wyman's suspicions the front door burst open and running along the passage was heard. Both Wyman and I grabbed our weapons and before the room door opened we opened fire. A scream from the other side announced that one of our bullets had found its mark. There was a burst of rapid fire from the other side of the door that splintered the wood. Bullets ripped into the furniture and into the wall opposite the door as our assailant sprayed the door with gunfire. I signalled to Wyman to go through the window. He nodded and cautiously followed the wall to the window. I then signalled to Jon to do likewise. I then opened fire with my weapon shooting through what was left of the door. I waited, but there was silence. Then the silence was broken as gunfire was heard on the other side of the door followed by another scream and a thud. The remainder of the splintered door gave way as the weight of a man's body fell against it. The upper torso slumped through it. On his head he wore a balaclava. The attack obviously bore the hallmarks of a Provisional IRA attack. So much for Jon's house being a safe house!

'Romeo you ok?' It was Wyman's voice using part of my call sign as cover.

'Yeah 222 I'm fine.' I did likewise using his agent number. 'How about you and our friend?'

'We're both sound. You can come out now.' I shoved the hooded body aside and opened what was left of the front door. As I came out onto the street a small crowd had gathered. I was just in time to notice a dark blue Volvo moving down the road.

'Did you get the reg. Number?' I asked waving in the general direction of the car.

'Shit. Sorry I didn't.' It was at this point that the cavalry arrived in the shape of the RUC and an army Land Rover.

Safely inside Lisburn barracks I was now recounting the catastrophic operation at Riley's farm.

'What actually happened out there at Riley's Richard?'

'I laid a double charge. I cut the telephone wires. Jock and Racain were in position. I counted down. The charge blew. Jock and Racain were in and I followed. There was already high-powered lights on and rapid fire on all sides. Jock screamed at me to get out. He took a packet. That's about it.'

'So if you blew the power like you say, then how come he had lights?'

'How the hell should I know?'

'Well are you sure you blew the transformer?'

'I'm certain. Are you sure that he didn't have a back-up generator?'

'Shit. Didn't anyone tell you guys?'

'Tell us what?'

'About his back up generator?'

'What? Hell no. Are you telling me there was a back-up power source and no-one thought to mention it?'

'I'm sorry Richard.'

'Sorry! Sorry! Is that all you can say! Fucking sorry! Well you best tell that to Racain hadn't you? Not only do we get half the information, when we do get out and to a safe house we end up losing our driver in a car bomb, we are attacked by the Provisionals and all you can say is fucking sorry. What good's that to the two men who are dead? They are dead because of bad information, lack of communication and piss poor back-up, no other reason.'

That was the end of my debriefing. Two hours later I was being flown back to Ashford for a meeting with Ash.

Chapter 8

Life had regained a sort of normality since that fateful night at Riley's farm. I had returned to the mundane life of a fruit farmer and contractor. Paul and I were busy with local contracts. Everything seemed fine in our sleepy little village in Kent, at least until I received a strange letter from Jean O'Donald.

Dear Richard,

        Sorry to contact out of the blue like this, but I desperately need to meet with you. I would telephone but I think my telephone is being tapped. I suppose I could drive into the town and phone from there, but I've recently been aware of a blue car following me when I go out. At first I put it down to my imagination, but after Sean's murder I'm not so sure. Call me paranoid, but I'm sure someone is keeping tabs on me and I don't know why. Other things have also happened, nothing major, but nonetheless unsettling. I can't put my finger on anything, but I'm sure I'm being watched, but by whom I don't know. Please say you'll help me. Whatever you do don't phone, write.
Yours truly,

Jean O'Donald

I read and re-read Jean's letter, not really sure what to make of it. One thing I was certain about and that was Jean was no fool. Scan had often said that he would have to go a long way to find a more astute and level-headed person. He often referred to Jean as his main back-up cell, his eyes and ears or his sixth sense. When it came down to his role within the Circus he always maintained she was the only one he would ultimately trust with any information and his life. So I took her letter very seriously, very seriously indeed. I decided that as much as I didn't like the idea of returning to Ulster so soon, I would nonetheless write back to Jean confirming my intention to see her within the next two weeks.

The plane banked steeply and turned for the final approach. I watched through the rain spattered window as the ground raced up to greet us. There was a groan from the hydraulics as the undercarriage was lowered followed by a dull clunk as the wheels locked into the down position ready for the landing. The aircraft twitched ever so slightly as the Captain started side slipping across the gusting wind. Suddenly the runway appeared to rush up beneath the wings and with a gentle bump and a slight shudder the wheels made contact with the runway. There was a tremendous roar from the engines as reverse thrust and brakes were applied simultaneously. Our speed was quickly reduced to a more leisurely pace and we turned off the main runway to taxi to our parking slot. The aircraft's public address system clicked into life.

'Ladies and gentlemen in the interest of safety please remain seated until the aircraft has come to a standstill and the seatbelt sign has been switched of. On behalf of the Captain, crew and Aer Lingus may I wish you a safe onward journey. Thank you for flying with us today and we hope to be of service to you in the very near future.'

The eagle had landed and I was now in Belfast.

Twenty minutes later I was through the arrivals lounge and out into the main body of the terminal. I had arranged to meet Jean at the airport information desk so as to avoid the crowded area near to arrivals, so I headed off following the signs for 'Information'. Fortunately it wasn't difficult to find and Jean was the only person in its vicinity.

'Richard'. She called to me. I made my way over to a tall slim brunette.

'Jean, it's lovely to see you.'

'You to Richard.' She gave me a light peck on the cheek. 'I hope you don't think it a cheek asking you to come all this way?'

'No it's fine.' I answered.

'You are sweet Richard, but the truth is I really needed to speak to someone. Someone I could trust and you were the only person I could think of. Anyway I'll tell you more once we get on our way. It's not far to the car park.'

'So what's been happening? I know you said you thought your phone was being tapped and you were sure you were under surveillance, but why?'

'I honestly don't know why. But it's not just the fact that I'm being followed in the car, or the phone is being tapped…ah here we are.' She took my hold all and opened up the boot of a red BMW. 'As I was saying. It's not just the fact that I'm being followed, or that my phone is being tapped. There have been other things happening.'

'Such as?' I asked as I got in the front passenger seat and pulled the door closed.

'Odd things, such as every morning over the last couple of weeks, when I've gone into work; I've noticed a red Ford parked near the entrance to the yard. Same car, same place and always two men in there.' The BMW accelerated away smoothly along the airport road as we headed towards the city. Out of habit I glanced over my shoulder and casually looked through the rear screen.

'Oh yes my shadow is there again.' Jean said. 'Did you notice the blue car a couple of cars back?'

'Hmm. Yes, is that the same one as before?' I asked.

'Yes it's always that one. Well leastways it's always that one I've noticed.'
'Are you positive it's that one Jean?'
'I'm positive.' I thought about this for a minute or two. Thoughts of the abortive attempt to take out 'Slab' Riley and the car bomb at the safe house, the gun battle and the dark blue Volvo that accelerated away from Jon's afterwards. Could this also be connected? I knew if it were one of ours then there would be more than just the one. Now was that red Ford up front part of the surveillance team? I wasn't sure. Jean had said a red Ford was always parked nearby to the haulage yard. I checked again on the blue car behind it was still with us. In fact even as we headed northwards along the city ring the blue car was still there. I was beginning to think that she was imagining about being tailed when, there it was, the switch. The blue car had gone and had been replaced by the red Ford. If my hunch was right then it would mean the red Ford in front will have disappeared. I turned to face the front and searched for the red Ford. My hunch was right. The red Ford was nowhere to be seen. I turned to look through the rear window expecting it to still be there, but it was gone. Damn it where had it gone. Suddenly it was there, going down the slip road into the city centre off to our left. So much for my hunch. I kept looking out of the rear window half expecting to see it reappear, but it didn't and neither did the blue car, so maybe I was wrong! In the end I gave up craning my neck round to see if I could see it and turned back to face the front. There in front was a dark blue Volvo. I was getting paranoid about this now. I again turned to look out through the back window and there two cars back was a red Ford. 'What the…'
'What's wrong?' Jean asked.
'Nothing really, it was just that I saw what I thought was the tail car go off back there down the slip road on the left to the city, yet it has reappeared behind us again. Unless they are using more than one red Ford.' As I watched I saw the red Ford get overtaken by a blue car which dropped in front of it. The red Ford disappeared from my view. 'They're good Jean whoever they are.'
'So I'm not imagining it? Someone is tailing me then.'
'I'm not certain but it looks like it.' Again I checked behind us, but both cars had gone where they had gone was a mystery. I kept watching all the way to the motorway, but still they didn't reappear. Perhaps I had been wrong all along. Perhaps it was pure coincidence and it just seemed like we were being tailed.

We swung through the open gateway and onto the drive of Jean's large detached house and parked outside the garage. She opened the boot for me to retrieve my holdall and as I reached inside to pick it up I noticed that a piece of the boot's carpeting had dropped down. I was about to push it back into place when I noticed a small metallic disk about the size of a ten pence piece with two leads attached to it. I carefully traced the pair of wires until I lost them amongst the rest of the car's wiring where they had been carefully concealed to make it look like they were an integral part of the wiring loom. It certainly wasn't rocket science to work out one lead was the feed and the other earth.

'Richard, have you got everything?'

'Umm. Yeah, sorry Jean just coming. Oh Jean…' I was about to tell her about the disk, then changed my mind.

'What did you say?'

'Nothing I'm coming now.' I had another look at the disk and I was convinced that what I was looking at was a tracking device and that would explain why the cars on the way did not appear to be tailing us all the time. It would also explain how it was that they could pick us up whenever they wanted to. In fact it would explain a lot of things. I decided that they had enough fun with Jean so grabbed hold of the disk and gave it a sharp yank causing the two leads to break away from their connection. I then put the disk in my pocket to dispose of later and closed the boot.

The following day we left for the yard from which Jean's haulage business operated and having removed the tracking device I was interested to see if we would be followed and surprise, surprise we weren't. Even the red Ford was nowhere to be seen. Either they, whoever they were, had stopped the surveillance or by my ripping out the disk I had foiled their plans unfortunately the respite was short lived and by mid-morning the red Ford was back. I decided that the time had come for me to have a little chat with Jean's shadows but as I approached their car they must have had other ideas because they suddenly took flight and drove off at high speed.

At lunchtime Jean introduced me to Chris Millar, the yard manager; evidently he had known Sean since his schooldays and had been with the company for years. A more loyal and true friend couldn't have been wished for according to Jean.

'Terrible do about Sean wasn't it Chris?' I said.

'Yes but I'm sure that someone, somewhere, must know something.'

'I'm sure you're right Chris. After all there's bound to be someone, somewhere who does, but Ulster is a big enough area in which to hide.'

'You misunderstand me Richard, I mean there's got to be someone in here, in this yard who knows something.'

'You do surprise me.'

'Why?'

'Because I thought everyone here had worked for Sean for years.'

'Most of them have, but that doesn't mean he wasn't betrayed by someone here.'

'True, but I thought they all liked him?'

'Yeah, but things change. People's loyalties change. Things happen out here.'

This last comment concerned me. 'Exactly what do you mean Chris?' I asked.

'Well the PIRA is becoming more powerful by the day, and what with Sean belonging to the UDR and all that...' He left the sentence unfinished.

'So are you suggesting someone purposely betrayed him?' I asked.

'People talk. Lads and their families have to be careful.'

'But everyone knew that Sean belonged to the UDR didn't they?'

'Apart from two.'

'Newcomers?'

'Relatively.'

'So who are these two and what do you know about them? I asked.

'Not a lot really. Anyway it just seems strange that shortly after they arrived on the scene things start to happen.'

'What sort of things?'

'Oh we have a truck which gets broken into and the fridge unit is sabotaged. We have had tyres slashed...'

'What in the yard?' I interrupted.

'No away from the yard.'

'Yeah but that could be coincidence.'

'Maybe. It just seems strange that these things have just started to happen.'

'Anything else?' I asked.

'We had one lad went off the road. He said someone had tampered with the brakes.'

'Well had they?'

'The police said nothing.'

'Did Sean get them checked out?'

'Yeah, but I never did find out from him, because just after that he was killed.'

'Have you said any of this to the Police?'

'Nah.'

'Why not?' I asked.

'A complete waste of time if you ask me, even the UDR is not interested.'

This last comment puzzled me and I wondered why the UDR wasn't interested there must be a reason but I just couldn't see it.

'What about Jean, have you spoken to her about this?'

'No.'

'Why not?' Chris just shrugged his shoulders, so I asked him again. 'Chris, you're not making too much sense at the moment so tell me why haven't you spoken to the RUC about this?'

'I've already said why.'

I was now getting a little annoyed at Chris. 'Look Chris I've asked you why you haven't mentioned this to the RUC, I've also asked why you haven't told Jean and up to now you haven't given me any good reasons, so what is going on?' I asked testily.

'Just leave it that's all.'

'I'll leave it only if you can convince me to leave it otherwise I'll speak to Jean and I'll sort it out...'

'All right, all right. I haven't spoken to Jean because I didn't want to worry her,' he said quite sullenly. 'Look Richard, I know you mean well but leave it with me I'll sort it.'

I thought about this for a moment or two before replying. 'Ok, on two conditions...'

'And they are?'

'That you keep me in the picture and if you've found nothing out by Wednesday then I'll started asking questions. Is that a deal?'

'Ok.' He answered somewhat begrudgingly.

The next couple of days proved uneventful except that Jean took me into Belfast and we lost our tail so it proved that the disk was in fact some sort of tracking device, then out of the blue on Wednesday Jean announced she was going out for the day on business and probably would not be back until late afternoon. This worried me, what with Sean's death and her been tailed I didn't like her being unaccompanied like this, but there was little I could do about it except perhaps find out where she was going.

'Whereabouts did you say it was?' I asked innocently enough hoping she would not notice my prying and tell me to mind my own business.

'I didn't say,' she smiled, 'but I'm going to Ballintur a small place near Killowen, do you know Killowen?'

'Killowen or Ballintur?' I asked.

'Either.'

I had to admit that I'd never heard of Ballintur although Killowen sounded familiar 'Isn't Killowen on the west side of the Province?' I asked.

'Yes not that far from Warrenpoint.'

'Ah yes of course.' I answered glibly as if I had known all along.

'Incidentally, would you mind dropping me off at your office?' I asked hoping she would agree without too many questions.

'Yes of course, but why the office?'

'Oh it's just that I arranged to see Chris this morning about something.'

'Oh?' She looked at me quizzically, 'anything I could help with?'

Now she was fishing.

'No it's just something we were talking about the other day,' I answered nonchalantly, 'it's nothing really important.' Hoping that my last remark would put her off the scent. I needed to see Chris hoping he would have some news by now.

'Yes ok.'

So it was arranged and shortly after dropping me off at the yard she left for Ballintur.

Left to my own devices I started by talking to Chris. He told me he had spoken with some of the old hands and he'd also done a bit of digging, but none of it turned up anything new. He'd also asked various people about the two new guys, but nobody seemed to know anything, in fact it seemed as if both men were without a past which bugged me. 'This is ridiculous Chris, there is no man in the world without a past unless...'

'Unless what?'

'Unless they are not who we believe them to be!'

'How do you mean Richard?'

'Have you ever heard of people being given a new identity?'

'Well yes, but that's done by the police isn't it?'

'Yes but can also be done by a number of other agencies and it's usually as a cover or to cover things up.'

'So what shall I do?'

'Precisely nothing.'

'How do you mean nothing?'

'Exactly what I say, nothing, besides what can you do apart from being aware that they are not who they claim to be. Just be a little bit wary that's all.'

Chris fell silent, thinking about what I said. His brow furrowed as he wrestled with this apparent revelation. 'Ok, I know you're right but it's a bit worrying all the same.'

'Don't worry about it, just act normally as you did before you knew. Besides we are assuming that they have been given a new identity because we don't know anything about them. We may be entirely wrong.' That seemed to convince him that we were probably doing them a grave injustice and that was how I wanted it.

Four o'clock came and went, but still no sign of Jean and by five thirty I was more than just a little concerned. I went to find Chris to ask if he'd heard anything from her, but this drew a blank, this worried me even more.

'Chris what time would you call late afternoon?'

'Hmm, about four why do you ask?'

I answered his question with another question. 'Did Jean say anything to you about what time she expected to get back?'

'No not at all why?'

'It's just that she said she would be back by late afternoon and it's now gone five-thirty, is she usually this late?'

'Tell you what Richard; if she hasn't returned by six then we'll phone the Police.'

With that I went back to Jean's office and phoned a mate of mine in Lisburn.

'Hi Jimmy, it's Richard.'

'Hi Richard and how are you.'

'I'm fine. Listen Jimmy I wonder can you do me a favour?'

'What is it?'

'A friend of mine has had some people hanging around her place and I wondered if you could put out some feelers. Also the same person is overdue from a business trip and I wondered if you could find out if there has been any…accidents?'

'What makes you think there may have been an accident Richard?'

'Well if I said to you that we are talking O'Donald here, Jean O'Donald, Sean's wife. You remember Sean who was blown up in his car don't you?'

'Ah yes the 'big man' of course I remember. Ok Richard give me a clue. Car…' Just then I heard footsteps approaching Jean's office. 'Jimmy I'll call you back.' I replaced the receiver just as Chris walked into the office. 'Hi Chris, any news yet?'

'Nope. Look Richard I'm going to call the Police see what I can find out, then I'll give you a lift back to the house. Ok?'

'Ok.' He went off back to his office, I gave him a moment or two to get there and then rang Jimmy again.

'Sorry Jimmy someone came in. Car registration you were about to ask…'

'Is it a BMW colour red?'

'Yeah why have you any news on it?'

'No but we know it. It was Sean's motor so we've got all the details on file. Where can I contact you if and when I need to?'

'I'm staying at Sean's place. Oh and could you arrange a car for me?'

'Now that maybe difficult!' He gave a little laugh, 'Of course I can. I'll get one over to you within the hour.'

'Thanks Jimmy, but a word of caution there seems to be an obs, on her place, anything to do with the department?'

'Don't know I'll find out. Anything else you need?'

'Some radio equipment and firepower, any chance?'

'Hmm, radio will be ok, but armoury could be tricky…leave it with me.'

'Cheers Jimmy.' I replaced the receiver and waited for Chris.

It was six-thirty by the time Chris dropped me back to Jean's, I thanked him for the lift and he agreed to phone me the minute he heard anything and on that note we parted company. I let myself in with the spare key that Jean had had the foresight to give me just after I had arrived. I hadn't been in long when there was a knock at the door. Moving quickly into the lounge where the windows gave an uninterrupted view of the front door and the drive, I eased back a corner of the curtain and looked to see who it was, it was my mate Jimmy.

'Hi Jimmy come in.' I said holding the front door open for him.

'How you doing Richard?' he asked as he stepped into the hall and I closed the door after him.

'I'm fine and what about you?' I asked.

'Couldn't be better, so what's been going on Richard?'

'Come through to the lounge where we can talk in relative comfort.' Jimmy followed me into the lounge and made himself at home. 'Did you manage to get the things?' I asked.

'Sure I did. We have one tasty Saab with an RT set plus your very own personal transceiver in the glove box.' he said as he passed me a set of keys.

'How about a weapon?' I asked.

'Voila,' he said as he produced a box. 'One browning 9.00 mm complete with holster, spare magazines and enough ammo for seventy rounds. Is that ok?'

'Hell Jimmy there's enough ammo to have my own private war.'

'Better to be safe than sorry,' he then passed me a record card for the weapon and rounds. 'I just need your autograph there for the armoury,' he said pointing to where I had to sign. I knew the score. 'Regarding the obs. team you asked about, all I can say for the moment is that they are not ours, but I hope to have some answers soon as we've got an obs team of ours watching theirs. I'll call you as soon as anything is known. Now about Jean, word is out but as yet still waiting, so what do you want to do?'

I was about to answer his question when his transceiver crackled into life

'Alpha Whisky are you receiving, Bravo two over?'

Jimmy pressed the send button and answered. 'Go ahead Bravo two.'

'Just receiving report of BMW sighted...standby...standby. Yes affirmative BMW our Charlie sighted off road Killowen area. Will you take from here? Bravo two over.'

'Roger Bravo two, this now assigned to Romeo Juliet to investigate Alpha Whisky out.' Jimmy had passed them my call sign.

'That was one of the helicopter patrols we seem to have a positive. It seems a little strange that nobody has reported it, wouldn't you agree Richard?'

'Hmm, just a little. Perhaps I'll find out more when I get to the scene.'

'Do you want me to come with you?'

'I'm not sure Jimmy; I think it would be better if you acted as my back-up?'

'Whatever you say, it's your shout.'

'Do you think we need to make this official?'

'I don't think so do you?'

It was close on eight o'clock when I eventually found the BMW. It had rolled down a bank coming to rest up against some trees, where it was completely hidden from the road. I had only stumbled on it through a lucky break. I had stopped to relieve myself and wondered a little way down the bank when something red and glinting caught my eye. As I went to investigate what it was that lay on the bank glinting I noticed the fresh grooves ploughed into the ground. All feelings of going for a pee had gone as I half slithered and half ran down the bank to a crumpled mass of tangled steel. I got the shock of my life because slumped over the wheel was Jean, I tried wrenching the door open but it was jammed. Her face was badly cut and she must have sustained an injury to her head because her hair was matted with blood. I smashed the side window with the butt of the Browning and searched for any sign of life. There was a faint pulse.

'Alpha Whisky, Alpha Whisky this is Romeo Juliet over.'

'Go ahead Romeo Juliet over.'

'Target barely alive, require assistance urgently over.'

'Roger Romeo Juliet ETA 5 minutes out.'

'Roger Alpha Whisky out.' Having acknowledged Jimmy's reply I now needed something to lever the door open with. The boot was already smashed open by the impact so tore out the false floor and tossed it to one side. It must have been my lucky day because there with the jack was an old tyre lever as used by a garage. This was the ideal tool for the job. I jammed the tyre lever between door frame and door and pushed as hard as I could, but it wasn't budging at all.

'What's the SP Richard?'

It was Jimmy. I had been so engrossed in what I was doing I hadn't noticed his arrival.

'Damn doors jammed.'

Jimmy didn't need a second invitation and with our combined weight and strength the door, slowly at first, started to give. Then suddenly with a bang it sprung slightly open. A little more effort by us and with a screeching of twisted metal the door opened.

'Right Richard I'll get back to my car and check the map for a grid reference and send for the Police and an ambulance, in the meantime you'd better make yourself scarce and get back to Lisburn. I'll report it as if I've just found her and I'll call you later and update you then.'

'Ok.' With that I started to scramble back up the bank to the road, 'I'll speak to you later,' I called back to Jimmy once I reached the top.

'Ok Richard.'

It was the early hours and still dark when the incessant ringing of the telephone wakened me.

'Hi Richard, Jimmy here.' Suddenly I was wide awake and focussed.

'Hello Jimmy what's the news?'

'Jean's been airlifted to Belfast. Got one of our guys with her and I'll let you know what is what as soon as I know anything.'

'Cheers Jimmy.'

Later that morning I drove to the yard to see Chris and was quite surprised to see one of the trucks still there. Usually all the trucks were left well before seven, but it was now getting on for ten. I tapped on the half open door of the yard manager's office.

'Come in.' Chris called.

'I just called in to see if you'd heard?'

'Heard what Richard?'

'Jean was in a nasty accident last night. She's been airlifted to Belfast.'

'What. Well I'll be… I haven't heard anything from the Police you'd have thought…'

'Well the RUC telephoned me last night…' I lied.

'You!' He exclaimed looking straight at me. 'But…' He paused and half closed his eyes, 'how did they know to contact you?' he asked a little suspiciously.

'Well when I say me, I mean they telephoned Jean's number.' I hoped it sounded plausible, but he was still suspicious.

'But I don't understand, why would they phone there, they know Sean is dead so what reason would they have to phone there?' He seemed to smell a rat and I needed to think quickly to divert his line of thinking.

'It wasn't the local Police.'

'If it wasn't the local Police, who was it then?' He still wasn't convinced.

'Warrenpoint. It was the Warrenpoint Police.'

'But they would have traced her back to here and the local Police would have dealt with it surely?'

'Perhaps they got the number from Jean's belongings, or something. Hell I don't know.' I shrugged my shoulders. 'Anyway they wouldn't know Sean was dead would they?'

I waited for his reply, he seemed to think about this for a moment or two, then nodded.

'I suppose not.' He answered all trace of suspicion was gone. 'Was she badly injured?'

'They weren't too specific. All I know is that the car was a write off so it must have been pretty bad. The main thing is she's alive.'

'Yeah, what a terrible thing to happen.'

'Terrible.' I agreed with him but I was far from convinced that it had been an accident. I quickly changed the subject, 'what's the wagon in for?'

'The driver had a slight mishap last night, bit shaken up so he's off today. Says he was hit by another truck, but it couldn't have been that bad though.'

'Why do you say that? I asked.

'Because there's only minor damage to our truck and if you ask me I would say it was the other way round, I would think it was our lad who hit the other truck.'

'What makes you so sure?'

'Because the damage is on the nearside that's why, still we'll see when he fills out the accident report form.'

The comment about the damage on the nearside interested me. 'Do you mind if I have a nose?'

'No help yourself.'

I sauntered over to the parked up truck. I looked carefully at the damage sustained. Chris was right, the damage was on the nearside and seemed fairly minimal, but the main thing that caught my eye was the red paint on the cab and along the side of the trailer, was it just a coincidence? My mind was racing, maybe I was doing the man a grave injustice but the damage was at the right sort of height for a car, I was no expert but I was sure that if it had been a truck then the damage would have been far greater and higher. Is this the culprit who hit Jean I wondered to myself as I went back to the office?

'Well what did you find?'

'It's as you said, minimal damage and on the nearside, I would say you're right about it being his fault. By the way, do you know where this accident happened?'

'Not really, well I'm still waiting for him to come in and make out his report. Why?'

'No particular reason I was just curious that's all. Is he one of the old crew?' I casually asked.

'No he's new. Why, what are you driving at?'

'Before I say what I'm thinking answer me one more question.'

'All right, what is it?' Chris looked at me through half closed eyes, trying to figure out what I was doing.

81

'Where was this driver last night?'

'Ballintur. Why?'

'Isn't that out through Warrenpoint on the Killowen Road?' I asked.

'Yes you go through Killowen...hey now hold on Richard, you're not suggesting...'

'I'm not saying anything except come and look at the damage.' I signalled for him to follow me out into the yard and over to the truck. 'Now look at the damage. You must agree, if he had hit a truck it would extend much higher than it does.'

Chris nodded, 'Ok, I'll give you that.'

'Also look at this.' I pointed at the red paint on the cab and trailer. 'Same colour as the BMW isn't it?' Chris nodded in agreement. 'And he was in the right area, now what do you think?'

'Shit. It can't be...'

'Look at the evidence Chris.' He looked at the truck again then back at me. 'Now, I bet you won't see this guy again.' We stood in silence for a moment or two before I spoke again. 'By the way, was he working here when Sean was killed?' Chris looked puzzled at my question, then realising what I was driving at he answered it.

'I'm not sure, but I think so. You don't think that...' He fell silent and studied my face for some clue. I shrugged my shoulders, and left the question hanging.

That night I got a call from Jimmy. Jean had regained consciousness, but had no recollection of what had happened. Slowly the surgeons started to rebuild her body.

I had been home for over three weeks and I had kept in touch with Chris. During this time Jean was making good progress. As to the truck driver Chris had not seen hide nor hair of him since that day. I gained little solace from knowing that my hunch about what had actually happened that day had been right. Chris had even gone to the address the driver had given to the company but all he found was an empty flat. Obviously the Police were informed, but the man had disappeared without a trace.

I dialled the telephone number for O'Donald's Meat Haulage and the phone was immediately answered by Chris.

'Hello Chris it's Richard James.'

'Hello Richard, how are you?'

'I'm fine, how's Jean progressing?'

'Oh she's a lot better now. She's been asking me to ask you to come over. I told her that maybe a problem, but I'll ask all the same.'

I thought about it for about thirty seconds, that's all it took for me to decide. 'Ok, tell her I'll come over at the weekend – just a flying visit though.'

'Thanks Richard I'll tell her.'

As a precaution I decided to make this an official visit so that I could legally carry one licensed Browning 9.00-mm automatic as personal protection and my transceiver. It also meant that a quick telephone call to Jimmy would ensure that I had a firm's car. Because I was travelling from a considerable distance away normal visiting hours at the hospital did not apply, so at 10:00 on Saturday morning I was sat in a small side room alongside Jean's bed.

'You certainly look a lot better than when I last saw you.' She gave a weak smile. 'Can you remember anything about your accident?' I asked.

'I'm not too sure. It's all mixed up. I keep having this dream that I'm driving along the road towards Killowen, it's a nice afternoon, so I'm not hurrying. When I'm suddenly aware of a truck driving at high speed coming up fast behind me. In my dream it's one of my trucks. It pulls out to overtake me then hits the side of the car. I try to swerve, then everything is upside down and the ground is rushing passed me and then blackness.'

'Jean, that isn't a dream.' I watched her face for some reaction.

There was a flicker of a smile, then a frown, a puzzled look. She shook her head. 'No Richard it is a dream, isn't it?'

I smiled reassuringly. 'Sorry Jean, but I have to say it isn't a dream. It was one of your own fleet. You were forced off the road and the bastard who did it left you for dead. It was no accident. Jean it was premeditated. Do you understand? Someone tried to kill you.'

She looked worried. 'Who would want me dead?'

'I'm not sure Jean, but whoever he is, he is probably the same person who killed Sean. I wondered if you would allow me to check out some of your drivers?'

'Of course Richard, but if what you say is true then you must be very careful.'

That night, armed with Jean's keys, I set off to the yard with the express intention of trying to piece together exactly who the two new drivers were. I was convinced that they were both in this together and working undercover for another agency leaving me in no doubt that they had been given fresh identities. Now if that were true then it would certainly explain why they had no past.

As I turned into the road leading to the yard my headlights picked out a red Ford parked less than fifty yards from the entrance. Alarm bells rang, it may be nothing, but I was sure it was the same car as Jean had seen there before. I purposely drove passed the car and noticed it was empty, careless of them, I thought they obviously were not expecting any callers at this time. As I passed the main entrance I noticed one of the gates slightly open. Hmm, I thought to myself, so we have company. I continued along the road a little further before driving over the kerb to park a short distance from the road. Reaching inside the glove compartment I felt for my transceiver.

'Alpha Whisky, are you receiving? Romeo Juliet over.'

There was a crackle of atmospherics and then Jimmy's voice came through loud and clear.

'Roger Romeo Juliet. Go ahead, alpha whisky over.'

'Alpha whisky back up required. Foxtrot to Jean's Alpha 2 over.'

'Roger Romeo Juliet ETA at Alpha 2 seven minutes, out.'

'Roger Alpha Whisky, will foxtrot to main office. Romeo Juliet out.'

So Jimmy will be here in seven minutes. I had told him that I was at Jean's yard and I needed back up so with a bit of luck we might find out who these scumbags are working for. At this particular time in Ireland there were so many different agencies at work one never quite knew who was with whom then, just to add insult to injury, they were not above nobbling each other.

I made my way around to the rear of the buildings, where a small rear steel door gave access into the cold storage depot. On one side of the depot was an external wooden staircase leading to some offices which sat above the smaller cold stores and looked out into the yard. I made my way to the first of these offices and from the window I could just make out a figure lurking in the shadows not far from the main gate; I had him down as a lookout. Over to the right were Jean's office and the transport office. Over to my left was where they normally park the trucks, but now this was empty so that was not the target. Initially I had wondered whether the trucks were to be the target, but as the yard was deserted then it must be something in the office. Yes, there it was the small glow of a flashlight. So one flashlight, one lookout and two intruders it was time for me to make my move.

The big steel doors rolled back almost without a sound. The electric forklift lurched gently forward virtually without a sound. It soon gained speed and with a whining from the electric motor I hurtled out of the depot towards Jean's office door. The lookout heard a sound and turned. Too late he realised. He launched himself towards me, but I swung the wheel round. The forklift tilted and for a minute I thought it would tip over. I spun the wheel back again and hung on as its tyres squealed in protest. Again it felt precarious as it teetered on two wheels only to slam back down with a body jarring crash. I was now passed my would-be assailant. Suddenly there was a crack of gunfire. Bullets whined as they ricochet of the metalwork. There was a loud crash and tinkling of glass. The headlights of a car lit everywhere up as it hurled through the main gates. Screeching to a halt pinning my would-be assailant to the wall. I launched myself from the forklift as it careered towards the office and hit the yard running. Before the second man had chance to think I was through the door. I let off one round from my Browning. He dropped the torch.

'Hit the floor NOW.' I shouted, 'arms outstretched and face down.'

He dropped where he was face down on the floor with his arms straight out in front of him. I pounced on him and with my knee bent I forced it hard into the centre of his back and jammed the barrel of my automatic up against his temple. 'One move and your dead, now tell me, who are you working for?' He remained silent. I grabbed a handful of his hair and yanked his head back as far as I could. 'Come on you bastard answer me, who do you work for?' Still nothing. Just then Jimmy arrived with a somewhat dishevelled second man. I dragged my prisoner up by his hair, slammed him face first into the wall. Still holding a handful of his hair I yanked back his head and again yelled at him, 'who are you working for?' He maintained a stony silence. Again I smashed his face into the wall. I repeated my question once more. 'Who are you working for?' His face was now a bloody mess, but still he said nothing. After more the wall treatment he eventually passed out without saying a word. He collapsed in a heap on the floor his face bleeding profusely from the treatment it had received.

In the meantime Jimmy had secured his prisoner with a plastic tie wrap around his wrists. He was going nowhere. With both of them immobilised it was now our chance to search them. This did not reveal anything. Both guys were clean out of identification.

'Well Jimmy what now?' I asked.

'We could try the car, it's a bit of a long shot I know, but it may just reveal something.'

We made sure our two 'friends' were secured, by tying them with plastic tie wraps to opposite ends of the desk. Jimmy stayed on guard whilst I searched their car. I had gone over it with a fine toothed comb, but like them it was clean. In fact it was too clean. It was almost sterile. I was about to give up when, bingo. I found a hidden compartment under the fascia panel. What I found next shocked me. In the compartment was a Browning 9.00-mm army issue, in fact if I wasn't mistaken it was the same as ours, non-traceable. This could only mean one thing; they were from our Circus or RUC Special Branch. So what were they doing here? What was their game? I removed the weapon and tucked it into my waistband of my trousers. As I entered the office Jimmy looked up.

'You know what, our friends sing from the same song sheet as us.'

'How d'you mean Richard?'

'Look what I found.' I waved the Browning in the air. Opened its breech then tossed it over to Jimmy. 'Same spec as ours.'

Just then a low moan came from the guy with the smashed up and bloody face as he regained consciousness.

'Well, well, well. Now I wonder whose armoury this is from. I think it's time for a little chat boys, don't you?' he said addressing our two prisoners. 'So which part of the Circus are you from?' They still played dumb. 'Come on guys. We've got your weapon. We can run checks. Are you from Belfast?' One of them looked up with a start. 'Ah, so Belfast is it?'

'So what are you looking for?' I asked.

The one with the smashed up face started to talk.

'We wanted documents.'

'What documents?'

'Copies of papers that O'Donald had kept.'

'How d'you mean kept?' Jimmy interjected.

'Well you must know. He was one of yours. He kept copies of everything he did. You see he didn't trust anyone.'

'Well with people like you around, who could blame him.' I answered.

'Yeah, but…' But that was all he said because he passed out again. I was puzzled. Why were they so worried about documents after all we were all fighting the 'good' fight together?

'What do you make of that Jimmy?'

'I'm not sure. But one thing I do know and that is they're not our lot.'

'So who do you reckon they are?'

'I think they are 'five' I'll take the gun and we'll try and do some tracing. Anyway let's bundle the pair of them back into their car and leave them there. Oh and we'll keep the ignition keys for good measure. Come on Tweedledum and Tweedledee.' He cut the tie wraps holding them to the desk, and dragging them to their feet we escorted them back to their car, a red Ford, where we left them.

I decided I would call in to the hospital again and tell Jean what had been happening. When I related what had gone on she managed a smile.

'So I was right after all. I was being tailed.' She gave a weak smile.

'Yes, but it is a little more sinister than that.'

On hearing this comment her smile quickly changed to a frown. 'How do you mean sinister, that's a bit melodramatic isn't it?' She gave a nervous laugh. Her eyes searched my face for some indication that I was joking, but she knew I wasn't 'Sinister you say,' her eyes again searching my face for some sort of answer, but found none. 'In what way do you mean sinister?' She asked.

'I mean sinister because one of them tried to kill you.' My last comment had shaken her and for a minute there she appeared frightened. 'Do you know of any reason why they should try to murder you?' I asked.

'I don't know.' Was all she said, but I had a feeling she was holding something back and an uneasy silence ensued. Then suddenly Jean said something rather strange. 'Richard, whatever you do be very careful.'

It was my turn to be puzzled. 'How do you mean Jean?' I asked.

'Just what I say be very careful, because if there's one thing that I learnt from Sean, it was not to trust anyone including our people. So like I say, be very careful Richard.'

'Why shouldn't I trust our people?' I asked a little naively.

'Oh Richard, Richard, do I have to spell it out for you. Our Government are 'past masters' at subterfuge and double dealing, after all it was us who taught the rest of the world. Just remember this everything you do they know about. They know every breath you take and every move you make. Look at how they reacted to Austen. How they categorically denied that he was working for us. How they sacrificed him and let him go to prison when all the time he was our agent. Why did they do it? I'll tell you why, because at the time it suited them, the faceless ones, the men in suits and the powers that be that's why.' She said fervently, 'so I say again, be very careful.' She paused to rest a moment before going on. 'Do you know Sean always, always kept copies of every single document, every single written sheet that he received. Even verbal instructions he carefully noted down in a log, names, dates, times and places. This was his insurance. You need to do the same Richard. Remember; keep copies of everything because that is the only insurance policy you'll have. Keep them safe. Do whatever is necessary and hide them away, preferably with a solicitor or someone you can trust, just in case.' She gave a gentle squeeze to my hand. 'Promise me you'll do it Richard, promise.'

I nodded. 'No I want to hear you say it. Tell me that as soon as you get back to Kent you'll do what I ask, if not for me do it for Sean.'

'All right Jean I promise for you and for Sean that I'll do it.'

'Good, now I know you will do it!'

'Jean.' She was looking tired now, but I was convinced there was more to this than what she was saying, and needed to know what it was.

'Yes Richard.'

'Is there something you're not telling me?' I asked.

'Look Richard, I know this sounds crazy, but I have been expecting this for a long time now. You see Sean probably knew too much.' She gave my hand another slight squeeze, smiled weakly and said, 'thank you for coming but you must go my friend and take care.' I could see she was exhausted so decided not to question her any further, but I was determined to get to the bottom of why an attempt was made on her life. Could it be linked to Sean's death, I just didn't know. I left her sleeping and returned to the airport to catch my late flight back to London.

Chapter 9

It had been a few weeks since I had visited Jean in hospital and I was just beginning to get back to normal when, out of the blue, I received a call from Jimmy over in Ulster.

'Hi Richard, how you doing? I've managed to unearth some info that I think you'll be very interested in.'

'About what Jimmy?'

'About our mutual friend and the two bravos we grabbed. I can't tell you about it now, will you be over again soon?'

'Not as far as I'm aware.'

'Aw shit.' The line went quiet.

'Jimmy, are you still there?' I asked.

'Yeah I'm still here, it's just that I was hoping you would be over in the near future that's all. Never mind I've a few days leave owing and I kept promising a mate of mine in Kent that I'd pop over to see him. If I come over how far are you from a place called Broad Oak?'

'About fifteen minutes by road, why is that where he lives?'

'Yeah…' He went quiet for a moment. 'Tell you what, I'll give him a call see what's what and call you again tomorrow. Is that ok?'

'Sure, what time?'

'About this time, would that be all right?'

'Yes it should be.'

'Ok 'till tomorrow then.' With that he put the phone down. I was intrigued and I wondered what it was that he'd managed to find out about the two toerags. Who were they working for and what was their brief?

It was twenty-four hours since I had last spoken with Jimmy when dead on six o'clock the phone rang.

'Hello Richard, Jimmy here. I've spoken to that mate of mine and it looks good for this weekend, is that ok for you?'

I quickly checked the work diary and it looked clear enough.

'Yeah should be ok, so when are you thinking of?'

'Saturday early evening – say seven or thereabouts?'

'How about seven-thirty?'

'Ok. Seven-thirty then. Do you know any quiet pubs where we could meet?'

'Yeah, I know just the place. The Red Lion at a place called Dunkirk.

'Where's that?'

'About ten maybe fifteen minutes from Broad Oak.'

'Good.'

'Do you want me to pick you up?'

'No don't worry I'll make my own way there. Dunkirk you say?'

'Yes. The Red Lion, its off the A2 on the way towards London, but you have to take the slip road towards Boughton come over the top of the A2 then turn immediately right as if you were going back to Canterbury. You'll see the pub on your left more or less opposite Howland's farm shop.'

'Got it. So I'll see you at seven-thirty on Saturday.'

'In the lounge bar. There are two bars so make sure you get the right one.'

'Ok, cheers Richard.'

'Yeah, see you Saturday.'

I parked my car in the car park of the Red Lion and as it was only twenty five passed seven and my car was the only one there I assumed Jimmy hadn't arrived yet, that was assuming he had a car and hadn't been dropped off by his mate. As I was a little early I decided to take a look inside.

The Red Lion was a large free house with an adjoining caravan and camping park, and in the days prior to the Canterbury bypass being opened it must have been a busy pub especially as it was situated on what was then the main route to the ferry terminals and docks at Dover. To cater for the trade it had a lounge bar and a separate public bar, but since those heady days passing customers had dwindled and the present owners had to rely on purely local trade. Even though I had stipulated the lounge bar I thought I had better check the public bar just to make sure Jimmy wasn't in there. The public bar was a favourite with some of the local lads and the bikers. It was a long narrow room with a small bar at the end, a darts board and a Juke Box on one of the side walls. I opened the only door and glanced around but the place was deserted.

The lounge bar was totally different, not only in style but also in clientele. To begin with it had two entrances, one at the front of the building and one at the back. It was the latter entrance I used. The back door was approached along a short path that ran between the public bar and the beer garden. Upon passing through the lounge door you enter an elevated area that would be a similar size to that of the average sitting room. The bar and main body of the lounge is found at ninety degrees to the entrance and is approached via three steps down from the elevated section. At the bottom of the three steps sits a 'one armed bandit' or fruit machine. Between the fruit machine and the bar were a couple of stools and it was here where I chose to sit and wait for Jimmy, where we would be tucked away in a corner and hidden from view.

The main body of the room ran full width of the building and was naturally divided into a dining area and bar area by a large wooden beam to the ceiling with upright oak supports. In the rear portion was an Inglenook fireplace that on a cold winter's day served to help heat the lounge by means of a large log fire. The second entrance to the lounge bar was at the front of the building through the dining area and from where I sat I could see whoever entered or left the premises, not only through this door at the front but also through the door at the back. It was here, in 1838 after the Bosenden Wood affray, that the body of Sir William Courtenay was laid out and rumour is that the place is haunted by his spirit.

At dead on seven-thirty Jimmy walked in through the rear door, walked passed where I was sat and ordered a beer. He was oblivious of me until the landlord told him that it was paid for and pointed out where I was sat.

'So there you are.'

'Yeah, it's a good place to sit and see who comes in without being noticed.'
I got off the stool and went over to Jimmy, 'how did you get here, by taxi, or did your mate drop you off?'

'No way, I've got the firm's car.'

'How did you wangle that?' I asked.

'Oh you know…' He left me to draw my own conclusions. 'Anyway how you doing?'

'Oh I'm fine, what about you?'

'I'm ok.' He casually looked around the lounge, 'grab your beer and we'll sit over there.' He indicated a table as far away from the bar as possible having now satisfied himself that there was nobody else around who could listen in on our conversation.

'So what have you got for me Jimmy?' I asked him in a low voice as we sat down.

'Well you remember Tweedledee and Tweedledum?'

'Yes what about them?'

'Well they are both ours.'

'What!' I exclaimed. 'Are you saying that they both belong to 'six'?'

'Not exactly.'

'Explain…'

'Have you ever heard of the FRU?'

'Tell me more.'

'Well FRU stands for the Field Research Unit or you may know it as the 'Detachment' and from what I can gather from a mate of mine in the Tactical Ops. Team, strictly off the record of course, FRU is a branch 'six'. Now things get a little complicated here because I've also learnt that both Tweedledee and Tweedledum are 'Detachment' trained yet belong to the Ulster Defence Association or the 'UDA' as it's called. Incidentally what's your knowledge of the UDA?'

'Fairly limited. I know that it's the Protestant's answer to the PIRA, a paramilitary organisation and I've also heard Sean talk about it, but other than that not a lot.'

'Did you know for instance that a lot of the UDA members have been SAS trained?'

'I had heard rumours, but I had always assumed that that's what they were, just rumours.'

'Well take it from me they aren't rumours.'

'So what you are saying is that the UDA has links with SAS?'

'Something along those lines, but then it gets more complicated, because the UDA is what it is, a sort of quasi-military operation and totally illegal, the FRU had certain of their agents infiltrate it. Tweedledee and Tweedledum are two of their agents and for all purposes act as UDA Intelligence Officers. Of course, on the face of it, they are handled by SAS but, in reality, their real task masters are the FRU and they are handled by 14th Int. Company.' Jimmy paused and took a mouthful of beer, 'are you with me up to now?'

I nodded. 'So to put it in a nutshell, we have two blokes Tweedledee and Tweedledum, both agents for HMG, but working for FRU a specialist unit, on top of which they are linked to SAS, handled by 14th Int. Company, and act as UDA intelligence Officers.'

I gave a low whistle

'Complicated isn't it?'

'You're not joking.'

'Now as I understand it Sean stumbled across these two and as our unit had not been told about them, he was about to blow the whistle on them, so having reported this information to his handler he had unintentionally signed his own death warrant...'

'What! Are you telling me HMG sacrificed a good operator to cover for these two?'

'It seems that way. It seems Sean knew too much.'

'The bastards! The fucking bastards! What chance do we stand when you have bastards like that around?' Jean's parting words immediately sprung to mind '...*You see Sean probably knew too much. Keep copies of every single document, every single written sheet that you receive, even verbal instructions.*' I realised now what she had meant. 'What about Jean, do you think there was also an ulterior motive there?'

'I'm certain there was and it's my guess that they thought she was getting too close for comfort. By the way, did you know Jean was one of ours?' this last remark shook me.

'Jeez, I had no idea she was a member of the Circus.' Never in a million years had I dreamt that she was an operator for Her Majesty's Government. 'Are you sure that's true?' I asked incredulously.

'Oh it's true all right, you see on the day that the attempt on her life was made she wasn't in Ballintur on business at all, she was actually returning from Ballykinler Army base.'

'Why Ballykinler base?'

'Why? Because Ballykinler Army base is where the UDR MoD are trained in counter-insurgency tactics.'

'So who do they use for instructors?'

'Some are from the School of Infantry at Warminster, some from the RUC and guess where else?'

'Don't tell me, the SAS.'

'You've got it in one, they send over specialist instructors from Hereford.'

'The camp at Bradbury Lines.' I said more as a statement than a question.

'Yes, as you say Bradbury Line, do you know it then?'

'I should say so. I did some of my training there.'

'Really?'

'Yes. Anyway as to Jean's situation, that doesn't prove a thing. I mean she could have been at Ballykinler to discuss…' Jimmy cut me off.

'Discuss what?'

'Sean.' I replied. Jimmy shook his head. 'Well I don't know she could have been there to…to discuss anything. Who knows?' I said lamely.

'No, no, no. Take my word for it; she is certainly one of ours.' Jimmy said as he continued to shake his head.

'So if she is one of ours then who was her handler?'

'Her handler?'

'Yes her handler?' I repeated my question.

'Can't you guess, it was Sean of course? After all who's better placed than her husband?'

'Bloody hell…' I was stumped for anything else to say and sat there in silence for a few minutes to gather my thoughts. 'Thanks Jimmy. You know when the shit hits the fan in this job you have no friends.'

'I know. The only thing you can do is to cover your back each time.' He glanced at his watch, 'Anyway I better be off.' Then as an after thought he added, 'By the way, I almost forgot to tell you, because of Sean's death you have a new handler, did you know?'

'Not as yet, but no doubt I'll find out next month as I'm scheduled for another training exercise. I suppose now you're going to say it's you,' I said jokingly.

'You're right.'

'How do you mean?'

'Exactly what I said, you're right. It's me.'

'You're joking, aren't you?'

'No I'm serious. It is me. I'm your new handler and now, I must go.' He stood up, finished off the last of his pint and shook my hand. 'See you Richard' he started to walk towards the door.

'Yes and Jimmy...' I called after him.

He paused and turned, 'Yeah?'

'Thanks for coming and for the info.'

'No problem, after all isn't that what mates are for? See you soon Richard.' With that parting comment he left me to finish the last of my pint and with my thoughts in turmoil I made my way to the bar to get another.

Some twenty minutes later I made my way over to my car, subconsciously noting a blue Volvo parked in the far corner of the car park. Out of habit, as I drove up the road, I checked my rear view mirror and noticed a blue Volvo behind me. Immediately my mind went into overdrive, was this history repeating itself? There was only one way to find out. I accelerated away towards Boughton and as I entered the thirty miles per hour zone for Dunkirk I slung a sharp right into Courtenay Road. The tyres squealed in protest. I floored the pedal and redlined as I had been taught. Changed up and redlined again. Now I was in top and my speed was well over 80 mph and climbing. The blue Volvo was still there. I knew this road ran more or less straight for approximately two miles. It then curved to the right. I also knew that on the right hand bend there was a narrow road to the left which led to the small village of Dargate and then on to the Margate road. As I approached the right hander I braked harshly, spun the wheel left and with screeching tyres, and a smell of hot oil and burning rubber I swerved into Dargate Lane. Again I redlined it. Again I was travelling at 80 mph, slinging my car into a right hander then a left hander. I was through the chicane and onto the straight. I now hit 100 mph as I hurtled towards Dargate. Stealing a quick glance in my mirror I saw the Volvo just coming out of the chicane. Up front was a tight right hand bend, almost a hairpin. I toe and healed, double declutching I changed down through the gears and I was round. On the apex I again floored the accelerator, redlining every time. Up ahead the road forked I took the right fork and headed towards the main Margate road. Just before the Margate road there was a narrow lane off to the right, which would take me out to Yorklets. I slammed on the brakes, the tyres screamed in protest kicking dust up off the road as the back end hung out to the left and the nose of the car entered the lane. A quick burst of speed straightened my line out and I now hoped that I had managed to put enough distance between myself and my tail. I continued at high speed along the lane with the car bouncing and bucking over the bumps in the road but I didn't let up. I was determined to shake off my pursuer. As I reached the hamlet of Yorklets I slowed down vaguely remembering that somewhere along here was another narrow turning which would take me back towards Hernehill and Boughton. As I rounded a bend I was upon it. I slammed on my brakes but just too late and I skidded passed. I wasted valuable seconds backing up, but before my wheels had stopped turning I dipped the clutch and selected first. Flooring the accelerator and with wheels spinning I was heading down the lane. I checked in my mirror there was no sign of the Volvo but I kept up my high speed driving all the way to Hernehill just to make sure I had lost my tail. At the cross roads I turned left and headed out along Staplestreet, there was still no sign of the Volvo, so I slowed to a more leisurely pace and I wondered who they were and with my thoughts once again turning to what Jean had said.

'*Be very careful. Do you know Sean always, always kept copies of every single document, every single written sheet that he received. Even verbal instructions he carefully noted down in a log, names, dates, times and places. This was his insurance.*' This last little episode convinced me and I decided that as soon as I got home I would put together a package and on Monday make an appointment with Gore the family solicitor. Ah! The best laid plans....

The summer was almost upon us when Paul told me that his uncle's will had at last been proven and the business was his, so he would be taking over within the next couple of days.

'You know, I'll miss this place Richard.'

'No you won't. After a few days you'll have forgotten all about fruit trees, grafting and such mundane things and be talking about radii, drill sizes and welds. It'll be a whole new world.' Paul laughed. 'Seriously Paul, if it isn't you for whatever reason, you know you can always come back. Besides what about your Irish colleen over in the Republic?' I joked.

'Who, Fionnuala?'

'No the girl from Dublin or wherever she was from?'

'Oh yeah hmm...' He left it at that. 'Anyway, I'm still up for the trips to the Republic if you need me, but I guess you're about sorted on that score.'

'Well you never know there maybe something come up.'

'Well I'm here if you need me.'

'Thanks Paul. I really appreciate the offer. Good luck mate.' I proffered my hand to my long standing mate.

'Cheers Richard and thanks for everything. How about going out for a beer at the weekend?'

'Yeah, yeah I'd love to, cheers Paul.'

That was that. After all this time we were both going to go our separate business ways.

Chapter 10

It had just gone seven-thirty when the telephone rang.

'Hello, James Fruit Farms Anne James speaking.'

'Richard James please.'

'Who is it calling?'

'That is unimportant. Just tell Mr James to be ready at the end of the road in fifteen minutes. Thank you Mrs James that'll be all.' With that the caller put down the phone.

'Richard.'

'Yeah.' I called back from the garden.

'I've just taken a most bizarre telephone call.'

'Oh in what way?' I asked as I came through the front door.

'Some man, he wouldn't give his name, phoned up and said you had to be 'ready at the end of the road in fifteen minutes' and then put the phone down. What's that all about?'

'Hmm, I'm not sure. But if it's what I think it is then it must be important.'

I waited until Anne was back in the sitting room and then I dialled the security telephone number that I had been issued with. All players in the Circus were issued with such a number to enable them to check out any calls they may receive purporting to be connected with the Circus or its operations, and this appeared to be just such an occasion. I let it ring the prescribed six times then put the receiver down. I checked my watch, it was seven-thirty two precisely at seven-thirty three I dialled a different number and was connected straight away.

'Control.'

'This is Ferryman I have a code red fifteen minutes, please confirm.'

'Please hold.'

The line went dead. I held on knowing that they had put a trace on my call which would confirm whether or not it was from a known insecure line, namely my home telephone number or not. I checked my watch. Thirty seconds, thirty-five, forty seconds there was a click.

'Thank you for holding, putting you through now.'

'Good evening I hear you want to speak to your mother, unfortunately she isn't available at present, but she has asked me to say a car is on its way to pick you up.'

'Thank you. Please convey my thanks to mother for arranging that and I'll see her later.' I put down the phone.

So the call was genuine. It could only mean one thing that either the proverbial had hit the fan, or there was a big one coming up and I was required urgently. I rushed upstairs grabbed my bag that was always packed ready for just such a situation. I clattered my way back down stairs to the living room and out to the kitchen where Anne was preparing our dinner. I knew I was going to be unpopular, but it just couldn't be helped. Although she didn't know everything that was going on she had a shrewd idea that I was involved with the Army in some way, but chose not to dig too deeply.

'I know don't tell me, you have to go.'

'Sorry love...' I grimaced and waited for some sort of reaction, but she took it all very well.

'So does that bizarre phone call have some bearing on this?'

'Yeah, I'm sorry love.'

'Ok.' She said with resignation then noticed the bag. 'I suppose that,' she pointed at the bag I was holding, 'means you won't be home tonight. So my next question is when can I expect to see you again?' But before I could say anything she quoted the line I'd always used, '*I don't know exactly love, but I'll let you know as soon as I know something.*'

I dropped the bag and held her tightly. 'I'm sorry, but there's nothing I can do.'

'Yes there is Richard James, there is.' She pulled away from me and turned back to her cooking as she tried to cover up the fact she was crying. I gently put my hands on her shoulders and turned her round to face me. She looked down at her feet. With my finger under her chin I raised her face. A tear rolled down her cheek and dropped on to the back of my hand. 'Yes there is Richard you could leave; you're married to me not the Army or the Government.'

I pulled her to me and gently kissed her wet cheek, her eyelids and then her mouth. I held her tight.

'Hush don't cry.' I kissed her neck and nibbled her ear in reassurance.

As we stood there in our embrace gradually her tears stopped and she looked up into my eyes and smiled. 'I'm ok now. You best be going otherwise you'll be late.'

I squeezed her to me and held her tight. 'I love you Anne and I promise I'll be home as soon as I can.'

'I love you Richard James.' With that she gave me a lingering kiss.

I gently pulled away from her, picked up my bag and gave her another quick kiss.

'I must go. I Love you and I'll call you later.'

I glanced at my watch I barely had three minutes to get to the end of the road where I was to be collected.

'Sit down Ferryman.' Ash indicated to the chair on the opposite side of the table to him.

'Thank you sir.'

Apart from the boss there were two other high ranking individuals, neither of whom I recognised, and a stenographer present. Ash sat between a Brigadier, who looked a lot younger than his years, and a very distinguished looking grey haired gentleman dressed in a pinstripe suit. On the table in front of the civilian lay a closed buff folder which was stamped in red capital letters TOP SECRET beneath this appeared 'Operation Orpheus'. As I sat down Ash turned to the civilian, 'Sir James, this is our agent Ferryman and he is the person whom I suggested is the best equipped for the Orpheus project. As you will be aware from the notes I passed over to you, Ferryman has considerable and intimate knowledge of the Dublin area, even in fairly recent times he was instrumental in bringing our Mr Austin home. Also he has been readily accepted by Breandán O'Shea, whom you no doubt are aware is one of the top people in the Official IRA. It's because of his knowledge and background that I recommend Ferryman to be the person who acts as our link man. That is assuming we want to scupper the talks.'

'There's no question about it Colonel, these talks must fail. Even your own Army Chiefs agree that the only way we can beat the terrorist is by outright military action, isn't that right Brigadier?'

'Yes I must agree with Sir James on this one Ash. The top brass are keen to see failure and a return to an all out military operation and that is why we need to get this project under way as soon as possible. As you know in the North we have already 'stepped up' our activities by passing information on Republican suspects to the Ulster Volunteer Force (UVF) and the UDA and this is 'helping' their cause and indirectly our cause. You know, the more Loyalist killings we have the greater the chance of these cease-fire talks failing.'

'So everyone is agreed then we start phase 1 of this project?' Ash looked to the Brigadier for his approval; the Brigadier for his part gave a slight nod of his head. 'I presume you're in agreement with phase 1 Sir James?'

'I certainly am.'

'In that case gentlemen may I have your authority to divulge the content of what is listed as TOP SECRET to our agent?' The other two gave a murmur of assent.

'So for the purpose of records, authorisation for divulging the content from a TOP SECRET file and communiqué by Colonel Ash of Military Intelligence to agent codenamed Ferryman, has been obtained from the heads of Military Intelligence MI6 and MI5. The document I am about to disclose to Ferryman is code named *Operation Orpheus* and for the record a transcript of this meeting will be held by central records classified as TOP SECRET. Also for the record Ferryman will now be addressed by Richard his first name only. All persons present will be addressed either by rank only or their first name. At this point I am passing a copy of the dossier over to Richard for his eyes only.'

Ash then removed a file from his briefcase and passed it to me. I opened the folder and quickly scanned the top document headed *Operation Orpheus* TOP SECRET. It gave a preamble about how the Military Reconnaissance Force (MRF) used Loyalist paramilitaries and Provisionals who had been 'turned'. It then outlined the training of the paramilitaries at Palace Barracks and the involvement off 22 SAS in the training programme. It went on to say how these organisations were 'actively deployed' as 'assisting the security forces' with tours of republican areas. It continued by outlining various activities of the MRF and how they used "whatever means, legal or illegal, to blackmail an involuntary 'recruit' to carry out operations which cannot be traced back to the handler." I then scanned the second page of the file and this was in a similar vein only this time concentrating on how the intelligence services, in liaison with the RUC's Special Branch, often masterminded Loyalist violence. It spoke of collusion between the intelligence services and the UVF and UDA being widespread and officially-endorsed. I quickly realised that should any of this information get out it was potential dynamite and the shock waves would reverberate throughout Whitehall and Her Majesty's Government doing untold damage. Page three covered the current discussions being held in secret between the IRA and the British Government. These talks were aimed at bringing about a ceasefire in Ulster. The last page in the TOP SECRET file was headed *Operation Orpheus* phase 1 & phase 2 but apart from these headings the rest of the sheet was left blank.

'Ok Richard, have you read through the pages?'

'Yes Colonel.'

'Have you any questions about what you have read; is there anything at all you're not clear about?'

'No I don't think there is anything at the moment Sir James.'

'Good.'

'Now Richard you have been selected for a very important task here and it is imperative that it works. We are relying on you and as such you will have our full backing. This operation must, no, it will succeed and failure is not an option do I make myself clear?'

'Yes Brigadier you do.'

'Good. Then the Colonel will give you the background and outline what we want you to do.' The Brigadier nodded to Ash to continue.

'Thank you Brigadier. As you can see Richard, the file gives a brief outline as to what is currently happening in Ulster and it also mentions the secret talks going on between HMG and the IRA. What is left out however is that the top aides and top brass have always been at variance with any peace process, as they feel such a process would not be good for Ulster or Britain as a whole.'

'But why not Colonel, surely a cease-fire is what everyone wants?'

'That's where you're wrong Richard. It's only the IRA who wants a cease-fire because we've got them on the run. Intelligence reports show that they are running low on arms and ammunition so if hostilities continue within a short space of time terrorism could well be crushed. It's felt that a cease-fire plays right into their hands. It buys them time, enables them to regroup and replenish their arms caches, so you see there is a hidden agenda there and the bottom line is they cannot be trusted with a cease-fire.'

'Ok I'll buy that. So where do I come into this?'

'What we have in mind is we attack the very heart of the operation. We need to unsettle their people, their supporters. We need something that shows even their most ardent supporters that the IRA are not strong, that they are weak, unable to protect their own people so shaking that support and bringing the IRA and what they stand for into question. We now take our argument to Dublin, the very core of the IRA's stronghold,' Ash turned to the Brigadier, 'wouldn't you agree Brigadier?'

'Couldn't put it better myself Colonel. In fact Richard, it is known as 'terrorising the terrorist' a tried and tested method used in Kenya.'

'So how do you propose to 'terrorise the terrorist' as you put it Brigadier?'

'Good question Richard.'

'We want you to act as an *Agent Provocateur*.' Ash stated in a matter of fact way.

'How exactly do you propose I do that?'

'Simple really, you've been booked on the ferry from Holyhead to Dublin and a room has been booked for you at the Tara, where you will stay for the next seven days. On Wednesday afternoon you will take this car,' Ash handed me a set of keys, 'and drive into Dublin city centre and you'll park in one of the main streets, lock it and walk away and that's all. You will then make your way to the Allied Irish Bank in Grafton Street where you will find your contact, a newspaper seller. Once you have located him you will use the following coded message. You will ask him if he still has a copy of Tuesday's Irish Times, he will reply and say 'no'. You will then ask him if he knows where you could get one; he will then offer to phone his distribution manager to see if they can send one over for you. Within five minutes your copy will arrive and you will be offered a lift, which you will accept. Have you any questions?'

'Where is this car?'

'It will be delivered to the Tara by a Seamus O'Neill one of our men over there so it's ready for you to take on the Wednesday. The car is a brand new red Ford with a Dublin registration so it doesn't look out of place over there. It's been registered to a Mr Fergal O'Hanlon, a resident of Dublin. Obviously the documents and address have been carefully done, but of course Mr O'Hanlon is purely fictitious as is the address. Oh there used to be such a place, but the house has been long gone and a car park has replaced it. It's not far from the Irish Supreme Court which is, under the circumstances, a little ironic. As for O'Hanlon, well he died a long time ago.

'So how do I get to the Tara in the first place?'

'You take your own car of course.'

'But that's at home.'

'Hmm. Have you got your keys with you?'

'Yes.'

'Thank goodness for that. For a minute there I thought we may have to do a 'rush' on making up a new set. Oh I forgot to mention it. I arranged with transport to pick your car up so it should be here anytime now, so unless you've any other questions I think I've covered everything...'

'I'm not totally clear on the arrangements for the Tara. You say I am booked in for seven days why?'

'Well you have a small contract to do at Seamus O'Neill's farm, he's quite well known in the area and a highly respected member of the local community.' Ash gave a little chuckle and his eyes twinkled mischievously. 'If only they knew him like we do, he wouldn't be so popular then. Still that's another story for another day.'

'I assume that Seamus O'Neill is not his real name.'

'Obviously not, that's his cover name. We fixed him up with a brand new identity when we moved him south from Antrim. He's a good team member and a useful contact for you Richard.'

'But why is it necessary for me to be there seven days?'

'Because we felt it would give you a good strong alibi and put you above any suspicion.'

'Then what after the seven days?'

'You return here for a debriefing and we then move toward phase 2. Have I answered all your queries?'

'I think that about covers everything, except for...'

'Yes Richard, is there something I've not covered?'

I would have liked more details about the car but then I changed my mind, 'No, it's fine.' I said hastily, 'I was only going to ask about my car but then I remembered you saying it's already over here in the transport section.' I then started to waffle on about my own car.

'So, when do I leave?' I asked.

'We have you booked on tomorrow night's ferry and I've arranged for you to stay on base tonight so you can take a leisurely drive up to Holyhead tomorrow.' Ash handed me a white sealed envelope with the name of 'James Fruit Farms' typed on the outside. 'This contains your tickets and one thousand pounds. The money is to cover your expenses and any emergency that may arise. Should you need additional funds then Seamus will arrange it and he will also supply you with a full set of gear once you are over there. It's been done like this in case there are any hic-cups. This way you are clean and there is non-traceability if you know what I mean. Anyway 'Bon Voyage' and have a safe trip.'

The arc lights seemed as bright as day after the pitch black of night. I was running through the undergrowth towards the light. Through the distant sound of rapid fire I could just hear Jock shouting something to me. The sound of rapid fire got closer and closer. Jock was shouting louder. I couldn't quiet reach him. Suddenly I could hear him distinctly. I woke with a start, my body covered in sweat there was someone knocking on my door and calling…

'06:30 Sir.'

Where was I? Gradually the last vestiges of sleep cleared and I remembered I was in the Officer's wing at JITC Ashford. Throwing off my covers and hastily slipping into my trousers and opened the door.

'Good morning Sir, Colonel Ash sends his compliments and asked me to tell you that breakfast is available in the Officer's mess from 07:00.'

'Thank you.'

'Sir.' He saluted, turned sharply to his right and marched away down the corridor. This was a novel idea me being elevated to 'officer' rank and treated as such.

It was bright and sunny as I pulled out of the main gate and turned left. Passing under the railway bridge I joined the traffic heading out of the town following the signs for London and the M2. In less than an hour I was on the M2 heading towards London and the Dartford tunnel and by mid-morning, with London and its 'rush hour' a thing of the past, I was cruising up the M1 at a steady 80 mph day dreaming about Ireland and my beautiful Irish colleen Fionnuala.

With a slight jolt, the car-ferry finally came to a halt and everywhere was a hive of activity. Gangplanks and ramps were hastily made fast so that foot-passengers could disembark. On the dock side a small crowd gathered and surged forward in order to glimpse a better view of friends and long overdue loved ones as they disembarked. Car ramps were lowered into place and the car-deck crew directed traffic with vehicles spewing from the belly of the ship. Everything was chaotic and very frenetic, a cacophony of sound. As I emerged from the chaos of the docks I headed north towards Swords and the Tara and it wasn't long before I was parking my car in the hotel's car park.

As I was unable to check-in to my room because it was still being cleaned I decided I to find Seamus O'Neill's farm and introduce myself. However in light of Jean O'Donald's and my past experiences I wasn't taking any chances and taped a small hand held tape recorder to my body in the hope that my clothes would not impair the quality of recording to any great degree.

'Testing one two three. Testing one two three.'

I spoke quite quietly to try and simulate someone a short distance away. Now the test was over, had it recorded successfully? I undid my shirt and rewound the cassette then pressed play. I held my breath. At first all I could hear was a loud rustling noise, which I assumed was the noise of my moving about then suddenly through all the background noise the metallic sound of 'Testing one two three. Testing one two three.' In fact it was quite loud and surprisingly clear. Happy with my crude but effective method of being 'wired for sound' I rewound the tape and switched off the recorder. Well that will cater for any conversation or verbal instructions, I thought to myself, now for the camera. I had taken the precaution of packing both the tape recorder and a camera so that I would have ample evidence from this trip to keep as insurance should anything go wrong.

O'Neill's place was a small farm about a mile to the west of the Tara. A nice little retreat, so I'd been told, complete with a small orchard of about thirty acres which would just about be big enough to substantiate my cover story. In addition to the orchard he had some acreage for grazing sheep which gently sloped down towards the river, which during the open season tended to be good for salmon fishing. The thirty acres of orchard were to the south and adjoined land belonging to a small hotel reputed to be used by the IRA as a centre for their rest and relaxation, this I found a little difficult to believe even with Dublin's lackadaisical approach to terrorism, but stranger things have happened.

Seamus was different to what I had anticipated. I had visions of a tall well built person, in his late fifties, but I couldn't have been further off the mark. He must have been in his late thirties of slim build and average height with fair curly hair, sharp features and wore spectacles, but the spectacles were purely for effect and were plain glass. He gave the impression of being quite meek and mild and the glasses added to this image. In fact his persona was far from meek and mild, but like everyone in the Circus this false image was created so he didn't stand out in a crowd. He was a 'nobody' and yet a lot of people knew him and knew of him. It took me about ten minutes to walk to his place and as I approached the door I reached inside my shirt and switched on the tape recorder. A black Labrador came bounding up to greet me, wagging its tail so hard its whole rear end moved from side to side.

'Come here my boy.' Seamus called to the dog, then he addressed me, 'it's all right he won't hurt.'

'Hi. Are you Mr O'Neill?' I called to him.

'Yes, how can I help?'

'I just thought I'd come and find you.' I'm Richard,' I said extending my hand in friendship. 'Just thought I'd pop over and have a chat about the work you wanted doing.' 'Ah yes top o' the morning t' yer.' He said as he pumped my arm up and down. 'Richard yer say yer name is?'

'Yes that's right.'

'Well, Richard it is then. I'm pleased t' meet yer.' He continued to shake my hand, 'B'jesus yer earlier than I had expected.' At this point he let go of my hand. 'Come in and have a drop of tea,' he said as he turned and headed off in the direction of the backdoor with me following. 'Will you have had yer breakfast yet? If not I can be fixing yer a bite of something.'

'A cup of tea will be fine Mr O'Neill.'

I followed him through the backdoor and into his kitchen where he had an open fire.

'Call me Seamus. All m' friends call me Seamus.' He pulled out a straight backed pine chair. 'Take a seat then.' He got a mug from the cupboard, 'Will a mug o' tea be ok for yer then, or would yer prefer a cup?'

'A mug will be fine Seamus.'

'Now Richard, I believe I have some gear here for yer just in case yer be needing it.' He opened his cupboard and lifted out a pile of newspapers. 'I always have plenty of papers t' light the fire with should it go out.' With the newspapers out of the way he carefully removed a small section of the cupboard's back wall revealing a hidden safe that had been cut into the solid stone wall. From the safe he withdrew a personal transceiver, a full mobile communication set and the obligatory Browning 9.00 mm with two spare magazines.

'It's surprising what yer can find under the trees nowadays.' He said and gave a wry smile; 'especially around this area!' He said as he closed up the safe and proceeded to replace the section of wood from the back of the cupboard.

I checked over the Browning, opened the breech to make sure there wasn't a round in there, and then checked the action.

'Very smooth action Seamus.'

'T' be sure. I lovingly oiled and cleaned it especially for you. It's one o' them special ones yer know. Non-existent!'

I checked the communications gear, all was working fine. 'Seamus can I leave this stuff with you and collect it when I'm in my car?'

'T' be sure yer can.'

'Good, then I'll drive over once I've checked in at the Tara. By the way where's the car I'm to use?'

'Oh way out of sight just in case.'

Damn, he wasn't very forthcoming on that one. Never mind it means I'll have to come back later and nosey about a bit. I looked at my watch it was getting on for quarter passed eleven.

'Well Seamus thanks for the tea and the chat but I had better make a move, I haven't checked in at the Tara yet.'

'Why is that?'

'It was just that I arrived too early and they hadn't cleaned the room or something so I took a walk over here to introduce myself. Well I thought it would kill two birds with one stone. I could meet you and introduce myself and it would give them time to sort my room out.'

'T' be sure, it was a good idea.'

I made my way to the door and back out into the open.

'Thanks again Seamus.' I called, raising my hand in a farewell gesture as I set off back to the Tara.

'No trouble at all,' he called after me, 'will I be seeing yer later then?'

'Yes, I'll come over in the car and pick those bits and pieces up.' I called back to him.

Being a regular guest at the Tara the girl on reception recognised my name and asked if I would like my usual room which was very handy indeed as it meant I had a ready made hidey-hole for my 'stuff'. Even though Fionnuala was not on duty when I checked in she would soon find out about my arrival, and sure enough, I had only just had my lunch and was lounging on my bed reading when there was a gentle knock on my door.

'Who is it?' I called.

'It's me Richard James.' The soft lilt of Fionnuala's Irish accent drifted to me through the closed door. I got up off my bed and opened the door; Fionnuala looked as beautiful as ever. I stood to one side and she entered my room closing the door behind her.

'And why are you here Richard James?' She asked in mock anger. I started to speak, but was cut off in mid sentence as her lips met mine in a passionate kiss.

In order to explain my visit away, I told Fionnuala that I had a small contract outstanding over at O'Neill's farm which would take about a

106

week to complete. Then to give my story further credibility I asked Fionnuala, when she went back down to reception, to tell her colleagues that if anyone wanted to contact me to take a message as I had had to go out on business. Two hours later I left the Tara and drove the short distance over to O'Neill' place.

In the ensuing hours Seamus and I carefully plotted and planned out the details of my cover story. Eventually we decided that in order to build up an alibi it would be necessary for me to have a daily routine that people would easily remember, that meant leaving my car parked at the Tara and walking to O'Neill's place at the same time every morning and returning at the same time every evening. In order to reinforce the plan I would always have to speak to the duty receptionist just prior to my departure so if anyone asked them they would have always seen me leave, then upon return I would have to check with the duty receptionist to see if anyone had left any messages and this way they would always see my return. A simple enough ploy really! There was only one slight flaw in the plan and that was Wednesday when I had to take the target car into Dublin. Originally it had been agreed that Seamus would bring it over to the Tara on the Tuesday night and leave it parked there but I felt that if it were spotted by some eagle eyed individual then I, along with the plan, could be compromised. Seamus agreed with me so we decided to modify the plan. So, as I had no need to be in Dublin until the Wednesday afternoon it was decided that on the Wednesday I would leave for 'work' at the same time as usual and after lunch Seamus would get the car ready for me to leave for Dublin. With this minor change I felt a lot happier, but I was still not totally convinced. In the main the plan now seemed sound with one niggling proviso and that was that my lift in Dublin would get me back to the farm or close enough to the Tara to enable me to walk back for my usual time. Timing was all important and it was this that was now causing me a problem. I couldn't help feeling that we needed more slack, after all there was no way that I could afford any deviation from my norm just in case the Gardai decided to visit the Tara and start asking a lot of questions about me. Having sorted out the details of my cover story and the finer points about the car I collected the items of hardware that I had left with Seamus earlier and drove back to the Tara.

Back inside my room I found the loose floorboard and prised it up. I then placed the hardware, which I had brought back from O'Neill's farm, into the space under the floor and replaced the floorboard. Now all I had to do was to remove the recorder taped to my trunk and listen to the recording. The quality of the recording although not brilliant was intelligible. The next job on my agenda was to wait for darkness then head back to the farm to try and find the car in order to get some photographs that would tie it in with O'Neill and the Circus. I glanced out of my window, it was almost dark. Ten minutes later and armed with nothing more than a small Maglite, miniature camera and tape recorder I set off to Seamus O'Neill's farm in search of the elusive car.

About twenty minutes later having followed the river bank for a short distance I turned left and struck a path due south heading up the gentle incline towards O'Neill's boundary. Now if I had got my bearings right then my route should take me a reasonable distance from the house so avoiding detection. I was now looking for some sort of outbuilding where a car could be housed. It had to be close to the main residence, yet far enough away so as not to be obvious. Suddenly not more than a couple of hundred yards away I could see a dark shape about the size of a garage, could this be where the target car was hidden. I stopped and listened, my ears strained for the slightest sound. The last thing I wanted to do was to run into O'Neill that would definitely take some explaining. I couldn't hear any sounds other than the occasional rustle of grass as some of his sheep moved out of my way. I reached a large irregular shaped mass that was big enough to be a building and yet from its silhouette it looked more like a mass of brambles and trees. Switching on my torch I could see why. In front of me was a huge camouflage net with tree branches and brambles interwoven into it. I was certain that this was the place all right and my suspicions were confirmed when I carefully eased up a corner of the net to reveal a large wooden shed big enough to house what I was looking for. No wonder he said it was parked out of sight. I bet you wouldn't even notice this in the daylight from a reasonable distance. I took out my camera and by using the infrared attachment I was able to get off a few shots. By torchlight I slowly and carefully eased away some of the branches and through the netting I could just make out two wooden garage doors. I stopped what I was doing and again I listened carefully for anything out of the ordinary, but nothing stirred, all was quiet. Within a few seconds I was inside and had pulled the door closed behind me. I stood for a moment or two thinking about my next move. I decided it maybe helpful to record what I physically could see and where I was situated, so reaching into my pocket I took out the handheld tape recorder and in a hushed monotone I started to record my findings. I started off by naming O'Neill as the owner of the property and a brief description of him and ended with where the outbuilding was situated in relation to the road. Having completed my recording, my next job was to take a series of shots of the car in the outbuilding. Finally I decided to put on to the tape, as a reference, the number of each of the photographs that I'd taken along with a brief description as to the subject. With my evidence collected I could now return to the Tara safe in the knowledge that should anything go tits-up then at least I had both photographic and recorded evidence as an insurance policy.

Suddenly I was wide awake. What day was it? Ah yes of course, it was Wednesday and already the adrenalin was starting to pump as I prepared myself for the day ahead. Having shaved and taken an early morning shower I now needed to let *Mother* know everything was moving forward according to plan, so once more I carefully removed the loose floor board and took out the satellite transceiver. I checked the time. It was now 06:30 which meant it would be a further eight hours before I left for Dublin. Switching the set on I quickly typed in my authorisation code and channel selection code. My message was short and to the point and read *'Top Secret Colonel Ash JITC Ashford Operations. Minor change to plan Ferryman now to collect rather than deliver stop Taxi needed to return to starting point by 1800 latest otherwise late for tea stop Phase 1 of Orpheus is 'T' – 8 hours stop Ferryman stop.'* There was little danger of the message being intercepted, but as a safeguard the system automatically encrypts anything sent by changing its structure and configuration as it passes through each secure link, therefore it was imperative that I had no typing errors. I checked my message for any such errors then pressed the send key knowing full well that in the blink of an eye it would arrive at Ashford whereupon the final switch unit will automatically decipher and reconstruct my message into plain language. The days of the enigma coding machine had now moved into the twentieth century.

Two hours later, having once again secreted my tape recorder, I was in Seamus O'Neill's kitchen drinking a coffee and going over the final details of the plan with him. On the table in front of me was a brand new rucksack containing a wig, sunglasses and a complete change of clothes, comprising of a pair of jeans, a brightly coloured shirt and a pair of trainers. The wig was blonde, curly and about shoulder length and the dark glasses were there to complete the disguise. The idea was that should a member of the public recollect seeing the target car being parked; their description would be of a tourist with blonde hair so sending the Gardai off in the wrong direction completely. We planned that once I had parked the car I would go to the nearest large hotel's bar and find the toilets where I'd be able to change out of my disguise, unfortunately I would still have to retain the rucksack to carry the discarded clothing in. I would need to make sure nothing was left behind in Dublin and to bring everything back here for disposal. Our calculations were that once I had changed out of my disguise I would still have a good hour to get to the Allied Irish Bank and I would be well away from Dublin before the shit hit the fan!

'So Richard this is the final plan.' Seamus started to run over the plan once again. 'Yer change into disguise at 14:00 hour we are at big-bang minus two and a half hours. At 14:30 yer drive the target car into the city centre, this should not take longer than forty to forty-five minutes, allow a further fifteen minutes to find a parking space that takes yer up to 15:30. This allows yer one hour to find a hotel; change and walk to Grafton Street, then get clear of Dublin. What d' yer think?'

'I'm not too sure. I like to have more time after parking an hour isn't very long.'

'Hmm. The problem is we don't want the car there for too long otherwise someone may get suspicious.'

'I know.'

Seamus thought about it for a moment or two and then suggested a compromise.

'Ok, say yer leave at 14:15 and it takes yer forty-five minutes to the centre plus a further fifteen minutes to find a space that then takes you up to 15:15. That'll give yer one and a quarter hours in which to get changed, across to Grafton Street and out. How about that?'

'Yeah, that would be better, but I still feel it's a little on the tight side.'

'Well I suppose yer could always call in to Mother on your way back here. That would save another few minutes. Say it only saves you five, at least it's now one hour twenty to get changed and across to Grafton Street and out. T'at should be plenty of time.'

'I'll see how the time goes otherwise it'll have to do.' I checked my watch. 'Right Seamus lets synchronise our watches. I'll be 09:15 in ten, nine, eight, seven, six, five, four, three, two, one NOW.'

'09:15 dead.'

'Have you checked the car Seamus?'

'Not yet.'

'So let's do that now.'

Seamus led the way to the camouflaged outbuilding that I'd previously found.

'So this is where you've hidden it.' I said with mock surprise, 'what a good idea.'

He pulled back the camouflage netting to reveal the entrance and on opening the door revealed a newly registered red Ford Cortina, the target car. He then produced two pairs of latex surgical gloves.

'Here you best be wearing a pair of these just in case.' I carefully pulled on the thin latex gloves and he did likewise. Once we both had our gloves on he opened the driver's door, reached under the dash for the bonnet release and with a slight clunk the bonnet sprung up. With the bonnet open I was now able to inspect the engine. Nothing looked out of place to the casual eye, in fact even to the trained eye it would pass muster. Seamus had done a good job of the wiring; Even though I knew it was wired and booby trapped I needed Seamus to point out what he had done. I was impressed.

'Once yer've parked it yer need to arm it and that is done on the anti-theft device.'

'Which is where?' I asked.

'Part of the door lock. All you need to do is to lock the drivers door as normal and t'at automatically sets the timer and the alarm, so whatever you do DON'T lock the car for any reason until you've finally parked, because you are then armed!'

'So that's why you left it unlocked then.'

'T' be sure it is. Oh and there is one other thing, both boot and bonnet are wired back to the main detonator, so once you've armed the device should anyone open the bonnet or the boot the timer is short circuited and the whole thing goes up in their face. So be careful, don't put anyt'ing in the boot just in case yer forget it, even by unlocking it yer will detonate the main device and b'jesus there'll be one helluva bang and Richard James would be no more!'

I had a good look round the car and the engine to satisfy myself that it was all in order.

'So are you clear on everything?' Seamus asked after a little while.

'Yes thanks Seamus, but there is one question?'

'What would t'at be?'

'Where did you learn about explosives?'

'Didn't I tell you? I was in the Royal Navy and trained as a frogman saboteur. Later I became an instructor first at Gosport then Hereford.'

So that explained it. Suddenly I viewed Seamus in a different light.

At 13:45 I went up stairs to change into my disguise, the wig was a bit fiddly, but I persevered and eventually got it right, donned my shades and looked at the result in the mirror. I must admit the disguise looked quite effective. Here I was a Mr Fergal O'Hanlon. Our plan had one minor weakness and that was the persona I was portraying. All the papers indicated Fergal O'Hanlon came from Dublin, yet my disguise was as a tourist. Still it was only a very slight risk and not really worth considering. It was only a risk whilst I was actually driving, so if I get stopped for any reason I'll just have to do some fast talking. All I needed now was a photograph, I wondered if I could trust Seamus to take one, after all as a tourist I would have photographs of different places an of me posing. I needn't have worried; Seamus thought it a brilliant idea. He felt it would add a little authenticity to the overall effect and willingly took a couple of me. It was now time for my departure, but before I left I had one more message to send and a favour to ask of Seamus.

'Should anything go wrong, make sure Fionnuala over at the Tara gets this.' I handed Seamus an envelope.

'Ok Richard.' He nodded, 'but I bet yer'll be back here to deliver it in person.'

'Of course I will Seamus.' I said confidently although deep down I felt nervous. The next thing was to send my coded message to let JITC Ashford know we were 'go'.

At 14:15 precisely a blonde haired tourist in a bright red Cortina turned out onto the main Dundalk to Dublin road and headed south towards Dublin. I made good time, in fact far better than we allowed for and at 14:50 I was into the city centre not too far from Grafton Street. I spotted the ideal place not far from the main shopping centre and at 15:04 precisely I had parked the car. The parking place I had found was unrestricted so the car would not be subject of too close a scrutiny. I double checked I had everything as I didn't want to leave incriminating evidence should anything go wrong. I picked up the rucksack and made sure the passenger door was locked. My heart was thumping. The adrenalin was rushing. The inside of my mouth felt dry. My hands in these silly surgical gloves felt clammy. As I got out of the car I suddenly felt very conspicuous. Beads of sweat started to form on my brow. I just hope you've got it right Seamus and I hope everything is connected correctly. I tried to look casual as I looked around me. I didn't mean to slam the door, it just happened that way. I gritted my teeth and screwed my eyes up tight just waiting for the flash, but nothing. Phew, that was close I thought to myself. Pull yourself together Richard, nothing is going to happen. I felt everyone must be looking at me as I checked the time 15:05. God I'll be glad to get out of this gear. I inserted the key into the driver's door. My heart was racing. Was I imagining it or was my hand shaking. People must notice me. I turned the key. It wouldn't turn. I started to panic. Calm down Richard I said to myself. I tried the key again, this time it turned. Clunk, the lock clicked down. I stood momentarily routed to the spot again waiting for the end, but nothing. Suddenly I realised I'd done it and I could again hear the traffic around me. Hear people talking. Smell all manner of things. I then realised all this time I had been holding my breath and let it go. I removed the key from the lock, took off the surgical rubber gloves and stuffed them and the key into my jeans pocket. I now unhurriedly walked back the way I had driven as I had remembered seeing a large hotel on the route in. There was a decided spring in my step and the time was only 15:08. At

15:10 I found the hotel and was now busy getting changed in one of the cubicles in the hotel toilets. At 15:15 I used the loo as a seat and composed my message on the satellite communication set, the message read

Top Secret Colonel Ash JITC Ashford Operations.
Message begins Phase 1 of Orpheus is completed big-bang now 'T' – 75 minutes stop Ferryman stop.

By 15:16 I had left the hotel and was on my way to Grafton Street. At 15:40 I approached the paper seller situated outside the Allied Irish Bank, everything, so far, had run like clockwork.
'Excuse me;' I said, 'I wondered if you still had a copy of Tuesday's Irish Times?'
'No. I'm sorry sir I don't have such a t'ing.'
'Oh dear, well could you suggest anywhere I could still get one?' I asked.
'I'm not sure, but if you'd be hanging on a minute I will phone my distribution manager he may have an idea.' The vendor gave me a wink and disappeared down the street a short distance to a telephone booth. In under a minute he was back.
'Ok I've spoken to the marn and he said he can get one over to you.' He looked about to make sure nobody was close enough to hear then said in a perfect BBC accent, 'transport is on its way Ferryman and should be here in about five minutes.'
In fact it was only a couple of minutes before a van pulled up and the driver dumped a pile of newspapers on the pavement alongside the news vendor. The driver looked at me and nodded, then gestured with his thumb towards the van. I nodded back and got into the passenger side. The driver got back in slammed his door and we drove off down the road. As we did I glanced in the wing mirror just in time to see the news vendor disappear in the opposite direction, dump a load of newspapers outside another kiosk as he walked passed then disappeared into the crowd. Within a few minutes we were off the main streets and heading down back streets around the twists and turns of the narrow back alleys then suddenly we were turning into the rear entrance of the British Embassy. Here we changed vehicles and I was whisked off in a blue Volvo heading out of Dublin on the road to Dundalk. At 16:40 precisely I was walking through the back door at Seamus O'Neill's farm.
'So what did I say t' yer Richard. I told you to deliver this y'self!' Seamus handed me the envelope I had given to him earlier. 'Now, first t'ings first, I've got the old incinerator going so lets burn the evidence.'
We both went out into his garden and placed one item of clothing at a time into his incinerator leaving it until that one item had been fully consumed

by the flames before adding the next item. By 17:30 every scrap of evidence had been destroyed and Fergal O'Hanlon and the tourist were both a figment of the past. Having destroyed the evidence it was now time to send in my final message which read

Top Secret Colonel Ash JITC Ashford Operations.
Message begins Phase 1 of Orpheus now completed successfully stop Ferryman safe stop returned to base stop Ferryman out

As I watched the Eamonn Byrne chat show the programme was interrupted by a Newsflash:

'We interrupt this programme for a Newsflash.
"News is just coming in about an explosion in central Dublin. At four-thirty this afternoon a large explosion rocked central Dublin killing several people and injuring many others. The Gardai have sealed off the area and have issued the following statement. 'At four-thirty this afternoon a large explosion occurred in central Dublin killing and injuring a number of people. The explosion occurred not far from Grafton Street. Although the cause is still being investigated the remains of a car have been removed from the scene for a more detailed examination by Army experts. At this time we cannot rule out paramilitary involvement.' There will be more on this item in the main news when we should have further details".
This is the end of this newsflash and we return you to the Eamonn Byrne show.'
How I wished I was back home. Suddenly Ireland had lost its appeal for me and after what I had done, so had the SIS!

Chapter 11

Ash looked up from my report. 'Well done Richard. Phase 1 of *Operation Orpheus* has been a resounding success. Not only did it bring the Dail to its senses about terrorism, it also broke up the secret peace talks that the Official IRA was involved in, so well done.'

'Will that be all then Colonel?'

'Yes thank you Richard.' As he placed my report inside the folder marked TOP SECRET *Operation Orpheus*. I got up to leave. 'Actually there is one more thing Richard.'

'Yes Colonel.' I said as I sat back down.

'I hope you haven't arranged anything special for the weekend have you?'

'I was hoping to spend some time at home with my wife.'

'Does she know you're back?'

'No not yet why?'

'Well let's keep it that way shall we?' He gave a quick smile. 'I want you to stay around here this morning, because later on today I want you to go to Warslow.'

'Where's Warslow?' I asked.

'Up in the Peak District, SAS are running a big training exercise up there specifically for the UDR and as you are UDR I think you should attend.'

I could have sworn I saw the trace of a smile, but perhaps I was mistaken.

'Are you able to tell me a bit more about it Colonel?' I asked.

'Sure.' He picked up a signal he'd received and read it out to me. '*It's specialist exercise in search procedures, ambush tactics and night patrolling in both urban and rural terrain,*' he read from the signal. 'Regard it as a refresher course like the next one.'

'The next one?' I asked.

'Sorry, haven't I told you about it?'

'No Colonel, you haven't.'

There was that slight smile again. I was sure he was enjoying this in a perverse sought of way. 'I am sorry Richard, how very remiss of me.' he said with such feeling, that I almost believed him. 'What it is, I have arranged for you to spend some more time at Fort Monkton, another sort of refresher course.'

'I see.' I said cautiously, 'and…?'

'And what Richard?'

'And what else is there that I should know?'

'Oh nothing. No, nothing at all. It's purely a refresher course, what you did before only more of it. Photographic skills, driving and pursuit techniques, weapons training and some explosives etc. does that answer your question?'

'Yes but when?'

'Ah, good question Richard. The answer is you'll go straight from Derbyshire to Fort Monkton, which is a seven day course or thereabouts, and once that's out of the way then I promise you that will be the last of the training and your time will be your own. Oh and by the way, I thought I would just mention that you have been promoted to the rank of Captain.'

I looked at him incredulously. 'Captain did you say?'

Ash nodded. 'Yes that's what I said but you can always refuse the promotion if you wish.' He gave a wry smile.

'With respect sir, you must be joking if you think I'm going to turn it down.'

'Somehow I didn't think you would.'

Over two hundred UDR members, of whom I was one, attended that particular training exercise run by the SAS in Warslow and in the Dales of Derbyshire. Our debriefing was held at Hanley, Stoke-on-Trent and late on the Sunday afternoon I was summoned to report immediately to Lieutenant Colonel Barrymore (Operations Planning) which I found was situated in block A3. I found out that the Lieutenant Colonel's office was on the second floor of the building to which I proceeded and knocked on the door.

'Come in.' A female voice called from the other side of the door.

I entered the office to be confronted by woman of about forty, her blonde hair pulled tightly back into a bun. On the front of the desk was a wooden block with the name Lt. Col. Barrymore inscribed on it. In front of her was a pile of papers and without even looking up from her work she said, 'You must be Captain James.'

'Yes Ma'am.'

At this point she looked up and smiled. 'Pull up a chair,' she indicated to the chair in the corner of her office, 'and sit down James.' I smiled back and moved the chair so it was opposite her and sat down. 'I'll be with you in a second.' She scribbled some notes on one of the sheets attached to the file of papers in front of her, then looked up. 'Sorry about that, but just needed to get this finished otherwise could end up sending equipment to Germany and men to Ulster, when it should be the other way round. Anyway that's my problem. Now let me see,' she shuffled through a pile of papers in a wire tray marked 'Pending' that was on a small desk to her left. 'Ah here we are. I have received a message from JITC Ashford, Tactical Operations, requesting that you be flown to Gosport where you'll be met by car and taken to Fort Monkton. Now the earliest we can get you off is 19:30 tonight. Where are you billeted?'

'Over in T block Ma'am.'

'T block.' She wrote the information on a message pad. 'In which case I'll arrange to have you collected at 19:20 and transported to the dispersal point where you'll be taken by helicopter to Gosport. So be outside T block by 19:20 with your kit ready for pick-up. Here you are James,' she passed me the top copy of her order/requisition sheet, which authorised my vehicle pick-up and flight to Gosport. 'Take that to the Admin Clerk in Movements and Logistics. You'll find them on ground floor, through the double doors second corridor on the right at the far end. Enjoy your flight.' She smiled. I smiled back, picked up the chair and moved it back to the corner. I stood to attention and saluted

'Ma'am.'

'That'll be all James thank you'

Fort Monkton was a highly secure purpose built training base set in Hampshire. Not only did it have the obligatory chain link perimeter fence topped with razor wire found at most military bases, on the inside it also had an eight foot high compact copper beach hedge and the whole was guarded by armed Ministry of Defence Police. Security was such that even our personal mail was forwarded, under separate cover, from various locations had to be shredded once we had read it. The camp operated under a well thought out cover story which explained away the strange goings on at all hours. This of course was my second visit to Fort Monkton, where specialist training in high speed driving techniques, weaponry, photography and surveillance were taught. Our instructors were specialists in their own field and were drawn from various Units.

Half way through my week and having already spent a tiring day of surveillance in and around the rough area of Portsmouth I was looking forward to getting an early night, when along with the rest of the group, I was summoned to the main lecture theatre. Once we had all settled down the chief instructor passed an A4 booklet to each one of us which contained a number of questions. A low murmur ensued as everyone started to flick through their booklet.

'Right everyone when you're ready.' Gradually the murmur of voices died away. 'Now over the next couple of hours we'll be doing a progress test just to ascertain how everyone is doing.'

'Bollocks,' I muttered, 'so much for an early night.'

'By the way,' the chief instructor was talking again, 'at some stage of the evening you'll all need to visit admin to sort out your travel documents. Once you've done that you can finish the test over a coffee in the dining room, so when you go take it with you.'

I started to read through and answer the questions, a lot of which seemed to be about photography characteristics, when every now and then the chief would call out someone's name and that person would leave to visit the admin block. Soon it was my turn. I picked up my booklet and headed off to the far side of camp towards admin.

As I walked along the path that followed the perimeter fence before it swung around passed the corner of the teaching block, I caught a glimpse of something moving out of the corner of my eye, and thinking it may be something important I glanced over in that direction. Too late I realised that something or someone was rushing towards me. I swung my head back round, my eyes were wide with horror and my mouth fell open with shock, but before I could utter a sound two bodies clothed in black slammed into me. Instinctively I brought up my arm as protection. My other hand immediately grabbed for my weapon.

The first of the two figures crashed into me full tilt, hitting me in my chest and abdomen so knocking the very breath out of me. I started to collapse completely winded. As I went down I was caught from behind and a hand closed about my weapon and wrestled it from my grip. A hood was roughly pulled over my head and I was slammed onto the ground. Within seconds I was forcibly gagged. Two or possibly three people pinned me to the ground whilst my ankles were tightly tied together. I was then rolled over on my front and my face forced against the earth. My arms were roughly yanked behind my back and bound tightly at the wrists with plastic ties and rope. The rope from my wrists was then looped around the plastic ties holding my ankles together and pulled tight forcing the soles of my shoes up against my buttocks. It was pulled so tight it felt as if my back would break. My breathing was laboured and I felt sick.

'Now you focker struggle if you can. Your moine!' said a soft, threatening Irish voice quietly in my ear. Jesus! I thought – what the hell.

Suddenly I was aware of being carried bodily. They were experts and had me trussed up like a chicken so I was unable to struggle. Who were they? The softly spoken, yet threatening voice was certainly Irish I was in no doubt about that. I was so confused that try as I could, I couldn't even work out the direction we were heading in. At first I assumed this was just another exercise and wasn't really afraid, then I began to wonder. How had they got in passed the tight security and in broad daylight? I then felt the scrape of wire against my clothes and that put a whole new slant on things. They must have cut their way through the fence and got passed the security. This was for real. Now I was really scared.

I was dropped into a small rectangular area and I heard a dull 'clunk' as a lid or door was shut above me. I tried to manoeuvre myself around but banged against a metal wall. I lifted my head and immediately banged it on the underside of a metal lid. My worst nightmare was confirmed when the engine started. I was in the boot of a car. The car accelerated away at high speed. I bounced and bumped against the boot lid and the petrol tank. I desperately tried to work my wrists free, but all that achieved was to cause me pain. Blind panic was closing in on me. My thoughts went back to an earlier time when I was in the Republic and I was bundled into the back of a car at gunpoint. There was one big difference between then and now, they were friendly. They were Special Forces who had crossed the border and grabbed me outside an IRA pub. Then it was all for effect as they took me to a Safe House to meet with Ash and the Circus. This time there was nothing friendly about these merchants.

Calm down Richard! Calm down! Come on plan! Think! Follow the twists of the road! Don't panic! It was easier said than done. I could here the petrol sloshing about in the tank somewhere behind me. This was scary. Petrol fumes seeped in and were making me feel nauseous. My scrunched up position was beginning to give me cramp and the rope was cutting into my wrists. Suddenly we lurched and bounced as we left the smooth road and headed along a rutted track. Then we came to a sudden halt and I banged my head against the inner wing. I heard doors open and heavy footsteps approaching, and then the boot lid was opened. I was yanked from the boot and carried a short distance before being dropped like a sack of potatoes. I landed on the ground with a thud and for a second time the breath was knocked out of me. I then felt a sawing and pulling on the rope that ran from my ankles to my wrists. Suddenly the tension had gone and I could unfold my legs albeit that my ankles were still tied together. I was roughly grabbed under the armpits and dragged. Then out of the blue my shirt was then ripped off. I was dragged into a sitting position and pulled up against a wooden post. My arms were yanked backwards and held around the post with my wrists crossed whilst somebody lashed them tightly together again. I then heard a dull snip as the binding around my ankles was cut. Hands then dragged off my shoes and socks. These were quickly followed by my jeans and pants. I now was left stark naked tied to the stake. Suddenly I felt very vulnerable.

Five maybe ten minutes passed and I heard another car approach and stop. Again doors opening and heavy footsteps shortly followed by more footsteps. Then a scuffing sound as if something was being dragged. Then silence.

A further period of time elapsed, it could have been five minutes, and more footsteps coming this way. Hands roughly pulled a sort of boilersuit on over my legs and feet. Someone grabbed me under the armpits and dragged me to my feet. The boilersuit was then pulled up to my waist. Whilst standing my legs were bound tightly to the stake and the boilersuit was pulled up and my arms were forced into the sleeves. My ankles were retied together, but the rope about my legs holding me to the stake was removed. Hands grasped either arm and dragged me forwards across rough gravel. I tried to hop to avoid my feet being dragged across the ground but I was unable to. We entered some sort of building with a rough concrete floor. My feet were scraped along the floor as my captors dragged me around the corridors. Eventually I was forced to sit on a rough wooden slatted area. Handcuffs were expertly snapped about my wrists and over one of the slats. All the time nobody spoke. It felt cool where I was and in the background there was the noise of machinery. I decided I must be held in some industrial area. Suddenly there was a deafening banging noise, which after the relative silence, made me jump. The noise was somewhere off to my right, but very close to where I was held. The banging settled down to a constant repetitive sound which I now recognised as the noise of an air compressor. So could I be in a garage somewhere? Suddenly I was grabbed from behind and the gag was removed and the hood was roughly pushed up my face uncovering my mouth. Someone then pulled back my head and forced a metal container between my lips and started to pour lukewarm liquid into my mouth. I tried to force my lips closed so the liquid ran down my front and onto my groin.

'Foking drink the water.' An Irish voice said threateningly. I was thirsty so I did exactly that. Then the hood was pulled back again. I tried to work out how long I had been held captive. Was it two or three hours? Damn it seemed like a lifetime. I now needed the toilet to relieve myself. Then without warning hands grabbed me under the armpits and there was the click of a key in the lock and without a word being said I was being dragged off through a door and down a corridor. Again I tried to shamble along but I was unable to keep up. Eventually I half stumbled and was half dragged up some steps into a carpeted room. I was forcibly pushed back into a chair where my guards pulled my arms back and padlocked them to the legs of the chair forcing me to sit up straight. The hood was yanked from my head and the light was so intense I had to screw my eyes up against it.

'Open your eyes.' A cold male voice demanded. But the light was still too bright and I held my eyes tightly shut.

'I said open your eyes.'

This time the voice had a slight edge to it. Squinting against the light I opened my eyes just wide enough to make out that sitting opposite me was a man dressed in a black sweater.

'Good, now look at me.'

My eyes had now adjusted to the brightness and I was able to stare at the face of my inquisitor. He held my gaze. He was a man in his forties sitting behind a shiny desk. In his hand he held a pen and in front of him on the desk was a writing pad. His face was pretty nondescript with no distinguishing features that I noticed. Three lights glared straight in my direction.

'You are my prisoner and provided you co-operate and answer our questions then we will feed and clothe you. What is your name?' He asked with pen poised. I thought back to my original training on interrogation techniques and decided for the time being I would say nothing. Then if it got messy all I would disclose was my date of birth, name, rank and number. We sat there staring at each other. He put down his pen. His hand rested gently on a length of rubber hose in front of him.

'I said, what is your name?' This time his voice was more menacing and his hand picked up the hose. He then started to gently slap the open palm of his other hand with it. I watched him and counted.

'Answer me. What is your name?'

'I'm sorry I can't answer that.' I said stalling. This must be an exercise I thought to myself. This guy is English not Irish, so the rubber hose is only there for effect. He won't use that. I gave an involuntary jump as he suddenly brought the rubber hose down onto the desk in front of him with an almighty crash. Up until now I had forgotten about needing to relieve myself, but the sudden crash that had made me jump nearly caused me to wet myself. I now desperately needed to go to the toilet.

'I need a pee,' I said.

'Answer my question and the guard will give you a bucket. So what is your name?' Once again he had his pen poised.

I hesitated but then I thought what the hell. I was desperate and what did it matter if he did have my name.

'James.'

As soon as I uttered my name the hood was whipped back into place and I was soon being dragged back to my cell. Again I was left alone locked to the slatted wooden structure. The compressor was still making a din. I tried to feel around as far as I could stretch for my bucket, when realisation dawned – no bucket. The bastards! I sat there fidgeting around trying to forget about the increasing urge. It was no good I was going to have to pee. This was the final indignity having to pee myself like a baby. I relaxed all I could, but nothing would happen. After years of conditioning ones mind from early childhood through to adulthood, I found that now I couldn't go. Eventually after relaxing everything and thinking of waterfalls and running taps I started to go. At first it was a mere trickle then the flood gates opened splashing down onto the concrete below me. The boilersuit was soaked.

Some considerable time had passed when suddenly without warning I was dragged off back to the room. This time when the hood was removed I was confronted by a female inquisitor.

'Your name, what is your name.' She screamed.
I waited before answering.
'James.'
'Don't lie. What is your name?' She screeched at the top of her voice.
'Richard.'
'Well done,' she said a little more calmly as she wrote it down on the pad in front of her. Then she looked down at my boiler suit and the damp patch that had spread across the front. She walked over and scrutinised it at close quarters.
'You dirty bastard. You've pissed yourself. A baby has more intelligence than you.' With that she went back to her seat. 'Guard!' She screamed, suddenly blackness again as the hood was pulled down. 'Take the dirty little baby away.'
I was hauled to my feet and dragged back to my cell. This time my arms were handcuffed behind me and I was placed facing the wall someone held my forehead against the wall whilst someone pulled my feet back a little at a time until I was at an angle and my head was supporting my full weight. The pain was excruciating. As time passed the pain got worse. I tried to manoeuvre around, but I started to slide and graze my face. I lost all track of time. Then again hands grabbed me from behind and I was dragged half stumbling and half shuffling back along the corridor to the room. Again I was pushed back onto the seat. Again the hood was whipped off only this time sat at the desk was the man. The interrogation followed the same pattern as before. Again the hood was replaced and once more I was half dragged and half stumbled back to my cell. This pattern of events was repeated many, many times until I eventually lost track of how many times. I reckoned that there was about thirty to forty minutes between bouts of interrogation. I continued repeating my answers giving only date of birth, name rank and number.

I had been padlocked to my slatted board for what seemed about an hour and the noise of the compressor or generator was still deafening when again I was dragged to my feet and half dragged off up the corridor. Only this time when I was pushed back onto the chair and my hood removed the person now sat behind the desk was the chief instructor
'Who am I?' he asked.
'The chief instructor?' I answered at which he smiled.
'Ok, Richard, this is the end of the exercise. You can relax now and well done. I'm going to release you now, do you understand?'
'Yeah, I understand.'
'One last question, how long do you think you were held prisoner?'

I thought for a little while whilst the handcuffs and padlock was removed, 'Oh...twenty-four hours?'

'No,' he answered, 'actually it was slightly over twelve hours. Funny how people, when subjected to this routine, always seem to think it has been much longer than it actually was.'

It didn't strike me as particularly funny!

At last without the padlocks, handcuffs and the plastic tie about my ankles I was able to stretch and move freely what a luxury. I stunk like a polecat, smelling of urine and stale sweat as I followed the chief instructor into another room where, on a table I found my clothes, shoes and my weapon. Once dressed, I was allowed to return to base whereupon I was given time to take a welcome shower before sitting down to a large evening meal.

As a group we were briefed on standard procedure for resistance of interrogation and it was apparent to me that the main purpose of my brief ordeal was to give me an insight into what it would be like to be captured and held as a prisoner under interrogation. It also served a useful purpose for those who acted as my interrogators, giving them some practice in interrogation techniques. I learnt later that we had all been subjected to similar 'snatches' carried out by SAS personnel from Hereford and that we had all suffered the 'in depth' interrogation in order to give us experience of what it could be like if we were ever taken prisoner. I found the experience both disturbing and scary so much so that I vowed that all the time I drew breath nothing like this would happen to me again. My personal security was paramount.

Chapter 12

'So Richard, how did your course go?'

'Oh pretty much as expected.' I replied with a nonchalant air.

'Oh I see, so nothing new then?' Ash studied my face.

'Well, you know what I mean...' I continued in my nonchalant way. 'Weapon training, setting up obs, unarmed combat all those sorts of things.' I fell silent. Ash continued to study my face. The silence started to close in and become oppressive. 'Oh, well there was one variation...' I noticed the beginnings of a smile on Ash's face then it was gone.

'Well Richard what was that?' he asked quietly.

'Err. Well they had a snatch squad from Hereford,' I tried to make it sound as if it hadn't bothered me, but the truth was it was still very vivid in my mind's eye and I still felt a little unnerved by the experience. I hurried on, 'Their brief was to grab us and take us prisoner. We were then dragged off to some place where we were treated to intensive interrogation where our captors used mind games in an attempt to break us. It was hmm... interesting first hand experience.'

'In what way?' Ash asked. His eyes narrowed as he studied my face.

'I'm not sure I can put my finger on it.' I thought about what had happened and tried to figure out how to describe what I had found unnerving. 'Well, put it this way. I know we don't use physical torture as such, but we apply certain psychological techniques that I found somewhat disturbing and what's more these techniques are alien to what HMG would have us believe. I suppose it is a form of torture – psychological torture.'

'An interesting point of view Richard.'

We sat in silence for a few minutes as Ash studied my face. I sat there impassively staring back at him, thinking to myself I can play mind games as well! Ash gave a slight cough. 'Well according to the report I received you certainly did yourself proud. You came away with flying colours. Anyway to more mundane things, 'Operation Orpheus', as you know the first part of the Op. was very successful, but we now come to the major prize.'

'Which is?' I asked. Ash picked up his pen and started to idly toy with it. Twisting the cap first one way then the next, he momentarily looked away from me at the window.

'I want you to form a new squad of blokes. They are to be trained by you and they will be under your command.'

'For what?' I asked.

Ash didn't reply straight away, instead he doodled on the paper in front of him on his desk. 'Oh hmm…they will be recruited for a special operation,' he remarked absently without even looking up.

'What's the special operation?' There was a heavy silence. Ash carefully laid down his pen as if it was very fragile, paused, then looked up at me and with eyes half closed as if he was trying to see inside my head he answered. 'Well shall we say a snatch squad… '

'Not Riley again?' I asked interrupting him.

'Yes Richard. We need 'Slab' Riley and quickly, and that's where you come in.' The Colonel went on to outline what he called the second phase of 'Operation Orpheus'. The backroom boys had dreamt up some crazy idea about me joining the local Territorial Army as a volunteer. I was then to get 'close' to a few of the men who I felt would be suitable material to use in a 'Specialist Unit'.

'This is…This is crazy.' I blurted out angrily. 'What do they take me for, an idiot?' I was annoyed and it showed.

The Colonel held up his hand.

'Just hold on Richard. Hear me out.' I fell silent as Ash continued. My cover story was that the Government now wanted a number of Specialist Units, which would be set-up in key places throughout the British Isles. Each unit would be trained in guerrilla tactics, the idea being that should the country be faced with a Russian invasion then these units would spearhead and co-ordinate the resistance movement throughout the United Kingdom. In order to carryout such a task it would be necessary for each unit to develop skills, not only in guerrilla warfare and urban warfare, but to also have many other skills. Such as covert intelligence gathering; manufacture of explosives; high speed driving techniques; specialist weapons and weapon training and of course the obligatory 'hostage' or 'snatch' taking techniques. Because of the 'Cold War' this no longer sounded as crazy as I had first imagined. As the details of the plan unfurled I gradually warmed to the idea.

'You know Colonel, this may just work!' I said enthusiastically.

'Richard, I have every faith in you to make it work. Have you any questions?'

I leaned back in my chair and closed my eyes. Different ideas tumbled through my mind. I gave an involuntary shiver as my thoughts turned to that fateful night in Ireland when the last attempt to snatch Riley failed. The operation had been a tragic failure. I remembered how we had not been informed about the back-up generators. How intelligence had been totally wrong about the numbers of men at his farm. How we had been let down by our back-up team. It had all been down to poor co-ordination and planning. I remembered how Jock took a packet and how I half carried and half dragged him to the road. All these memories came flooding back as if it had been yesterday and they were all down to someone not doing their job. I also remembered how we were nearly killed at our safe house. My thoughts now turned to this present scheme and I knew that although it was dangerous it could work. All I needed was the right team and well laid plans. I wondered who they had as my number two, because this time I needed somebody who was reliable and somebody like Paul who I could trust.

'Well Richard?' The Colonel's voice had a slightly edge to it and quickly concentrated my mind.

'Yes Colonel, I have a question. Who is my number two?' I expected Ash to have somebody already lined up for the job and was taken completely by surprise when he told me that it was down to me.

'You mean you've no-one in mind?' I asked

'That's right Richard. You're choice. It's your show.'

My mind went into overdrive. I was amazed that I was being allowed this freedom. Then I started to look for the catch, but there was no catch. I knew who I wanted and that was Paul. But I wasn't convinced the Colonel would agree. So with some trepidation I put it to the test. 'Well, I've given it some thought and I would…'

'Well get on with it man.' Ash said irritably.

'I have one suggestion. It's an old friend of mine. Paul Jones, we were both in…'

'The Para's,' Ash interrupted me. 'I know. Well Richard, do you think you could convince him to join?'

I looked at Ash incredulously. Had I heard him right? Did he mean what I thought he meant? 'Sorry Colonel, did I misunderstand you. You did say that provided I could convince Paul Jones to join the TA then you would be happy for him to be my number two, didn't you?'

'Yes Richard that's correct. But you need to convince him first and that may not be as easy as you think.'

'What about his clearance?' I asked.

'What about it?'

'Well doesn't he need to be cleared?'

'We already know everything we need to about Mr Jones…Yes we know everything there is to know about Paul Jones. So let's just leave it at that shall we?' Ash smiled.

'But…but when, when did you do his clearance?' I asked.

'At the same time we did yours, after all it's no good having just the one person in mind, you must always have a back-up eh Richard!' Ash gave a wink and a broad grin. 'So if you want Jones then you need to persuade him to come on board, and I think that you will have your work cut out there.'

I had to secretly agree with Ash on this, but there was no way that I was going to let him know about my misgivings. 'One last question Colonel. What is the timescale and do we operate out of Ulster or the Republic?'

'That's two questions,' he said with a trace of a smile, 'the timescale is down to you, but I prefer sooner rather than later. Obviously it will take some months before your group is ready for operation. Now as to where you will operate from, it will definitely be out of Ulster that way we can have a springboard from where you can take off. I think it would be easy enough to take a couple of civilian registered cars south of the border, as sightseeing tourists don't you? Still we can look at the details closer to the deadline. In the meantime you will get regular updates on Riley's movements. So unless there is anything further…'

'No Colonel I think we've more than covered it, except when do I report to Broadstairs?'

'In two weeks time. I'll arrange for them to be notified that you will be arriving there.'

It was the first time I had been to Paul's workshop, but having been told the name of the industrial estate and roughly where it was it didn't prove too difficult to find Jones Engineering. It was a small brick built unit down a cul-de-sac easily recognisable by Paul's car parked outside and the finished steelwork waiting for collection.

The small metal door set into the larger steel door at the unit's entrance opened outwards and straight ahead was a steel stairway up to a mezzanine floor where a small office was situated. To my right the area opened up into a reasonable sized engineering workshop. Around the walls were various items of capital equipment such as capstan lathes, milling machines, grinders and upright drills. There was also the obligatory gas welding gear, mig-welding set and what looked like a plasma cutter, quite a nice little set up really. The radio was blaring out some rock number that I didn't recognise but no sign of Paul, in fact apart from the radio playing the place seemed deserted. I turned to go up the staircase when the small metal door opened and Paul entered.

'Hey Richard, how you doing? Long time no see. Where've you been hiding?'

'Oh you know Ireland, Ulster, Hereford, Gosport, London and Ashford. Oh and I forgot Derbyshire.'

'Whoa, hold on. What's with Hereford, Gosport and so on and so forth?'

'It's a long story Paul.'

'Well…I've got some time. Come up top,' he indicated to the mezzanine floor, 'and tell me the story.'

I thought about it for at least thirty seconds, but decided this was as good a time as any to tell him everything, especially as I wanted him to be my number two. 'Ok, lead on my friend.' Our footsteps clattered noisily as we both ascended the metal staircase up to the mezzanine floor and Paul's office.

'Grab that chair.' Paul indicated to the old easy chair in the corner. 'Want a coffee?'

I nodded and Paul put the kettle on and grabbed two clean mugs from the small cupboard under where the kettle sat and plonked them on a ring marked coffee table in front of me. From the same cupboard he produced what was left of a packet of wholemeal chocolate biscuits. 'Help your self to biscuits.'

'Cheers Paul.' I took a couple from the packet. Paul brought the coffee tin over and put a spoonful of coffee in each mug then returned it to the cupboard, just in time to pick up the boiled kettle. He poured in the water, returned the kettle to its place and passed me a spoon to stir the coffee with whilst he hunted for the milk. 'Sorry mate it will have to be Coffeemate. No milk.'

'That'll be fine.' He spooned a couple of spoonfuls into each mug and dumped the tin on the table.

'Now tell me what you've been up to.'

'How long have you got Paul?' I asked, 'because this could take a long time.'

'I've got as long as it takes, all night if necessary, so fire away.'

'Well it all started when we were over in Ireland.' I paused to see what his reaction was.

'Go on.' He said his face not showing any reaction at all. I didn't know what I expected so I carried on.

'As I said it started over in Ireland. You remember when I went with Terry and Mick up to the 'Holiday Camp'...'

'Yeah...'

'Well being me I was curious....' I continued to tell him about how alarm bells had rung when I saw the tractor with milk churns, diesel and fertiliser. How Pat and Kelly had the dog compound yet no dogs, and how O'Shea had introduced me to Eamonn the local IRA commander.

'So what did you do when O'Shea said about this Eamonn bloke?'

'Well I had to make my excuses to Mick and Terry and go and meet him.'

'Sounds a bit dodgy to me...'

I hurried on with my story so as not to get side tracked; especially now I had decided to talk. 'You haven't heard the best of it yet.' I took a sip of my coffee. 'So I met up with Eamonn and that was fine, but it was later when things really fell into place in a manner of speaking.' I took another bite of my biscuit and a swig of my coffee.

'Well what happened?' Paul leaned further forward intent on hearing every detail.

'When this tractor turned up with all the paraphernalia on it I got halfway up the field when I realised what it was that bugged me. It was the milk churns. Now why would they have milk churns on a fruit farm? So I did no more than go back. By then the tractor had gone and the place seemed deserted so...' I took another sip of coffee.

'Yes go on...'

'I inspected the dog compound...'

'And?'

'It led to a door that opened into the cellar. In there they had masses of fertilizer, diesel and milk churns. Through another door was the proper cellar, I suppose it had been a wine cellar in its day, but it was used for something other than wine storage. It was being used by O'Shea's family as a bomb making factory. There was mixed compound already in milk churn lids, there were detonators, soldering equipment the whole works! Paul it made me realise that there I was working for O'Shea and yet here was his family actively making bombs for use in Ulster.'

Paul's eyes narrowed and his face looked like thunder. 'The bastard. The murdering bastard...so what did you do?'

'I did what you would have done, I informed on him...'

'How?'

'Well do you remember Sean?' Paul nodded. 'He was in the UDR...'

'I know he was, so...'

'But what you didn't know was he was Military Intelligence. 14th Intelligence Company to be precise, so I called him.'

'How did you manage that especially as there was no telephone there?'

'Well Mick and the lads had gone down to the village in my car for some grub, and never returned so I was worried about them, but had to wait until the brothers returned before I could get a lift into the village to look for them. In the end I went to Eamonn and enlisted his help. I also had seen a telephone box on our tour round so under the pretence of having to phone Anne I got Kelly to drop me at the phone box. I made a quick call home, got Sean's number then phoned him.' I then went on to tell Paul how I had been picked up by the SAS guys and taken to meet Ash and O'Rourke at the safe house. How I had been recruited by them to work for Ashford. I did leave out the fact that I along with Sean and others were in fact MI6 not just 14th Intelligence Company. I explained away my visit to Hereford as a training exercise with the UDR as I did with the other places and left it at that.

'So, have I got this right? Ash wants you to form a 'snatch' squad to go over to Ireland to grab this 'Slab' Riley character?'

'Yeah that's the gist of it.'

'So why have you told me all this?' Paul looked at me suspiciously.

'Well…' I paused looked Paul straight in the eyes and said, 'there's no easy way of saying this, but I want…no I don't mean that.' I started again, 'I mean I would like it very much if you would join me…' I held my breath and waited. Paul looked down at his nails, reached for what was left of his cold coffee and unconsciously took a mouthful.

'Phew…I…I don't know what to say mate…'

'There's no rush. Think it over and let me know…maybe in a couple of days eh…'

'No…'

'Oh…' the disappointment must have sounded in my voice because Paul was quick to start again.

'No, I didn't mean 'no' I meant no I wasn't going to let you know in a couple of days, we need it sorted now. Shit Richard, you and I go back a long way…just give me a second or two.' I honoured his request. We both sat in silence, a silence heavy with expectation on both sides. Suddenly Paul spoke. 'Ok…count me in!'

'You mean it?'

Paul drew in a deep breath. 'Yep, I mean it; I'm your first recruit.'

'In that case I will make you my Sergeant Major and I'll make sure you get paid accordingly.'

'At least Sergeant Major and damn right I get paid accordingly.' A huge grin spread across Paul's face. 'Just like old times partner.'

It was close on midnight when I eventually stepped through my front door. The place was in darkness save for a tiny glow of light from under the bedroom door. I crept upstairs as quietly as I could with the idea of trying not to disturb Anne from her sleep, but to no avail. I opened the bedroom door and was greeted by a shriek of joy. 'Richard…it's really you!' Anne leapt from the bed and rushed to greet me, she threw her arms about my neck and squeezed and hugged me as tight as she could. 'Mmm my love it's good to feel you close.' She looked up into my eyes then gave me a lingering kiss. 'My darling at last you're home.'

All around me darkness! Not even the faintest glimmer of light penetrated my surroundings. I could smell petrol fumes. I could feel the panic welling up inside. My face and head are covered and I struggled against invisible straps. Where was I? Ah yes, the room. That smell. The noise of machinery. 'My name is James. My date of birth is….' I'm back in the room again.

130

Why is everywhere so dark? It's so hot it's stifling. Phew that's better I can breath and someone has switched on the lights. Suddenly I'm alert, my eyes wide open. The room is bathed in sunlight and I'm sweating. Where am I? Then it all comes flooding back to me, of course I'm at home in bed. So what was that all about? Slowly I piece together the images and realise that I was, or should I say had been dreaming about the exercise when I was taken by the SAS team. The pictures in my mind fade into oblivion as I think about the next phase I'm entering. The second part of the operation. I rolled over in bed towards where Anne should have been but her side was empty, she had already got up. I felt the sheet where she had been but it was already cool so she must have been up for a little while. Damn! I wondered what the time was. I rolled back to my side of the bed and checked my watch it was already seven-thirty and I had a lot to do. Just then the door opened and Anne appeared with a welcome mug of tea.

'Here you are,' she put the mug on the small bedside unit and leaned over kissed me lightly on the head. 'Oh Richard James it's good to have you home.'

I made a playful grab at her, but she nimbly side stepped out of reach wagging her finger at me and smiled. 'Now, now Richard James don't you start taking liberties just because you've been away.' I made another grab at her and she laughed at me. 'You'll have to be quicker than that to catch me. Anyway breakfast won't be long.'

I lay back on the pillow and smiled back at her. 'Why didn't you wake me?' I asked my mood becoming more serious.

'Well you were sound asleep when I got up so I thought I'd leave you for a while. You were obviously tired. Anyway what's the panic?'

'Nothing much, it's just that I've got to get on with some paperwork and I need to arrange to see Brian Gore the solicitor about something, that's all.'

'What do you need to see Gore for?'

'Oh nothing much, just some papers to do with the contracting side that's all.' I lied.

'Sorry love. If I'd have known I would have woken you earlier.'

'No problem.' I picked up the mug and drank my tea.

It was just after eleven when I pulled up on the street alongside a neat picket fence. The fence surrounded a small garden in the centre of which stood a lovely grade two listed Tudor cottage. This was the office of Jackson, Harper and Gore Solicitors of which Brian Gore was our family solicitor, a fine example of a country cottage that many couples would give the earth for to own as a house, let alone use as their office and place of work. The entrance to this quaint office was approached by way of a path that passed under an arch covered in Honeysuckle whose delicate fragrance lay heavy in the mid-morning air. The cottage was of timber framed construction under a Kent peg tiled roof. The front of the building was virtually covered by the blooms of an old English climbing rose, the scent of which mingled with the fragrance of the Honeysuckle to give a most delightful aroma. I opened the front door and entered what was tantamount to a reception room, in which two desks were placed. One desk just inside the front door was for the receptionist, a young lady I would guess at being in her early twenties, who answered the telephone an did some of the typing. The second desk was for Brian's secretary – a mature lady in her late forties – busy typing Brian's dictation from an audio tape.

'Good afternoon sir. May I help you?' the young receptionist asked as I entered.

'Hi, I have an appointment with Brian Gore.'

'What time is the appointment Mr…?'

'James, Richard James. My appointment is for eleven fifteen.'

'Thank you sir, please take a seat.' She indicate to some antique looking upright chairs. I made my way over to the chairs she had indicated, selected a copy of Country Life magazine and sat down to wait, thinking it funny that wherever there's a waiting room, whether it is the GP's, Dentist or a solicitors they all have a similar cross-section of magazines.

'Mr Gore, your eleven fifteen appointment, Mr James has arrived…certainly.' The receptionist replaced her phone and smiled sweetly in my direction. 'Mr James, Mr Gore will see you now if you'd care to go through sir.

'This office?' I indicated to the door to my left.

'Yes that's right Mr James the office on the left.'

'Thanks.'

I gave a gentle tap on Brian's office door and pushed it open.

'Ah Richard, come in, come in. Take a seat.' He indicated to the chair in front of the desk. He was a tall slim-built individual with wispy sandy coloured hair and about three or four years my senior, but nevertheless been our family solicitor for more years than I care to imagine, as was his father before him. His office was full of character, a fairly large square room with an Inglenook fireplace and a wealth of oak beams. Along one wall he had placed a green button back leather Chesterfield with a low level table strategically placed in front of it. His desk was a large square affair on which were placed bundles of documents tied up with red tape and neatly stacked to one side. As I sat down on the chair at his desk, he closed the file he'd been working on and raised a quizzical eyebrow. 'Now what is this all about?' he asked.

I placed a manila file on the desk in front of me, turned it around and gently pushed it across the desk toward him. 'In that file you will find a number of different items. There are reports, copies of official documents, copies of logged telephone conversations and a list of contacts. All of which I would ask you to keep in safe custody for me.'

Whilst I was talking Brian opened the envelop file and took out the various items. 'Who's this?' he asked holding up a photograph of O'Shea.

'That Brian, is Mr Breandán O'Shea a top official in the Official IRA. You will find he is referred to a lot in my log.'

'And this photograph?' he showed me the photographs I had taken of the car I used for the bombing of Dublin.

'That car was the one that HMG provided for me to use in the bombing of Dublin.'

He glanced through the other documents and photographs of different people and different places. I had even got photographs of me in various disguises, including as a tourist in Dublin the day of the car bomb.

'What's this all about Richard? What have you got yourself into?' he asked. His pale blue eyes fixed me with a searching look.

'If I told you that I was involved in certain things that even my family don't know about, then how would you react?'

'That's a strange question to ask of your solicitor and friend. Of course I would not divulge anything, after all as your solicitor I observe strict confidentiality at all cost, but you already know that so why the question?' He looked puzzled.

'Because Brian…just because.'

'That's no answer. Richard you will have to level with me and trust me. So what is it?'

'Really Brian the less you know the better. If I said it could be dangerous for you if I told you, then that could well be an understatement on my part.'

'Let me be the judge of that. So come on Richard out with it, tell me what's going on.'

For the next thirty or so minutes I explained what had happened back in the Republic. How both Paul and I had got caught up with O'Shea and how he had tried to recruit me into the IRA.

I told him about my discovering the bomb making plant at the 'Holiday Camp', my time with the Devlin brothers and how O'Shea had introduced me to Eamonn. Where Eamonn fitted into this, how in recent times I had been used as an *agent provocateur* etc., etc. I finished off by bringing him up to date on my latest situation, how HMG wanted me to train a 'snatch' squad and return to Ireland to grab 'Slab' Riley. In fact having started to tell him I took him into my confidence and told him everything. I trusted him implicitly. 'So there you have it Brian, warts and all.'

'Hmm…very interesting. So are you working for the Secret Intelligence Service (SIS) or MI6?'

'Well I was trained by MI6 and I am officially a member of the UDR as you see by the copy of the documents there, so officially I am military Intelligence, but unofficially a member of SIS. So you see it is very, very dangerous for you now that you know!'

'I'm sure you're exaggerating the dangers, but whatever the danger my lips are sealed and of course I'll keep these documents for you. In fact I'll lock them in the safe right now.'

With that he took the manila envelop file and went to the safe housed out of sight in a floor to ceiling cupboard. 'And just in case you're wondering the whole of the premises is alarmed and of course the cupboard is not what it seems. The door is lined with steel and has a latticework of alarm wires sandwiched between the steel and the outer skin. So it should be well protected!'

'There are two more things I need to ask of you before I go…'

'Fire away Richard.'

'One is probably quite obvious to you, but I'll ask anyway and that is…should anything ever happen to me pass a copy of all those documents to Anne and the Police they are my insurance policy.'

'Ok what's your second thing?'

'As I said I have been tasked to set up this secret operation with this new 'group' or 'squad' and in order to protect them and myself I intend to get photographs of each and everyone of them plus I intend get them transferred into the UDR. Once I have all this documentation I would like you to keep copies with the stuff you've already got, would that be all right?'

'It's as good as done.'

'You're sure you don't mind holding this stuff?' I asked him again for the umpteenth time.

'Richard stop worrying. Now go and leave me to do the worrying.' At this point he stood up with an outstretched hand. 'Don't worry. It's all in hand.' I shook his hand and thanked him once again for being so accommodating.

I closed the outer door to Jackson, Harper and Gore Solicitors and the delicate fragrance of Honeysuckle again drifted to me on, what was now, the warm afternoon air. The time was approaching one o'clock as I drove up the street towards the Queens Head, just time for a pint, I thought to myself, before going home. Ah Richard, I heaved an inward sigh of relief, that's a good job done even though it was well overdue. As I turned into the car park of the Queens Head I knew I was now ready for that pint of Shepherd & Neame bitter!

Chapter 13

It's several months past since I lodged my documents with Brian Gore, the solicitor, without any repercussions and life in general has been fairly quiet of late. Paul is now very much part of the Circus and between us we have managed to put together what we feel is a reasonable unit, a total of sixteen men including ourselves. Each man has been selected for 'specialist' training from the TA barracks in Broadstairs and has already been involved in the occasional night exercises and map reading, both of which would play an important role in the forthcoming operation.

Everyone had been sworn to secrecy and 'encouraged' to believe in the idea that they were being trained in gorilla warfare because of the constant threat of a Russian invasion. We, that is Paul and I, perpetuated the idea that if an invasion did take place our unit would spearhead the resistance movement in Kent and this was readily accepted without question – well so we thought. After many hours of weapon training and marksmanship the unit eventually achieved a standard that Paul and I felt happy with. Once this level of competency had been reached we moved on to explosives along with bomb making and it was at this point one member, George Imanos, came to our attention. He seemed to have a natural flair in this field and it wasn't long before it became apparent that he was a very useful asset. After much discussion with Paul, I decided to reward his ability by contacting the Colonel and recommending him for promotion to Sergeant and within a short space of time George was summoned to attend Ashford for an interview with Major O'Rourke and to sit his Sergeant's exam shortly after which he was promoted.

In civilian life George Imanos owned a medium sized hotel on the Dover side of Canterbury and came in contact with many people from many walks of life. We knew very little about George save that he came to us with very good references, which contained a comment that 'Major O'Rourke spoke very highly of him' and that 'he and Imanos had worked together in the distant past'. There was however little else in his records of any note. The records were squeaky clean, too clean. I suppose I should have realised something wasn't quite right then, but I didn't give it a thought. Although George was a man in his forties he was in remarkable shape for his age and maintained a strict regime of physical fitness. He was of average build and height with dark brown hair and eyes, of swarthy complexion and with a bushy moustache that gave him a somewhat intimidating appearance. He had very few friends and he kept himself very much to himself. All in all he was a bit of a dark horse, but this was to our advantage and suited us perfectly. As a Sergeant, George became part of the leadership group which necessitated him knowing certain aspects of the operation and our 'real' objective. Any information imparted to him was always done on a 'need to know' basis and as such was fairly limited. He took on board his extra responsibility like a duck to water, and within a couple of weeks he had the guys eating out of his hand.

A couple of weeks after George's promotion we had a particularly gruelling Saturday training day after which Paul and I decided to go for a drink and I invited George to come along.

'No thanks Richard I'll give it a miss tonight if that's ok.'

'No problem. There'll be another time.'

'Sure, maybe another time. It's just that I need to get back as I've got a number of guests in tonight, but thanks all the same.' Then as an after thought he casually asked, 'where do you usually go for a drink?'

'The Red Lion along with a couple of other places.'

'Why have you changed your mind?' Paul asked jokingly.

'No, just wondered that's all. Tell you what, what about tomorrow?'

'Tomorrow's out for me, what about you Paul?'

'No tomorrow's out for me as well.'

'What about next week George?' I asked.

'That maybe a possibility, but I can't promise.' He looked at his watch, 'is that the time! I must go, see you both.'

'See you George.' Paul called after him as he disappeared through the door.

'What do you make of him Paul?' I asked.

'He's ok, a bit of a dark horse though. He doesn't say a lot.'

'No he doesn't say much.' I replied thoughtfully. I had a strange feeling about George, but couldn't quite put my finger on why.

'That's not a bad thing is it besides it could be useful in certain situations don't you think?'

I was miles away, too engrossed in what it was about George that I wasn't sure of when Paul brought me back to what he'd been saying.

'I said it could be useful in certain situations. Or don't you think so? '

'What could?' I asked.

'George, not saying much, haven't you been listening?'

'I have, but I was just thinking…'

'About what?'

'George. I can't put my finger on it but I can't help feeling there's something odd there.'

'Such as?'

'Don't really know what it is about him, it's just a feeling I have…what about you Paul?'

'In what way?'

'Well what do you make of him?'

'He seems ok to me.'

136

'Must be my imagination then. Come on let's go for that drink, where do you fancy going?'

'How about 'The Three Tuns' in Canterbury for a change?'

'Fine by me.'

Ten minutes later we walked into the Three Tuns, a sixteenth century coaching inn situated within the city walls on the London side of Canterbury. The pub was the haunt of the younger set and was usually frequented by students from the university and some of the younger soldiers from the local barracks. With bare brickwork forming the inglenook fireplace, walls of wattle and daub, low beams and bare floorboards the pub had a certain ambience about it and was an extremely popular meeting place with tonight being no exception. Paul and I pushed our way through to the bar where I ordered a couple of pints and as I went to pay for them I noticed George Imanos standing over the other side of the room. He was talking to a bloke wearing what looked like sunglasses with black shoulder length hair. I nudged Paul and said, 'Isn't that George over there?' He looked over to where I indicated.

'Yeah. I thought he said he was busy?'

'He did. Maybe he's been home and come out again.' I suggested lamely giving George the benefit of the doubt.

'Oh do me a favour Richard. There's no way he could have got over the other side of Canterbury, back here and have drunk half his pint in that short space of time. After all we weren't far behind him leaving were we?'

'Don't be silly, I'm not serious. Perhaps he just didn't want to come with us and was too polite to say!'

'What, George too polite…you're having a laugh. No I reckon he had other arrangements, like our friend over there, that he didn't want us to know about.' Paul grinned and winked, 'Perhaps he has a secret life that we don't know about! What do you think?'

'Probably.' I grinned and left it at that.

The following morning as I came in from the orchard for my mid morning tea, Anne asked me if I'd seen the red Ford parked just up the road from us.

'What red Ford?' I asked

'There look.' She pointed to a car parked right across the access to Seeboard's sub-station. 'It's been there since early this morning.'

I casually looked over at the car. 'Huh, I hope Seeboard don't need to get in there in a hurry.'

'Well they shouldn't have a problem, there's somebody in it.'

Suddenly I became more interested. 'You say there's somebody in it, how do you know? You can't even see it properly from here.'

'I know because I saw them stop there. Someone got out from the passenger side and walked off up the road but the driver didn't get out.'

I stared out at the car trying to see if I could see anyone sitting in it. In the end I decided from where we stood it was impossible to see properly. 'Anyway he or she could easily have got out whilst you weren't looking.'

'I know that silly, but what I meant was when it first stopped. Since then I've seen him get out walk round the car and get back in.'

'And he's been there ever since?'

'As far as I know. It just seems strange that's all.' With that she lost interest and went into the kitchen to pour herself another cup of tea.

'What did he look like?' I was now far from disinterested.

'Oh just a bloke.' She called back, 'why?'

'Well was he big, small, black or white?'

'He was white.' She called back the irritation sounding in her voice, 'he had shoulder length hair for what it's worth.'

'Don't get cross...'

'Well...I don't know, I only mentioned it because it's been there for a long time. No other reason.'

With the mention of the long hair I began to wonder...no it must be a coincidence, but all the same I had a strange feeling about this. Who was the other bloke, could it have been George? My mind was in a whirl. In the end I decided to put a quick call into Paul.

The phone rang several times then the answer phone clicked in and the dulcet tones of Paul's voice announced, 'hello, this is Jones Engineering. I'm sorry no one is available to take your call at the moment, but please leave your name and telephone number and someone will call you back as soon as possible. Please speak after the tone, thank you.'

'Hi Paul it's me, Richard. I'm at home for the next thirty minutes please give me a call urgently. Thanks.' I was about to put the phone down when there was a click.

'Hi Richard, what's the problem?'

'I just thought I'd let you know that I think our house and farm is under some sort of surveillance.'

'How do you mean and by whom?'

'Can't talk now, but can you come up here?'

'Well...sure but why the mystery?'

'I'll explain when you get here. In fact come in through Dargate and leave your car down the road, and cut across the orchard on foot and I'll meet you in the farm office say in half an hour?'

'Make that forty five minutes. That'll give me time to finish off what I'm doing and tell the lads what the next jobs are.'

'Ok see you in three quarters of an hour then.'

Paul parked his car in the gateway to the main orchard, locked it up and made his way across to the main body of the farm and the farm office. As he did so Mr James senior crossed the yard, glanced toward the orchard and saw Paul as he came towards him and the farm office.

Lifting his hand in acknowledgement he called out to him. 'Hello stranger, how you doing?'

'I'm fine Mr James. How are you?'

'Not too bad Paul, not too bad. How's the new career going?'

'Very well. We're very busy at the moment.'

'So what brings you up here? Can't you keep away from the old place then?'

'No, you know me Mr James after all this is my second home.' Paul grinned, 'I've just popped up to see Richard, is he in the office?'

'Yes I think so. I better not keep you.' Mr James slapped Paul on the arm, 'look after yourself Paul. Hope to see you again soon.'

'See you Mr James.' Paul raised his hand as he set off towards the single story brick built building that was used as a farm office.

'So what's the big mystery?' Paul asked as he walked in the office. I didn't answer, instead I motioned for him to follow me and set off towards the back door of the house. We entered the kitchen and went straight through to the front room. I took him over to the window and pointed to the red Ford still parked in the entrance to the Seeboard's sub-station. 'Do you recognise the car?' I asked.

'No, should I then?'

'Not particularly. I just wondered if you'd seen it anywhere before?'

'Can't say that I have why?'

'Well it's been parked there all morning and from Anne's description I would say the driver is the same bloke who we saw talking to George Imanos last night.' Paul went to speak but I held up my hand. 'Hang on a minute before you say anything. Just listen to what I've got to say and you may know why I'm more than a little touchy about that car. A few months back I met up with someone out at The Red Lion. That person worked in a sensitive job, in fact he was over from Ireland…you can draw your own conclusion as to what he did. Anyway he arranged to meet me with some news from Ireland and as I said I met him at the Red Lion. When I left the pub I picked up a tail, a blue Volvo, they were good I'll give them that, but I eventually shook them off. Now I suddenly find a red Ford sitting just up the road from me. I don't think I'm being paranoid and I'm beginning to wonder what's going on.'

'Hmm…Do you want me to take a walk over there?'

'Not so fast Paul. Now I don't think the two incidents are connected but, when I was over in Ireland at Sean's haulage yard there was a red Ford with two occupants keeping the yard under surveillance. In fact it was with the help of a mate of mine, the contact who I recently met up with at the Red Lion, that I grabbed the two over there. Now it seems to me more than a little suspicious that having broken up that little party I have suddenly become the centre of attention over here, especially just after meeting with my contact. Ok, before you say it, I know that it was a blue Volvo and not a red Ford that tailed me, but I now suddenly find myself looking at a red Ford sitting on my doorstep with its owner keeping tabs on me just like the red Ford was doing over at Sean's. Now I ask you don't you find that just a little more than a coincidence?

'I can understand your concern, but I'm not sure that I would definitely connect the incidents.'

'Oh do me a favour Paul, just look at the facts…'

'They are?'

'First of all, a red Ford over in Ulster keeping tabs on Sean's place and two of us take the drivers out. Two I meet with my contact from Ulster and I am tailed. Three a red Ford miraculously appears outside my house and the description of the driver is George's pal from the pub…'

'No I don't accept that.'

'Accept what?'

'The driver being George's mate. How do you know he's a friend of his Richard?'

'Because he was in the pub with him.'

'Yeah I agree, but just because he was talking to him doesn't make him his friend does it?'

'Ok, ok so he may not be his friend, but he was talking to him all right, so don't be so bloody pedantic.' I was getting annoyed with Paul, 'anyway number three. Matey, whoever he is turns up on my doorstep and has been there all morning. I think that makes it a little more than just a coincidence. Oh and just for good measure number four, there was a second person in the car, now was that George and if so what has he got to do with this? Tell you what Paul; I think we need to get to the bottom of this little game.'

We both stood in silence looking out of the window.

'What about this for an idea. I go back to the workshop and as I drive passed the Ford I get the number and then I can phone it through to you, at least that way you can get a vehicle check done.'

This seemed like a good idea to me, in fact it was the only idea. There was only one problem, the other person, his passenger.

'What about his mate? He could quite conceivably be Imanos and he knows your car as well as mine and what's more he would recognise you.'

'So all that does is confirm that I was out this way.'

I knew he was right and reluctantly I had to agree with him after all I had no other plan of action. So I went to see Paul off as he left through the back door, but by the time I had returned to watch from the front window, the red Ford had gone. So much for getting the number!

Sunday saw me at the Red lion having my usual tipple. I always met up with a couple of the locals in the lounge bar for a few pints before lunch. I took my usual stool positioned next to the bar in the corner hidden away behind the fruit machine. I sat there drinking my pint and listening to Bert and his old wartime buddy reminiscing about their exploits whilst on active service when in walked a bloke with the shoulder length hair and dark glasses. It was the same person who we saw drinking and chatting with Imanos in the Three Tuns the other night. Now I wonder why he should suddenly turn up here. I could hear Bert's voice droning on in the background, but I was no longer paying attention to what he was saying. I was more interested in the newcomer then Bert turned to me and said, 'so what do you reckon Richard?'
I had to admit it, I hadn't listened to a word he'd said, 'sorry Bert, what was that?'
'I said what do you reckon about all this?'
'All what Bert?'
'Richard, you haven't being paying the slightest bit of attention,' he gently chided me. 'I was talking about all this trouble in Ireland. I was just saying to Fred here, it didn't used to be like that. I remember Ireland back in the fifties and there was none of these here car bombs and the like…'
'Sorry Bert, will you excuse me, I've just remembered something I needed to do urgently.' I finished the last of my pint and disappeared out of the rear door. There in the car park was a red Ford and on the back of it was an Irish Ferries car sticker. So who was this mysterious person and what was his interest in me? There was only one way to find out and that was to run a vehicle check, so armed with his registration number I set off to the nearest telephone box to phone 'Mother' for a vehicle check, but to no avail as the answer came back as 'We have no record filed on a red Ford of that registration.' So maybe it was pure coincidence that he had turned up here, and I was reading too much into it.

We were now Operation Orpheus minus ten, just over one week left to make certain that our operational squad was ready for the big day.
'Ok men, welcome to the briefing for today.' We had gathered the team together in the TA drill hall and I was now going to tell them the real reason for their training. 'Now as you all know we have worked hard at our training. You've all exceeded the expectations and are now ready for a real

operation. Up until now we have done exercise after exercise. You have always been led to believe that this was in preparation for a Russian invasion, well that has not been strictly true.' A low murmur rippled round the room then slowly subsided. 'The training was not in case of a Russian invasion it was for a different reason all together. Gentleman in one week's time we go to Ireland.'

There was more murmuring. 'We leave for Ireland and will be stationed at Lisburn Barracks. Once we reach Lisburn we will split into two groups, one group will be deployed as decoys and back-up, whilst the second group will be deployed as a 'snatch' squad whose target is in the Republic. Any questions?' I watched intently to see what reaction I got, but I had no need to have worried. 'Right as there are no questions, may I remind everyone that this is classified information and loose tongues cost lives. So remember keep your mouth shut! Even wives, lovers and girlfriends are not to be told. This operation and the outcome as such is your responsibility and it is on a 'need to know' basis. Thank you, that'll be all gentlemen.'

Two days later, Operation Orpheus minus five, Paul and I were sitting chatting in the office at the TA Barracks after drill when there was a knock on the door.

'Come in.' I called. The door opened and framed in the doorway was John Rains. He was one of the quieter members of the unit, a Traffic Warden by day who had a son in the Army. 'Come in John.' I could see by the look on John's face that something was not quite right. 'What's wrong?' I asked.

'Sorry to trouble you sir, but the other evening…' His voice trailed off.

'What about the other evening?' I asked.

'Well, did you mean what you said about us going to Ireland next week?'

'Of course why do you ask?'

'Well…' his brow furrowed, 'I'm not sure how to put this…'

'Spit it out John, what's bothering you?' Paul asked.

'Well Sergeant Major, I'm not too happy about what was said. In fact I'd rather not be part of it.'

'What do you mean; you'd rather not be part of it. Pull yourself together man. You can't pick and choose.'

'Hang on Paul,' I said holding up my hand. 'Now what's troubling you Rains?'

'Well it's like this sir; the Sergeant isn't all he seems to be.'

'What do you mean by that?' I waited for his answer. 'Well come on, tell me.' I said impatiently, 'because at the moment you're not making much sense.'

'He's a mole,' Rains blurted out, 'he's working as an intelligence gatherer for the IRA.'

'What!' Paul exclaimed, 'I've never heard such a load of crap. How do you mean working for the IRA?' He said in a derisory tone. 'I think you've lost it Rains.'

'No I haven't.' He answered quite belligerently. 'With respect sir,' he addressed me, 'I know it sounds far fetched but I do know he is a fully paid up member of the Irish Republican Socialist Party, you know the IRSP and as such he has been feeding information about us back to his Lord and Master.'

'How can you be certain Rains?' I asked.

'Well sir, as you know, my son Jamie is currently with the lads out in Ulster, this is his second tour out there, and before he left this time, he told me about a bloke called Lamar…'

'Who's this bloke Lamar,' Paul interrupted, 'and what's he got to do with it?'

'Lamar is known to be an activist in Irish Republican Socialist Party (IRSP), originally from County Louth. Anyway, according to Jamie he is also known to be IRA and when he was out there last time Special Branch was taking an active interest in Mr Lamar. Unfortunately rumour has it that about six months ago he disappeared off the face of the earth only to resurface a couple of weeks ago over here in the Canterbury area. So you see Imanos cannot be trusted.'

'Hmm.' I looked at Paul who was deep in thought at this little bombshell. 'Well what do you think Paul?'

'Don't know what to say or think. What about you?'

'If what you say is true Rains, and I've no reason to disbelieve you, then why hasn't something been done?' I asked.

'I don't know sir.'

'Tell me Rains, how do you know Lamar is in the Canterbury area?' Asked Paul.

'And what's more,' I interjected, 'how do you know he is connected to Imanos?'

'Because one of the lads in my Jamie's unit had been out drinking one night before they left, had too much as they do from time to time, and started mouthing off about Ireland to some stranger. A fight broke out and the police were called. One of those present was Lamar…'

'So why wasn't he nicked?' I asked.

'Evidently in all the confusion, he managed to get away.'

'How can you be sure it was Lamar? I mean to say, I know your son told you, but how did he know it was him?'

'Because that was the name the lad from his unit remembered him being called.'

'Which lad?'

'The one who had been shouting his mouth off about Ireland.'

'Surely if he was that drunk he wouldn't have remembered?'

'According to Jamie he, the lad, remembered Lamar quite distinctly, evidently it was Lamar and the bloke with him who supposedly started the ruckus in the first place.'

'So didn't he, the lad that is, tell the police?'

'Sure he did, he even gave them a description of him. He also told his C.O, but everyone chose to ignore it.'

'Why?'

'Well I suppose because he was steaming at the time.'

'Maybe, anyway how do you know he is friends with Imanos?'

'Well sir, earlier in the evening my lad, Jamie, remembered seeing Imanos with a bloke fitting the description of Lamar. Both of them were in he same pub as my lad. Buying drinks for a couple of Army lads.'

'Lads from your son's lot?'

'He didn't say, but I would think so.'

'Which pub was this?' Paul asked.

'The Volunteer.'

'Was that where the fight was?' I asked.

'Oh no, that happened much later...' he paused, 'Jamie did say, but I'm sorry I can't for the life of me remember it now.'

'Ok, not to worry.'

'Did the Police speak to your son?' Paul asked.

'No, but why should they?'

'Well if he was involved in the fight...'

'Oh no, nothing like that. He wasn't involved at all. He along with some of the others had returned to Barracks well before that all happened. He needed to get on with some things; after all they were due to ship out to Belfast within forty-eight hours.'

Paul and I sat in silence for a few minutes thinking about what Rains had just told us.

'Why didn't you tell me about all of this before now?' I asked

'Because I didn't know until tonight.'

'What!' I exclaimed, 'you didn't know until tonight, how come?'

'Well after you told us about the Op. I wrote to my son...'

'You did what!' I didn't give him chance to finish. 'You idiot, don't you realise what you've done? Not only have you broken Queens Regulations, you have committed a court martial offence. You have breached security and have endangered a planned operation of Her Majesty's Government. You have put your colleagues' lives at risk as well as your own. I now need to consider what action to take. You are dismissed. Get out man.' I was fuming.

'Well where do we go with this Paul?'

'Your shout Richard.' We both sat in silence pondering over what we had been told.

Paul broke the silence, 'shit! The stupid sod. All that time and training all for nothing.'

I wasn't convinced that we had done it all for nothing. 'I know we have had a breach, but I'm still going with the original plan only we move it forward.'

Paul frowned. 'I don't know Richard. Could be a bit dodgy don't you think. What if Imanos has leaked it to the IRA then the target will be expecting a hit, won't he?'

'Not if we pull it forward to tomorrow straight after training. We will still have the surprise element. Anyway all Imanos knows is that we are going as a 'snatch' squad, but he doesn't know the target so it could be anyone.'

Paul thought about this for a moment or two. 'Ok, you've got a point there. So what do you propose?'

'I'll contact Ash and bring Orpheus forward. Tell him we leave tomorrow midday. We'll tell the men tonight to report here for 07:00 hours, full kit inspection. Tell them to pack kit away. We'll arrange for it to be stowed on the vehicles here. Regroup for full exercise at the woods for 08:00 hours. At noon we'll ship out.'

'But we'll have to tell them before then Richard.'

Paul had a point, after all this was the TA not the regulars, also they were 'Home Guard' this made a difference as well. 'I suppose you're right, in that case we tell them tonight. Agreed?'

'Agreed.'

With the night's training over Rains left the Drill hall in Broadstairs with a worried look about him. He thought long and hard about his next move before deciding, then he got into his car and set off towards Canterbury, his mind made up. He kept turning it over in his mind, every last detail, of what he was to say when he got there. There was no way that he was going to Ireland and he knew it. This was the only way he knew that would stop it and get him out of this suicide mission. After all he had his wife and family to think of, and that was why he had written to Jamie, and that was why he got such a bollocking off the 'old' man Captain Richard James. Yes sir, his mind was made up all right.

It didn't take too long for him to drive from Broadstairs to Canterbury and in next to no time he swung his car onto the forecourt outside the Police station.

'Good evening sir, can I help you?' the Police Constable on the front desk asked politely.

'Yes, I wish to speak to the duty Officer.'

'May I ask in what connection?' The young constable asked.

'I want to report a possible firearms offence.' He answered keeping a level voice which did not betray his nervousness about what he was about to do.

'Hmm, I see sir. Could you be a little more specific?'

Damn you just get me the Chief Inspector you little shit, he thought to himself, and let me get this over and done with. Rains smiled calmly. 'Tomorrow there is going to be a unit of men, armed with Self Loading Rifles and other weapons and using live ammunition who will be training in woods not too far from here. Now would it be possible to speak to the duty officer?' Rains gave a smile.

'Certainly sir, I'll be back with you in a minute.' With that the young constable disappeared through to the back office. 'Here Sergeant I've got some sort of nutter out there telling me about a group of blokes who are going to be training with live ammo and SLR's etc. out in the woods tomorrow.'

The Sergeant, a rather rotund individual with a round face of ruddy complexion, was just taking a mouthful of tea as Rollins said about the live ammunition.

'What... Live rounds... Firearms...' the Sergeant spluttered. 'Right Rollins, I'll deal with this.' The Sergeant slammed his mug of tea down so hard he slopped some onto the report he was reading. With a curse he pulled out a voluminous handkerchief and proceeded to dab at the spilled tea on the report. His chair scraped across the floor as he hurriedly pushed it back. 'Live ammo, whatever next?' he muttered to himself. 'Jardine.' He shouted, but not getting an instantaneous response he shouted louder, 'Jardine...Wpc Jardine.' His tone was one of exasperation. He quietly cursed the fairer sex, then shouted her name again. 'Jardine...anyone seen Jardine?'

'I'm here Sergeant.' A female's voice came from behind a row of filing cabinets.

'Right. Keep an eye on the front desk.' He said curtly.

'But Serge...'

'Just do it Jardine.' He said brusquely. He knew that her shift had finished and she was just finishing off a report but the situation demanded action and he didn't have time to argue. 'Rollins show Mr...er... what is his name?'

'Sorry Sergeant I didn't think to ask...' The sergeant cut him off in mid sentence.

'What the...didn't they teach you anything at Police school? Quickly, get it sorted.'

'Yes Sergeant. Sorry Sergeant.' With that he was gone, only to reappear a few minutes later with a name.

'Well Rollins, what's the man's name?'

'Rains Sergeant. A Mr John Rains.'

'Right…' The Sergeant paused to think. 'Right Rollins, take our Mr Rains to IR 1 and wait with him there, I'll join you both in a couple of minutes.'

'Yes Sergeant.'

The Sergeant went across to the computer and logged on. He needed to run a check on Mr Rains such as, who he was and if there was anything known. In a matter of seconds he knew John Rains was a Traffic Warden, he knew his number and the office he worked from. His home address and the fact that he was also a member of the TAVR were logged. From that moment the Sergeant knew that the complainant was a very reliable and trustworthy source and the 'incident' as such had to be taken seriously.

'Jardine be a good girl and phone the Chief at home.' The Sergeants tone had softened. 'Offer my apologies for disturbing him at this time but tell him that we have a potential major incident brewing and ask him…no… tell him that it would be advisable for him to be present. He shouldn't do, but if he does ask why, then tell him we have a possible security alert involving firearms. Also you can tell him that the potential incident has been brought to our attention by a trustworthy source.' With this latest turn of events Police Officer Jardine, who had already forgotten about her earlier protestations, now dialled the Chief Inspector's home number and waited patiently for him to answer.

Pc Rollins held open the door that allowed entry into the main body of the 'Nick'. 'Would you like to come through sir?'

John Rains nodded 'Thank you.' And walked through the open door and entered a corridor.

'If you would come with me sir we'll find an empty office just along here.' The two men walked along the corridor in silence. 'Here we are sir.' Pc Rollins paused outside a small office the sign on the door indicated the room was IR 1. He tapped on the door and waited. There was no reply so he opened the door to reveal a room of about average size painted in neutral colours. There was a small window set high up in the wall, but on the inside of the window were steel bars to either keep people out, or more than likely to keep the inhabitants in as this was one of the main interview rooms used for interviewing persons suspected of being involved in some sort of criminal activity. Beneath the window and placed end on against the wall was a single table with two chairs positioned either side thus enabling two interviewing officers to one suspect plus a solicitor. Set into the wall midway between the facing chairs were twin cassette tape decks for recording interviews.

'Please take a seat sir.' Pc Rollins indicated to one of the chairs at the table. 'The duty Sergeant will be joining us shortly and you'll be able to give him more details about what you were telling me.'

John Rains looked around the sparsely furnished room and gave an involuntary shiver.

'Did I hear you correctly Constable, did say the duty Sergeant will be joining us?'

'That is correct sir.'

'But surely in a matter such as this, a more senior person would seem to be the appropriate choice, wouldn't it?'

'I'm sure the sergeant will be quite capable to deal with this matter sir. Now if you wouldn't mind taking a seat.' Again Rollins indicated to the chairs at the table and John knew there was now no going back.

Chapter 14

It was already promising to be another warm day as the early morning mist, a product of a hot summer night, was already dissipating rapidly in the rays of the morning sun. At least there was a slight breeze this morning, which would be a godsend to us out in those woods on exercise. Today was to be of major importance to the unit, we were to rehearse our final set piece using live ammunition prior to our departure for Ulster. Today was to bring everything we had learnt together. Today the men would be told the details of their trip over the water. If everything had gone according to plan, I had envisaged telling them a complete fabrication which was, that they were to going to go on manoeuvres joining up with a number of other units and head off for a long weekend away. I would not even have mentioned Ireland until the very last minute, but the facts were that I had had to tell them about what was planned and it had all gone a bit pear shaped. Now, because of our friend Mr Imanos everything had to be pulled forward so I had decided, once we were on the move I would then open the sealed orders – of course the opening of a sealed envelop was purely to add credence to it being a secret operation that even I knew nothing about. A bit of a fairytale really. The fact was both Paul and I knew the full story and based on a 'need to know' George also knew we were to head off to Ireland, even though he didn't know the details, he still knew enough for it to be a problem. So that was the plan as it now stood. In the meantime the men should be arriving at this, our rendezvous, in the next few minutes. We had briefed them earlier and split the group up into four man 'bricks' or 'cells' and each cell was issued with a map, a compass and a brown envelope. Inside the envelope they would find a grid reference and a time. The grid reference was their target and the time was the time they had to arrive at the target. Once they reached the target they would find another similar set of instructions and this sequence of events would be repeated many times until they all eventually reached here. Once here they would then each be expected to use their training to 'snatch' back a member of their team who had been taken prisoner. They would need to quickly identify 'friend' from 'foe' and to shoot the enemy pop-ups with live ammunition. Each cell will take it in turn to be the 'snatch squad' whilst the other members of the unit would patrol the perimeter to make sure no member of the public inadvertently strayed into the target area. The problem was that although this land was leased by the MoD it still bordered on to privately owned woodland.

We had been up and running for some considerable time when it came to my turn at the 'killing game'. As I slowly edged forward through the undergrowth, I checked to my right and could see the two giant concrete blocks as they rose majestically out of the undergrowth surrounding them.

They were all that remained of the Anti Aircraft Gun emplacement used during the Second World War. Straight ahead of me was nothing but bracken and trees. The gentle breeze tugged at my open neck shirt. I scanned the sector from right to left. Even though I headed up the unit on this part of the course Paul had been the one to set up the various obstacles etc. After all it was only fair that everyone, including me, was ignorant as to where each pop-up was. I had done a similar scheme for Paul, and both of us had set up the course for all the others.

Suddenly I tensed. Out of the corner of my eye I saw a movement. I eased my Browning from its holster, dropped to the prone position and carefully parted the bracken and undergrowth so I had a clear line of sight. For some time I stared at where I had thought I had seen the movement, but to no avail. I slowly edged forward. A rabbit hopped out into the clearing ahead of me. I stared straight ahead into the clearing. Still nothing. I watched the rabbit for any clues, but nothing, save for another rabbit joining it in the clearing. Slowly my muscles relaxed. I scanned the area again. Yes, I was certain this time. I watched intently. Was I seeing things? Was it the breeze? I watched, concentrating my gaze on a place that looked to be about forty-five metres away. There it was again, the slightest of movements. I was now tense like a coiled spring. Suddenly with a swishing sound and a flash of white a pop-up sprung through the bracken. I squeezed the trigger and a loud crack rang out as I unleashed a single shot. Everywhere was pandemonium. The whole woods came alive as birds screeched…the rabbits bolted…all around me panic…In an instant the pop-up was gone. Once more to be hidden in the bracken. It was over in the blink of an eye. Had I shot a friend or foe? I was certain it was foe. I eased myself forward, pausing now and again to listen and watch for any other tell-tale movement. There was nothing and everywhere was still. I heard the staccato message from the unit acting as Control, as it drifted up from my personal transceiver.

'Alpha, Whisky, Bravo 1 down.'

As soon as I heard from Whisky, the call sign for Control, that it was Bravo 1 down, I knew it was a 'good' hit. I had taken out a foe. I replied in the same style to acknowledge the receipt of the message. 'Alpha'. I lay still for a moment or two whilst I carried out further reconnaissance of the area. Once I was certain the way was clear I continued to inch forward through the undergrowth moving off around the clearing until I had completely circumnavigated it. On reaching the other side of the clearing I carefully made my way through the undergrowth toward the gun emplacement and where I had seen the pop-up. Once there I checked for myself that it was as stated, an enemy pop-up, and confirmed the information back to Control. I then slowly moved off deeper into the woods.

Two hours later I put a call in to Control on my transceiver in order to speak to Paul. 'Whisky, Alpha, over.' I waited but the only response was the crackle of an open channel. I repeated the call. 'Whisky, Alpha, over.' Again nothing. This puzzled me. Perhaps I was in a dead area, so I moved off to where there was less cover and tried once again. 'Whisky, Alpha, over.' Still nothing. Shit I muttered under my breath, Control's bloody set must be down. I stomped off back up through the woods towards where I knew Control was situated. Halfway there I paused again and tried calling them on my transceiver knowing I was definitely within range now. 'Whisky, Alpha, over.' Still the result was the same, nothing!

I eventually entered an area of concrete blocks, which had at one time had housed the nerve centre for Dover's radar defence. I was suddenly struck by how deserted it was. No men, there should have been at least six, and where was Paul? He should have been back here by now. In fact they all should have been here for debriefing. Where the hell were they? Suddenly the peace was shattered by the metallic voice through a megaphone.

'Halt. Armed Police, move into the open with your arms raised.' What the...Again the metallic voice...'I repeat... armed police move into the open with arms raised or we shoot...' A frown creased my forehead, what the hell is going on I thought to myself. Suddenly there was a crack of a high velocity weapon and the whine of a bullet as it ricochet off one of the trees nearby, spitting wood splinters in all directions.

Again the metallic voice.

'I will not warn you again...move into the open with arms raised.'

'Ok, ok...' I shouted back as I raised my arms above my head and moved into the centre of the clearing.

'Lay face down on the ground. Now!' The metallic voice barked. I carried out the instruction. The smell of fresh earth filtered up through the shoots of bracken.

'Arms outstretched in front of you.' Again I did as I was asked. I heard the sound of many feet running and then felt a knee in the small of my back as someone roughly grabbed my arms and jerked them back behind me. This was followed by the snap of handcuffs as that person deftly clicked them over my wrists. From my position of limited view I could just about see three pairs of black high ankle boots and dark coloured trousers neatly tucked inside the ankle gaiters of the boots. I was hauled to my feet and for the first time was able to take in the scene before me. Around the periphery of the clearing was about ten armed police and a further two flanked either side of me with their weapons covering my every move. The one who had been the arresting officer quickly frisked me, removing my Browning and the personal transceiver. These he passed to one of his colleagues. I stood there nonplussed not sure what was actually going on.

'Richard James I am arresting you on suspicion of being illegally in possession of firearms and of explosives. You do not have to say anything, but it may harm your defence if you do not mention when questioned something which you may later rely on in court, anything you do say maybe given in evidence. Is there anything you wish to say?'

'No,' was my curt reply.

With that the arresting officer nodded to one of his colleagues for him to radio on ahead.

'Control, this is Red leader, over.'

'Red leader go ahead, Control over.'

'Control this is Red leader. Latest situation is that we have Target two in custody and returning to base. I believe total arrests are sixteen. Red leader over.'

'Roger Red leader, and well done. Control out.'

I was still utterly confused as to what was going on.

Most of the unit was released during the morning with the exception of Paul and me. We were both charged under the Firearms Act and held in custody pending further enquiries. Both of us were given the opportunity to make a phone call, but because of the sensitive nature of the operation and my position within SIS I was left in a quandary as to what to do exactly. If I used my contact number, which was classified information, then my true operation and my controller's identity would be blown and if I contacted Brian Gore then that would be of little use as he was not privy to the bigger picture. There was another option and that was to telephone O'Rourke at the London desk, but again that would mean using a sensitive telephone number which could cause massive repercussions. In fact I suddenly felt very much alone in all of this but I decided that for the time being I should play it by ear, knowing full well that if things did look really black I could always get a coded message to the Colonel.

'Richard, it would be better for all concerned...'

The voice droned on and on, but I was too busy trying to figure out what to do rather than concentrate on what he was saying. Then I had an idea. I would phone Anne and ask her to do two things, one to phone Jean O'Donald and tell her to telephone my mate Jimmy, the second thing was for Anne to contact Gore, just in case I needed a solicitor.

'Sorry Chief Inspector may I make a phone call?' I asked politely.

'Yes, you are allowed one telephone call and that is all.'

I smiled warmly. 'Thank you Chief Inspector.' I mentally rehearsed what I was to say to Anne, making sure that she repeated it back to me word for word.

'What number do you want to call?' asked the Chief Inspector.

'My home number that's all.' I dialled my home number.

'Hello…'

'Anne,' I interrupted her, 'listen to me carefully and write this down. I am in Canterbury Police station….'

'Why?' She cut me short.

'I've been arrested…'

Again she interrupted me and I was running out of time. 'What for?'

'Just listen and write this down,' I said curtly. 'Two things to do. One telephone Jean O'Donald and give her this message 'I'm in Canterbury nick and I've been arrested tell Jimmy! Have you got that?'

'Yes, you want me to telephone Jean O'Donald and tell her that you're in Canterbury Police station, you've been arrested and for her to tell Jimmy.'

'Good girl. Now the second thing. Contact Brian Gore and tell him I've been arrested and I'm at Canterbury. Ask him to come over just in case. Have you got that?'

'Yes, tell Brian Gore you've been arrested and for him to go to Canterbury Police station.'

'Good, and don't worry, it'll be sorted!'

'Oh Richard I hope so…'pip, pip, pip, pip, pip.

I didn't hear the rest because of the pips. 'I've run out of money. See you love, bye.'

'Bye darling…' the phone went dead.

'Right Mr James, is there anything you wish to say?'

'Only that I am working for Her Majesty's Government and I was acting under orders.'

'Yes I know Mr James and I'm the Chief Constable of Kent. Now do us all a favour and tell me the truth. I'll ask you once again, is there anything you wish to say.'

'I am working for Her Majesty's Government acting under orders and I have nothing further to add.'

'Well perhaps a spell in the cells may help. Sergeant…'

'Yes sir?'

'Escort Mr James back to custody.'

'Yes sir. Mr James.'

I stood up and was escorted by the constable already present in the room and the Sergeant back to the cells.

Some two hours later I was taken back to the interview room where once again I was interviewed by the Chief Inspector, and just as before, I said nothing except the bit about being a member of Her Majesty's Government and acting under orders. Try as they might they got nothing more and nothing less. This interrogation was child's play to me.

There was a tap at the door. 'The interview is suspended as Police Constable Dodsworth has entered the room.' The Chief Inspector stopped the tape. 'Yes Dodsworth, what is it?'

'There's a solicitor wishing to speak with the defendant sir. A Mr Gore.'

'I see. Well bring him through.'

A few minutes later Brian was ushered into the interview room with a look of consternation on his face. 'Excuse me Chief Inspector I must object that this interview with my client was started in my absence, why?'

'Because Mr Gore we were not aware of your attending.'

'Hmm. In that case I will ask for some time in private with my client thank you.'

The Chief Inspector motioned the constable to wait outside the interview room, curtly nodded in Brian's direction and with the Detective Inspector in tow vacated the room.

'Now Richard, what's all this about?'

'Oh it's a long story, but basically I and Paul have been held on some trumped up charges. Firearms charges to be precise. The whole unit was taken in this morning...'

Brian cut me short. 'This morning! Why wasn't I told sooner?'

'Because it wasn't necessary. Anyway it's really complicated; it involves Her Majesty's Government and my job with them etcetera, etcetera. So you see there's not a lot you can do except make sure fair play is observed.'

'Ok if that's what you wish. What about your, what do you call it, your control man, does he know?'

'My controller...Now there's a problem...' I didn't have time to finish what I was saying before the Chief Inspector returned his face like thunder.

'Chief Inspector I do take exception to this interruption...'

'Mr Gore, if you would allow me to explain...'

'Well explain Chief Inspector, explain.'

'It appears your client was telling the truth Mr Gore. He is working for Her Majesty's Government and as such we have been advised that he is entitled to carry firearms, in fact he is well known by Special Branch and MI5. Therefore the firearms charges have been dropped. Incidentally Mr James, does the name O'Rourke, Major O'Rourke mean anything to you?'

'Major O'Rourke, did you say?'

'Yes Major O'Rourke.'

I smiled and shook my head. 'Never heard of him.'

'So Chief Inspector; does this mean all the charges have been dropped?' Brian asked.

'It appears so. Evidently according to my bosses everything about your client had to be referred up the line and everything has been dropped.'

'Everything?'

'Yes everything. Even the illegal drilling charge has come back as not in the publics interest. So he's free to go, well unless this Major has some other reason for him to be held.'

'One question Chief Inspector.'

'Yes Mr James, what would that be?'

'Who tipped you off?'

'Now Mr James, you should know better than to ask that. All I will say is that we had received a report about your activities from a reliable source, and that Mr James, is all I am at liberty or prepared to say.'

Outside the balmy night air felt good on my face as I shook Brian Gore's hand. Paul had already set off back home a few minutes earlier.

'By the way Richard, I had a visit from some gentlemen this afternoon. They told me they were from the government, something about MI5 or 6 they said that they knew I was acting for you and wanted to know what information I was holding on your behalf.'

This bit of news concerned me. 'What did you say Brian?'

'Oh, nothing much,' he smiled and said, 'I just told them I'd never heard of you and left it at that.'

'Do you reckon they believed you?'

'Bah, never in a thousand years,' he laughed out loud. 'Good night Richard.'

From what I could gather we had been arrested because someone had 'leaked' our operation to the Police, saying that a group of men dressed in army clothing were using real firearms and shooting people. So based on this report an anti-terrorist unit of armed Police had been sent along with other police to investigate, with instructions to apprehend and bring in for further questioning. This was the story as given to me, but I wasn't convinced and as sure as hell I was determined to get to the bottom of it.

As soon as I got close to home I found a telephone box and called the emergency number for my Controller, in this case Jimmy, but all I got was number unobtainable. I was even more puzzled. I then tried the number for Ash the result was the same. As a last resort I tried O'Rourke's direct line, again the continuous tone of number unobtainable. This did not make sense. I drove to another telephone box and went through the same procedure and got the same result. Exasperated I then asked the operator to check the numbers for me, and each time the story was the same.

'Sorry sir this is a spare line.'

'It can't be,' I replied, 'I only used it twenty-four hours ago!'

'Sorry sir according to my records this line has been a spare line for some considerable time now.'

'What do you mean by a considerable time?' I asked, 'weeks…months…or years?'

'Hmm, I'm not too sure as I don't have access to the full records, but based on the information at my disposal the subscriber to the last number gave up that line over six months ago.'

'You're joking...I only called it less than twenty-four hours ago...'

'I'm sorry sir, you must be mistaken. This line has not been in use for some considerable time...'

'But...'

'There's nothing more I can tell you. Sorry sir, goodbye.' With that the line went dead.

'Shit...' I banged my fist against the wall. It didn't make sense. I suddenly felt very vulnerable. I had been stitched up, but what could I do? I decided I would try and see Ash first thing in the morning and with that I slammed the car door and with wheels spinning I set off home.

Chapter 15

It was dead on the dot of nine-thirty when Brian Gore entered the grade two listed house used as the office of Jackson, Harper and Gore solicitors. 'Good morning ladies,' he said addressing both his secretary and the receptionist as he closed the outside door behind him. 'Would you bring me a coffee Elizabeth?' he asked his secretary as he entered his office closing the door behind him. Placing his brief case on his desk, he picked up the pile of mail and hastily shuffled through its contents. Nothing desperately urgent there he thought to himself as he moved round the other side of the desk and sat down. It was at this juncture he noticed the open door of the safe. 'Elizabeth, Elizabeth…' He was up and over to his office door in three big strides, 'Elizabeth…'

'Yes Mr Gore.' A female voice floated to him from the kitchenette where his secretary was making his coffee.

'Forget the coffee and come to my office immediately.'

There was a sense of urgency in his tone, which had Elizabeth abandon the coffee without giving it a second thought. 'Just coming Mr Gore just coming.' She quickly rushed to his office and closed the door.' Yes Mr Gore, is there a problem?'

Gore sat down at his desk and motioned Elizabeth to do the same, picking up a pencil he idly tapped his teeth with it as he looked up at the ceiling. All the time Elizabeth, his secretary, sat there in silence. He stopped tapping and looked straight at her. 'Hmm…Elizabeth have you been in here this morning?'

'Of course Mr Gore.' She answered, 'I brought in the post, why?' Her face looking puzzled.

'Did you notice anything odd?'

She thought for a little while before answering. 'I can't say that I did. Well nothing out of the ordinary why?'

'Have you touched the safe?'

'No. Why would I?'

'Hmm.' Once again Brian looked up at the ceiling, 'Well if you haven't and I haven't, then who has?'

'How do you mean Mr Gore?' Brian looked back at Elizabeth and didn't speak for a moment or two. His gaze moved from her face to the safe. She followed his gaze. Suddenly she saw the open door of the safe and gave an involuntary start. 'The safe is open!'

'I know Elizabeth, that's why I asked if you had been to it this morning. Now you're quite sure you haven't been to it?'

'Of course I am Mr Gore.' Her annoyance at not being believed was apparent in the tone of her voice.

Brian hurriedly tried to smooth her ruffled feathers. 'That's fine Elizabeth. I'm sure it was all locked up when I left last night.' He said more to himself than anyone else. He fell silent trying to think back and retrace his movements just prior to his leaving the office the previous night. He got up from his desk and picked up a couple of imaginary files. Yes that's right, he made his way over to the safe. He remembered placing a couple of his client's files into the safe. He paused there for a moment and feigned to push the door closed. Yes he remembered doing just that. At this point he stopped dead in his tracks. What happened next? Ah yes of course the phone rang. He retraced his footsteps back to his desk and sat down, pretended to pick the phone. That was it, it was Anne James phoning about Richard's arrest, he then replaced the imaginary phone, stood up and went back to the safe, picked up an imaginary file then started to walk back to his desk when he changed his mind. All this time Elizabeth his secretary watched on in silence and somewhat bemused.

'What on earth are you doing Mr Gore?' she asked unable to contain her curiosity any longer.

'Shh Elizabeth, I'm just retracing everything I did last night before I left.'

'Oh I see,' she said nodding her head, 'and have you covered everything?'

'No not yet. Now where was I? Ah yes of course, Mrs James had phoned and I went over to the safe and picked up a file...' Brian walked to the safe and once again picked up an imaginary file and walked back towards his desk and paused. 'Got it! I didn't take the file, I returned it to the safe and then closed the door.' Brian turned and headed back to the safe and pretended to place the file back inside and shut the imaginary safe door and locked it. 'Yes, that's it I placed the file back in the safe and locked the safe door. Bingo, I came back to my desk,' he walked back to his desk, 'checked the window was closed and locked, I then made sure everything was switched off and that I hadn't left anything on my desk and I then left my office closing the door behind me. By the way Elizabeth, the burglar alarm, was it on or off when you arrived this morning?'

'It was on Mr Gore.'

'And windows?'

'How do you mean Mr Gore?'

'This morning when you arrived were there any windows left open or anything like that, any sign of a break-in?' He subconsciously jangled the safe keys in his pocket as he spoke then realisation dawned on him. 'Sorry Elizabeth, I definitely locked the safe because here are the keys.' He pulled his hand from his pocket and held up a bunch of keys. 'Now the windows, were any open?'

'Not that I noticed. Anyway if there had been any the alarm would have been going wouldn't it?'

'Hmm. You're right it would, unless…'

'Unless what Mr Gore?'

'Nothing...' His mind was racing away, had this anything to do with the two visitors from Her Majesty's Government he wondered. Was it anything to do with Richard James' predicament? He wasn't sure but suddenly he had a sneaking suspicion that this would turn out to be far from the normal petty criminal. He wouldn't mind betting that the men from the ministry had more than just a passing interest in the office of Jackson, Harper and Gore solicitors! 'Elizabeth I want you to keep this quiet for a little while…'

'But what about the Police Mr Gore, we ought to phone the Police and report it…'

'All in good time, but for now do as I say. Anyway coffee,' his voice took on a lighter note, 'come on Elizabeth chop, chop I need my caffeine.'

He waited until Elizabeth was out of the way then he picked up the phone and telephoned James Fruit Farms.

The loud jangle of the farm's telephone could be heard right the way into the orchard where I was busy setting up the irrigation plant.

'Are you going to get that Richard?' Mr James senior asked.

'No Anne's there she'll get it.'

The jangling stopped and a couple of moments later I heard Anne calling me. 'Richard, telephone.'

I waved to her in acknowledgement and made my way to the farm office.

'It's Brian Gore on the phone.' She said as I got within earshot. 'Will you take it at home or in the office?' She asked.

'I'll take it in the office.' I went into the farm office and picked up the phone. 'Hello Brian.' There was a click as Anne replaced the phone indoors.

'Hello Richard, can you pop down to see me?'

'When?' I asked

'Now if possible.'

'Is everything all right?' I asked wondering what could be wrong.

'Of course Richard, it's just that something has come to light that needs your urgent attention.'

He sounded tired and his voice sounded strained, which led me to believe all was not well, so with this uppermost in my mind I agreed to leave straightaway.

As I opened the front door to the offices of Jackson, Harper and Gore I was greeted by the young lady receptionist with on over zealous smile. I immediately sensed she was trying her hardest to put on a brave face. 'Good morning can I help you sir?'

'Good morning, I believe Mr Gore is expecting me.'

'May I have your name sir?'

'Yes it's Richard James.' I replied.

She immediately scanned through the morning's appointments. 'I'm sorry sir there seems to be some mistake. You did say your name was Mr James didn't you?' Again she looked down her list of appointments and shook her head. 'I'm terribly sorry Mr James; would you tell me the time that Mr Gore was expecting you?' At this point Brian's secretary, Elizabeth, came out of his office and recognised me.

'It's Mr James isn't it?' she enquired.

'Yes that's right; I believe Mr Gore is expecting me.'

'I was...'

The young receptionist was about to say something but was interrupted by Elizabeth 'Wendy would you get Mr Gore some coffee please, and Mr James, would you like coffee or would you prefer tea?'

'Coffee would be fine.' I answered.

Elizabeth smiled and indicated to the open office door. 'Please Mr James, go through and Wendy will bring your coffee in a minute.' She turned her attention to Wendy, who was still waiting to advise her about my not being on her list, 'Come, come Wendy Coffee for two, there's a good girl.' With that she turned on her heel and went over to her desk where she sat down, put on her headphones, pressed her foot down on the foot pedal under her desk and started to type.

I gently closed the door behind me as I entered Brian's office. He immediately looked up from what he was doing and invited me to sit down in the chair positioned in front of his desk. I had barely had time to sit down when there was a gentle tap on the door and Wendy, the receptionist, entered carrying a tray with two cups of coffee and a plate of biscuits, which she placed between us on Brian's desk and quickly withdrew back to the outer office closing the door behind her.

'Richard good of you to come so promptly, and I know it was very short notice but I really felt that in this instance it was necessary.'

'Sure Brian, but why, what's the urgency?' He didn't answer straightaway but pointed behind me. I turned in my chair to see what he was pointing at.

'That was how I found it this morning when I got here.'

He was talking about his safe, but I didn't understand what he was really on about. I turned back to face him and asked, 'So what's wrong with your safe?'

'Nothing apart from being wide open.' He replied.

I snivelled around in my chair and took a second look, then turned back to face him, shrugged my shoulders and said, 'So what? Don't you usually have it open during the day?' I still couldn't see what he was driving at.

'Of course I have it open during the day, but that's not what I'm on about. What I am saying is that when I arrived at work this morning and came in here I found the safe wide open, and that was laying there.' He indicated to a manila folder lying on the floor in front of the open safe with some documents poking out.

'Is that folder the one I brought down to you a little while back?' I asked. Brian nodded. Slowly I started to realise what he was saying. He had had a break-in and the possible repercussions started to dawn on me. I got up from my chair and without speaking walked slowly over towards the safe. 'Anything missing?' I asked.

'Nothing that I'm aware of, but the question is do I tell the Police?'

'The Police haven't been told about this then?'

'No, I thought it best to leave them out of it until after I'd spoken to you.' He fell silent waiting for my reaction but for a moment or two my mind was full of confusing thoughts.

'Do you want me to call them in Richard?' I was still silent as I thought about whether or not to involve the Police. I wasn't sure. Slowly my thoughts cleared and rightly or wrongly I decided not to call the Police and slowly shook my head. 'Ok then no Police. The next thing is to check through your papers and see exactly what's gone if anything, wouldn't you agree?'

'Before we do that how did they get in, any idea?'

'I'm not sure.'

'Perhaps I could have a bit of a poke about then.'

'Help yourself Richard.'

The first thing I did was to scrutinise the window for any sign of forced entry, not a thing. Next I carefully examined Brian's office door but again nothing.

'What about your alarm wasn't it on?' I asked.

'Oh it was on all right. When I first saw the safe open I thought I had forgotten to lock it, but then I distinctly remember doing so because after Anne telephoned and told me what had happened I was going to bring the file with me to Canterbury. In fact the safe was unlocked then because I was about to lock it when she phoned me. I took out your file, thought better of it and put it back and locked the safe. I even questioned Elizabeth. I asked her a couple of times just to make sure she hadn't been in it this morning, in fact she got quite upset about it.'

'What about the alarm Brian, didn't it go off?'

'Not according to the alarm panel.'

'I presume the alarm was set?'

'Of course it was!' Brian snapped 'What do you take me for Richard some sort of idiot? It's more than my job's worth not to set the alarm.'

'So tell me Brian, why didn't it trigger?'

'I don't know I'm not an expert on alarms. Anyway for all I know it could have gone off but according to the alarm panel the alarm was not activated.'

'Hmm.' my gut feeling was this was a professionally organised job and had all the hallmarks of the department, unless of course it was from across the water. 'What about strangers? Have you noticed anyone taking an unhealthy interest in your offices here?'

'I can't say I have.'

'No strangers, no sign of a break-in and no alarm tripped.' I repeated loudly to myself.

'There was something...'

'What was that then?' I asked.

'The two men from the ministry who asked about the information I was holding for you. I don't expect it's connected, well not with the break-in anyway.'

'What did they actually say?'

'I can't remember their exact words, they said they were from some Government Department, MI5 or MI6 can't remember now anyway they had official I.D. with them.'

'What did they want exactly?'

'They said they had heard about your arrest and seemed to know I was acting for you. They then asked me what information had I got as they wanted to help. All that sort of stuff, why do you think they had something to do with the break-in?'

'I'm not sure...'

The more Brian told me about them the more convinced I was that they had something to do with it. I was convinced they were from the either 'Five' or the 'Circus', either way it was not good, but it would explain the professionalism of the job. In fact the chances were that they had not forced an entry, they had in fact over-ridden the alarm and walked in through the front door by unlocking it.

'So where do we go from here Richard?'

'I'm not sure, but I need to know what has been taken so let's have a look through the file.'

'You're sure you don't want the Police involved?'

'I'm certain Brian. No Police.' With that he retrieved the file from his safe and brought it over to his desk and placed it in front of me.

It took quite some time going through each piece of paper and each photograph, but eventually the task was completed and everything seemed

162

to be there. I had just put the last piece of evidence away when I suddenly remembered I hadn't seen the photographs of the car I used for the bombs in Dublin. Again I took out all the papers and again I went through them piece by piece and sure enough that photograph was missing along with two or three others such as one of me dressed as a tourist in Dublin, the car's registration and the ones I had surreptitiously taken of Seamus. I was now almost certain it was the work of the department and something was going on but I didn't know what. It puzzled me why they had gone to all that trouble and only taken a couple of photographs and not the whole file, unless I was right about it being someone from across the water! The more I thought about it the more I warmed to the possibility, after all there had been collusion for years between loyalist paramilitaries and the security forces.

A couple of days after the so called break-in at the solicitors I received a telephone call. 'Sorry to trouble you sir, British Telecomm engineers here I'm just giving you a quick call from the exchange as we have had a fault report outstanding on this line.'

'Have you?'

'Yes sir. I was wondering if you've been having any trouble making calls from this number?'

'No, why?'

'Oh, it's just that I've carried out a number of checks at the exchange but everything seems fine at this end. Unfortunately whoever wrote up the docket left some of the information off so I'm a little lost as to what the actual fault could be. It rather seems to be at y…' just at that moment there was a click and the line seemed to go dead.

'Hello…hello…' I rattled the receiver rest, but the line was as dead as a dodo. 'Damn.' I slammed the phone down and was about to walk away when it rang. I grabbed the phone.

'Hello…'

'Sorry about that I lost you for a moment or two. It does appear that there is a fault somewhere between the exchange and your phone. We're checking it out right now. Sorry for the trouble sir, goodbye.' With that he hung up. What a strange conversation I thought to myself. I picked up my phone just to check that it was working but all I could get was a series of clicks. I frowned. Strange it was working fine until British Telecom phoned and now it's faulty, but there again he did say it had been reported faulty. Still not a lot I could do about it. Just at that precise moment there was a knock on the front door. On the doorstep stood a medium sized bloke with short ash blond hair brushed straight back. He wore a pair of rimless spectacles and a pale blue shirt with the words British Telecomm emblazoned across the breast pocket.

'Sorry to trouble you sir British Telecom, I believe the engineers spoke to you a short time ago about a reported fault on this line. It appears that the fault may well be with your installation at this end sir, may I come in and check the hand set.' He smiled and waited to be invited in.

'Well...err...of course.' I held the door open.

'Technology, what would we do without it!' He quipped as he went straight to the phone picked it up and rattled the receiver rest. 'Hmm, this bit of technology sounds is if we need to do without it. Dead as a dodo. Sorry about that I'll just pop to my van and get a new handset, be back in a mo,' with that he was gone.

I sensed all was not what it seemed and opened the door to check on my visitor, but outside was a British Telecom transit van with its back doors open. At this point I decided I was getting paranoid and closed the door. Perhaps I should have followed up my instincts?

'Was he all right about it John?' The voice on the van's radio said to the BT engineer.

'Yeah, no problem swallowed it straight away.'

'Don't be too sure my friend. Don't underestimate Mr James. He's a shrewd cookie and I have it on good authority that he is one of the better ones. So be careful, one slip and our cover is blown and you know we can't afford that. The department doesn't suffer fools gladly.'

'Ok, ok. So he's a shrewd operator but he hasn't a clue. Tell control we should be clear in...say five minutes. Where's Frank?'

'He should have the tap in place by now.'

'Ok. Give me two minutes and I'll be out of there.' With that there was a metallic click followed by a lot of white noise. The BT engineer started to whistle as he picked up the new hand set unscrewed the base, checked the internal connector block and replaced the base. Well, all over now bar the shouting, he thought to himself, it's not a bad life in working in this section of MI5. He remembered when he was posted to Ulster back in the 70's working in that theatre of 'black operations' that was particularly 'dirty' so much so that it was known as dirty tricks department. Funny how things move on. Out there he had worked in the Information Policy Unit under Mr Smith and here he was now in MI5 which was headed up by Mr Smith, strange old world wasn't it? He shut the rear doors of the transit van and made his way back up the path to the house.

'Well that should do it sir,' he said as he screwed the last screw into the line box, 'what about extensions? I just need to check them.' Again he smiled at me as if to reassure me. I nodded.

'Of course.' I said. 'There are two extensions, one's upstairs in our bedroom and the other's over in the farm office, so if you'll follow me I'll show you the one upstairs first.' I started up the stairs in front of him; again I had that niggling feeling that he wasn't who he purported to be. In the bedroom he picked up the receiver listened a second or two shrugged his shoulders and said, 'That's fine. Now if you wouldn't mind showing me where the other one is I'll get this all wrapped up for you.'

Just over a mile away in a small telephone exchange a British Telecom engineer was just tidying up after completing his last job. All his time in working for British Telecom he'd heard of some strange goings on, but this was the strangest. After all why would some research engineers from Martlesham Heath want access to this tiny exchange in the middle of nowhere? He could have appreciated their interest in somewhere like Ashford, Canterbury or even somewhere like Faversham, but not a tiny village like this. After all how could the level of traffic through this exchange justify their interest. Ah well it wasn't his problem, he'd done what they had requested, he'd made available a pair on the two subscribers so they could fit their equipment. They'd said it was so they could monitor traffic from an average household, but to him it looked remarkably like a phone tap. There again they have some very sophisticated equipment in Martlesham, but that was only to be expected after all it was the main research centre for British Telecom. He gave one last look around, did a final gas check and signed the exchange book before pulling the doors closed.

'Thank you Mr James just one more thing I need to do before I leave,' the engineer said as we made our way back to the house. 'I need to use your telephone to call in. Would that be all right sir?'
'Sure it would.' I stood close enough to see the number he dialled without being too obvious, I still was not totally convinced of this man's credentials.
'By the way, what did you say your name was?' I asked.
'I didn't sir.' He grinned at me.
'Well would you give me your name?' His grin now turned to a frown and his eyes grew hard.
'Why sir?' he asked
'Because…'
'Smith sir.' He said hurriedly cutting me short. 'It's John Smith.' He gave that smile again. 'I'm down here for a few days from Martlesham Heath. On relief you know. Why don't you phone 151? In fact why not do it now?' Before I could stop him he had dialled the number. 'Hello, faults this is the engineer at James Fruit Farms, I have Mr James with me and he would like

165

to speak to the line manager. Yes I'll put him on now, thank you.' He thrust the phone towards me, 'Here you are sir. Just to put your mind at ease have a word with the line manager.'

I took hold of the phone just as a young lady's voice came on the line. 'Putting you through now.'

'Hello my name is James, Richard James and I wondered if you could confirm that you have a Mr John Smith working here on relief from Martlesham Heath?' I paused and waited for the answer.

'You did say Martlesham Heath didn't you sir?'

'Yes that's right Martlesham Heath.'

'It was a Mr John Smith you were enquiring about wasn't it sir?'

'That's right...John Smith.'

'Hold on please sir.' There was a click and the line went dead for a moment or two as the operator seemed to search some sort of database. 'Hello sir,' the operator came back on the line. 'Yes I can confirm that we do have an engineer by that name here at Martlesham Heath.'

'Thank you.'

'No problem sir. Is there anything else I can help you with?'

'No that's all thank you, goodbye.'

'Did they confirm it then?' The engineer enquired.

'Yes they did, sorry for doubting your story.'

'That's ok. Better to get these things confirmed. You can never tell who is who nowadays;' he said smiling knowing full well that the name John Smith would always be confirmed at any exchange, after all that was the procedure as laid down by the corridors of power.

Hmm, I thought to myself, they may have confirmed the name but I'm still not totally convinced. I watched as he dialled 151 again and asked them to test the line on ring back. In less than thirty seconds the telephone rang. 'Hi, yes thank you. Bye. Right Mr James all fixed, would you please sign here.' He indicated to a box at the bottom of his worksheet which he passed to me.

'What's this for?' I asked, 'I've never had to sign before.'

'Sorry Mr James. I should have said, it's only for the new handset.'

'Oh I see,' but I didn't see. 'I suppose it's...normal nowadays?'

'Yeah, it's getting so we have to sign for everything now. Tightening up all round. Procedures bah, more like jobs for the boys! Thanks Mr James, good bye.' With that he let himself out and was gone. I watched him drive off down the road before I picked up the telephone; there was a click and then dialling tone.

Not too far from James fruit farm the British Telecom transit van pulled into the side of the road. John Smith BT engineer got out, walked to the side of the van and gently peeled of the vinyl BT signs and motifs. He now went to the back of the van opened the door to reveal a few reels of telephone wire a small box of clips and the handset he had removed from the home of Richard James. One by one he tossed the items over the fence into the woodland beyond all were quickly swallowed by the thick carpet of undergrowth and brambles. However that was not all the van held, in fact set further back towards the front seats of the van was some of the most sophisticated electronics equipment around. In fact the van was a veritable mobile GCHQ more than capable for what it had just been used or what it was about to be used for. Jack Carmody, alias John Smith next stripped off his pale blue shirt to reveal a black T shirt beneath. He carefully removed the ash blond wig to reveal closely cropped dark unruly hair. The last vestige of John Smith was the plain glass rimless spectacles which he placed with the wig and the shirt into a small holdall on the front passenger seat. Just as he had finished removing the final traces of colouring from his eyebrows a white Sierra pulled in behind him. To an idle onlooker the car appeared to be nothing other than a standard white Ford Sierra, but had they taken the time to scrutinise it then they would have noticed little things which set it apart from the every day family car. There was the detail on the instrument panel that showed turbo pressure. The car, had it been placed alongside the standard Sierra, sat approximately an inch lower than normal and the tyres were designed for speeds in excess of 140mph. yes this was not your average Sierra, this car was designed for speed and was one of the new breeds of Sierra an RS Cosworth. As cars go, although it did not advertise itself as such, this was one of the best. Jack turned and greeted the driver.

'Hi Jimmy. All set from our side, it's now up to you and your lot.'

'Ok Jack so far so good.' The man in the white car spoke with a slight Belfast accent. 'You know the score we always win in the department, you of all people should know that Jack.'

'I know Jimmy, I know. So tell me what's the set-up with these two characters?'

'In what way?'

'Well this James bloke, he seems quite a decent bloke, bit slow on the uptake but decent enough.'

'Listen sunshine, Richard James is far from slow on the uptake. Be very careful, he's a shrewd person and more than a little handy. In fact he's one of the best operators in the Circus, so just be careful. You forget I know how he works; I know his strengths and his limitations. I know what makes him tick. You don't work as a field operative's controller without knowing a bit about your operator, and where James is concerned I know everything there is to know. You of all people should know, that in this game you have no friends, you can't afford that sort of luxury and in this world dog eats dog!'

'So who is going to eat you Jimmy?'

'Not you Jack, not you.' Jimmy answered his voice soft and menacing, then just as quickly his mood changed and his tone now became very business like, 'right, it's the department's show now. Thank you for your and Five's help in this matter, and good bye Jack.'

Chapter 16

The more I used the telephone at home the more convinced I was that it had a tap on it. Every time I picked it up to use there would be a click as if someone, somewhere had picked up a party line and was listening. I even contacted faults and got it checked out to be told that there was nothing wrong with it. I also queried the possibility that it had become a party line and again BT confirmed that this was not the case, but I remained unconvinced. In the end I got so paranoid about it being tapped that I used to always make important calls from the call box in the village. What with the break-in at the solicitors and now this telephone situation I was not surprised when I noticed a white Sierra parked up the road from the house. At first I didn't take too much notice of it, it was just a car parked on the other side of the road, until Anne commented about how she had seen it parked there for the last three or four days and wondered who it belonged to. In the end I decided I would investigate it by going over there to see who, if anyone was in it. As I walked up the road towards it, whoever it was decided the time had come for them to go and with squealing tyres they roared off down the road before I had chance to get a good look at them. Convinced that would be an end to it I decided to leave it for the time being.

'Did you see who it was love?' called Anne.

'No, they shot off before I could get close enough, but I don't think they'll be back now they know I've spotted them.' But I was wrong. Within the hour they were back. Again I set off up the road and just as before they drove off at high. I hoped that they would soon tire of this silly game but that was not to be and the routine was repeated many, many times throughout the week, in fact it got so bad that, as a last resort, I telephoned the Police. However, the Police were far from helpful and at one point it was even suggested that we were imagining it. I pushed it as far as I could but they said, "Without proof there is nothing we can do." Yeah, I thought to myself, nothing you can do, my arse! It's more a case of you won't do anything rather than you can't do anything. I now had the distinct feeling that we were, or undoubtedly I was, more the just a passing interest to somebody out there. Wherever we went and whatever we did we were under constant surveillance and it certainly appeared as if I was now the subject of what was tantamount to 'mind games.' It was as if I was being specifically targeted by the department of Psychological Warfare a department which had been set-up in 1971 within the Information Policy Unit in Ulster and was based in Lisburn headquarters along with the intelligence service. In the end these 'mind games' got so bad that I decided desperate measures were needed to put an end to them. So on the Friday, five weeks to the day since all of this started, I set off to Ashford and JITC

Barracks where I was determined to see Ash, and at just after eleven-thirty I turned into the main entrance and went into the gatehouse to sign in.

'Thank you Mr ...err...James.' The Corporal on duty looked up from the visitor's log and handed me a visitor's car pass. 'Place the disk in the windscreen of your car and park it over there by the Guardroom. Once you've parked your vehicle check in with the duty Sergeant who will contact the officer concerned and issue you with your visitor pass.'

'Thank you Corporal.'

The Corporal raised the barrier and I drove over to the allocated visitor's space. Now I felt I was getting somewhere. I may not be able to get through by phone, but at least I can get in to see you Ash, I thought to myself as I parked out side the Guardroom.

'Good morning sir. Print your name there and sign here,' the Sergeant indicated on the visitor's log book. 'Over here enter the person you wish to see, and car registration.'

I did what was asked of me and then the Sergeant checked that everything was correctly entered.

'Thank you sir. I notice you wish to see Colonel Ash. Do you have an appointment?'

'No I don't have an appointment Sergeant, but I'm sure he'll see me.'

'I'm sorry Mr...' he again turned the log book around to look at my name, 'Err Mr James, he doesn't see anyone without an appointment.' With this response I looked through my wallet for my old Identity Card. The Sergeant looked on with mild amusement as I shuffled through a mound of pieces of paper and eventually uncovered my UDR Identity Card. He picked it up and peered at it for what seemed an age. He smartly came to attention.

'Err, sorry Captain James, sorry about that sir I didn't realise. I'll try Colonel Ash now.' He immediately picked up the phone and dialled the Colonel's internal extension. 'Hello, Guardroom here. I have a Captain James to see the Colonel.' The Sergeant waited patiently for an answer. 'Sorry to trouble you Colonel but I have a Captain James here to see you...My name is Brown, Sergeant Brown Sir...' He paused and listened to what the Colonel had to say and then replied. 'Yes Sir... I see Sir...' He then looked across at me and nodded. 'Thank you Sir.'

He slowly replaced the receiver and looked me straight in the eyes; his face gave nothing away as he reached for the bell on the desk. Suddenly his hand froze and instead of ringing the alarm he started to talk in a controlled even voice. 'I'm sorry sir according to the Colonel, you are to leave the barracks immediately and should you persist in this constant charade of purporting to be a Captain in Her Majesty's Forces I must warn you that you will be arrested for imposing as an officer of the realm. I must insist that you return to your vehicle and leave these barracks immediately. In fact to make sure you do leave you will be escorted by an armed guard from these grounds. Also I insist on having the identity card that is in your possession....' His hand once more reached towards the bell push but before he could finish I was out of the guardroom and into my car. Engine running and heading back to the gate. As I approached the barrier went up and I shot out onto the main road, swung to the left and headed off towards Faversham. 'Shit' I muttered to myself, 'so where does that leave me now?' I checked my rear view mirror half expecting some sort of pursuit, but there was nothing. I decided I had better ease up just in case some hawk-eyed local copper clocked me, because the last thing I needed right now was to be involved in a Police chase.

Half an hour later I entered the outskirts of Faversham, turning right off the London road I headed off towards Oare and the small industrial complex where Paul's workshop was situated. As I turned into Hall road I was surprised to see a Police car parked on the workshop car park and another unmarked car alongside. Now what have we got here? I wondered as I drove passed and stopped a discrete distance from Jones Engineering. I manoeuvred my car into a position where I was able to observe the goings on without attracting any attention. As I watched two guys in grey suits got out of the unmarked vehicle. They must be CID or Special Branch I thought to myself, as they were joined by the two uniformed blokes from the Police car. At that moment a Police personnel carrier swung round the corner into Hall road and pulled onto the car park. The side door slid open and another half dozen uniformed coppers appeared and stood in a group not far from their colleagues. Once they had arrived on the scene, the two plain clothes coppers entered the building followed by the two from the Police car whilst the second group just stood around chatting. Well, well, well. I thought to myself, what are those bastards after you for this time? This looks remarkably like a shake down to me and it looks as if someone is trying to fit you up my old mate and all I can do under the circumstances is to sit tight and watch.

Paul was just finishing off some paperwork when he heard the metallic ring of footsteps as people hurriedly climbed the metal stairs towards his office. Suddenly the office door flew open and he was confronted by two men.
 'Please, do come in.' He greeted the two interlopers sarcastically, 'a rush job is it?'
 'Police. I'm Detective Sergeant Hall,' the man held up his warrant card, 'and this is Detective Constable Denstrode,' he said indicating his to colleague who also produced his warrant card, 'I believe you're Mr Jones, Mr Paul Jones. We would like to have a chat with you'
 'About what?' Paul asked.

'Oh about this and that,' came the vague reply from Hall whilst Denstrode, his colleague, busied himself looking around the office.

'Which 'this' and what 'that' in particular?' Paul countered sarcastically.

'Anything of interest?' Hall addressed his colleague.

'Not at present Sarge, but maybe a closer look with Forensics would reveal something.'

'Excuse me,' Paul interjected, 'I asked you what this was all about?'

'Oh don't you know sir?' Hall smiled ruefully.

'If I did then would I be asking?'

'I suppose not sir. Do you mind if we have a look round?'

'Why?'

'We could always get a search warrant if necessary sir, but I don't think that will be necessary will it sir?' He smiled again.

Paul shrugged his shoulders, 'Will it make any difference if I say no?'

'Sorry sir, you did say that would be all right didn't you?'

'No I didn't say it would be all right.'

'Oh sorry, I was sure you agreed. Mr Jones did say that he didn't mind, didn't he constable?'

'I thought I heard him agree Sergeant.'

'There Mr Jones, it appears as if my colleague also heard you agree. So it's all right if we take a look round then?' Hall didn't wait for Paul's answer. He nodded to Denstrode who opened the office door and called down the stairs to someone out of Paul's sight.

'Ok, have a look round and bag anything that looks as if it could be of interest. Now Mr Jones, I think it's time we all had a little chat, don't you?' Hall directed his gaze at Paul.

'Like I said, about what?'

'A white van, France and a young man. Ring any bells?'

'No.' Paul pulled a face, shrugged his shoulders and shook his head. 'Can't say they do, why should they?'

'Now you do surprise me Mr Jones. Perhaps if we go to the station it would help?'

'Help what?' Paul frowned. He didn't like this sarcastic bumped up fart of a copper. Who the hell was he to walk in here and start throwing his weight about? 'So what's this all about? You come in here like you own the place and start talking in riddles, then you decide that you're going to take a look around whether I agree to it or not. What's your game?'

'Sorry sir. I would have thought that was obvious. We are investigating a crime and you are kindly helping us with our enquiries. Does that answer your question?'

'What am I supposed to have done?'

Hall ignored him and called down stairs to the team who were searching the workshop. 'Anything lads?'

'No, not as yet,' came the reply.

'Ok, leave it for now. Mr Jones is coming along with us for a little chat about things.' He turned to Paul, 'aren't you Mr Jones.'

'On what grounds are you arresting me?'

'Who said you were under arrest? No Mr Jones, you're merely helping us with our enquiries. Now if you'd be so kind as to get your coat and lock up your workshop then we will take a ride to the station.'

'Not so fast. So what happens if I refuse?'

'Then that would be very foolish Mr Jones wouldn't it?'

'Why would it?'

'Because I would then have to arrest you.'

'So I am right then. I am under arrest.'

'I wish you wouldn't keep saying that Mr Jones because that is not true. You are helping us with our enquiries and that is all. Now shall we go Mr Jones?'

Paul picked up his jacket, and followed Hall out of the office and down the stairs to the small entrance door of his workshop. 'Just one thing before we go...'

'What's that Mr Jones?'

'Is it all right if I pop to the loo?'

'Of course Mr Jones, of course.' Hall gave him a patronising smile, 'we can wait.'

Paul made his way to the back of the workshop and to the toilet. Once inside he shut the door and as quietly as he could he slid the bolt home. Quickly he went through his pockets looking for something to write on and with. "Ah just what I need" he thought to himself as he pulled out a stub of pencil and a piece of chalk. Now Richard my friend, if I write a cryptic message will you find it and will you recognise its significance? All I need is something to write on. Then it struck him, the toilet roll. Carefully he unrolled a portion of the roll and carefully wrote a letter and a figure on each sheet rolling it back up as he did.

'Come on Jones, what are you doing making your will?' The dulcet tones of Hall's voice floated to him through the closed door of the toilet. Someone tried the handle and then there was banging on the door.

'Come on open up.' Denstrode shouted to him through the closed door. 'If you're not out by the time I count to five then we'll force the door.' He hammered on the door again. 'Do you hear me?'

'Ok, ok. Just coming.' Paul called as he rolled up the last part of the message, flushed the toilet and unbolted the door. 'So what's all the excitement about, can't a bloke have a crap in peace?'

'Come on Jones let's go.' Denstrode grabbed Paul's arm to hurry him along choosing to ignore Paul's comment.

'All right, I'm coming.' He said pulling his arm free of Denstrode as he made his way towards the front of the workshop. Outside Hall and Denstrode escorted him over to their car where he was invited to sit in the back with Denstrode alongside him.

The interview room in Sittingbourne Police station was small and compact. The décor was Home Office regulation magnolia and the room was furnished simply with a table and four chairs, two chairs situated opposite each other on the long sides of the table. Mounted on the table, which had one end pushed up against the outer wall, was a cassette tape recorder, to one side of this was a telephone and mounted on the wall a large red button. This was a 'Panic Alarm' button to summon assistance in an emergency. In fact the layout and furnishings of the room could have been in any Police station throughout British Isles. The door of the interview room was closed with Hall and Denstrode seated facing Paul across the table.

'Now Mr Jones, as I said earlier, you are helping us with our enquiries into a serious crime that happened over in Lyon in France…'

'What crime?' Paul interrupted, 'I've never been anywhere near France, let alone Lyon.'

'If that's the case Mr Jones then no doubt we'll have this sorted out in no time at all. Now if I may continue Mr Jones?' Hall raised an eyebrow, 'thank you. As I was saying, the French Police have asked us to assist them in tracing the whereabouts of the driver of a white van with a British number plate. This van was seen by a witness at the scene of an armed robbery during which shots were fired and a security guard received multiple gunshot wounds from which he has since died. Now Mr Jones I would like you to think very carefully before you answer my next question…where were you Friday 21st?'

'At my workshop why?'

'Are you sure Mr Jones?'

'Of course I'm sure.' All this time Denstrode sat looking at Paul and not saying a word. In front of him on the table was his open notebook, in which he wrote the occasional comment and this he did now…'the witness replied in my workshop, and when asked again he answered "Of course I'm sure." '

'All right Mr Jones. Do you recognise this vehicle?' Hall pushed a photograph of a white van across the table to Paul.

Paul looked at the photograph and shook his head, 'Not particularly, should I?' he asked.

'Take your time Mr Jones. Now look at the registration. Tell me what does it say?'

Paul looked at the photograph again, and again he shook his head. 'Means nothing to me.'

'What's the van's registration Mr Jones?'

'E245XUJ'. Why?'

'Isn't it true that you hired a white van week ending the 21st with that registration?' Denstrode watched carefully as Paul stared at Hall.

'I don't know.'

'Well I suggest that you had better think a bit harder Mr Jones. Now did you or did you not hire a white van of the week in question?'

'I'm not sure. I'm always hiring vans...'

'Well you had better be sure. Did you or did you not hire a white van? Answer the question Mr Jones.'

Paul tried to remember. He had hired a van recently, but whether or not it was on the 21st he couldn't say without checking back through his paperwork.

'Well Mr Jones, I'm waiting?'

'All I can say is that I hire a lot of vans, white, blue, black all different colours but as to whether I hired one when you are asking about I can't say without checking back through my paperwork. Ah, wait a minute 21st you say...yeah I think I did hire a van that week and it was white, but there again there's thousands of white vans aren't there?'

'But only one with the registration E245XUJ Mr Jones and it's that one that we're particularly interested in. Now I'll ask you once again, did you or did you not hire that van?'

There was silence. Paul looked first at Hall then at Denstrode with half closed eyes, what was going on he asked himself. 'No I didn't...'

'Hmm, that's strange Mr Jones because we have traced that van to a hire company called 'vans-R-us', now according to the rental company's records you hired that van last and it was not returned to them until after the weekend that was after the 21st...' He let this fact sink in before speaking again. All the time Denstrode watched Paul's expression. 'Now Mr Jones,' Hall's voice held an edge to it, 'let's stop playing games. I know you had that van. That van was seen in Lyon on the Friday of that week. That was Friday the 21st, so Mr Jones lets cut the crap tell me where you were on the Friday in question?'

'I've already told you. I was not in Lyon. I was not even in Fr....'

'So where were you Mr Jones if you were not in Lyon?' Hall fell silent. You could have cut the atmosphere with a knife. 'You were seen Mr Jones...'

'No I wasn't in Lyon, I was in...'

'Yes Mr Jones, you were where?'

'I was...'

'Well Mr Jones...I'm waiting.'

'I was in my workshop.' Paul said lamely.

'Rubbish Mr Jones, we have a witness...If you were in your workshop you can of course prove it can't you?'

Paul racked his brains as to what he'd done that week. Then he remembered, he had been to Cheltenham to deliver some metalwork to GCHQ. 'Got it,' he grinned triumphantly at the two stone-faced coppers, 'I went to GCHQ that day. I delivered a job there.'

'If that's the case Mr Jones then it should be simple enough to prove your alibi.' Hall signalled to Denstrode to pass him a page from his notebook, scribbled something about GCHQ, folded it and pushed back his chair and got up. Opening the door of the interview room he called to a young constable, 'Here lad, take this to CID and get someone to call them and check it out and tell them it's urgently required.'

'Yes Sergeant.'

Hall shut the door and returned to his seat to await the outcome of the telephone call, he didn't have long to wait before there was a tap on the door which was then opened. Framed in the doorway was a fresh faced young constable, probably not much more than twenty-one and still wet behind the ears.

'Sergeant Hall, here's the reply from GCHQ.'

Hall took the piece of paper proffered by the young constable. 'Thank you constable that'll be all.' As he returned to his seat he unfolded the paper quickly scanned the page then he passed it over to Denstrode. The paper stated categorically that nobody with the name of Jones had signed in at GCHQ at either site in Cheltenham on the date in question, nor for that matter at any time in the previous two weeks. Hall looked up at the ceiling then back to Paul. Pushed back his chair and stood up. Denstrode did likewise.

'Mr Jones, I now want you to listen carefully to what I have to say...'

Paul instinctively knew by the tone of Hall's voice what was coming next.

'Mr Jones I am arresting you on suspicion of armed robbery and murder. You do not have to say anything, but it may harm your defence if you do not mention when questioned something which you may later rely on in court, anything you do say maybe given in evidence. Do you understand?'

Paul looked dumbfounded. 'This cannot be true. GCHQ took delivery of metal-work. I booked in so someone, somewhere is lying!'

Denstrode grabbed his arm and smartly snapped hand-cuffs about his wrist, yanked the arm behind him and snapped the other cuff around his other wrist.

'Come on Mr Jones, let's go.'

Paul, flanked either side by Denstrode and Hall, was escorted from the room and taken to the cells situated to the rear of the building.

It had been quite some time since Paul had left with the two non-uniformed blokes, but whilst I sat there another van appeared and a man and a woman got out went to the rear of the vehicle from which they removed a large case. Both then proceeded to put on white disposable boiler suits and made their way through the door into the workshop. I must have been there for at least an hour before they re-emerged carrying some polythene bags which I assumed contained items taken from the workshop. I waited until the last vehicle had left before I made any move. Fortunately Paul had the foresight when he took over the business to have an extra set of keys cut and gave them to me as a precaution against loss, or for use in emergency, and tonight was just such an occasion. I checked just to make certain that there were no Policemen lurking nearby, and having satisfied myself that the coast was clear I let myself in. Once inside I closed and locked the door, switched on the lights and started a painstaking inch by inch search of the premises. I didn't know what I was expecting to find, but all I knew was if there was something then I would recognise it when I saw it. The workshop revealed nothing, so the office was the next obvious place. Again after a painstaking search I drew a blank. I sat down and tried to think what I would do in the same situation, where would I leave a message that would not easily be discovered. I riffled through the desk, nothing. In the end I was convinced that I was chasing an imaginary message and decided to call it a day, but before leaving I needed to use the toilet. As I entered the loo a thought struck me, I wonder, I thought to myself, if...I started to carefully unroll the toilet roll...was it my imagination or was there something written on it? I tore off one sheet of toilet paper and looked at it closely. Bingo! There it was the letter 'G' followed by a figure'0'. I unrolled more of the toilet roll and it was now making sense, well sort of. The letters read Gore, but the figures 0194789 didn't mean anything to me. Perhaps Brian Gore knew something.

Through the steel door Paul could just about make out the sound of approaching footsteps and muffled voices. They stopped outside his cell door followed by a short rasping sound as the small aperture was opened and a pair of eyes stared through at him.
'You can have five minutes Ben that's all. If this ever gets out then I'll deny all knowledge.'
'Don't worry Frank, it won't.' There was a fresh noise. The sound of a key turning in a well oiled lock. The cell door swung open silently and there

framed in its doorway was Hall. He entered the small cell and the door closed behind him.

'Now Paul, it is Paul isn't it? We've checked through everything so start telling us what happened in Lyon…'

'But I keep telling you I have never been to Lyon. On the day in question I was making a delivery to Cheltenham, to GCHQ…'

'I'd love to believe you Paul, but the truth of the matter is that had you been to GCHQ then you would have signed in. The registration of your van would have been recorded and there would be a record of your visit, but there's nothing. In fact GCHQ have sent us copies of the visitor sheets for that day and the days either side of it and your name does not appear anywhere.'

'What about the bloke I saw…Didn't he confirm my visit?'

'You told me you saw a Mr Buckle, is that correct?'

'Yes a guy called Jim Buckle. He was my contact there.'

'Hmm. I see.' Hall paused as if deep in thought before speaking again. 'I'd love to believe you Paul, but you see that's impossible…'

'Why?'

'Because no such person works there…'

'What!'

'Like I said no such person works there. Jim Buckle does not exist! He is a figment of your imagination. GCHQ confirmed that there is no such person as Jim Buckle and there never has been, so I think it's about time you started telling us the truth. Don't you?'

'But I am telling you the truth…'

'Like you did about the van…'

'Well, three weeks ago I ask you. A lot has happened since then…'

'I know, like an armed robbery and murder in France. So come on the sooner you tell the truth the better…' Hall left the rest of the sentence hanging. He turned and knocked on the door. Again the scraping noise as the trap opened and a pair of eyes looked through, then the noise of the key turning and the door swung open.

'Thanks Frank…'

'What about my telephone call?'

Hall turned with a puzzled look on his face he asked, 'What telephone call. You're only allowed one and you made that.'

'So where is my solicitor?'

'How should I know sunshine?' There was a dull clang as the door slammed shut and the noise of the key turning in a well oiled lock. This was followed by another dull clang as the trap was slammed shut. Paul knew that he was being held on a trumped up charge, but for what reason he didn't know. He needed to prove his innocence and the only way to do that

178

was by getting a message to Brian Gore, if he failed then they, the faceless ones, will win.

Big Ben was striking the last of the ten 'bongs' at the start of the Ten o'clock news on ITV when the telephone at Brian Gore's house rang.
'Hello, Brian Gore speaking.'
'Hello Brian, sorry to call you at such a late hour…'
'Not at all Richard. What can I do for you?'
'It's not for….' A series of pips interrupted the conversation and Brian could hear the click as more coins were inserted. 'Sorry Brian, as I was saying it's not for me. It's for Paul. He's been arrested, but I don't know where they've taken him and Canterbury nick isn't being very helpful, nor is the HQ.'
'What about your contacts Richard, can they find out anything?'
'No good. When we got arrested before, they closed down the net so I've been isolated, you know the sort of thing. I no longer exist!'
'Ok, can you meet me at my office in, say twenty minutes?'
'Yes no problem.'
'Good I'll see you there.'

Dead on twenty minutes past ten Brian Gore arrived at his office and I followed him down the shingle path to the front door. In a matter of minutes I was seated at Brian's desk recounting how I'd gone to Ashford with a view to seeing Ash and how I had been refused entry. I told him how I had grabbed my ID card back off the Sergeant and done a runner. Then went on to recount the events that I'd witnessed at Paul's workshop.
'You know Brian; I'm beginning to sense that there is a conspiracy going on here and that both of us are the scapegoats for something but for what, I don't know…I mean let's face it your office is broken into and documents from my file are taken, both Paul and I are arrested. I am accused of impersonating an officer in the armed forces. Paul has now been arrested for the second time…oh and I almost forgot; I'm sure my house is under surveillance, so what's going on?'
'Hmm, I see what you mean. So apart from Paul, where do I come into this?'
'Sorry Brian I was rambling on. I think the main thing is to find out where Paul has been taken, don't you?'
'I agree,' he paused for a moment then said; 'doesn't it seem strange to you that if Paul has been arrested he hasn't telephoned?'
'Perhaps they haven't allowed him to use the phone.'
He thought about that for a moment. 'No that's not the reason.' Then as if on cue the telephone rang. 'Brian Gore speaking.'

'Sorry to trouble you Mr Gore, this is Kent Police Sittingbourne. We are holding a Mr Paul Jones who claims he is a client of yours and would like to speak to you...'

'Hello, is that Mr Gore?'

'Yes. Hello Paul. What's the problem?'

'I'm being held on some trumped up charge...'

'Sit tight and say nothing until I arrive. Do you understand, say nothing?'

'I understand.'

'Good I'll be there as soon as possible.' There was a click as the line went dead. Brian Gore replaced his handset and looked at me with the trace of a smile. 'That was fortuitous wasn't it? At least we know where he is being held. Was there anything else Richard, because if not then I better get of to Sittingbourne?'

I suddenly remembered the message, which was my main reason for calling Brian in the first place. 'Yes he left me this message.' I pulled out yards of toilet paper at which Brian raised a bemused eyebrow. 'On each sheet he wrote one letter and one figure, see.' I pointed to the 'G' and the '0' on the first sheet. I unravelled the mass of paper being careful not to tear any of the sheets. 'I worked out the first part of the message as your name, but the second part 0194789 means nothing to me. Does it mean anything to you?'

'I'm not sure, but wait a minute.' With that he unlocked his safe and took out a green coloured envelope file with Paul Jones written neatly across the front. Inside the file were various documents.

'I thought you had all Paul's stuff in my file.'

'Most of it, but he brought these extra bits and pieces in the other day. Now let's see...' he tipped the contents onto his desk. 'Ah what's this?' Brian unfolded a white receipt with the serial number 0194789. Stapled to the top left hand corner of single sheet of white paper was a small white vehicle pass for GCHQ and stamped MoD Police Gate 3. On the 'Vehicle Pass' it showed the registration number E245XUJ as being a white van from Vans R Us the driver's name given as P Jones and signed by Paul. At the bottom of the pass in bold lettering it stated "This pass is to be surrendered upon leaving by order MoD Police." It was obvious Paul had failed to give up the pass and knowing these establishments it was dependant on who was on the gate and how busy they were as to whether they enforced the surrender of paper passes. So that was what the number stood for. Even the delivery note showed the signature of the recipient, a Mr Jim Buckle!

'May I suggest something Brian?'

'Of course you may.'

'Knowing past form of HMG and how they have treated me, perhaps you ought to take a photocopy with you and keep the original away from here in a safe elsewhere, just in case.'

'I think you're right Richard. I'll keep both yours and Paul's information in our office in Canterbury.'

At eleven-thirty Brian Gore was taken by Ben Hall to the cells at the back of Sittingbourne Police station where Paul was being held. The custody Sergeant opened the door and Paul was given back his belongings and escorted back to the front of the Police station where accompanied by Brian Gore, he was ushered into an interview room. Both Paul and Brian Gore were invited to sit down at the table opposite the two officers, Denstrode and Hall, to await the arrival of the Chief Inspector.
'Sergeant Hall, on what grounds is my client being held?'
'I think you are fully aware of the situation Mr Gore, but for the record, Mr Jones stated that on the day in question he was visiting GCHQ. He also stated that whilst at GCHQ he visited a Mr Jim Buckle. According to our information your client, Mr Gore, never set foot inside GCHQ on the day in question, in fact GCHQ even deny the existence of a Mr Buckle, whom your client assured us he visited. Now Mr Gore, if your client had visited GCHQ, on the day in question, then surely GCHQ would have a record of such a visit wouldn't they?'
'Have you checked with GCHQ Sergeant?'
'Of course we have, so what exactly are you driving at Mr Gore?'
'Is it possible you mad a mistake?'
'Mr Gore,' Hall sounded annoyed, 'what do you take me for? We have got photocopies of their Visitor's Log for the day in question. I suppose you would like to see them?' He said somewhat sarcastically.
'Certainly Sergeant, I would love to see them. Have you got them to hand?' Brian didn't like Hall and he wanted to make him look as foolish as possible. Hall pushed back his chair, got up and left the room only to reappear a few minutes later with the faxed copies of the pages in question.
'There you are, just like I said.' Hall dumped the sheets in front of Brian then resumed his seat at the table, feeling rather good about having one up on this snotty solicitor. But his feeling of euphoria was to be short lived. Brian scanned down the sheets.
'Hmm. You're absolutely right Sergeant.'
'I know I'm right sir.' Hall gave a patronising smile. 'You see we are thorough, when we do something we do it right. Don't we Denstrode?'
'Yes Sergeant.'
'I see.' Said Brian, 'So tell me why didn't you go to Cheltenham and do a little digging?'
'As I said, we had no need those sheets say everything.'
'Ah, I see. The sheets say everything.' Brian leaned back in his chair; half closed his eyes and nodded. 'Yes of course. The sheets tell the full story.'

181

He fell silent, but something in his tone made Hall and Denstrode feel a little uneasy. A slight smile touched Brian's lips then it was gone. He suddenly sat upright, eyes wide. 'Did it never occur to either of you that there could be an error? That perhaps a page maybe missing or maybe somebody is bending the truth?' With that he pulled out the photocopies of the two pieces of paper, the vehicle pass and the 'Delivery' note with Buckle's signature both and pushed them across the table. 'Gentleman, all those pages of names say is that a number of people visited GCHQ on the day in question. True they do not show my clients name. True you may have spoken to them, but I think that someone, somewhere is trying to set my client up and these sheets will prove his innocence.' He gave both men a broad smile. Hall picked up the papers and scrutinised them carefully, then passed them to Denstrode. 'Now gentleman, having seen the evidence, you can be rest assured that Mr Jim Buckle does exist and that the Vehicle Pass confirms my client's story, and if you continue with this persecution of my client and you see fit to prosecute then I feel sure that when we produce these signed sheets in evidence there will be a lot of red faces in the court room, and especially yours gentlemen. In view of this I suggest we finish this stupid charade and that you contact your Chief Inspector immediately. Please advise him that my client wishes to make an official complaint about wrongful arrest, and tell the Chief Inspector that if needs be, we will pursue this complaint through the law courts up to the highest level.'

After reading the two pieces of paper and hearing Brian Gore's plan Hall was galvanized into action and rushed from the room to phone his Chief Inspector, only to return a few minutes later to announce that his boss, Chief Inspector Blake, was on his way.

A few minutes later the door was opened by a well built man with greying hair with a round face of fresh complexion.

'Mr Gore,' he extended an outstretch hand, 'I'm Chief Inspector Blake. Pleased to meet you,' Brian shook hands with him. 'Ah, you must be Mr Jones.' Again he proffered his hand, but Paul chose to ignore it.

'Chief Inspector, I must protest most vehemently about the arrest of my client.' At this point Brian picked up the copies of the GCHQ gate pass and the 'Delivery' note and passed them to the Chief Inspector. 'As you can see Chief Inspector my client has been detained based on incorrect information. 'Not only was he wrongfully arrested, he was also delayed from making his rightful telephone call to me and his place of work was searched without a warrant and without his express permission. In fact it appears to me that all in all, my client has a very good case against the Police, and I cannot protest enough about this blatant disregard for the procedures. I must point out to you Chief Inspector that it is my clients wish and my intension to take this matter further and the very least I would expect is some form of explanation and an apology.'

'Mr Gore, Mr Jones, I can understand your frustration, but I cannot nor am I prepared to comment on what has happened, but please be assured that I will investigate this and I will be only to happy to communicate my findings to you in due course. However your client is free to go and I will be in touch with you as soon as possible.'

'Chief Inspector, I do feel that there has been a grave injustice to my client in this matter and I want your personal guarantee that this will now be addressed and there will be no further harassment.'

'Mr Gore I take your various points on board, but I'm sure you would agree that until I have had chance to investigate it fully I am unable to comment further on this case.'

'Accepted Chief Inspector, so how long before you will come back to me with a report on your findings?'

'Shall we say a week Mr Gore.'

'A week then Chief Inspector.'

'Thank you Mr Gore.' The Chief Inspector gave a fleeting smile, 'now if you'll both excuse me.'

'Of course.' Brian stood up and extended his hand. 'I look forward to hearing from you in due course. Good night Chief Inspector.' The Chief Inspector shook Brian's hand then showed both men out through the front door of Sittingbourne Police station.

Paul sat in the office of Jackson, Harper and Gore Solicitors waiting to see Brian in the hope that he had further news about his arrest seven days ago.

The door to Brian's office opened, 'Come in Paul.' Paul followed Brian into his office and sat down at his desk. 'Right Paul, I've now had a letter back from Blake at Sittingbourne and although he admits that it appears as if you were the innocent party in all of this. He does state that on the evidence presented at the time there was a case to answer. Now what that means is that with the evidence they had they were within their rights to arrest you, but having further investigated the alleged sighting of the van and the proof you offered all charges have been dropped.'

'So what about wrongful arrest, can I get any compensation?'

'Sorry Paul, as they say "there was a case to answer." '

'I think it stinks. It's a whitewash and you know it is Brian.'

'I agree Paul. It does stink, but knowing it and proving it are two different things entirely. I agree it looks more and more as if someone somewhere was trying to have you implicated in something that was nothing to do with you. In fact I would even suggest there is a distinct feel of a conspiracy here. Perhaps something to do with your stint in the woods, what do you think?'

'Hmm. You could be right, I certainly have the distinct feeling somebody tried fitting me up. Good job I had that vehicle pass and that delivery note and more to the point that you had them here in your safe otherwise I would definitely have had a problem big time. You know I did have a file copy of the delivery note in my GCHQ file, but that's been removed by the Police, but of course they have no record of that nor has Hall any recollection of it being taken. Bah the whole things a cover up and what's more they're getting away with it.'

'I know Paul, but there's not a lot you can do at present. My advice to you is to forget it and to watch your back. You know this country is a past master at subterfuge. We, after all, taught the rest of the world this particular game.'

Paul nodded, 'I know. Anyway thanks for trying.'

Chapter 17

For ten days now BT engineers had been working at the end of the road. Sure to the passer-by it looked genuine enough with the little red and white striped apex tent set up over a manhole and a guy sat there pouring over thousands of multi-coloured wires but was it? The tent, the workman even the BT truck looked the part but the way things had been going my instincts told me otherwise because the Circus had, after all, used similar ploys before as observation units so why not now?

The BT truck was fitted out as a mobile workshop to support a team of field engineers. On the left-hand side it had rack after rack of tools, instruments and drums of multicoloured wire. Even the front bulkhead had racking divided into storage bins which held soldering irons, hard hats, line testing equipment, a gas ring for melting lead and of course the obligatory kettle for the mid-morning brew! All in all a genuine BT workshop, but it had one subtle difference and that was that the front rack formed a cleverly concealed door that opened into another compartment, which, although small, had just enough room for two engineers and the sophisticated electronic listening and recording equipment that it housed. This was not your average BT truck.

The engineer sitting on his canvas stool shielded from the elements by the striped awning of the small apex tent was busy carrying out various line tests. On his head he wore a single earphone which also had a microphone attached to it. As he used what appeared to be a meter he talked to someone via his microphone.

Inside the small claustrophobic compartment within the body of the truck sat another engineer. He was intently listening to various clicks as a dialled number was pulsed along the cable to the exchange. There was a click then the ringing tone. The recording equipment kicked into life and the red, yellow and green light emitting diodes (leds) on the electronic equipment flickered on and off as different signals were detected.

I was engrossed in reading an article in the Sunday paper when the jangling of the telephone disturbed me. 'Hello James Fruit farms.' There was that click again, I was sure that someone was listening in.

'Hello, is that Mr James?' A muffled voice I didn't readily recognise at first greeted me.

'Who wants to know?' I asked warily.

'Never mind who Mr James, just listen to what I have to say that's all.' The voice although muffled as if someone was trying to disguise it now sounded vaguely familiar. I was sure I could make out traces of an Irish accent.

'Ok, I'm listening.'

'Be very careful. Someone who you've trusted wants you out of the way. You're an embarrassment to them...'

'Jimmy is that...' I cut across his talking but too late the line went dead.

Inside the BT van the engineer pressed the record button on a reel to reel tape recorder as he simultaneously pressed down the transmit button on the microphone in front of him.

'Alpha 1 to Control over.'

'Control receiving, over.'

'We have contact on target's phone trying to trace now over.'

'Roger Alpha 1, can you patch through?'

'Roger Control.' The engineer flicked a switch. 'How's that Control?'

'Loud and clear Alpha 1. Thank you.'

The engineer flicked another switch and called to his mate via the microphone. 'We're on Simon...'

'Got it...'

'Damn!'

'What's up?' Simon asked via his microphone.

'Lost him. He's cleared down.'

'Did you get chance for a trace?'

'Nah...he wasn't on long enough. Sounded like he was trying to disguise his voice though, I can't be certain, but I would say he was Irish wouldn't you?'

'Not sure, but there was definitely a trace of an accent there. Who did James call him, Jimmy or something?'

'Yeah Jimmy, but that could be anyone. He didn't seem to acknowledge the name.'

There was a crackle as the VHF set came to life. 'Alpha 1 this is Control over.'

'Go ahead Control.'

'Any trace or was it too short?'

'Negative Control.'

'Ok, but we need to stick with it for now. Control out.' The speaker went dead.

My brain went into overdrive. I was certain that the call had come from Jimmy my old controller and friend from over in Ulster. Who was he alluding to when he said 'someone I trusted' wanted me out of the way? Did he mean Ash or was it closer to home? My brain was in a whirl. I went through all the people I had been in contact recently. There was Jean, could it be her, no she was too remote from me. What about Paul, I dismissed that as being absurd. Of course Imanos was a possibility, I never did really trust

186

him, nor did Paul for that matter but he was too obvious. Hmm, Brian Gore, I suppose that was a possible, but for what reason? Then there was Ash, but then there was anybody and everybody in the Circus. None of it made sense; in fact they could all have their own hidden agenda and want me out of the way for some reason. The more I thought about it the more confused I became until in the end I decided to call Paul and arrange to meet with him at the pub in the village.

'Hi Paul, it's me. Do you fancy a beer?'

'Yeah ok, where?'

'I'll walk down into the village if you like.'

'Ok.'

A mile away at the Red Lion public house a white Sierra pulled into the car park. Its three occupants, probably in their late twenties to early thirties, were smartly dressed in grey suits and looked every bit like business men, but as it was Sunday they would pass as men from the local Jehovah Witness church. The passenger in the front pulled a map from the glove compartment and appeared to be engrossed in sorting out a route of some description whilst the driver sat fiddling with the controls of a radio.

'Bravo 2 are you receiving over?'

The passenger picked up a small handset. 'Roger Bravo 1. Go ahead, over.'

'Target leaving. He is foxtrot toward A2, believe he is headed into village over.'

'Roger Bravo 1.' The passenger in the front passed the map to the occupant in the back, who placed on the seat next to him.

The driver looked in the mirror and gave a slight nod of the head.

'Right lads here we go. Remember nothing too obvious, I'll pull up slightly in front. You Chris get out and get on his right hand side and ask him the way to Whitstable. You Mark,' he looked over his shoulder to the one in the back, 'as soon as Chris engages him in giving directions you get out and take up your position on his left hand side. If he starts to move off go with him. Warn him about things. Tell him to keep his mouth shut about things, about Ireland, what he was doing, suggest that he has attracted some unhealthy interest and last of all he should forget about us, Imanos and company otherwise his family could have major problems. In other words put the frighteners on him. Understood?'

'Yes Gov.' Chris the front passenger answered.

'What about Jimmy?' Mark asked.

'Leave the boss to take care of him. We have our job to do and that's all there is to it, besides he's back over the water now. Anyway let's go.'

The driver eased the white Sierra out of the Red Lion's car park and turned towards Faversham.

I was walking down the hill towards the village and the pub when a white Sierra drove slowly passed me as if looking for somewhere then stopped a little way ahead. The minute I drew close to the car the front passenger door opened and a youngish bloke in a dark grey suit got out and called to me.

'Excuse me I wonder if you can help us?'

Without giving it a thought I walked over to him.

'What's the problem?' I asked.

'We're strangers around here and we've been told we can get to Whitstable this way, is that correct?'

At this juncture I was vaguely aware of the back door opening and another youngish man joining us. Like the one I was talking to, he was also dressed in a grey suit. He stood on my left whilst the other was on my right. Alarm bells started to ring, but it was too late. I suddenly felt the hard steel of the gun barrel jammed hard into my side. The one on my left steered me away from the car and gently but firmly urged me to walk on down the hill with both of them. All this time the gun was jammed firmly against my side.

'Now listen to what I have to say and listen carefully.' He spoke in a low authoritarian way.

I didn't reply, but continued to walk on down the hill.

'You,' the other one spoke for the first time, 'Mr James, are way out of your depth. Remember there are much bigger fish than you, so if you step out of line it will be curtains for you and your family. Keep your mouth shut about everything. You've never ever been to Ireland…'

'Don't be stupid people know I've been to Ire…'

'Shut it and listen.' His pal snarled.

'Like I was saying Mr James, there are much bigger fish than you. Be careful and do as we tell you. You have no knowledge of Ulster. Do you know that the job you were doing has attracted some unhealthy attention, but of course you would know that by now wouldn't you? So Mr James I'll repeat it once more. Forget everything, is that clear? After all you wouldn't want anything to happen to your family would you?'

By the menacing tone in his voice I felt that he meant every word.

'So Mr James,' the other one started to speak, his voice was quieter but equally as menacing, 'if not for you then for your wife's sake forget everything, you even need to forget this conversation. After all Mr James we do have some very powerful and influential friends and let's face it who have you got to protect you now?'

He was right and I knew it, but it still didn't stop me reacting angrily to his threats. 'Who the hell are you to tell me what to do?'

'Who we are is of no consequence,' he replied with another jab of the gun as a reminder, 'just remember we are watching you twenty-four hours a day seven days a week. We know where you go and who you see, and what is more, we know every little move your wife makes. So be warned!'

I had been so involved with our little tête-à-tête I had not noticed that the car had pulled passed us and had stopped a little down the road ahead of us. As we drew level with it and before I could say anything the front passenger door was open and the one on my right was in. I went to grab the other bloke, but he was too quick for me. In a flash he had the rear door open and as the car started to accelerate away he launched himself backwards. As his backside hit the seat he swung his legs into the car and slammed the door. A classic move that we had all been trained to do and he executed it perfectly. With a roar from the engine, squealing of tyres fighting for grip and the smell of burning rubber the car accelerated away down the hill and they were gone.

'Shit!' I shouted after them. 'You bastards. Who do you think you are?'

That fateful Sunday lunchtime a couple of days ago, had worried more than I cared to admit and no matter what I did it was there niggling away at the back of my mind. Who were those guys? Was it coincidence that on the same day I had received a phone call warning me about someone I trusted? Who was the stranger who had made that call? Was it Jimmy or not? I didn't know what to think or who to trust any more. I needed to speak to someone, but who should it be? In the end I decided to start back at basics, back where all this had begun. I decided to retrace my footsteps, figuratively speaking, back through Ireland. I couldn't help feeling the answer lay in Ulster somewhere, so with my mind made up I drove into the village and telephoned Jean O'Donald. I telephoned Jean from a call box because after Sunday I was more than ever convinced my telephone was being tapped and the BT truck was still there at the end of the road. Today, however, was the first day that there was no sign of a white Sierra and this convinced me that my 'friends' from Sunday were the ones who had been keeping tabs on me so did this mean that the BT truck was from another team?

Because of my experiences over the last few weeks I decided to park in the George Inn car park which only had one very narrow access road into it. This would mean that anyone following me would have to pass by and park where they could on the street, by which time I could be parked and have a number of options open to me. I could leave via the rear gate which would take me into the recreation field near the Village Hall, or I could go through the lounge door and out through the public bar, or enter the pub through the back door and exit through the front door. It was the latter I took, telling Dave the landlord I would pop back in a couple of minutes and I was soon in the telephone kiosk putting my call into Jean.

'Hello Jean it's Richard speaking.' I pushed a couple of fifty pence pieces into the box.

'Hello Richard how are you keeping?' She asked.

'Oh I'm fine…listen Jean I haven't got much time so I need to be brief. I desperately need some help, your help. I don't know how much you know, but things have gone pear shaped big time for me. The Circus has shut me out, my solicitor has had his safe broken into and some of my documents have gone. I am being watched and I have been getting strange phone calls. The last was on Sunday, thought it was Jimmy but…not sure. In fact I'm not sure of anything anymore…not sure who to trust. Jean I desperately need your help to find out what's going on, can you help me?' There was a silence. 'Jean…'

'Yes Richard…'

'Oh you're still there…'

'Yes I'm still here Richard…how can I help?'

'Jean I know about you, Jimmy told me. So can you use your contacts and also contact Jimmy for me. Find out what you can. Tell Jimmy the last operation went sour. Tell him Orpheus, Operation Orpheus closed down, hopefully he may be able…' I was cut short by the pips. I managed to find a couple of ten pence pieces and pushed them in. 'Will you do that for me?'

'To be sure I will Richard; I'll call you Thursday evening…'

'Don't call me at…' Too late the pips cut me short so I was unable to warn her about the possible tap on the phone. Damn it, I hadn't any more change. I went straight back to The George and got David to change me up a note, again I told him I'd be back. By the time I had got my change and walked back again to the phone box ten minutes had passed add to that another five minutes waiting for a young girl to finish her conversation on the phone and all in all a good fifteen minutes had gone by. I dialled Jean's number and let it ring for a good two or three minutes but no reply. I then tried the haulage yard.

'O'Donald's Haulage.' A man's voice answered.

'Hello, is Mrs O'Donald there please?' I asked.

'No I'm sorry, can I give her a message?'

'No thank you.' I answered and replaced the handset. Bollocks I thought to myself, what now. I tried two or three more times on her home number but to no avail until in the end I had to give up. I decided I would have to try again tomorrow and Thursday, it was imperative I stopped her from phoning me at home.

Unfortunately I tried and tried to reach Jean but was unsuccessful. In fact I even tried early Thursday evening on the off chance I could intercept her before she called me at home, but my luck had finally run out. She seemed to have disappeared from the face of the earth. At seven o'clock the telephone rang, I picked it up hoping that it would not be Jean, but that was just too much to expect.

'Hello Richard.' It was Jean all right.

'Sorry I think you've got the wrong number.' I said and put down the receiver. Jean was not put off, the phone rang again.

'Hello...' Before I could say anything or warn her she cut me short.

'Richard, listen to me. Spoke with you know who and they are finding out what they can...'

'Jean, Jean...'

'What's the matter?'

'The phone is tapped...'

'Oh shit...' was all she said. 'Well too late now. All I can say is be careful of someone high up over there. Also you are being targeted by the department of Psychological Warfare but I don't know why. Must go, will be in touch. Bye.' With that she hung up.

So that was it, I was right; I was being targeted by the Department. Who could be behind this, Jean had said someone high up?

There was a frenzied knocking on Jean O'Donald's front door. She eased back the curtain of an upstairs room in order to get a clear view of who it was creating all the noise. Outside was parked a Volvo car but the registration was obscured from her view. On the doorstep stood a clean shaven youngish looking man dressed in well cut dark grey suit. He knocked again, stepped back from the door and gave a cursory glance up at the upstairs windows. Jean let the net curtain fall back into place just in time. He was a young fair-haired lad she guessed he was late twenties early thirties, but his face was not familiar to her. She looked over to the Volvo and could just make out the dark outline of another person sitting in the driver's seat. She didn't like it. There was something not quite right. She ran to her bedroom and dialled a number.

'Square four laundry.'

'Good morning,' she said quite calmly, 'I have a red dress that needs cleaning urgently. Could someone arrange collection?'

This was a coded message advising her control she needed help urgently.

'Certainly madam. Just one item or more?'

'One urgently but I have a possible second dress you could take at the same time.'

This indicated to the telephone operator that there was one definite threat possibly two.

'Your name and address please?'

'Solitaire at chequers.' Jean gave her code name and her coded address as her home.

191

'Thank you madam, we'll arrange collection within fifteen minutes, can you please make sure someone is there?' He wanted her to keep the one on the doorstep busy until help arrived.

'I think so.' She replied as she started to think about how she could keep this young man busy. 'I'll expect your pick-up in fifteen minutes, thank you.' She put down the phone and paused, slowly a plan of action started to form.

In Lisburn barracks the phone on the Northern Ireland desk rang. Jimmy picked it up.

'Hi home desk.'

'We have received a coded alert. Level top priority. Action immediate,' the voice on the phone said, 'operator requires assistance.'

Upon hearing this Jimmy signalled across to one of his assistants, 'Jane switch to line one take some details operator in trouble.' Jane reacted accordingly. She curtailed her conversation and switched to line one. She could now hear her boss Jimmy talking.

'Codename?'

'Solitaire,' the voice replied.

'Place?'

'Chequers.' The voice replied.

'Problem?'

'Coded message reads "has red dress needed cleaning urgently possibly could have two." She asked for collection, we've advised fifteen minutes.'

'Roger, got that. What about the one definite?'

'She says she will detain there.'

'Good.' Jimmy looked over to Jane and placed his hand over the mouthpiece, 'Did you get all that?' Jane nodded. Jimmy uncovered his mouthpiece and continued talking to the voice at the other end. 'Ok, we have that. We are now go and thanks.' He replaced the handset. 'Right Jane, who've we got near there?'

'Nearest is Eamonn.'

'What! He's miles away in Louth. Shit why does JITC do this to me. Check if anyone is here on base even if we have to nick someone from London sector. In the meantime I'll take this.' Jimmy was already pulling on his jacket as he headed for the exit. 'I'll give you a test call when I'm mobile.' Just then another operator came in through the swing doors. 'Ah Gary you'll do.'

'What's up gov?'

'You're on with me. Operator needs back-up. Come on.' Both men hurried out through the swing doors.

Jean knew that if her plan was to succeed there was no time to waste. Quickly she pushed the clothes aside in her wardrobe to reveal a small wall safe. Deftly her fingers spun the dial to the correct combination and she opened the safe revealing a small handgun and a box of live ammunition. Precious seconds ticked by as she had loaded the Walther PPK and jammed it into the waistband of her skirt. Further seconds were lost as she hurriedly closed the wardrobe door. She then removed her shoes and ran silently and swiftly to the stairs. Again there was a hammering on the front door. She knew it was only a matter of minutes, perhaps even seconds, before he would decide to go so she could not afford to lose any more time. Within a matter of twenty, or maybe thirty seconds, she had reached the front door and as quietly as she could she eased back the deadlock. At last she was into the final stages of her plan. With the front door now unlocked she quickly and silently returned to her bedroom and her ensuite bathroom where she turned on the shower. Once the shower was on all she had to do was to conceal herself behind the slightly open bedroom door. Had she done everything? Front door was unlocked, shower on and bedroom door slightly open, yes that was everything now all she had to do was wait. She was certain that it wouldn't be long before her unwelcome visitor tried the door. The plan was to entice upstairs and then to take him prisoner, or to shoot him if necessary, seems simple enough she thought to herself, but would it be? She didn't have too long to wait before she heard a slight noise that indicated someone had entered the house.

'Mrs O'Donald.' The young man paused in the hallway and listened for any reply. 'Hello, anyone at home?' Again he stood and listened but nothing. 'Mrs O'Donald, hello.' Again he strained his ears for a noise, any sort of noise that would indicate she was here. It was then he heard the faint noise of the shower and nodding to himself he slowly and purposefully climbed the stairs. At the top of the stairs he stood on the landing undecided exactly which way to go. He listened intently trying to make out exactly from which direction he could hear the running of the shower. Behind the partly opened door Jean could just see through the gap near the hinges. She held her breath as she watched her would be intruder as he stood at the top of the stairs looking first to the left and then towards her. Which way would he go?

A thought occurred to the young man as he stood there pondering. Perhaps he ought to take a moment or two to check out all the rooms and see what he could get on her that would boost his standing with his boss. He paused a moment or two longer and decided that the noise of the shower was from the room off to his right, the one with the door ajar. Having decided that was the room he would take the opportunity to search the others, so he set off down the corridor to his left and the first closed door.

He paused outside the door and listened to see if he could detect any movement from within.

From her position behind the open bedroom door Jean watched him as he set off down the corridor to the first of the spare rooms. She watched as he paused outside the closed door. Slowly and carefully he opened the door and disappeared from her view. She was now on the horns of a dilemma, did she stay where she was and wait for him here, or should she try for him in the spare room. She considered the situation and decided that it was too risky so she would stay put and in the meantime she hoped that her back-up would arrive soon. Whilst he was in the room she managed to steal a moment to check the time and was surprised to see that it was already five minutes since she had made her call.

'Jon, hey Jon where are you?' A muted voice called from downstairs. Shit, Jean thought to herself. That's done it. Now what do I do. She racked her brain for some ideas as to what she could do now. Just then she heard the spare room door close and she could just see the young man through the gap in her door. Again his mate called to him, 'Jon, Jon where the hell are you?'

'Shh Mick.' He called softly to his mate and waved to him some sort of signal. Jean gave a slight frown, what on earth was happening she wondered? She could still see the one called Jon, now what was he doing. He had decided to set off down the stairs he'd only gone down two or three and he stopped. He was now talking to his mate. Unfortunately all she could hear was them talking in low voices, she could not make out what they were saying nor could she see his partner. Ah some movement. The murmur of voices had stopped and she distinctly heard footsteps as someone went down the stairs. Jon, the one who had been upstairs was now on his way back up, this time there was no hesitation, he turned left back along the corridor. Jean gave a sigh of relief.

'Christ Garry is this the best you can do, Jean was told fifteen minutes and already we've nearly taken ten.'

'Sorry gov, but what can I do in this traffic?'

'I know.' Jimmy picked up the radio microphone, 'Control, Alpha Whisky 22 over.'

'Go ahead Alpha Whisky 22.'

'Any news on our man in the RUC over.'

'Yes, he's on his way over.'

'ETA for him? Over.'

'He gave five minutes over.'

'Tell him no siren and to wait down road to rendezvous with us, over.'

'Roger Alpha Whisky 22. Control out.'

'Roger Control. Alpha whisky 22 out. Right Gary how long do you reckon?'

'Not long now we're clear of the traffic, ten minutes.'

'Ten minutes, that's no good. Can't you do better than that? Tell you what take the next right then in about three maybe four hundred yards a left...'

'Of course, I know it...' There was a squeal of protest from the tyres as Garry swung the car sharply to the right and with the tail swing wide, reverse lock applied, he jammed his foot hard to the floor. The car twitched slightly then straightened up. Jimmy grabbed the grab handle to stop himself being thrown towards Gary. The car accelerated to ninety, then hundred soon they were over a hundred and braking to take a sharp left. Again the car hung out its tail and Gary piled on the gas with reverse lock as the rear end threw up a cloud of loose dirt. They were into the home straight and Gary was redlining as he chopped it into fifth gear. The speed now topped one hundred and fifteen miles per hour. They had about three minutes to go if they were to make it in the fifteen minute time frame. As they rounded a slight left hand bend they could see the profile of their Police contact's vehicle up in front. They started to slow down and Gary pulled in behind the Police vehicle. They had made the rendezvous with time to spare.

Jimmy wound down his window and spoke quickly to their man in the RUC. 'We have one of our team in there needs back-up. Believed to have two unwelcome guests. Plan is we'll go in you block entrance, ok?' He didn't wait for the reply. 'Right let's go.'

Jean tried to see where the young man had got to, but there was no sign of him. What was that? Had she imagined it or was that the front door. She checked her watch, according to that it was only just ten minutes ago she had phoned so she must have been hearing things. Suddenly the young man came into view he was now heading her way. She took a deep breath knowing it wouldn't be long now. She could feel the adrenalin build up as he got closer to her room suddenly he was there. The bedroom door pushed open. Jean tensed like a coiled spring. He walked in without even looking behind him.

'Mrs O'Donald, hello, Mrs O'Donald are you the...' He never finished the sentence. Suddenly the door swung closed and he started to turn but too late. There was a glimpse of a body as an arm descended in a ferocious swing then a blinding flash of light and blackness. He felt his knees begin to buckle; he felt something or someone grab him from behind. There was a subtle smell of perfume then nothing. He couldn't have been out too long, but when he came too he was lying on a bed. Slowly his eyes came into focus and as they did he saw for the first time the very person he had been looking for. Jean O'Donald. She was a lovely lady, he thought to himself.

'Pleased to meet you Mrs O'Donald,' he croaked to her and smiled weakly. Then his eyes caught sight of the snub nose of the Walther PPK directed at him. The smile quickly disappeared. 'Now what have we here/' He asked, 'you're not likely to use that.' He said in almost a derisory tone as he started to get up from the bed. It was at this point he realised that Mrs O'Donald had stripped him of his trousers and pants. There he lay naked from the waist down. Suddenly he felt a little silly and more than a little embarrassed

'I suggest you lay back down and keep quiet.' Jean's voice was soft yet menacing, 'after all we don't want to attract you mate's attention do we.' At this point she proceeded to rip her blouse open so it would look very much like he had attacked her should they be disturbed. 'Now what exactly do you want?' she asked him.

'It's about …'

'No don't talk loudly, keep it low. Understood?'

'Ok.' He answered in a quiet voice, 'it's about Richard.' Jean frowned. 'You know Richard, you know who I mean don't you Mrs O'Donald?' Jean shook her head.

'Richard who? I don't know any Richard…'

'I think you know full well who I'm talking about. Richard James.'

'But I don't know any Richard James.' She lied glibly, 'who is this Richard James and what has he done?' she asked innocently.

'Ok Mrs O'Donald. So you say you don't know this man. I'll play along with you if that's what it takes. All I will say is that this man is highly dangerous and very ill. Now should he try to contact you then you need to let us know straight away…'

'Who is "us" then?'

'I'm sorry Mrs O'Donald, I forgot to say. I work for the Government.'

'Which Government, the British Government?'

'Yes the British government. Now as I was saying…'

'But how do I know you work for the government? Prove it to me. Can you prove it; do you have a card or something?'

He was now beginning to realise she was playing a game, just extracting the proverbial and he wasn't happy. Again he started to make a move.

'This is loaded and I will not be afraid to use it, and use it I will. The first shot will be through your knee and you must know that even a little Walther at this range can do untold damage. Now tell me more about Mr James.'

'Like I said Mrs O'Donald I work for London and you will take notice of what I have to say if you know what's best for you? 'You need to understand he is ill, mentally ill. He has become unstable and an embarrassment to the Government. Not only an embarrassment but he's also a danger to you and everyone he worked with. Look I'll show you my ID then perhaps you'll believe me.' He moved his hand towards his inside pocket.

'No you don't, leave your hands where I can see them out on your lap. To be honest I couldn't give a two-penny toss who you work for at this precise moment in time. I'm more interested in what's going on with Richard James, so come on out with it.'

Richard James is a liability. It will be proved that he is mentally unsound. It will of course be proved that he has never ever worked for Her Majesty's Government and anything he says will be the ramblings of a man suffering from a complete breakdown…'

'So let me get this right, you're telling me that Richard James, one of our people, is to become a persona non gratia, on whose orders?'

'You know better than to ask me that. Now what I can say he is a very ill man and although he has helped us a great deal, unfortunately he now requires medical attention. So please Mrs. O'Donald stay out of this, it is nothing whatsoever to do with you.'

'And if I refuse?'

'Well I can't say what will happen, but I'm sure you appreciate that if you do continue with your present attitude then no doubt the powers that be will see to it that you are justly rewarded for your efforts.' He gave a half smile, 'and I'm sure you wouldn't want the sort of reward that they would be inclined to give. I mean some of the things you read about today are scandalous and it makes you wonder how these people get away with it. Also cocaine is a really bad habit. Do you know how many girls take to the streets to fund their bad habit? No Jean, may I call you Jean?' Jean nodded more interested in what he had to say rather than the niceties of etiquette, 'I don't think you would want that type of reward. After all you do have a lovely body, it would be a shame to see such an exquisite form become defiled.'

Mick had completed his search down stairs and came back to the bottom of the staircase and in a low voice called for his mate, 'Jon, Jon where are you?' and waited for a reply. Jean put her fingers to her lips. 'Jon, where are you?' There was no reply, he listened intently for any movement, but there was none, not even the sound of the shower running. Funny he thought, he was certain he had heard the shower earlier. Then it occurred to him that perhaps Jon had found Jean O'Donald and a smile crept across his face, 'why you dirty little sod, I know what you're up to, that's why you not replying.' With that he decided to surprise them both and quietly and carefully he set off up the stairs. He had got about half way up the stairs and with the picture of both Jon and Jean still vividly displayed in his minds eye he was oblivious of the front door being slowly and silently opened. He was too busy with his imagination and anticipation to even sense the closeness of Gary until he suddenly felt the cold steel of the gun barrel against the base of his skull. A voice rasped out the words 'Stay where you are.' Expert hands frisked him and removed his Browning 9.00mm. Then he felt a searing pain as he was hit from behind. Strong hands grabbed him and eased him down the stairs. The slight noise and the voice had not gone unnoticed upstairs in the bedroom.

'Mick, I'm in here.' The young lad shouted.

Jean fired a warning shot into the bed beside him. 'I told you shut it.'

Too late the door burst open. 'Thank god and about time to Mick...' Jon stopped in mid-sentence. It wasn't Mick; in fact he'd never seen this person before. 'Oh my god, who are you?' He uttered as Jimmy came into full view with his Browning pointing straight at him.

'Let me introduce you,' said Jean, 'this is a very good friend of mine Jimmy and Jimmy, this is someone whom I believe is called Jon. He's also got a mate downstairs called Mick. There I have introduced you.' Jean smiled sweetly as if butter wouldn't melt in her mouth. 'Jon was telling me a very interesting story about a Richard James. Do you know a Richard James Jimmy, because I don't. In fact I've never heard of him have you?'

'I can't say I have Jean. Now are you all right?'

'I'm fine Jimmy; sorry about having to introduce Jon without his trousers, but you see you caught him with his pants down.'

'What happened to your blouse Jean? I suppose...No.'

'What Jimmy?'

'Just a thought, perhaps a photograph of you two would be useful, just as a guarantee for your safety of course Jean. I think if we took a photograph of our friend here like he is and with your blouse ripped as it is we could maybe use it as some sort of evidence that he had raped you. After all the RUC could take it further, what do you say Jean?'

'Why I do believe you're right.' Jean replied warming to the idea.

'Gary, bring in a camera.' Jimmy called downstairs.

A couple of minutes later Gary appeared with a standard issue camera. He took one look at Jon and said, 'What's he been up to then?' and smiled knowing full well what the boss was up to as it had been done before.

Twenty minutes later the photographs had been taken and the two men, Mick and Jon had been bundled into the back of the Police car and whisked away to Lisburn where they would be interviewed by the RUC. Meanwhile Jean changed her blouse whilst Gary and Mick drank their coffee.

'Who do you reckon they are gov?' Gary asked Jimmy.

'Not too certain, but they're not from this side that's for sure. In the meantime I'll get Jane to run some checks on them.'

198

'What's that Jimmy.' Jean had just entered the room.

'Oh Gary was just asking if I knew who they were and I was just saying I wasn't too sure, but I was going to get Jane to run some checks.'

'Are they from here do you think?' asked Jean.

'I wouldn't swear to it but I am almost certain they're from across the water, but what I am sure of is that someone somewhere doesn't want Richard James around and what's more I think it's at a very senior level.'

Chapter 18

It was now a week since I had spoken to Jean and I was beginning to wonder what had happened. There had been no more strange incidents and even the BT engineers had gone. Perhaps that was an end to it and we could get back to something approaching normality.

Months had been flying by without me even realising it and it was now well into autumn. Anne had gone off into Canterbury to do her weekly grocery shopping and I was busy sorting out the pickers ready to start the apple picking, when there was a knock at the front door. I opened the door and on the doorstep were three strangers.

'Mr James, Mr Richard James?' the nearest of the three addressed me.

'Yes.'

'Ah Mr James we're from the Ministry, may we come in?' When they said Ministry I immediately assumed that they meant the Ministry of Agriculture and Fisheries, so without giving it a second thought I let them in.

'So you're from the Ministry of Agriculture and Fisheries then, is that the Canterbury Office?' I asked. The three of them looked at me a little strangely and the one who had addressed me on the door step spoke again.

'No we're not from the Canterbury office, we're from London.'

'Hmm, that's unusual.' I said, 'they usually send someone from Canterbury not London. So what are you here for then?'

'Mr James please sit down we need to have a quiet chat about one or two things.' I sat down in my usual place a single easy chair opposite the television near to the fire.

'So what do we need to chat about?' I asked as I rolled up the sleeves of my shirt. 'I sent in all my latest returns to Canterbury office about two weeks ago. Is there a problem with the returns?' I asked.

'No Mr James. I see you were in the Parachute Regiment.' He said indicating the tattoo on my arm.

'Oh, this you mean?' I said pointing to my tattoo, 'yeah had that done a long time ago when I was in the mob.'

'How long were you in?' asked one of the others.

'Five years. Why all the questions?' I asked. I was then aware of someone standing closely behind me, 'Ay, who are you lot? I thought you said you were from the Ministry of Agriculture?'

Suddenly the guy behind me had whipped a leather strap around the top part of my body and with a 'click' he had it fastened. I lashed out with my feet hoping to make contact with someone or something but all I caught was thin air. It was then that I felt the prick of a needle as the one behind me deftly injected some sort of serum into my arm. Gradually a warm glow started to dissipate throughout the top of my arm and my shoulder which then spread throughout my body. My thrashing and struggling weakened until all my fight had subsided and I sat their quietly.

'Now that's more like it Richard. I don't like violence. I prefer people to be amicable and quiet don't you Richard?'

'F..F..' I tried to speak but the words wouldn't come. I knew what I wanted to say but try as I might I just couldn't form them properly. "Why don't you fuck off you bastards" I thought to myself. I tried to speak again. 'Fu...F...from where?' I heard myself say as if from a long way off. No, no, no I don't want to say that. I want to say 'Fu...off...' that's right, 'off...office where.' It didn't matter how much I tried whatever I thought was not what I said.

'No we are not from Canterbury Richard. In fact we are not even from the Ministry of Agriculture. We are from the Ministry of Defence. Now don't try to speak, just listen to us.'

I tried to tell my legs to kick this person, but all that happened was a very slight movement of my foot.

'As I was saying, we are from the MoD and Richard, you need to listen. It's no good fighting it because we've given you a strong muscle relaxant, so just listen. Unfortunately Richard you have had a breakdown and it's in your interest that you are treated for this breakdown. Do you understand?'

'Stupid bugger,' I tried to shout out, 'you think you're going to get away with this don't you,' but nothing came. I was powerless. My mind would work, but my mouth wouldn't. They had managed to rob me of my power of speech.

'Of course you do understand don't you Richard. You will now be taken into hospital where you will be assessed.'

I made one huge effort to overcome the cotton wool in my head and shouted as loud as I could. 'Fuck off you bastard,' but my shout was a mere whisper so I tried again. 'Fuck off.' I croaked, 'You'll never get away with it.' He leaned closer to me so he could hear what I was saying. 'You arsehole.' I licked my lips and made another superhuman effort to speak. Again my voice croaked. 'You won't win. P...p...people will stop you.' I was soaked through with sweat from my effort and worn out.

'Very interesting Richard, but I'm afraid the Government will win. You see we cannot afford not to. It's for your safety as much as anything.' He nodded to the one behind me, again there was another prick and a further shot was administered. The third one, who had said very little during this time, went into the hall to make a phone call to reappear minutes later. 'Ok the ambulance is on its way.'

'Good, now Richard you will begin to feel drowsy but don't worry you'll soon be safe in hospital.' That was the last I remembered.

Just after five Anne returned from Canterbury laden down with her weekly shop.

'Richard I'm home.' She called up the stairs but there was no reply. She pulled a face and walked through to the kitchen and checked outside in the back garden, but still there was no sign of him. Assuming he must be out on the farm she started to unload the car herself expecting him to return in due course, but he still was conspicuous by his absence even after she put all the shopping away. That job done she started to make tea and it was only then she started to wonder where he had got to. 'Richard, tea will be ready.' She called from the back door, but twenty minutes went by and still no sign. Now she was getting annoyed by his absence deciding enough was enough she set off towards the farm office. She tried the door of the office but it was locked. A slight frown crept across her brow. Where on earth could he be she wondered?

'Richard,' she called him again, 'tea's ready.' She stood there for a few moments and called him again. Still there was no sign of him. Now she was getting cross 'Richard James where the hell have you got to?' she said out loud. As a last resort she decided to check out the cold store, and with a purposeful stride she headed off away from the house to the large building next to the pack house on the edge of the orchard. The door to the pack house was open so she quickly checked inside, but it was deserted. Closing the door she marched over to the cold store, he had to be in there she thought to herself, after all there was nowhere else for him to be. The door to the cold store was open so she marched in there guns blazing, 'Richard James your tea is on the table and spoiling...' She stopped in mid flow, the place was deserted. This didn't make sense. Suddenly she heard footsteps behind her and expecting it to be Richard she turned round and let fly. 'Richard James this is beyond...' Seeing Richard's father standing there instead of Richard took the wind right out of her sails.

'Hey, steady on Anne. What's wrong?'

'Oh sorry dad for a minute I thought you were Richard, I can't find him anywhere. I don't suppose you've seen him have you?'

'No sorry love. As far as I know he was indoors sorting out the pickers ready for the off.'

'Hmm, strange. He's not there now.'

'Well don't worry; he'll not be far away.' He gave her a smile, then as an after thought, 'I wonder, has he gone off to see Paul?'

'Not unless he's walked, his car's still here.'

'I suppose Paul could have picked him up.'

'Well anything's possible I suppose.' Anne thought about it for a moment. 'Yes I'm sure that's what's happened. Thanks dad.' With that she headed off back towards the house.

'Give Paul a ring love.' He called after her.
'Yes I will, I'm sure that's where he'll be.'

The phone gave three rings and then it was picked up, 'Jones Engineering, Paul Jones speaking.'

'Paul it's Anne'

'Hello love, and to what do I owe this pleasure?'

'It's Richard, he's not here and I wondered if he was there with you?'

'No sorry love, I haven't seen him for a few days now. Still he can't be far away. You know him; he's probably gone out somewhere.'

'Without his car?'

'Ah, perhaps he's around the orchard somewhere. Don't worry he'll not be far away.'

'I know. Thanks Paul bye.'

'Bye love.'

At seven-thirty and having thoroughly checked everywhere for a note, even to the point of unlocking the farm office and checking there to no avail, Anne decided to call the Police.

'Good evening Police.

'Hello my name is Anne James. Mrs Anne James and I'd like to talk to someone about a missing person.'

'Thank you Mrs James. Where are you calling from?

'Oh sorry, the Canterbury area.'

'Thank you Mrs James, hold the line please while I try to connect you to Canterbury.' The line went dead for a moment or two then another voice answered.

'Good evening Canterbury Police. DC Fletcher speaking.'

'Yes good evening I would like to report a missing person.'

'I see and who am I speaking to?'

'Sorry, Mrs James.'

'Your relationship to the missing person?'

'He is my husband.'

'First name Mrs James?'

'Anne.'

'No, your husband's first name Anne, may I call you Anne?'

'Yes of course. His name is Richard.'

'Right, so it's Richard James and he has been missing for how long?'

'I'm not quite sure, but he was here this morning when I left to go into Canterbury…'

'Hang on a minute Mrs James. Let me get this straight. You say he was there this morning, well that's not even twelve hours…'

'Yes but it's very unusual...'

'I understand what you're saying but it's hardly a missing person until 24 hours has elapsed and even then with an adult there could be all sorts of reasons. No I'm sorry Mrs James there's nothing we can do as yet. Tell you what if you haven't heard anything by this time tomorrow give us another call.'

'But I know something has happened to him...'

'Mrs James I'm afraid our hands are tied...'

'Can't you do anything at all please?' She was getting frustrated with not knowing which way to turn and the tears started to trickle down her cheeks. 'Please help me,' she whispered. The line went quiet for a moment.

'Tell you what Mrs James I'll make a couple of calls and see if there has been anyone by that name admitted to any of the hospitals around here.'

'Thank you.' She said eagerly knowing she was grabbing at straws, 'thank you so much.'

'No promises mind. Leave it with me and I'll give you a call back within the hour, but that's all I can do.'

'That's fine and I do understand, it's...well it's just that I've contacted everyone I can think of and they haven't seen him and now I don't know what else to do...'

'Try not to worry Mrs James I'm sure that Mr James will turn up safe and well and as I said I'll make a couple of telephone calls and call you back within the hour.'

'Thank you DC Fletcher and I will of course phone you if he turns up in the meantime.'

'If you would that would be helpful. I'll speak to you again soon, goodbye Mrs James.'

'Goodbye and once again thanks.' Anne heaved a sigh of relief as she replaced the handset, at least he's agreed to help she thought to herself, but no matter how much she tried to 'think positive' deep down she had a bad feeling about Richard's disappearance.

The signature tune played out 'Coronation Street.' It was the one soap on television that Anne always watched but tonight, because of Richard's disappearance, her thoughts were elsewhere as she went through the motions of watching it. No matter how many times she went over it in her mind she still drew a blank. Suddenly the telephone rang and hoping that it would be Richard she rushed to pick it up.

'Hello.' She answered eagerly, 'Richard is that...'

'Hello Mrs James Canterbury Police, DC Fletcher here.'

'Oh.' The disappointment sounding in her voice, 'I'm sorry DC Fletcher, I thought it was Richard.'

'That's all right Mrs James. I presume that you've heard nothing as yet.'

'No.' She sighed, 'have you heard anything?'

'I'm sorry Mrs James, like you nothing. Now I know it's of little consolation to you but the good thing is that he is not in hospital so there is a good chance that he will be in touch before too long. Once again I'm sorry I can't be of more use.'

'I know, and I know you've done what you can but it's so unlike him to…'

'Well I'm sure there's a good explanation for his momentary disappearance, now if you'll excuse me Mrs James I must get on.'

'Oh, of course, I do understand and thank you.'

'Not at all, goodbye Mrs James.'

'Bye.' Anne said quietly as she put the phone down in a daze. She fought to hold back the tears as she slowly walked back into the sitting room unsure as to what she should do now. She stood staring at the television with unseeing eyes as the coloured picture flickered in front of her. She went to switch it off, but changed her mind because in a funny sort of way it gave her some comfort to hear the talking. At least with the television on she didn't feel so totally alone. Suddenly it dawned on her that the programme was a drama about a missing person, how ironic. She gave a silly little half laugh as she watched the drama unfold, the woman on the television was going frantic, and she was turning out all the drawers of the desk looking for something. Slowly it dawned on Anne, the bureau, perhaps there was something, a clue or something in Richard's desk. Of course that's what I'll do she thought to herself, I'll go through the bureau. 'Thank you television for the idea,' she said out loud to the television screen and proceeded to open drawers, hunt through papers and farm files. Every last piece of paper she scrutinised in case it held some sort of clue, but nothing. She was just about to give up the search when a small piece of paper fluttered to the floor she bent down to pick it up to throw it in the bin when she noticed the number 028728227 written in pencil. As she stared at the number it occurred to her that what she was looking at was a telephone number, but one she was unfamiliar with. Now why wasn't this in the telephone book she wondered, perhaps it is someone that Richard doesn't want me to know about, she thought to herself. Well Anne, go on phone the number and find out. So with hands shaking and heart pounding she went to the phone and dialled the number, brr brr, brr brr, brr brr the phone rang three times.

'Seven two eight two two seven.' A man with a strong Belfast accent answered the phone. 'Hello, hello…'

'So…sorry to trouble you,' she stammered, 'but I found this telephone number in my husband's bureau and…' The Irishman cut her short.

'And who would you be?' He asked brusquely.

'Umm, m…my name is Anne. Anne James…'

'Hello Anne. You'd be Richards wife then?'

'Y...yes. Who are you?'

'I'm Jimmy.'

She was sure she'd heard Richard speak of Jimmy in the past and was so relieved to hear his voice for herself. Perhaps he could shed some light on Richard's disappearance and without thinking she just blurted it out, 'Oh Jimmy please help me Richard's missing and I know you...' He cut her short.

'Can't speak to yer now. Phone from a call box tomorrow night at seven o'clock and I'll speak to yer then.' There was a click as his phone went down and the line went dead. She looked at her handset in disbelief and screamed.

As arranged, dead on seven the following evening, she dials Jimmy's number from the telephone box near the Queens head and within moments of being connected Jimmy answers.

'Hello Jimmy, it's Anne.'

'Hello Anne, sorry yer had t' phone back but yer can't be too sure in today's climate. Now listen to me carefully...'

'Yes I'm listening.'

'I want yer to give me yer telephone number...have yer got that?'

'Yes my telephone number is...hang on ...it's 01227 725728.'

'Good, now put the phone down...'

'What...no, Jimmy you don't under...'

'I understand only too well. Now do as I say...' she cuts him short.

'But please Jimmy please. Please, oh please listen. You...'

'Anne you must listen to me and trust me. I need you to put down your phone and I'll call you back within five minutes.'

'If I do that promise me that you will phone back.'

'I have said I will, so do as I say.' His voice was quiet but firm, and something in the way he spoke reassured her that he meant what he said. Slowly and hesitantly she does as he asks, she puts down the handset. Oh Richard where are you but before she can dwell anymore on her thoughts the phone rings.

'Hello, is that you Jimmy?' she asks eagerly.

'To be sure it is, who else were you expecting?' he asks light heartedly.

'Jimmy, what's going on? What's happening? Where's Richard, I haven't seen...' Jimmy cuts her short.

'Slow down Anne, slow down. Give me chance to find out and I will be able to answer all your questions, but I need a chance.' He waits a couple of moments for her to gather herself together before he speaks again. 'Ok, now that's better. First of all I'm sorry that I had to go through all that malarkey with yer, but my telephone may not be too secure so I needed to phone yer back from t'is number. Now have yer got some paper and a pen 'cause yer best write down this number?'

'Hang on a minute Jimmy.' Anne rummages through her bag. 'Ok I'm ready.'

'Right t'en this number is zero two eight six five six seven six five, have yer got that?'

'Yes I've got it.'

'Good. Now one t'ing more. Always phone me from a call box, understood?'

'Yes ok.'

'Now I need some time to find out some information, so tomorrow night I'll call you at seven o'clock on this number …'

'But what happens if there's someone in this call box?'

'Don't worry; I'll try again at five minute intervals up until seven fifteen. If the worst comes to the worst and I haven't got through then wait until seven thirty and you call me on the number I've just given you. Have you got that?'

'Yes I understand. Thanks Jimmy.'

'That's ok and Anne,' he waited a second, 'don't worry I'll find out where he is.'

'I know,' she gave a faltering smile. 'Thanks Jimmy. Bye.'

'We'll speak to you tomorrow. Bye Anne.'

As Anne approached the call box opposite the Queens Head she could just hear the faint ringing of the telephone. She glanced at her watch; it was just after seven o'clock and over forty-eight hours since she had seen anything of Richard. She was nearly to the box when out of the blue a young girl, on hearing the phone ring, decided to enter the call box. Her action took Anne completely by surprise, and before she could call out to stop her, the young lady she had picked up the phone. Why you little… Anne muttered to herself as the girl came out of the kiosk.

She smiled at Anne and shrugged her shoulders. 'Huh, whoever it was hung up.'

'Well, was it for you?'

'No, but…'

'Well why answer it if it's not for you, you should have left it alone shouldn't you?'

'Huh, some people…' With that she glared at Anne and continued on her way up the hill. Anne checked her watch again it was now 7:05, and according to what Jimmy had said he should phone anytime now, so she opened the door of the kiosk and waited. Another five minutes went by but still no call. Anne looked at her watch again. It was now 7:15 and still

Jimmy hadn't phoned. Should she ring him, she wasn't sure what to do. Damn that girl, why couldn't she mind her own business she thought to herself, if only she hadn't been so nosey then this wouldn't have happened. She had now been waiting in this smelly telephone kiosk for what had seemed an age and still Jimmy hadn't phoned. Something must have gone wrong, she thought to herself, and if that's the case then I'll just have to phone him. She looked at her watch for the umpteenth time and at last it said 7:30. She took out the piece of paper that she had written the telephone number on and dialled it, she heard the exchange click its way through the sequence; there was a momentary pause followed by a click then she could hear the distinctive brr-brr, brr-brr of the number ringing. It rang once, twice, three times and now four times in fact she counted up to eight rings and was on the point of putting it down when Jimmy answered.

'Sorry about that, I was held up.'

'Was that you who rang earlier?' she asked.

'Yes, but that wasn't yer earlier. It was a women's voice all right, but it sounded different somehow, so to be on the safe side I left it knowing full well that if I didn't telephone by seven-fifteen then you would call me by seven-thirty as we arranged. So was it you?'

'No it was some girl just walking passed. I was just about to go into the kiosk but before I could stop her she shot in and picked up the phone. You can't have said anything because she was out again almost immediately.'

'Ah well no harm done.' He paused and wondered how to broach the subject of Ireland and Richard's connection. How much did she know he wondered after all there was the security aspect to be considered? 'Tell me Anne did Richard ever talk to yer about Ireland and his work over here?'

'What you mean his connection with Breandán O'Shea?'

'That among other t'ings, does the name O'Donald ring any bells with yer?'

'I knew Sean O'Donald and I know of Jean. I know Sean was in the UDR. Unfortunately he was killed a while ago why?'

'Ok so you know a little bit about what Richard was involved in.'

'Well yes, I know he was also in the TA and he was connected to Ashford. He spoke about a Colonel Ash from time to time and that's about it, why?'

'Why don't yer tell me what yer t'ink he was doing whilst he was over here?'

'As I said, I know that when he first went over to Dublin to work for Mr O'Shea, he worked with Paul Jones, Do you know Paul?'

'I know of Paul, but carry on Anne.'

'Well Paul is a long standing friend of his and they were in the Parachute Regiment together…'

'Yes ok Anne, but do yer know anyt'ing about O'Shea?'

'Not really why?'

'Oh it's not important. Now yer say yer knew Sean O'Donald?'

'Yes, Sean has stayed here with us…'

'So tell me about Sean because Sean was a friend of moin as well.

'Well as I said earlier he was in the UDR but I think he was something to do with Military Intelligence? I'm not too sure.'

'And where do yer t'ink Richard fits in with all this?'

'How do you mean?'

'Well yer said about him being in the TA fer example which unit?'

'I know he joined the UDR whilst working in the Republic, something to do with O'Shea I think. I know about Colonel Ash at Ashford and how he sent Richard on lots of different courses. In fact come to think he used to get mysterious telephone calls from time to time, but I thought he'd finished with the Army because the last time he came home he said he was home for good. One of the mysterious phone calls was at two in the morning and shortly after that he had to go off somewhere. He told me afterwards that he had to go to Heathrow to meet someone. It was all very secretive and whenever I asked him what he actually did he'd just shrug his shoulders and say "it's another exercise," or maybe "another contract to look at in Ireland." In fact he's not the person I married, he's become secretive, evasive and I don't seem to know him anymore…'

'Listen Anne,' Jimmy stopped her from going any further. 'If I tell yer something yer must swear not a word to anyone otherwise it could be moi life as well as yers. I'm talking dangerous t'ings now. Do yer understand what I'm saying to yer now?'

'I think….' Suddenly her reply was interrupted by a series of rapid pips. 'Damnation hold on Jimmy while I find some more money.' She scrabbled in her purse and found two ten pence pieces which she pushed into the box just in time. 'Ok, as I was saying I think I understand what you are saying, but why do you say it could be our lives on the line?'

'Because Richard, like me, works fer the British Intelligence Service now I believe someone somewhere wants him out of the way. As to why I'm not t' sure, and as t' where they've taken him at the moment I don't know. But be rest assur'd I will foind out. Because we're dealing with the twilight zone and fighting with shadows it's best you don't say anyt'ing to anyone about this conversation otherwise I won't be able to help yer at all. Do yer understand Anne? No-one must know about me or my involvement. This has to be unofficial; I'm doing this to help you and Richard who's a good friend of moin…'

'Oh thank you Jimmy and I do understand, not a word…'

'Good, then yer need to phone me tomorrow night at the same time on this number and maybe I'll have something fer yer them.'

'Thanks Jimmy, you'll never realise how much I appreciate this help…'
Again the pips cut her off, 'good bye Jimmy, goodbye.'
'Goodbye Anne, speak to yer tomorrow.'

Chapter 19

I sat like a zombie; my eyes were glazed and emotionless as I studied the face of the man sitting behind the desk opposite me. Although I was heavily sedated I was sure I had seen his face before, but as to where, I could not remember. Damn this wooziness, if only I could clear the fuzziness from my head then I'm sure I'd remember.

The room to which I'd been taken was a large office and was situated at the front of the building. A large desk had been placed in front of French doors that led out onto a large well maintained lawn. The lawn gently sloped down towards an area of rhododendrons which helped to conceal the fifteen foot high chain link perimeter fence. It was a sunny day and Richard, who had now forgotten about the man's face, watched the antics of a grey squirrel as it made its undulating run across the lawn to the rhododendrons where it quickly disappeared into the leafy cover.

'Now Richard,' the man in the white coat looked up from his file and spoke for the first time, 'you say you were involved in a top secret Government operation. If so, and you are a…what did you call it…an operator, then why were you arrested?'

'I don't know,' I answered in a flat monotonous voice.

'But, wouldn't you agree, that if you are, or were, such a person then surely the Government would have…hmm…avoided something like that happening at all cost?'

I looked vacantly at my inquisitor; his voice seemingly distorted and echoing as it droned on and on, asking silly questions, probing and making statements. Somewhere, in the depths of my mind, I vaguely remembered being told something about rank and number. What was it now? Ah yes of course, that was it. 'Whatever you do if you are captured,' a little voice in my head said, 'only give your name, rank and number,'

'My name is Richard James and I am a Captain in…'

'Richard you are ill, now listen to me…'

'My name is Richard James, Captain Richard James…'

'Richard, listen to me...'

'My name is Richard James, Captain James and my number is H4283742…'

I woke with a start and found myself in a strange bed dressed in striped pyjamas. 'What the…' I racked my brains but couldn't remember a thing. I looked around my unfamiliar surroundings, a small and sparsely furnished room with a single light bulb under a white plastic shade in the centre of the ceiling. The furnishings were pretty basic and apart from the bed I now found myself in, there was a small bedside locker and a single wardrobe.

Apart from the single light bulb the only other source of light was through the small barred sash window opposite my bed. The room's décor did little for me, it was painted in the obligatory green and cream found in many of the older Government establishment. I had woken with the mother and father of all hangovers and just wished that the pounding would cease. Slowly the fuzziness in my brain started to clear and through the fog I started to get some clarity of thought and things started to come back to me. I vaguely remembered three men calling on me at home but was it today or yesterday, I wasn't sure. Where was I, was I in hospital I asked myself. If only I could fill in the many blanks. This room with its small window, and the bars on the outside, was I in prison, or some sort of secure unit, and what was I doing dressed in these pyjamas? Where are my own clothes? I just didn't know. Slowly I pushed back the bedclothes, swung his legs out of bed and gingerly stood up. How I wished that the pounding in my head would stop. I slowly walked over to the small sash window hoping that the view from it would give me some idea as to my whereabouts. Outside it was a sunny day and from my vantage point I looked down onto a beautiful manicured lawn. There were a handful of people all wondering about aimlessly in the sun and seemingly oblivious of each other. The way they looked and acted reminded me of how films portrayed zombies. Suddenly two men in white coats appeared and escorted one of these wretched people away and realisation that I was in some sort of psychiatric unit dawned on me. This left me with three, as yet unanswered questions, why was I here, did Anne know where I was and finally if she did know then why hadn't she done something to get me out? However these concerns were short lived and paled into insignificance as suddenly the glass in the window exploded into thousands of pieces. Instinctively I threw myself sideways and hit the floor as shards of glass flew everywhere. Shit, I thought to myself, why is some bastard is trying to kill me? I lay on the floor motionless half expecting a quick burst of automatic fire but after a couple of minutes and no further shots I cautiously raised my head to check out the damage. There was glass everywhere but at least I was unscathed. I needed to move away from the window and his line of fire and I felt that if only I could get over to the bed then I would feel a lot less vulnerable. Having satisfied myself that nothing further was about to happen, I slowly and carefully cleared a path through the shattered pieces of glass and crawled across the floor to the refuge of the bed. Here I sat and pondered over this latest development and concluded that either someone was a terrible shot and had missed, or it was by design. In fact I decided that the miss was intended because even the world's worst shot could not miss a target framed so neatly in the window, no it had to be a damned good marksman to miss and I believe it was their intention to do just that. The more I thought about it the more convinced I became that this was a warning and that someone, somewhere, desperately wanted to scare me. Well, warning or not I concluded that here was not the place to be right now and I needed to get out and as far away as possible. With this in mind I slid off the bed and once again all fours I carefully crawled through the broken glass towards the wardrobe over by the door. Cautiously I stood up and flattened myself against the wall so presenting as smaller target area as possible to any would be sniper. Holding my breath I moved inch by inch along the wall half expecting at any moment to hear the unmistakeable crack of a high powered rifle, but it never came. I stretched out my arm and felt for the handle on the wardrobe door. My fingers closed around the small handle, I paused, took a deep breath then in one quick movement I was in front of the wardrobe. I threw the door open and dropped to the prone position just in case the sniper was still out there. Again I waited, half expecting to hear the crack of a high powered rifle, but nothing happened. Encouraged by this and using the door to screen me from view I checked inside the wardrobe. You can imagine the relief I felt when I saw my clothes and shoes in there, now all I had to do was to get dressed and find some way out of here, it seemed to be too easy!

Anne looked at the clock for the umpteenth time; it was now 7:15 pm. Again she looked out of the window half expecting to see Richard walk up the path at any moment, but still it was deserted. In fact even the road was deserted apart from the red Ford parked in the gated entrance to the Seeboard substation and her own car, a blue Citroen. With a despondent sigh she went into the kitchen and in order to pass the time she busied herself washing up the few things left from earlier in the day. Once more she checked the time. It was still too early for her to leave for the village and the phone box, unless of course she walked, but that would take her at least fifteen minutes and Jimmy had said 7:30. No she would wait, after all couldn't afford to be late. She went back into the front room and again looked out of the window still nobody. Still the road was deserted except for the red Ford. That's strange; she thought to herself, that car has been there all day. I wonder who it belongs to. Seeboard will be annoyed if they need to get into the substation.

Slowly, ever so slowly I turned the door knob and pulled. Imagine my surprise when it opened, after all I had half expected the door to be locked. Inch by inch I opened it a little further until it was just wide enough to allow me to make a cursory examination of the immediate vicinity. Yet another surprise, no guard and the corridor was completely clear. One more check to make doubly sure that no-one was coming and that was it, I was out into a wide dingy green and cream painted corridor. I looked first to my left, then

213

to my right but neither way gave me any clue as to which way would lead me out of this place. It was down to the toss of a coin, heads left, tails right, it came down tails. With my heart pounding I set off on my quest for freedom knowing full well that with every step I took I ran the risk of discovery.

The corridor ran in a dead straight line, with doors that punctuated the walls on either side, some opened to reveal storerooms others revealed small bedrooms similar to the one I had just left. I was just beginning to think that I should retrace my footsteps and try in the opposite direction when up ahead it appeared that the corridor turned to the right. Now this, I thought to myself, looks promising and with my confidence restored I hurriedly pressed on. As I approached the corner I heard the sound of voices and unseen footsteps echoing eerily around me, and afraid of discovery I hastily looked for somewhere to take refuge, but there was nowhere to hide. I was trapped.

Anne sat down and switched on the television, a quiz show was on one side, with Emmerdale on the other but she was unable to settle to either. At last it was twenty-five past seven and time for her to set off to the village to make her call to Jimmy. It only took a couple of minutes to drive to the short distance to the Queens Head where she parked her car before crossing over the main road to the telephone box. As she opened the door to the red telephone kiosk a white car pulled off the main road and parked. The driver watched carefully in his rear view mirror as Anne entered the box to make her call.

The voices and footsteps were getting louder, so I knew they were heading towards me and with nowhere to hide I was left with no option but to grit my teeth, keep walking and hope that I would get away with it. Trying hard to take on an air of authority I walked purposefully forward towards where the voices were coming from and as I rounded the corner a man and a woman, deep in conversation, walked towards me. I held my breath, looked straight ahead and continued to walk unfalteringly towards them. Lady luck must have been on my side because they seemed oblivious of my very existence as they walked passed and on around the corner. Gradually the sound of their voices and footsteps receded into the distance and once again I was alone, phew, I let out the breath I had been holding. Another corner came into view, but no voices this time. I rounded the bend and there ahead of me the corridor ended outside yet another unmarked door. With fingers crossed I turned the handle and pushed on it gently. The door swung open noiselessly into what appeared to be a large sitting room or lounge. This room differed from everywhere else I had seen. It was light and airy with a large television set stood at the far end. Arm chairs and occasional tables were positioned informally about the main body of the room and from somewhere I could hear softly playing background music. As I entered this large informal room I could hear the soft drone of distant voices and for the first time since arriving in this place I could hear the bird's singing. As I moved into the main body of the room I saw the open French Doors over to my right. Ah, my chance of escape. I made a bee line for the doors and out onto a very colonial styled veranda, at last I was outside and freedom. However it was short lived, lady luck had finally deserted me.

'Ah Richard so you're awake at last.' A voice addressed me from behind.

I stopped dead in my tracks and swung round to see who the owner of the voice was. He wore a white coat and was of average height and stocky build with a shock of ginger hair. The owner of the voice walked across the room towards the French Doors and where I stood on the veranda.

'Come in Richard. Come in. There's no way out that way save into the gardens. Then where will you go?'

'I'll …I'll get out outside and then home, that is unless you're going to stop me.' He laughed. 'Why do you think that's so funny?' I asked.

'Because Richard that way certainly leads to the garden but that's as far as you would get. You see, around the garden area is a fifteen foot high chain link fence and I doubt that even you with your capabilities or resourcefulness would easily overcome that obstacle. No Richard you would not get out that way. The only way out is through the front door and that is manned day and night. So come on, come back in here and have a wee chat with me.' He indicated to a couple of chairs just inside the French Doors. 'Come on Richard, come in here and sit down.'

'Why?' I asked, 'why should I want to sit down?'

'Ah well, I just thought it would be nice to have a wee chat that's all.' He was softly spoken with a faint Scottish accent. 'You see, I thought you maybe like to know what has been happening since we last spoke.' Oh I wanted to know what was going on all right, but who was he? I certainly had no recollection of seeing him before let alone talking to him. 'So Richard will you join me?'

'You say we've spoken before, but who are you?'

'All in good time Richard, all in good time. Now come on, sit down and let's have a chat.'

Anne dialled the number and let the phone ring. Jimmy had told her to wait until it had rung eight times then replace the handset; she then had to wait for one minute before re-dialling the number again. The line connected and Anne counted the number of times she heard it ring as soon as she herd the eighth she replaced the receiver and waited. She checked the second hand on her watch thinking how long a minute seemed. Dead on the minute she picked up the phone and re-dialled the number and true to his word Jimmy answered on the third ring.

'Hello Anne'

'Hello Jimmy. Have you any news?'

'I've...' he started to say something then changed his mind, 'well sort of...'

'Well tell me then, where is he Jimmy?' Anne couldn't hide the excitement in her voice.

'He's been taken to a place of safety...'

'Yes but where?'

'Err...from what I've heard he's in hospital...'

'Why, what's happened? Jimmy tell me...' he could hear the agitation in her voice, 'Jimmy, Jimmy. Hello, hello, Jimmy. Are you there?'

'Calm down Anne I'm here, I'm here.'

'So Jimmy please tell me, where is he, where have they taken him?'

He wasn't too sure how to play this, after all his contacts hadn't told him everything he needed to know yet. All he knew was that Richard had been taken out of circulation but as to where and by whom was still unknown. He needed to stall her; he needed more time, twenty-four hours should do it. He decided on his plan of action.

'Look Anne it's very difficult fer me because I don't know how much yer know. In fact yer could be anybody...'

'Of course it's me, who else would it be?' she answered full of indignation at his insinuation that she was not who she claimed to be.

'Please understand, I don't know yer nor do I know your voice so put yourself in my position, how would you react?'

'Well...err...'

'Exactly my point, yer would have certain doubts as I have. Now don't take this the wrong way, but say I gave out Richard's whereabouts to the wrong person what do yer think would happen?'

'I suppose you'd be in trouble...'

'Oh that would be the least of the problems. Just suppose Richard was in danger and I gave out his whereabouts to the wrong person, then he could end up DEAD. Is that what yer'd want?'

'Don't say that Jimmy. Tell me it's not true; please tell me he's not in danger...'

Jimmy could tell by the way she had reacted that Anne was genuine all right. However he still was short of information but he was convinced that he would have it by tomorrow so he took a gamble. His next question threw Anne completely.

'What sort of car do yer drive?'

'Why, what's that got to do with Richard's disappearance?' She asked totally bemused by his sudden change in tack.

'Tell me the make and registration.' He persisted in his line of questioning.

'It's a Citroen why?'

He answered her question with another question. 'What's the registration and colour Anne?'

'It's blue and the number is C517OKP. Now will you tell me what this is all about?'

'This is the deal Anne,' his voice sounded hard, no longer did he sound Mr nice guy. 'Tomorrow you phone me at eight in the morning on this number and I'll give you further directions. I plan to be over there to meet with you or I'll arrange something else, but I can't do anything further until tomorrow. Do you understand?'

'Yes.' She said with resignation.

He could feel the disappointment in her voice, but there was little he could do about that. 'Anne.'

'Yes.'

'Keep your chin up and I'll have something definite for you tomorrow.' He'd gambled on a long shot and hoped for her sake it would pay off.

She got back to her car even more confused than she was before the phone call. What on earth was going on, what was Richard involved in? Her head was spinning with the events of the last few weeks never mind the last few days and Jimmy's conversation had not helped one little bit. The only thing she was sure of was that he had said Richard was safe but for how long, that she didn't know. As she drove out of the Queens Head car park and set off up the hill towards home a red car pulled out from where it had been parked and followed at a discrete distance.

I sat down in one of the easy chairs opposite the softly spoken ginger haired man.

'Richard, do you remember me?'

I looked at him and thought about his question. I racked my brains and yes there was something vaguely familiar about this man, but I couldn't put my finger on it.

'No.' My voice sounded strange as I answered in a flat monotone. 'Who are you?' I asked. My voice sounded as if it didn't belong to me. What was happening, there was something very odd about this guy, something very odd was happening to me as I sat opposite him. I wanted to fight against it but didn't know how.

'Don't worry about me Richard. I'd like to talk about you. Is that ok?' He asked in his soft Scottish accent. I felt really strange; it was as if he was controlling my very mind. I stared blankly ahead and felt myself nodding with approval. Shit Richard what is happening, what are you doing? Come on snap out of it, tell him to fuck off. I opened my mouth to do just that but the words wouldn't come. I summoned up all my will power and slowly my mouth began to work. Go on Richard, go on. Tell him, tell him. Slowly I started to speak. It was strange how my voice sounded very distant as if it didn't belong to me.

'F...from where should I start?' No, no, no. Not that. Try again. FUCK OFF I screamed silently to myself. Again I opened my mouth to speak. 'F...fine. Yes ok.' No matter how I tried it was as if I was no longer in control. It was as if he was controlling me.

'Then that's good. Now I'd like you to come with me.' He stood up and I did likewise. It was uncanny what was happening. What had they done to me? It was as if his voice was some sort of trigger mechanism to my mind. Had they drugged me and taken control of my mind by some sort of hypnosis and subsequent auto-suggestion? The stranger, with ginger hair and a soft Scottish accent, took my arm and gently guided me back through the door and along the dingy corridor to my room.

'Well done Richard, here we are.' The stranger opened the door for me and I shuffled into my room. It was my room all right because there lay my pyjamas exactly as I had left them thrown on the bed, but the window was undamaged. I shuffled over to the window and ran my hand over the glass in disbelief.

'The window, it's ok.' I said in that detached monotone voice.

'Yes Richard, the window is ok why, was there something wrong with it?' He asked.

'Of course there was,' I answered, 'it was broken. It was shattered.' I remembered being shot at. 'Yes it was shattered. Glass everywhere. I was shot at.'

'Yes, yes, yes.' He said in a patronising way, 'of course you were Richard, of course you were.'

I knew from his tone of voice he was only humouring me, he didn't believe a word of what I was saying. I got down on my hands and knees and started to scrabble around trying hard to find something just to prove to him that what I said was true. 'Really, I was shot at.'

'I know Richard, now come on be a good chap and get up.'

'No. No there's glass here somewhere, I know there is.' I scrabbled about even more desperate to prove now. Was I going mad, I was certain I had been shot at, but I couldn't prove it. Slowly I stopped scrabbling about; there was no glass, not a single piece. There was nothing, nothing at all. The window had been repaired and every splinter of glass had been cleaned up. All the evidence had been removed. I slowly stood up. 'No glass.' I said in a matter of fact way.

'No glass Richard. There never was any glass. Now why don't you get back into bed there's a good chap.'

'Because I don't want to.'

'Ok just sit there then.'

'But the window was broken…'

'No Richard you only imagined it. You see you have not been yourself lately and what was very real to you was only in your mind. In your imagination, it was probably another of your flashbacks to something that happened to you earlier in your life.' He sounded very convincing. Perhaps he's right, perhaps I had dreamt it, but there again did I? I was confused.

'Do you understand Richard?'

'Do I understand what?' I asked.

'The broken window never existed. It's all to do with your illness; it was something you imagined happened but never did. You see Richard, you've been very poorly and we are here to help your recovery.'

'How do you mean poorly?' I asked.

'Well you've not been quite yourself recently. You've been imagining lots of things, people, and different places. You've been suffering from hallucinations. Seeing things that are not there, like the broken window for example in fact you have become quite paranoid about some things, but don't worry we'll get you better. Now why don't you do as I suggest, slip into your pyjamas and get into bed? You need to rest for a little longer.'

'No I don't want to get into bed.'

'Ok then just rest there.' He gently yet firmly helped me lie down on my bed, talking all the while in a soft low voice. Gradually I could feel my eyes getting heavier until eventually I found it difficult to keep my eyes open any longer. I heard the click of the door close as I drifted off to sleep.

Chapter 20

There were still a couple of minutes to go before Anne was supposed to call Jimmy, but as he had promised to have definite information for her she got to the telephone box early so as to make sure she could call him on time. On the stroke of eight Anne dialled the number.

'Hello Anne.' The familiar sound of Jimmy's voice answered after the first ring.

'Hello Jimmy. Have you managed to find anything out?' She asked excitedly.

Instead of answering her question straight away Jimmy started to give her some instructions. 'Anne, you need to listen to me very carefully and don't interrupt as I have very little time if I'm going to help you. Do you understand?'

'Of course, please tell me what you have.'

'Tonight at seven o'clock I want you to take the road to Faversham. At Brenley corner you go around the roundabout then take the A2 towards Canterbury...'

'But...'

'Yer agreed not to interrupt and I've got a plane to catch and time is running out.' He said curtly, 'now take the A2 towards Canterbury. Do you know the turn off to Chartham Hatch?'

'Yes why?'

'Well turn right towards Chartham Hatch. Now do you know the public house called the Chapter Arms at Chartham Hatch?'

'No, but I'll find it.'

'Well do that and sit at the first table inside the door and just so I know it's yer, take a copy of the 'Fruit Grower' with yer. Do yer understand my directions?'

'Yes but...' that was all she said and the line went dead. She rattled the receiver rest up and down but to no avail. 'Damn, damn, damn.' She had expected more than just a lot of silly directions, the very least she had expected was for him to tell her where Richard was, but all he had done was give her a load of rubbish directions for what. She was angry and frustrated and now she was frightened. She threw back the door and ran to her car parked in the Queens Head car park. Slamming the car door she started the engine of the little blue Citroen. Grabbed the gear shift and crashed it into reverse. With engine roaring and wheels spinning she shot backwards. She stamped on the brakes and with a crunch selected first gear and accelerated out of the car park towards home. Why this, this entire charade, this silly game, why couldn't he just tell me? All these and a myriad of other thoughts tumbled through her mind. What the hell was going on? Suddenly another, more sobering thought, struck her, could it be a trap she was blindly walking into after all she didn't know this person called Jimmy? Out of the blue another phone box came into view and at the last minute she decided to phone Paul. Braking violently the car slid to a halt. She grabbed her purse and ran from the car leaving the door wide open and the engine running. She ran to the phone box too preoccupied with her own thoughts to notice the red Ford which had had to brake harshly and swerve to miss her Citroën, let alone see the driver, a man with black shoulder length hair and wearing dark glasses. The red Ford continued along the road for a short distance before turning off to the right.

The radio blared out 'Papa don't preach' as Paul measured up some steel ready for cutting when the telephone rang. Paul took the stairs two at a time up to his office to take the phone call. 'Hello, Jones Engineering.'
'Paul, it's Anne, do you know someone called Jimmy?'
'Jimmy?'
'Yes Jimmy, an Irish man?'
'Jimmy,' Paul repeated the name, 'Jimmy, no I can't say that I do. Who is he?'
'I think he is something to do with Richard and Ireland...'
'Ah, yes. Now that rings a bell.'
'So you know him then?'
'No I don't know him personally but I'm sure I've heard Richard mention his name before why?'
'Well it's just that he's been promising to tell me where Richard is for the last couple of days but all he said to me this morning was that he wants to meet me at Chartham Hatch...'
'Where in Chartham Hatch?'
'A pub called The Chapter Arms.'
'The Chapter Arms, I know it well. What time are you supposed to meet him?'
'At seven. Paul I'm worried, what shall I do?'
He thought carefully about what she had just told him before he answered. 'Tell you what. Keep your date with him and I'll be there in the bar as well.'
'Are you sure Paul, I don't want to impose on you?'
'Of course I'm sure. Don't worry Anne, I'll be there.'
'Thanks Paul.' She now felt happier in the knowledge that Paul would be there as well.

I woke with a start. Where was I? The fuzziness in my head slowly started to clear and gradually my mind began to focus. I looked around, nothing had changed. I was still in the same dreary little room that was painted in Ministry green and cream. My memory started to return. How long had I been out of it, an hour, two hours or was it a day I hadn't a clue; it could have been a week for all I knew. I remembered returning to this room with some ginger haired bloke, I remembered the gun shot. Shit, the gun shot! That was it, the gun shot and the window. I lay there for a moment or two, my eyes darting from left to right whilst the significance of the gun shot slowly dawned on me. Other snippets of memory starting crowding in, the long corridor, the large sitting room, the veranda but the most important item was the shattered window and how on my return it had miraculously appeared unscathed. Yes I remembered it all now. I swung my legs off the bed and checked the time; my watch said 8:00. Bloody hell, I must have slept for hours. Cautiously I looked out of my window, half expecting it to explode, but nothing happened. Below was a vast area of deserted lawn and I could vaguely hear the birds singing. Judging by the lack of shadows being thrown up I decided it was 8:00 in the morning, I unconsciously ran my hand across my chin as I thought about what had happened and could feel the stubble. On feeling the growth I immediately knew that I must have lost at least a day, or was it more than a day? I wasn't sure of anything anymore. At least I was still dressed now all I needed was my shoes. I reached down under the edge of the bed where I was sure I had left them, but it seemed as if they had gone. Funny, I was sure they were right here under the bed, unless they have got pushed further under. I knelt down to have a look under the bed for my shoes when I saw something glinting in the light. I was curious as to what it was and stretched my arm under the bed to retrieve it. As I'd reached under the bed I pressed on something sharp. 'Ouch.' I yelped and withdrew my hand rapidly to find a small sliver of glass sticking out of my finger. I pulled out the sliver and laid it in the palm of my hand. So if the gun shot that shattered window was only imagination, as they would have me believe, then how did that get there? I laid it carefully on my bedside locker and went back to look for more evidence. After a few moments of careful searching I found two more pieces of broken glass that they had missed when clearing up. I was now convinced that there was some sort of cover up going on. Having discovered the pieces of glass all thoughts about my shoes was forgotten and with renewed energy I started an inch by inch search of the wall. I was now looking for evidence of where the bullet had lodged, but there was nothing. Out of the blue a thought occurred to me that I may well be looking in the wrong place, after all the projectile was not aimed at me. Had it been meant for me then I would, at the very least, have been wounded if not killed. So, if someone was aiming to miss me then the trajectory would have been at a totally different angle. Again I started to search only this time I searched along the top half of the wall and the ceiling, but even after my meticulous searching there was no bullet hole. I was on the point of giving up when bingo! I noticed, high up on the wall just below the ceiling line, a small area of plaster where the paint was a slightly lighter cream; could this be what I was looking for? I needed to take a closer look and the bedside locker was the ideal step-ladder. I carefully wrapped my pieces of glass up inside my handkerchief and placed them in my trouser pocket for safe keeping then moved the cabinet into position. Then a thought occurred to me that if I was being stitched up by the Government, as I suspected, then it would be quite conceivable that I was being watched. So standing in the centre of the room I carefully looked for anything that closely resembled a camera, but there was nothing, it was clean.

Carefully I climbed onto the cabinet to take a closer look at the area in question. I was just about to reach out to touch the lighter coloured paint when the door to my room was opened. The door crashed into the cabinet, I lost my balance and ended up on the floor with cabinet on top of me.

'Oh my goodness, Richard are you all right?' I lay there feeling slightly dazed and very stupid looking up at a young lady looking down on me. 'What on earth were you doing up there?' she asked.

'Err nothing…I was looking for my shoes.' I added lamely.

'Where on top of your wardrobe?'

'Err yes. Yes on top of my wardrobe, I'm sure that's where I saw them last.' I smiled.

'Really, and you expect me to believe that, how about looking inside the wardrobe?' she said opening the door and pointing at my shoes.

'Thanks. I must have…well you know…'

'Sure I know. I'll tell you what I do know and that's the smell of bull shit when I hear it and there's an awfully strong smell of it in this room. Anyway enough of this nonsense you have a visitor so if you'd sort your room and yourself out I'll wait in the corridor for you.' A visitor, I thought to myself, now I wonder who that can be. I grabbed my shoes and hurriedly tied the laces and in a flash I had my cabinet upright and back next to my bed. Within seconds I was out of my room and into the corridor to be met by two burly individuals. I had been fooled. Even before the door to my room had closed I was being gently yet firmly assisted along the corridor to my left and a few minutes later we passed under an archway and out into a large open reception area. In the centre of the large hallway was the receptionist's desk, a large, ornately carved oak desk positioned facing two half glazed doors which I assumed to be the main entrance. Immediately to the rear of the receptionist's desk was a wide sweeping staircase which led to a galleried landing. To the right of the staircase was another archway which gave access to another wing of the building. On the opposite side of the entrance foyer were two oak panelled doors and it was in this direction my escorts and I headed. We stopped outside the door nearest to the main entrance and one of my 'friends' rapped smartly on it. Without waiting for a reply he opened it and we entered a large well furnished room. Heavy burgundy velvet curtains hung at the bow fronted window in front of which was positioned an antique oak desk. As we entered the man sitting at the desk looked up and smiled. He looked to be in his fifties with steely grey hair and dressed in a mid-grey suit that could easily have come from Seville Row sat. He indicated the middle one of three chairs already positioned in front of the desk. 'Richard, please sit down.' He acknowledged the presence of my two 'friends' with a fleeting smile and then motioned them to sit either side of me. 'Now Richard, let me introduce myself, I'm Doctor Ferris and I gather from the notes you have not been too well of late. So how are you feeling now?'

So this was there little game!

'Well Richard, how do you feel?' he repeated the question as he looked at some papers on the desk in front of him and read the notes scribbled in the margins. 'According to your records here you have been very ill and because of this I have been asked to talk to you.' He looked up from the notes he had been reading and studied my face for a moment or two. 'Are you aware of how ill you've been?' He asked.

Ok so you want to play this game I thought to myself. In that case I'll play along with you and perhaps I may learn something. 'No, I didn't know I'd been ill.' I said, 'but please tell me what has been wrong with me?' I asked.

'Well Richard, you've had a type of breakdown. Do you understand what I mean by a breakdown?'

Cobblers, I've had no breakdown. I said to myself, but the truth of matter is I've been drugged and I've been made to look as if I'm ill by you lot. 'How do you mean a breakdown?' I asked and waited to see what sort of story he would come out with. We both sat there in silence whilst the Doctor thought about my question..

'Well Richard,' he eventually replied, 'the mind is a complicated and a very complex part of our body...'

Oh yes I agree, and you're doing your best to try and bend mine, I thought to myself.

'Now sometimes things don't always work as they should...'

I'd heard enough of his patter.

'Bollocks.'

'Excuse me.'

'I said bollocks, you're talking utter bollocks. There is nothing at all wrong with me and you know it. The truth is I've been set-up by the department. Why, I don't know but you…'

'How do you mean set up?' he enquired interrupting me in full flow.

'What I say, I've been set-up. You know I work for the Government and you and your mates,' I indicated the minders sat either side of me, 'are all in it together. I know what's going on. You are all trying to discredit me. The department or someone wants rid of me because things didn't quite go according to plan and suddenly I'm an embarrassment. So come on Doctor at least be honest and admit you work for the department, because I know your game.' I suddenly thought I may have gone too far and waited for my two minders to grab me and drag me away back to my room, but to my surprise nobody moved.

'You see Richard, there you go again.' His eyes never left my face as he spoke to me in a quiet even tone. 'Let me explain to you…'

I wasn't as calm as him and I certainly didn't want to hear any more of the so called party line. 'No you listen to me.' I said raising my voice above his, 'I work for the Intelligence Service, and as far as I'm concerned I still do. I am a member of the Ulster Defence Regiment and have worked undercover in Ireland, so bollocks to your party line.' He slowly shook his head and the trace of a smile touched his lips as I ranted on. 'Think of another excuse for holding me here!' At this juncture all trace of any smile disappeared as soon as I intimated that I was being held as a prisoner. I must have touched a nerve, because for a second he looked slightly rattled, but then he regained his composure and when he spoke his voice was steady and quiet.

'Richard, Richard. Nobody is holding you here, but this idea that you work for the Government and that you are a member of the intelligence service is …shall we say all in your mind, it is no more than that…'

I shouted at him, 'Crap, absolute crap and you know it is.'

He held up his hand and shook his head. 'Ok, if that's the case and what you say is true then it can easily be proved by telling me who your controller was.'

'Why?'

'Because we can then telephone him…'

I started to laugh, 'You must be joking! Do you think I'm stupid enough to fall for that, no way?'

'Well if you're not prepared to do that then who should I telephone?' He asked pulling a pen from his inside pocket ready to make a note of a name.

I knew that I was beaten because all the telephone numbers that I had for the Circus no longer existed and he knew that to. 'You know I as well as I do that my communications net has been shut down. How do I know that you know? Because you work for the same firm, you also work for the Government.'

'I see,' he said nodding his head, 'so you agree that you are unable to give me a name or telephone number of anyone who could verify your story.'

'You know I can't.'

'Exactly my point Richard, you are ill and we are here to help you. Now if you will allow me to explain what it is…'

'Piss off, I know all about explanations. I know your little game; this has the hallmark of the Department of Psychological Operations. You're no more a doctor than I am.' At this point I sprung from my chair and made a dash for the door.

The calm façade of the so called doctor was now dropped. 'Quickly grab him, he mustn't get out.'

My two escorts were across the room like lightning and had quickly overpowered me. Within seconds I was restrained and lying prostrate on the floor, the sleeve of my shirt was roughly pulled up and the man called Ferris swiftly administered an injection which in next to no time was having the prescribed effect. I could feel myself slowly becoming more relaxed. I remember a warm comfortable sensation working its way through my body then nothing.

'Richard, Richard…' I could hear someone calling my name. The sun was shining. It was a lovely sunny day and everywhere was peaceful. 'Richard, Richard,' there it was again, someone was calling to me, but who? Slowly ever so slowly I gradually surfaced. The sunny day slowly receded and eventually disappeared as I opened my eyes and squinted in the glare of the light shining on my face. I turned away to hide from the bright light. 'Ah, at last you're awake.' A soft female voice spoke to me. At the same time the bright light disappeared as she switched off the ophthalmoscope she had been using. 'It's time for your medication Richard.' I turned towards the owner of the voice and a pretty young girl in a nurse's uniform handed me a small plastic tub containing some pills and passed me a beaker of water. 'Here you are Richard, now be a good chap and make sure you swallow them.' Still woozy from whatever they had injected me with I took the little tub and tipped the contents into my mouth, took a drink of water and swallowed them in one go. 'Good man,' the pretty nurse smiled, 'the Doctor will see you now, so up you get there's a good lad.' I smiled back at her as she helped me up. I swung my legs off my bed and thought to myself, what a kind and considerate girl. She took hold of my hand and I slowly shuffled along the corridor with her to see the Doctor.

I looked about my new surroundings and couldn't help feeling that there was something oddly familiar about the room; it was as if I had been here before. The room itself was large and well furnished with expensive heavy burgundy velvet curtains at the bow fronted window. Positioned in front of the large window was an old English oak desk behind which sat a man of about fifty years old with steely grey hair and dressed in a mid-grey suit. I stood where I was waiting, waiting for what I wasn't sure.

'Sit down Richard.'

The pretty young nurse guided me to a chair where I sat down, perhaps that was what I had been waiting for! As I sat in front of the desk I had the weirdest feeling that this all seemed so familiar, could it be déjà vu?

'How are you feeling Richard?' I smiled at the man in the grey suit. 'Do you remember me?' he asked.

I frowned at this question and wondered if I had seen him before somewhere. There it was again, that feeling of déjà vu, but this time I hurriedly dismissed the feeling as being absurd; he was being silly, of course I'd never seen him before so how could I possibly remember him!

'No.' I replied

'What about earlier today for example, did you see me then?'

I was totally bemused by this question and shook my head. The grey haired man in the suit smiled.

'Tell me Richard, why are you here?' he asked.

'Because the nurse brought me here.' I answered and smiled.

'No, I don't mean in this room. I mean, why are you in this building?' He smiled benignly.

Hmm, that's a good question, I thought to myself as I scratched my head and smiled back. I knew I didn't live here but I wasn't sure why I was here either. Now if I don't live here, then where do I live? No I must live here.

'Because I live here.' I answered in a matter of fact way.

'I see.' He smiled again. 'Now Richard, I want you to think very hard before you give me an answer to this next question.' He paused and studied my face, 'now how long have you been here?'

I thought long and hard about his question and all I ever remember was living here. I was about to say something when somewhere in the dark recess of my mind reminded me of another place I'd lived. A place with lots of trees, ah yes an orchard, but that was many years ago when I was a child. 'I don't know how long I've lived here.' Again my thoughts turned to my childhood and the orchard, 'I think I've lived here for years.' My speech sounded strange and far away to me. It was as if it was somebody else speaking and I was just an onlooker. I heard the door behind me open and someone else came into the room but I didn't look round.

'Now Richard, I'd like you to meet someone else.'

I heard someone's voice from behind me. 'Hello Richard.'

I turned in my chair to see who it was who had spoken to me.

'This gentleman is a Major in the Army Richard.' I smiled at him.

'Do you remember me Richard?' the stranger asked.

You seem a nice sort of person I thought myself, but that's a silly question to ask especially as I've only just met you, so how could I possibly remember you. 'No should I remember you?' I asked the Major.

'Not necessarily, it's just that your face seemed familiar and I just wondered whether we had met before somewhere that was all.'

'No I don't think we've ever met.'

'In that case let me introduce myself. My name is O'Rourke, Major O'Rourke. Do you remember me now?'

'No I can't say I do. That's a nice accent.' I said.

'Thank you.'

'Whereabouts are you from?' I asked, 'I've heard that accent before, but I don't remember you.'

'I'm from Belfast, have you ever been there?' he asked.

'No, I've never been to Belfast, well not that I remember.'

'What about Ireland, have you ever been to Ireland?' he asked with interest.

'Can't remember,' I paused deep in thought for a moment then said, 'no, never been to Ireland. I Would like to go though.'

'Well Richard perhaps one day. Now if you'll excuse me I need to talk to the Doctor.'

I smiled at the Major as the pretty young nurse helped me to my feet. She took hold of my arm and I shuffled slowly toward the open door and off to my room.

Major O'Rourke waited until the young lady had closed the door and he and Doctor Ferris were alone before he spoke. 'So what's the verdict, do you think we've managed to cover everything, do you think he's been neutralized, or do you think he is playing us along?'

'I think we have covered all angles and he is no longer a possible threat.'

'I hope you have because if not you'll be in real trouble, there must be no cock-ups otherwise…' He left the sentence unfinished.

'No problem Major, I'll stake my life on it.'

'Hmm, you may have to.' An uneasy silence ensued. The Major was the first to speak.

'So how long do you still need to keep him here for?'

'An hour maybe two at the most.'

'Then what?'

'Well we'll follow the plan that you and I agreed, to have him taken into Chartham under section 2 of the Mental Health Act. After all he has been sectioned by a Doctor and an Approved Social Worker hasn't he?'

'Yes, yes I know all that but do you think we're watertight? Do you see Chartham giving us any problems?'

'No, why should they? They have our version of his medical notes that show he has suffered from a breakdown and that for some time previous to him being sectioned he was paranoid. It could be said he is suffering from Paranoid Schizophrenia, so you see I don't envisage any comeback from Chartham Hospital.'

'Good. Let's hope your right. No cock-ups and no loose ends. In which case I'll get off and leave you to make the necessary arrangements.'

'One thing before you go Major.'

O'Rourke paused with his hand on the door knob. Turned and looked back at the Doctor. 'What about his wife?'

'Don't you worry about her Doctor, that's all in hand, just you worry about getting him into Chartham and leave the rest to me. A couple of hours you say?'

'Yes Major two hours.'

'Thank you Doctor.' With that O'Rourke left.

Major O'Rourke allowed himself a pat on the back and smiled to himself safe in the knowledge that Richard James would no longer be a threat to him, Imanos or other members of his little group. Now all he had to do was to get back to the London Desk and hope that the good Doctor was right. He flagged down a passing black cab. 'Victoria please.'

'Yes guv.'

O'Rourke shut the door of the cab and settled back in the seat as the cab moved off along Wimbledon Common Road towards Putney and Victoria.

At 7:00 pm precisely a light blue Citroën registration C517OKP went around Brenley roundabout and headed along the A2 towards Canterbury. At 7:15 the same Citroën turned right, across the dual carriageway and down the narrow country lane that was signposted to Chartham Hatch. Anne checked in her rear view mirror to see if there was anyone following her but there wasn't a soul in sight.

Within a couple of minutes of turning off the A2 onto the Chartham Hatch road Anne was turning into the car park of The Chapter Arms. The Chapter Arms being a popular pub meant that already there were a number of cars in the car park, any of which could belong to the contact she was to meet. She slowly drove round the car park trying hard to guess which of the many cars maybe his. Suddenly she saw Paul's grey Ford parked over in the corner and she heaved a welcome sigh of relief. At least Paul had arrived she thought to herself as she parked her Citroën in a space nearby. Quickly she checked her face in the mirror and pulled a comb through her hair. Having picked up 'The Grower' magazine that was lying on the passenger seat she locked the car and hurried into the pub. On entering the lounge bar she looked around for Paul and eventually caught sight of him sat on one of the stools at the far end of the bar. Paul was seated hidden by a large plant, but in an ideal spot right opposite a mirror in which he had an uninterrupted view of the entrance. He had already seen Anne arrive and watched her in the mirror as she made her way to a spare table to the left of the door, where she placed her coat on one of the seats and 'The Grower' magazine on the table. Having now made sure of her seat Anne made her way to the bar and ordered a glass of white wine then returned to sit and wait for her contact already happy in the knowledge that Paul was close to hand. There seemed to be a constant flow of people arriving in twos and threes, but as of yet there was still no obvious sign of anyone looking for her. She checked the time, it was getting on for 7:35 and still no contact. Having drunk the last of the wine she was just about to give up when a man over at the bar talking to a couple of others broke away from his party and came over to her table. Her heart started to thump as he approached her.

'Excuse me, are these seats taken?' he asked. She was just about to answer thinking Jimmy wasn't coming when she heard another voice.

'T' be sure they are.'

She immediately recognized the voice of Jimmy, but she still couldn't see where he was, then he appeared from behind a group of men stood between the young man who'd asked and his friends at the bar. The young man turned to see who had answered, smiled at the Irishman as he approached carrying a glass of beer and a white wine.

'Ok, sorry about that I just wondered if they were free that's all.'

'Oh don't yer be worrying now, I'll give yer a shout when we're going if yer haven't found somewhere by t'en.' Jimmy gave a grin at the young man and sat himself down opposite Anne. 'So at last I meet the lovely Anne.' He extended his hand, 'I'm pleased and honoured t' meet yer. I'm Jimmy who yer have spoken to over the last couple of days.'

Anne took his outstretched hand and shook it. 'I'm pleased to meet you Jimmy.'

'White wine is it yer be drinking?'

'Thank you Jimmy. I shouldn't really as I've already had one and I'm driving.'

'It'll not hurt t' have one more. Now first t'ings first. Sorry about all the palaver but I needed to know yer were clean...'

'What do you mean by clean?' Anne asked looking puzzled.

'T'at yer weren't being followed. Anyway I can now tell yer I've tracked him down.' He looked around the bar to see if anyone was listening and having reassured himself that nobody was taking any notice of the two of them he continued. 'Yes our Richard has had a spot of bother!'

'Bother, how do you mean?' asked Anne.

'Well I called in some favours and spoke with a few contacts; it appears as if Richard has been taken ill. According to the bush telegraph he's in hospital.'

'Hospital you say.' Jimmy nodded. 'But, but I don't understand. Surely if he was in hospital I would have been contacted, wouldn't I?'

'True. If he'd been physically ill t'en they would've been able t' trace yer, but yer see it's not so straight forward as t'at. From what I've heard Richard was found in London just wandering around…'

'In London?' Anne asked incredulously.

'Yes in London. He was found just wandering. It seems he's had some sort of breakdown, and as such nobody knew who he was.' He took a drink of his beer all the time he was watching Anne's reaction to what he was telling her. 'Yer see he didn't seem t' know where he was or who he was. Tell me, has he been all right at home, or has he been acting differently?'

'In what way?'

'Well doing odd things. Seeing t'ings that were really innocent but to him, he saw them as threats. Was he paranoid about anyt'ing? Has he been getting agitated about anyt'ing? Any of these sort of t'ings.'

Anne thought back over the preceding weeks, yes there had been odd times when he seemed on edge. There was the time he was sure that they were under surveillance, and all those times he went into the village to use the public call box because he was certain the phone was being tapped. Oh my, if only she had realized what was happening to him. Still too late now to cry over spilled milk, all she needed now was to know where he was and let the doctors do the rest. 'Now you come to mention it, there have been signs. It wasn't long ago he was sure we were under surveillance and there was the time he was convinced the phone was tapped. So yes I suppose your right and I just didn't take any notice.' Jimmy smiled inwardly. 'So where have they taken him Jimmy?'

'Oh dear me, it's worse t'an I thought. Yer see they found him in London wandering around. They say he just looked vacant and was talking gibberish about being in the Secret Service or something like t'at. In fact my contacts told me it was the police that picked him up but as he had no identification on him they didn't know who to contact, or where he lived so they sent for an ambulance and had him taken to hospital.'

'But he was…' Anne was about to say something then changed her mind.

'He was what Anne?'

'Oh nothing.' She changed the subject. 'I suppose with the farm, the contracting business and then Sean's death it all got a bit much for him.'

'Yes I'm sure yer right. Still he'll be in the right place now.'

'Yes you're probably right, so which hospital is he in?'

'I'm sorry Anne didn't I say. Well it's Chartham of course.'

'Chartham! But I thought you said he was found in London?'

'I did, but they transferred him down here to be closer to home.'

'But how come they knew he'd be closer to home?' Anne smelt a rat. 'You said he had no identification on him, so if they didn't know who he was then how did they know where he lived?'

Too late Jimmy realized his mistake and he now had to try and cover his tracks. 'Ah well, I expect he had some lucid moments and from what I've managed t' find out from my contacts he was able to tell the hospital t'at he came from Kent.'

'How come they didn't contact me then?'

'I suppose he couldn't remember his address or whereabouts in Kent he actually came from. I t'ink he managed to remember he lived near Canterbury and t'at was about all. Obviously t'at must have been the reason because if he had been more lucid then the Police would have known who to contact.'

'Oh I see. Well I suppose your right and thanks Jimmy for your help at least I know where he is now.'

Jimmy heaved a mental sigh of relief as he drank the rest of his beer. He was thankful that Anne believed him. Shit, he thought to himself that was close, still she believed me in the end. He took a casual look at his watch as Anne sipped her wine.

'Sorry Anne,' he pointed at his watch, 'I must get going now yer see I'm due to meet with someone up in London and it'll take me a good hour to get there.'

'I understand. Anyway it'll take more than an hour by road so you best get off.'

'I'm going by train, but yer right I'd best get off or I'll not make it tonight.' He smiled as he got up and extended his hand, 'nice meeting yer Anne and give my regards to Richard when yer see him won't yer?'

'Yes of course, and by the way how do you fit in to all this?' She asked smiling. Suddenly Jimmy's smile dropped. He was sure he'd sold her the breakdown story but now he was no longer so sure. He slowly sat back down.

'How do you mean 'fit in' to all this?'

'Well, Richard never spoke about you. You see when he disappeared like that I found a piece of paper with your telephone number on. I knew you had worked with Sean and I also knew Richard had worked with you in Ireland. Of course I knew Richard was involved in something, but what it was I wasn't sure. Incidentally you do know that he was in the UDR don't you?'

Jimmy was taken back by this last few comments having already convinced himself that she knew nothing, but now he wasn't so sure. 'Ah...' he paused, 'The UDR you say?'

'Yes.'

'Was he?' he tried to feign surprise.

'Yes and I know he went on a number of courses with them. So Jimmy is that where you fit in?' Anne smiled.

Jimmy was no longer sure of his ground and felt that he needed to get out whilst the going was good. 'Sorry Anne, I'd really love to stay and chat,' he made a point of looking at his watch again, 'but the truth is I haven't got time. Perhaps another day?'

Anne smiled sweetly. 'Of course Jimmy, I do understand. You have a meeting in London so maybe another day. Bye now.' With that Anne picked up the two glasses and carried them to the bar, making sure she put them down close to where Paul was seated. She smiled at the man on the stool and watched Jimmy in the mirror as he left The Chapter Arms.

'So what did you find out Anne?'

'That Richard is in Chartham. They say he's had a nervous breakdown.'

I sit quietly watching television in my new surroundings and the people here are very nice. I've already made friends with one of the 'old' boys who told me he has been living here for a couple of months now. They say I've had a breakdown, something about London, but I don't remember much at all. All I know is that it's nice and peaceful here.

'Hello my love.'

I wonder who the voice is addressing, I ask myself. It must be me as I'm the only one in the lounge. I slowly turn to see who it is.

'Richard it's me Anne.'

'Sorry should I know you?'

'Of course you do. It's me Anne, your wife. Surely you remember me?'

I stared vacantly at the women addressing me but couldn't place her. I slowly shook my head and turned back to watch the television.

'But Richard you must remember me. Please Richard think.'

Again I turned in her direction and studied her face, but I still couldn't place her.

'Come on Richard time for your pills.'

Now that voice I recognized and I looked towards the nurse and smiled as she handed me a small plastic tub containing three tiny pills and a beaker of water to help me swallow them.

'Thank you.' I said as I handed her the tub and beaker back.

'Hello, do you know Richard?' she asked the woman who had just been talking to me.

'Of course I do, he's my husband.'

Somewhere in the depths of my mind her voice seemed familiar.

'He's my husband. My poor, poor Richard what has happened to you?' Suddenly she started to cry. I didn't like seeing her cry whoever she was.

'Please don't cry.' I said as I reached into my pocket for a clean handkerchief. 'Ouch!' I yelped as something stuck in my finger. I quickly pulled my hand from my pocket to see what it was that had caused the pain and sticking from my finger was a splinter of glass. In that instant of pain something deep in the recess of my mind stirred. A memory, a window exploding, there was glass everywhere. I stared at the sliver and tried hard to remember. I gingerly touched the splinter of glass; again I felt the sharp prick as I pressed on it. Her voice, I had definitely heard it before. Slowly I pulled the sliver of glass from my finger and sucked the blood from the small cut it had left. I passed her the handkerchief and stared at her, looking for something familiar that would unlock my memory of where I had heard her voice. As she wiped away the tears, she tossed her head and gave me a smile.

'Thank you Richard.'

I continued to suck the cut on my finger and study her every move. She reached up and rubbed the side of her nose. A gesture I had seen many times before, but where?

'What's wrong?' She asked as she noticed me staring at her.

'Nothing' I said. 'It's just that you did something that reminded me of someone I once knew.'

'Who was that Richard?' Anne asked trying hard not to be too optimistic.

'That's the problem. I don't know...I don't know.' My voice trailed away to a whisper. 'I just don't know.' I looked down at my finger and the red spot of blood as it slowly oozed from the small cut. Again I saw the exploding window. Again there was glass everywhere. Then another memory, this time I was in a room somewhere. The room looked familiar, but where was it?

'Richard.' Anne called softly, 'Richard. What are you thinking?'

'I am trying to remember. There's a room... a chair...a television in the corner...a window. It's a large room...there is a woman looking out of the window but I can't see her face. She's telling me about a car that's been parked opposite...her voice...why... it's your voice... it's you.'

'Richard, listen to me.' I turned to face her. 'The room you are remembering is our front room. We have a farm, a fruit farm.'

'A fruit farm?' I asked.

'Yes a fruit farm. Think hard now and tell me what else you remember?' Gradually my mind started to reawaken and my memory began to return. With a little prompting I started remembering different things. At first they were just snippets of memory and very confused snippets at that, but as time went on I managed to get a logical pattern to the process and things became less confused.

It's now number of days since that first day in Chartham and images from the past are still coming back bit by bit. The arrest, George Imanos, Operation Orpheus, the Major and my time in Ireland all of these I remember. I am now well and truly on the road to recovery which was all down to a splinter of glass. All I have to do now is to prove that I, Richard James, was a victim of Psychological Operations, the Dirty Tricks Bureau and Department of misinformation. I desperately need to prove that someone, somewhere within the Government had set me up. Because then, and only then can I get my life back and the pension that is rightfully mine.

Today is the beginning of the rest of my life and I am determined that I will find out who betrayed me. I know that once I get out of here and with Paul's help I shall win!

Also available in *Quill Publishing*

Who Pays The Ferryman?

Pat Monteath

As the Land Rover rounded the bend the driver spotted what appeared to be a wire at about six inches above the ground stretching across the road in front of him. Too late he realised what it was. He slammed on the brakes locking all four wheels, everything then went into slow motion. With all wheels locked up the vehicle slithered forward over the surface of the road. The driver saw the wire disappear from view. As the front wheels made contact and he sensed the wire go taught there was a blinding flash of light and an almighty BOOOM, then blackness. The force of the explosion picked up the Land Rover and tossed it in the air as if it were a toy. It landed a broken twisted wreck upside down some forty feet along the road. The blanket of silence that followed was almost deafening as the pitch black of the night closed in once again.

"He tells the truth behind the headlines in his trilogy of books"
Barbara Argument *Evening Gazette*

"Subject matter great, interesting story. Nothing irritated me about the story, in fact I loved it. The phrase I would use to sum up this book is 'Intriguing'".
Mark Druce *Ex-serviceman.*

'Who Pays The Ferryman?' ISBN 0-9545914-0-2